CLA

Clark, Jean.

The marriage bed

83 02400

DATE			

© THE BAKER & TAYLOR CO.

THE MARRIAGE BED

THE
MARRIAGE
BED

A NOVEL BY
JEAN CLARK

G. P. Putnam's Sons
New York

Van Badenswyck and its residents are fictitious. It was, however, enterprising and ambitious people like the leading characters in this novel who, along with people of prominence from Holland and England, eventually established some of the well-known dynasties in New York's Hudson Valley.

Copyright © 1983 by Jean Clark
All rights reserved. This book, or parts thereof, must not be reproduced in any form without permission. Published simultaneously in Canada by General Publishing Co. Limited, Toronto.

Library of Congress Cataloging in Publication Data

Clark, Jean.
The marriage bed.

1. Dutch Americans—Hudson River Valley (N.Y. and N.J.)—History—Fiction.   I. Title.
PS3553.L2855M3   1983   813'.54   82-13134
ISBN 0-399-12746-1

PRINTED IN THE UNITED STATES OF AMERICA

I wish to express my gratitude to Marceida Lopez for her invaluable help in manuscript production.

For A. Raymond Rogers,
who led me to this subject

THE MARRIAGE BED

Chapter 1

The tide flowed with them; the wind blew from the southwest. The sloop, having left Manhattan at noon, sailed northward past the steep-sided chain of cliffs that guarded the western shore. Except for two cows strapped before the mast, Margretta Van Dyck, sitting with her back against the deckhouse, her sunbonnet shielding her skin and the dark gold of her hair from the brightness of the June sun, was the only passenger.

As she watched porpoises tumble about the boat and a sturgeon break the water with a silvery leap, she thought of how stirred Henry Hudson must have been as he journeyed in his small square-sailed craft up this river that now bore his name. It was said that he, like other skippers of his era, had kept an elaborately embroidered mandarin robe in his cabin so that, should he be the one to discover a new waterway to the Orient, he would be properly attired to greet Chinese notables.

Margretta owned no such robe. Now, in the early 1740's, most people doubted the existence of the northwest passage that had so long excited the hopes of explorers. Yet within her, as richly embroidered with dreams of the future, lay a similar desire for adventure and achievement.

Believing that such fancies were well concealed and unaware of how much wistfulness and an eagerness for life her dark eyes betrayed, she folded her hands demurely as befitted a woman of eighteen on her way to Van Badenswyck to teach the dominie's children

11

for a year. Although hardly an adventure, it was a step toward the future.

Besides, she had heard that life at the great manors was enlivened by many festivities. As a member of the dominie's household she would doubtless be included, pleasures denied her while living in the city with an ailing grandmother.

With her grandmother dead, Margretta was glad to leave the congestion of Manhattan. Ships crowded the harbor, sailors the streets. Rarely had she hurried from one teaching job to another without having at least one sailor grasp her arm.

"Hey, pretty lass. Where did you get that golden hair and those dark eyes?"

One had even boldly slipped an arm around her. "Hey, pretty lass, let us go somewhere and enjoy ourselves."

If they were too persistent, she had a standard reply. "Go on down to the main battery at the fort. You will find plenty of courtesans there as soon as it begins to get dark."

As the city had grown more crowded, the crime rate had risen. And yellow fever and smallpox struck again and again. Some said the ships loaded with immigrants brought the fevers. Others said overcrowding had made water from wells and streams unfit to drink. Certainly few streams within the city sparkled like the one now pouring its freshness into the brackish Hudson.

The boom whooshed over her head as the sloop turned and sailed slowly up the river toward a long wharf flanked by a huge waterwheel and a mill.

"The Pocantico River," Captain Abrams called down to her. "That's Philipsborough Manor ahead."

While the sailors unloaded the rum and sugar, Margretta moved so she could see the stone manor house with its gambrel roof and tall chimneys. Gardens and green fields lay beyond it. Was this what Van Badenswyck would be like? Excitement made her heart beat faster.

Later, back on the Hudson, they stopped briefly at Cortlandt Manor, where the cows were taken off. North of there, the river— nearly three miles wide, one of the sailors said—resembled a huge lake shimmering in the afternoon sun, a passage to and harbinger of a future that surely would be no less splendid.

They sailed until the sun had set behind the rounded hills to the west and the gold it had cast over the river faded. The breeze ceased then, the tide ebbed, and they dropped anchor in a cove. Margretta ate the supper of bread and cheese she had brought with her. Some of the sailors swam and had a ration of rum. Afterward, two of them sat beside her, conversing idly. Fireflies glimmered over the water, some settling on the rigging and one on the fine bobbin lace at the wrist of her brown linsey-woolsey dress. It flashed a fiery sparkle, then faded.

One of the sailors said, "I think that one is a female. She is saying: 'See how bright and pretty I am? Come over here and love me.'" He slipped an arm casually around her. "But you do not need to send such signals."

"No, indeed," said the other. "All you have to do is sit here with your hair like honey and—"

"I think that's enough, men," Captain Abrams said. "Miss Van Dyck may not appreciate your compliments, however well-intentioned. Time enough for enjoyment when we get to Albany."

Reluctantly the sailors got up and walked away. Then, to Margretta's surprise, the captain sat down by her.

"Is this your first journey on the Hudson?"

She nodded. "What a beautiful river."

"Yes. The queen of rivers. Beautiful for navigating, too. Even when she narrows, she still has a deep channel going all the way to Albany. And the tide. How many rivers can you sail up as we did today, at least twenty-five miles, without using oars?"

He talked a while longer about the river and his love for its idiosyncrasies, until he saw her stifle a yawn. Quickly he rose. "You must be tired."

"Somewhat. It has been a long day. The packing, crossing the city with all my things in a cart . . ."

"Of course. You must go directly to your cabin. I thought only to relieve you from perhaps unwelcome attentions. Some of my sailors are young and untutored. You are the only woman on board, very pretty, and under my protection."

"Thank you, I am grateful." She held out her hand. He clasped it warmly, then to her surprise lifted it to his lips and kissed it briefly. "Yes, very pretty," he murmured.

Her cabin was so small she could barely turn around in it, yet her bunk was comfortable, and the boat rocked her as gently as in a mother's arms.

They started out early the next day with the change of the tide, moving soon into a narrowed section of the river with mountainous shorelines. "These are the Highlands," one sailor said. He pointed to the east. "If the clouds weren't hanging so low, you'd be able to see Anthony's Nose up there. Over on the other side is Bear Mountain."

A few miles farther upriver, as they approached a large island on the east side, the river made an abrupt right-angle turn to the west, overlooked by a huge rocky prominence.

"Here at West Point we are always slowed down the most," the same sailor said.

Margretta could see why: the wind constantly changed direction, sometimes stopped altogether. It was late afternoon by the time they reached broader waters, but by then the tide and wind had subsided. Progress with oars was slow; they finally dropped anchor.

"With a good wind I could have got you to Van Badenswyck tonight," Captain Abrams said, sitting down beside her. "Are you a relative of the Van Badens'?"

"No. I am going there to teach the children of Dominie Hardenbroeck to read, write, and cipher."

"Dominie Hardenbroeck. I heard him preach some years ago in New York. A fine preacher. As a man . . ." He paused. "Oh, a good man, I am sure. Perhaps a bit opinionated." He stood up. "But then, a man as learned as he is has a right to hold firm opinions."

"And his wife—do you know her?"

"No, but I have heard that she knows more about herbals and medicines than most physicians do."

He left her alone then. She rather wished he had stayed . . . or allowed the sailors to stay. Harmless enough, they helped to make the time pass. She felt restless, confined. Now, far to the northwest, towering over the hills that stood close to the river, rose the Catskills. But though their splendor charmed her, she was tired of scenery, tired of sitting still, more eager than ever to move forward to grasp the future that lay ahead of her.

Later, as she lay wakeful in her bunk, she thought of Captain Abrams' remark about the dominie. Opinionated, was he? Perhaps difficult to get along with? Her father had never said so, but he had probably enjoyed the stimulation of a clash of opinions. All she knew

of the dominie was that, widowed, he had remarried and had begun
a second family, and that in the years before he had left the city he
and her father had spent long hours together smoking their long
Dutch pipes and talking about philosophy, religion, and the latest
books.

"New York," her father had said bitterly, "is not a city where ideas
flourish or where education is valued. Hardly a town in Connecticut
or Massachusetts lacks a public school, and each colony has a univer-
sity. Here what is valued is money, possessions, land."

A teacher noted for his scholarship, he had begun Margretta's instruction when she was five. By the time she was fifteen, she had her
own clientele.

"If anything ever happens to me or your grandmother," her father
had said before he left on his ill-fated journey to Holland, "write to
Dominie Hardenbroeck. I know that for my sake he will do all he
can for you."

She had done so after her grandmother's death. Although the dominie's reply had been formal, she had been sure then that in person
he would be warm and friendly. Yet recalling the coolness of his
letter, she began to entertain doubts about the wisdom of embarking
on such a questionable journey.

The next morning the sun shone brightly—a good omen—and
again the future became an adventure, impeded at the moment only
by a northerly wind that fought against the tide. The captain ordered
the sailors to tack; even so, the small islands and the narrowness of
the passage made sailing difficult. They finally had to anchor and
wait for a change in the wind.

Despite the delay, Margretta was able to find some amusement in
the winks and smiles of the young sailors who were so attracted to
her. In their three days of confinement together they had become
almost like a family.

Just before noon, a southeast breeze came up and they set sail
again, taking advantage of the last of the tide.

Margretta ate the remainder of her bread and cheese. The bread
was hard now, the cheese soft and its surface greasy, but she was so
hungry that it hardly mattered.

"Not long now," Captain Abrams said. "Up on the bluff there—
see it?—that's the Van Baden manor house."

What she could see through the trees was a long roofline with many chimneys. Below it a windowed second story peered down-ward. Was an interested gaze fastened on the sloop from up there? Was anyone else in the world seized at this moment with such a stirring mixture of curiosity and eagerness?

They continued sailing, more slowly now, and edging inland. Captain Abrams said, "There. That dock—the long one with the storehouse next to it—that's the landing for Van Badenswyck. We'll be leaving you there . . . with much regret, my dear." He turned away then, barking commands as the sloop slowed further and eased in toward the landing.

Some workmen in loose, ill-fitting clothes came out of the store-house and waited next to an empty wagon. Beyond it stood a carriage, sleek and black.

Also waiting on the dock was a tall man with graying hair. He carried a gold-headed cane and wore a long black surtout over his waistcoat. His bearing was so impressive that at first Margretta thought perhaps Lord Baden himself had come to greet her.

The captain leaped to the dock, shook hands with the man, and handed him a packet of mail. Then, helping Margretta off the sloop, he said, "Dominie Hardenbroeck, this is Miss Margretta Van Dyck. I believe you were expecting her."

The dominie greeted her with a perfunctory smile and a formal handclasp. She had expected more from a man who had been her father's closest friend.

"Was your trip a pleasant one?"

"Very pleasant."

"We took good care of her," Captain Abrams said.

"Thank you." He granted the captain a brief smile, then turned. "Come, Margretta. The carriage is waiting."

"But my things. . . ?"

"They will be unloaded and brought to you."

"But my *kas?*"

"You brought a *kas?*"

"It was my grandmother's marriage chest. I could not leave it behind."

Ignoring his faintly suppressed impatience, she smilingly directed the sailors as they unloaded the huge, handsomely carved oak piece and placed it in the wagon. Almost ten feet high, it contained the linens she had woven for her marriage, each piece bearing her cross-stitched initials. It also contained six silver spoons and a pewter porringer that had been in her father's family for a hundred years, her clothing, a brass clock she had inherited from her mother, a small wall mirror, her books, and the pillow, bobbins, and fine linen thread she used for making lace.

When the *kas* had been carefully placed on its back in the wagon, along with other supplies from the sloop, she shook hands with all the sailors and thanked them for their courtesy. One of them impetuously lifted her hand and pressed it to his lips. She withdrew it with a laugh.

"She is very pretty," Captain Abrams said to the dominie. "I am hardly being a prophet when I warn you that it will not be long before you'll find yourself performing a wedding. I had to watch my sailors all the way."

"I hope her behavior was circumspect."

"Indeed. Completely so."

The captain shouted an order now. At the same time, a florid-faced man emerged from the carriage and hurried toward the sloop. Dominie Hardenbroeck spoke briefly with him, then led Margretta to the carriage.

"How splendid," she said. "I have seen two or three of these in Manhattan, but I never expected to ride in one." Warmed by his thoughtfulness, she added, "This is certainly a very elegant welcome for a poor schoolteacher."

"It was quite by chance. The carriage belongs to Lady Van Baden. She suggested it be used to take her lawyer, Mr. Sulzer, to the sloop. The poor man was widowed only ten days ago. As long as the carriage was here, it seemed logical to take you back in it." He frowned. "Especially since every inch of the wagon is taken up with that *kas*."

"I see," she said softly. Then, determined not to let his words diminish her pleasure, she flashed a bright smile at the young purple-turbaned Negro holding the reins.

Dominie Hardenbroeck frowned again. "We are ready, Jupiter," he said.

As the horse began a labored walk up the sloping road that followed a stream at the left, the dominie cleared his throat. "As you know," he said, "I am a man of God. As such, there must be no hint of immorality in anything I do or say."

"Of course."

"The same is true of members of my household."

She looked at him, puzzled.

"And especially," he said, "of someone who is constantly with my children."

"Of course. And certainly there is no hint of immorality in anything I have ever done."

"You say that. But already I have observed behavior that is less than circumspect. I am referring to your easy way with the captain and, worse still, with those sailors."

"I was merely thanking them, saying good-bye."

"You exhibited a flirtatiousness, a lack of restraint, very much like that of a loose woman."

"Dominie Hardenbroeck, I am *not* a loose woman."

He lifted his hand. "I am sure you are not. At least, I am *reasonably* sure. But as your father's friend, I feel I must counsel you. I would not, like the captain you were so friendly with, call you pretty. You are not a true blond, and you lack the blue eyes that make for real Dutch prettiness. But you apparently have a quality that makes young men turn their heads. Perhaps you are unaware of the conclusions men leap to when a woman responds so impetuously to their attentions." After a pause that gave her time to speculate about those conclusions, he added, "While you are in my home and under my protection, I must ask you to curb such impulses. Thus you will avoid the appearance of evil."

Sitting as straight as possible, her fingers curled into her palms, she said in a voice that to her ears was full of false notes, "Thank you for your advice. I assure you my behavior in the future will be above reproach."

"Good." He patted her hand, but the gesture lacked warmth. It had nothing of the father in it.

As the carriage proceeded up the road, the dominie pointed out, through the dust stirred by the horse's hooves, a grist mill on the left. Beyond it, at the top of the slope near the sawmill, they turned right. The road, on level ground now, ran through a community of shops and homes, most of them built of stone and shaded by locust trees. She noted some of the signs: the wheelwright, the blacksmith, the dressmaker, the tavern. After passing the last house on the left, an imposing two-story wood structure with a sign in front that said "GUSTAVUS SULZER, LAWYER," they drove another hundred yards and, at a crossroad, turned right onto a narrow lane. Here, beyond a field and an orchard, she saw on the right a long, low stone house, its slanting roof extending over a porch that ran across the front. Beyond it stood a church with a high, pointed roof, and across the lane, barely visible through the trees, the manor house.

Again anticipation stirred within her. How different this would be from the life she had known as she had hurried through Manhattan's crowded streets, later returning to a home where all evening she had sat with a padded board on her knees working on the bobbin lace her grandmother had taught her to make and listening to the old woman as she talked about the past and complained about the present.

Although Margretta loved her grandmother and enjoyed producing a fine piece of lace, her thoughts all too often had wandered to others of her age who were experiencing the pleasures of family activities as well as the joys of courtship and love—and she was torn with restlessness and longing.

Yet when her grandmother had died, she had been brokenhearted. She missed the droning voice still, regretted her failure to say "I love you" more often and with more feeling.

She had remained silent and preoccupied during the remainder of the ride, more than a little angry with the dominie, merely nodding as he had pointed out shops and homes in the village. Once or twice he had glanced curiously at her.

Now, as he helped her down from the carriage, he said, "Do not be downcast. You probably did not realize what an unfavorable impression your forwardness created. I have tried to advise you as your father would have done."

"Thank you," she said, aware that the lack of humility in her voice made a mockery of her words.

Looking at the complacent expression on his face, she felt an urge to break away, run back to the sloop, and ask for a ride to Albany. She ought to be able to find work there.

But the wagon with her belongings was already lumbering down the lane, and on the porch a tall, angular woman was rising to greet her. Besides, the sloop would have set sail by now in order to take advantage of the wind.

It was too late.

Chapter 2

Although Margretta knew this was a second marriage for the dominie, she was unprepared for his wife's youthfulness: the un-
lined skin, the smooth brown hair. She went forward to meet her,
hoping to be greeted with warmth.

"My wife, Judith . . . Margretta Van Dyck." Immediately after the
introduction, he left them alone.

Judith smiled briefly, inquired in a perfunctory way about her
journey, and expressed regret for the deaths of her father and her
grandmother. "Your room is just off the parlor," she said. "You'll use
it for the schoolroom also. There's a *slaabauck*, so your bed won't be
in the way. But why not have a cool drink before I show it to you?
You must be thirsty."

"Thank you. I am. But first I want to see to the unloading of my
things from the wagon."

Judith gazed thoughtfully at the *kas* as the men carried it up onto
the porch. "That's quite elegant."

Margretta said without apology, "It's my wardrobe, my trunk . . .
and my marriage chest."

She was surprised and pleased to have a room of her own where
she could shut herself away from these people who had greeted her
with such restraint, and dream of a future in some as yet unknown
place where she would not be forced to lower her eyelids and express
thanks for criticism that she neither appreciated nor deserved. It was
furnished with a chest, a washstand, four straight chairs, and a rec-

tangular table, had a small corner fireplace and one window that looked to the east.

"Is there anything else you need?"

"A shelf for my books, if possible."

"I'll have Abraham put one up. And take out the chest." She went to the door. "I'll wait for you on the porch."

Alone, Margretta unpacked her books, changed to a lightweight blue muslin dress, returned to the porch. Soon a young light-skinned Negro woman with pretty features and delicately arched eyebrows came out with two cups on a tray.

"This is Alicia," Mrs. Hardenbroeck said. "She's pretty much in charge here. Alicia, this is Miss Van Dyck."

Alicia smiled with lady-of-the-manor graciousness. After she had gone, the two women silently sipped their strawberry-flavored drinks for a few moments before Margretta said, "Where are the children, Mrs. Hardenbroeck?"

"Please do call me Judith. I dislike formality."

"All right, if that is what you wish. And call me Margretta, please."

Judith said vaguely, "The children. You wanted to know where they are." She waved toward the woods behind the house. "Somewhere out there. They've been gone since early morning."

"When have they been doing their lessons?"

"Well . . . not too often. I don't have much patience for that sort of thing."

"What do they know, then? Are they able to read?"

"The girls know their letters. Most of them. Frederic"—now she smiled ruefully—"I'm afraid all he knows is how to make his way around the woods. Oloff leaves everything to me. Then he says I spend too much time in my garden." She looked hopefully at Margretta. "Are you by chance interested in herbs?"

"I know very little about them."

"Then I won't bore you by showing you my garden. It's too hot anyway." She finished her drink, then said, "Tell me how things are in the city."

"Crowded. New people coming in all the time."

"Here too. More and more foreigners. Huguenots, Walloons, Germans, even Irish. It's terrible. And of course many English. Too many. Most of them come over from Connecticut or Massachusetts. Our land here is of course so much better."

"Well, New York *is* an English province."

"That may be. But we still think of this section up here as Dutch. We see no reason to forget Dutch customs just because some greedy English upstarts are in control."

Margretta had thought only old people like her grandmother felt this resentment.

"When I was young," her grandmother used to say, "everyone I knew spoke Dutch. Even though the English had recently taken over, I was brought up to consider myself Dutch. The English are uncouth. At public gatherings the men spit on the floor. Their women do not scour and scrub as we do."

Always she spoke of the English as if she were unaware that Margretta's mother had been English. Reminded, she would say, "Yes, but well bred. Delicate in health, however."

Margretta had heard it over and over: the story of her mother's long wait for pregnancy, the miscarriages, the long labor that had produced the one baby girl, herself, and then the tired breathing out of too short a life.

Judith was saying, "You were there, of course, during the Negro conspiracy two years ago. Was it very frightening?"

"Yes. It was frightening to hear they were going to kill all the white men in the city and divide the white women among themselves. But still . . ." She paused, remembering a statement her father had once made: *There is no justification for one human being holding another in bondage.* "I cannot help thinking," she said, "that we all want to be free to do as we wish, go where we wish. And Mary Burton, that young girl who revealed the plot in return for a hundred-pound reward—much of her testimony didn't stand up. Even so, they hanged twenty-nine Negroes and a few whites and burned thirteen at the stake. Those who confessed were sent to the West Indies."

"The West Indies, yes. That's where we send our slaves. But only, of course, if they become unmanageable."

"I've heard they're worked so hard on the sugar plantations that they don't live long."

Judith rubbed the back of her neck. "But, as Oloff says, if they behaved, they wouldn't *be* sent away. Anyway, the slaves here are very well treated. Ours are comfortable in the attic, and the Van

Badens have fine quarters for theirs in their cellar." She gave Margretta an intent look. "I see you are a young woman of strong opinions. And sympathies."

Meeting her gaze with directness, Margretta said, "I sympathize with anyone deprived of independence."

"You're young, Margretta. As you get older, you learn to accept the realities of life. I don't even think about anything if I can't do anything about it." She stood up. "I should attend to some things. Perhaps you'd like to rest."

"Not really."

"Well, look around. Do as you wish."

Wanting activity, Margretta went out the drive and along the shaded lane toward the river. The lane, soon dwindling to a path, sloped upward. About five hundred feet to the left, she could see, more clearly now, the manor house. Though made of stone, the front that looked toward the village road was faced with brick.

What, she wondered, was it like inside? Would she really be invited there? She envisioned herself in a full-skirted, paniered gown, dancing with a handsome young man across a polished floor. Music, laughter, talk.

These thoughts lightened her steps as she moved toward the top of the incline. From there she could see the river, its surface like satin now that the afternoon breeze had died. Though tempted to follow the path down the steep grade to some benches and a small dock, she decided against it.

For a while she sat on a rock. A misty blue in the late-afternoon light, the Catskills beyond the river thrust upward toward anvil-shaped clouds. Less downcast now, she sat a long time and let herself dream of the future. Would she find someone here to love, to share the adventure of life with her? Would they travel to some new, exciting place? Would she have children of her own to teach and a home surrounded by a great stretching out of pastures, orchards, and plowed fields?

She was glad she had decided against going down to the river, for when she returned, the family was already seated at a table by the windows, food in trenchers in front of them.

The dominie looked up. "I see you are back . . . finally."

"I am sorry to be late."

"It is quite all right." Having made his point, he could afford to be magnanimous.

"Is she the one?" one of the girls asked.

"Yes, Gertrude." Judith indicated a chair. "Sit down, please. The children are eager to meet you. Antonia, stand up and curtsy. *Antonia*, I said to stand up. This is Miss Van Dyck. Antonia is nine. Gertrude here is eight, Frederic seven. Make a little bow, Frederic."

"When do our lessons begin?" Antonia asked.

"Tomorrow," Margretta said.

"That soon? For how many minutes?"

"From eight o'clock until noon."

"That long?"

"Unless, of course, you fail to do your work. In that case, we will have to continue into the afternoon."

"Mama!" They all spoke at once, united in appealing this effrontery, this threat to their freedom.

Judith lifted her hands helplessly. "Discuss it with your father. He is the scholar in the family."

"Papa. Do we have to have lessons all day?"

The dominie slowly chewed a piece of roast duck, swallowed it, cleared his throat, and finally spoke.

"Miss Van Dyck is your teacher and will be making decisions about your learning. I do think, however, that if she began with two or three hours a day and then—"

"Two hours. That's enough," Antonia said triumphantly.

Controlling her anger, Margretta said, "How many minutes are there in an hour, Antonia?"

Antonia shrugged. "What difference does that make?"

And Frederic said, "I don't like this teacher."

"Me neither," Gertrude said.

Margretta turned to the dominie. "Do you suppose we could discuss this after supper in your study?"

"That is a good idea."

Though her first bite of the crisply roasted duck tasted delicious, Margretta found it hard to swallow. She forced it down, smiled, even contributed to the conversation—all to prevent the children from discovering they had upset her. Although she knew their outburst reflected no more than their reluctance to study, what they said had put her in a bad light with their parents. Worse still, the dominie had made her lose face in front of them; it would make her work more difficult.

At last she faced him in his study, where he was already seated at his desk. "Dominie Hardenbroeck," she said, "I found that scene at the table very disturbing."

"So did I. Sit down so we can discuss it."

"I'll stand. What I have to say will not take long. You brought me here to teach your children. It is clear that no three children ever needed a teacher more. They are rude and undisciplined; they cannot read. I could read and write in two languages by the time I was Frederic's age. But only because I worked several hours a day. One learns through discipline, not indulgence."

"There is some merit in what you say. But . . ." He pulled at his collar with his index finger.

She understood how he felt. With this second family he was like an indulgent grandfather. When he did not continue, she said, "Dominie Hardenbroeck, do you want your children to spend their lives slinking around the woods like Indians, knowing nothing of the treasures that lie within books? Surely you, as a scholar, want more than that for them." She waited. "What is your decision? Do I have them for the morning? Or do you wish me to leave?"

From the mountains beyond the river came a drumroll of thunder. The dominie went to the window. "We'll have a storm before long," he said. He gave her a thin smile. "You may have them for the morning."

Detecting a note of respect in his voice, she softened her attitude. "I do not think you will be sorry."

He nodded, dismissing her, but as she moved toward the door, he said, "One more thing. You are here to teach them to read, write, and cipher. As for molding them in other ways, that is our job. You are not to indoctrinate them with your opinions about life, politics, religion . . . anything."

"I understand."

She found Judith still at the table, absorbed now, in the fading light, in a large tome propped up in front of her: *Pharmacopoeia Londinensis*.

"I'm going to my room now," Margretta said.

"Is it settled about the children?"

"Yes. I will see them at eight in the morning."

"Well, good night, then." Judith bent over her book.

Margretta took a lighted candle with her to her room, its small flame yielding a measure of reassurance. Thunder rumbled again as she closed her door. How grateful she was to have her own room, to be able to close the door on this family that was in no way her own. Although tired now, she forced herself to sit down and plan the first day's lessons and to lay out books and writing materials. By the time she was finished, it had grown dark. She stood a moment by the window. Would she someday stand here and watch someone turn down the lane prepared to sweep her up onto his horse and carry her away to a life of adventure in some new uncharted land?

Foolish dreams of faceless people and unseen places.

"I am afraid, my dear," her grandmother had said, "that you are doomed to comb St. Catherine's hair. That is what happens when a young lady has no parents to present her to society, no dowry large enough to attract the right kind of man. You must accept this single state as I have accepted the deaths of my husband and my son. Acceptance is all."

Easy enough to practice acceptance when your life was practically over, Margretta thought. Meanwhile, she would continue to nourish her hopes for a love great enough to accommodate all the longing in her heart.

She undressed, washed methodically, unhinged the door that hid the *slaabauck*, let the bed down, fastened the legs, and slid in between the sheets.

Immediately after she had blown out the candle, the storm broke with a flash of brilliance. The earth trembled in the thunder that followed; the house rocked in a fierce gust of wind. Rain hammered on the roof and trees creaked and groaned. Almost without letup, the sequence of lightning and thunder continued. It was far worse, this Hudson Valley storm, than any she had experienced in the city. She waited it out, her body tense until it spent itself, or, perhaps unspent, raced on to terrify people in the Housatonic Valley of Connecticut.

Her room was black and silent now. She turned restlessly, aware in every curve of her body of her aloneness and of her loneliness. What would it be like to have a young man holding her or making love to her? Often she wondered whether the act of love was as unpleasant as her grandmother had said.

"Perhaps you can find an old man," her grandmother had told

her. "An old man doesn't ask for much. Young men want to be on top of you all the time, making babies all night."

"And the women find no pleasure in this?"

"I never did. Nor would a nice girl like you, I'm sure. No, find yourself an old man."

A knock sounded on the door. "It's me. Judith."

"Come in, the door isn't latched."

Judith put a candle and a cup down on the table. "Are you all right? I've just checked on the children. That was the worst storm we've had in several years."

"I'm fine. I didn't enjoy it, but I'm all right." She sat up and put her feet down on the floor.

"I came to apologize for remaining silent before." Her face above the candle flame was all light and shadows and sharp angles. "People will tell you I'm odd. I guess I am—a woman who cares more for gardening than for housekeeping. Not the best of mothers. But I do hope we'll be friends."

"I hope so too."

"I thought you might be dispirited, so I brought you a special drink. Wine with some sprigs of borage steeped in it. It will lift your spirits."

"Thank you very much."

"Well . . . I'll leave you now. I see you have the morning's work laid out. You seem very efficient. Good luck with the children."

"Thank you. And for the wine."

She drank it slowly after Judith had left, then lay down again. Whether inspired by wine, the borage, or the expression of friendship, she felt a lift of the heart as she closed her eyes and prepared for sleep.

Chapter 3

Immediately after breakfast the three children appeared at the doorway of her room.

"Good morning," she said pleasantly.

They raced in and scrambled for seats.

"Stand up," Margretta said. "The first thing you do upon entering this room is say, 'Good morning, Miss Van Dyck.' Then you wait until I tell you where to sit."

The two younger children looked at Antonia. She nodded. "Good morning, Miss Van Dyck," they all said.

Ignoring the sullenness, Margretta said, "I want you, Frederic, to sit at the end. Antonia on this side, Gertrude on that. You will take these same seats every morning."

When they were seated, she continued. "Next I want to find out whether you can tell time." She held up a model of a clock face and quizzed them as she turned the hands. She moved the hands to nine o'clock. "When my clock says nine, you may leave for ten minutes. But you must be back by this time." She moved the hand ahead. "I'll do that at the end of each hour. At twelve o'clock we will stop. If you have been rude or have failed to do the work I have assigned or failed to return promptly, you will have to spend an hour with me in the afternoon."

They exchanged glances. The girls sighed to show her how much her arbitrariness tried their patience.

"Now, you will find writing materials in front of you on the table.

I want each of you to write as many of the letters of the alphabet as you know how."

While they worked, she walked around the table checking, correcting, praising neatness and accuracy.

The girls did well, but Frederic did so poorly that she had to write them out for him and put him to work copying them.

At nine she let them go. The girls returned at ten after, Frederic at quarter past.

"I'll see you this afternoon at one," she said to him.

"On the first day?"

"Absolutely."

Again at ten she let them go. The girls were back at ten-ten. Frederic, grinning, returned at ten-thirty.

"I'll see you this afternoon from one o'clock to three o'clock," Margretta said.

"You said one hour."

"But you've been late twice."

"It counts each time?"

"Of course."

"You see?" Antonia said. "I *told* you."

After that, Frederic returned on time, even appearing exactly at one o'clock for his afternoon session. The heat by then had grown oppressive. He wriggled restively. "Couldn't we do this tomorrow? It's so hot."

"No. Remember, Frederic, it was you who made the choice to come back here this afternoon."

"No, it was you."

"Not at all. I said you would have to come only if you were late. You chose to be late, despite my warning."

"I thought maybe you didn't mean it."

"I always mean what I say, Frederic."

The two hours were a duel of wills, his to leave, hers to make him work. He was so appealing she was not surprised Judith had given him such free rein. She had to resist her own impulse to make him happy by releasing him early. Looking down at the pale curls clustered around his head, she was filled with longing. Would she ever have a son like him? Was she really doomed to comb St. Catherine's hair?

Gradually she settled into the routine of the dominie's household and the way it revolved around his churchly duties. On her first Sunday she stood outside the church with Judith, waiting, she learned, for the two older Van Badens to appear. Nicolaus, their son, Judith told her, was now in Europe. "Moving in society, absorbing culture at the art museums. It would not surprise me to discover he is getting most of his education in the brothels." She rubbed her forehead. "Oh, dear, it's so hot. I do hate this waiting."

"Does everyone wait outside like this every Sunday?"

"Everyone except the dominie."

"Why?"

"Who knows? They've always done it. As a courtesy to our lord and lady, I guess. Besides, it gives the young people a chance to do some courting."

Looking around, Margretta saw young couples on the benches behind the church or walking near the graveyard, holding hands, touching. She sighed softly.

The Van Badens' carriage came down the lane to the church, Jupiter alighting first.

Judith whispered, "Have you noticed? The Van Badens like to dress up their slaves so they look like Oriental potentates. It's considered the thing to do."

As the sea of waiting people parted, the lord and lady, as confident of God's approval as the Israelites, paraded past them, Lady Van Baden in mauve silk, a faint smile on her narrow, haughty face; Lord Van Baden in a long, dark red coat with a white ruff showing at throat and wrists. As he walked, the full-skirted coat swung wide and the metal buckles on his knee breeches shone like gold.

Margretta took an instant dislike to the arrogant lift of nose, the distinctive curve of eyebrow, and the unsmiling nod when, as he passed, the parishioners—including Judith—bowed and murmured, "My Lord Patroon."

Inside the church with its small-paned, hooded windows, the congregation sat on long, backless benches. Lord and Lady Van Baden, however, sat on raised chairs that looked like thrones and were curtained for privacy.

During the service Margretta thought about those murmured words, "My Lord Patroon," trying to recall what her father had told her about the patroonships, remembering only that in the seventeenth century the West India company had given some of its members tracts of land on navigable rivers in return for the promise to bring settlers to the area. But hadn't the English abolished the system?

Later, she asked Judith about it—Judith, who was beginning to confide in her with more and more frankness.

"No, there aren't any more patroons," Judith said. "Not since the English set up the manor system in 1664. But some of the old property owners still like to hear the words."

"What's the difference between a patroonship and a manor?" Margretta asked.

"Not a great deal. The patroons were allowed to establish civil and criminal courts and to appoint officials. Those powers have been limited somewhat, but each of them sends a representative to the Assembly. Our representative is Gustavus Sulzer. He's the man who lives in the modern-looking house on your right on the way into the village."

"Yes, I noticed it the first day."

They passed it a few days later as they walked to the village, where Judith was to see her dressmaker. It was a fine day: the air clear, the flowers bright, the village street shaded by the arching branches of the locust trees.

Margretta went briefly into the dressmaker's with Judith. The woman, Antoinette Renault, a brisk, bright-eyed young widow, looked at the lace edging her sleeves.

"How lovely that is. You got it in Manhattan?"

"I made it."

"You can make bobbin lace like that? If you ever plan to sell any, come to me."

"For the time being, she'll be busy enough trying to teach my little Indians," Judith said. Then, turning to Margretta, she added, "Why not go out and look around? These fittings will take a while. And you've been confined all morning."

It was good to get out in the air again. Margretta strolled down the street, looking at the shops. When she came to the sawmill on the corner, she paused and watched the wagons pull up and unload long sections of tree trunks. Others were leaving with straight-sawed boards. The clean, sharp smell of freshly sawed wood drifted across the street.

Some of the younger men looked at her with frank curiosity, others with a boldness that went beyond curiosity. Only one of them touched his hat in the gesture of a gentleman. He was a big light-haired man who lifted the stacks of boards and set them in his wagon with ease and grace.

Who knows why one person is attracted to another? She found it hard to analyze, largely because the emotion that seized her existed so far outside rational thought. Nor could she prevent herself, during the next few days, from reliving that respectful gesture: the hand lifted to the hat. And her reaction. Her father had taught her to value two qualities in a man: courtesy and intellect.

He was married, of course. By the time she and Judith had reached home, she had persuaded herself that was the reason he had tipped his hat with respect rather than giving her the bold evaluation of a young man seeking a wife, or, like the sailors in Manhattan, an evening of pleasure.

She looked for him the following Sunday at church and each Sunday thereafter, each time suppressing disappointment when he did not come. After a while she stopped looking, stopped her foolish dreaming.

As the days passed, the children grew more tractable. The girls were easy to teach, eager to please and show off their knowledge, but though they presented fewer problems, Frederic gave her more pleasure. One day when they were alone she said to him, "If you do not learn to read and write fluently, how can you expect to be a success when you grow up?"

"I don't care. I want to be an Indian."

"And do what?"

"Paddle around in my canoe. Run in the woods. Hide behind trees. Shoot the enemy."

"What enemy? We have no enemies here."

"But the Indians have. Our Indians hate the Algonquins and the Hurons. They are the real savages."

"Silly boy," she said, resisting the impulse to give him a hug. "Those days of warfare are all in the past."

In time she discovered that Judith had not been joking when she had said she was a poor housekeeper. What pleased her was to work in her garden, a large rectangle laid out in neat geometric shapes at the side of the house. Fortunately, the dominie was able to afford half a dozen slaves who took over the care of the house. When Margretta arrived in June, the glow of red and yellow tulips from Holland had begun to fade, but the fence that kept the animals out sagged with the heavy blooms of roses. The perfume of their petals permeated the air, as did the subtler scents from the herbs that were Judith's main interest.

During the spring, summer, and fall, Judith cultivated her herbs, picked and dried flowers, leaves, and roots, or extracted the oils and scents by steeping, distilling, or stamping. Amid the beds nestled bulbous, narrow-necked glass bottles full of green herbs, each placed upside down on a lower one so that the distillation from the leaves would filter through a cloth to the bottle below. Others dried on wooden trays. Some merely steeped in the sun in bottles of water or wine or were decocted using the greater heat of the kitchen fire.

At other times Judith studied such books as Gerard's *Herbals*; and Culpeper's *The English Physician, The Queen's Closet Opened, Incomparable Secrets in Physick, Chirurgery, Candying and Cooking*; and others, many over a hundred years old.

Several times Margretta found her in the kitchen drinking chocolate with an Indian woman and questioning her about the qualities and uses of native plants and barks.

"Quite a few of their remedies are good," she told Margretta later, "but some are based on the doctrine of signatures. That's when some part of a plant looks like the organ it's supposed to treat, as with the liver-shaped leaf of the liverwort. Or assuming a parasitic plant will cure cancer."

Margretta had been able to muster little warmth for the dominie, a man of fixed opinions and moral judgments, but her admiration for Judith grew as she realized that when Judith made her oils, waters, powders, and decoctions, and dispensed them, often with surprising success, to manor residents, she was filling a role that nicely complemented the dominie's.

Their friendship grew throughout the summer as if nourished by the same beneficence of sunlight that ripened the herbs. Yet Judith was a woman of moods, who sometimes withdrew completely. At other times she was given to bursts of confidences. Once in the early fall when Margretta was helping her gather herbs and tie them into bundles for drying, they saw the Van Baden carriage. Judith with a twist of mouth said, "There goes my Lord Patroon. How he loves to hear those worshipful words. If only he knew how little worship lies behind them." Then quickly she added, "You must immediately forget anything I say about the Van Badens. It is my husband's job to cater to them. He enjoys it. As his worthy helpmeet, I of course share his feeling." She paused, rubbed her forehead with the back of her hand. "I am so glad you came, Margretta."

"I'm glad I came too." She could not deny her growing affection for both Judith and the children. Yet she was not really happy. "But I think," she added, "I might be happier if I were married and no longer dependent on anyone." It was the first time she had ever confided her feelings in anyone.

"That is quite natural. Perhaps in time we can find someone suitable for you to meet." She placed a spray of pearly everlasting in her basket. "These will keep the moths out of the wools." Then, straightening and glancing toward the manor house, she said, "Soon now the parties will start. You never saw such beautiful clothes. Everyone important along the Hudson comes. The Schuylers, Van Renssalears, Livingstons, Philipses, Van Cortlandts. No one from here in the village, of course, except for us and Gustavus Sulzer."

"And no teachers, I suppose."

"Oh, definitely not. Surely you did not think. . . ?"

"No, no. Of course not." Yet she was disappointed. Despite having no desire to mingle with the wealthy, she did long for new experiences, even if only to see the inside of the manor house. Was life here to be no more than repetition of her life in the city, with only the settings changed? It was true that it was beautiful here. But a woman of eighteen wants more than sunsets and views of a shimmering river, a river that now seemed static rather than a pathway to the future. Just as in Manhattan, she was still marking time, still longing for change.

Then quite abruptly change occurred, at least at the big manor house. Early in the morning of the first Sunday in September, Lord Van Baden died quietly in his sleep. A courier was sent to Manhattan with a message to be sent overseas on the next ship to inform Nicolaus of his father's death. Mr. Wortheimer, the agent, stood outside the church when the people gathered and told them the sad news. He said there would be no service, since the dominie was with Lady Van Baden, but that any who wished to do so would be welcome to go inside to pray.

That same day Margretta once again saw the young man she had seen outside the sawmill and once again felt an acceleration of heartbeat as he looked at her and lifted his fingertips to the brim of his hat.

Chapter 4

The following Sunday she saw the young man again. Standing outside the church in a pool of red and gold leaves that rustled and sent up a woodsy odor each time she moved, she found herself breathing more deeply and more quickly than usual.

He was with a young man and woman. His wife, or the other man's? Round-faced, dark-haired, pretty, she was talking rapidly, looking back and forth from man to man, now touching one on the arm, now poking the other. She held a baby in the crook of her left arm. Two small girls wandered in and out around the legs of their elders like kittens waiting to be fed.

The young man looked across the crowd; his gaze found Margretta's. Once again came that gesture, more common to the English than to the Dutch, of tipping his hat.

Lady Van Baden in her somber widow's weeds and black veil appeared then, leaning heavily on the arm of Mr. Wortheimer, the agent who managed the Van Baden properties. The crowd bowed with silent respect for her bereavement before moving to follow her into the church.

The next Sunday the young man appeared again with the same people. This time when he lifted his hand to his hat Margretta smiled. Immediately he crossed over to her, stirring the leaves as he walked, bringing their woodsy odor with him.

Removing his hat, he said, "I am Stephen Warner. I believe I saw you in the village early in the summer."

He spoke in nicely inflected English. His name was also English. Strange—he looked so Dutch with his straw-colored hair and blue eyes. He wore the leather breeches, loose, unruffled shirt, and heavy shoes of a workingman, but intelligence deepened the blue of his eyes, and his crossing over to speak to her showed, in its risk of being treated with condescension, initiative and courage.

"Do you serve the dominie's family?"

So that was it. Seeing her here and in the village with Judith, he had thought she was her personal servant.

Pride made her say stiffly, "I am a teacher. I teach the dominie's children."

Never mind that few people held teachers in high esteem. It was an honorable profession. "Food and shelter can guarantee survival," her father used to say, "but without education a person, a country, a world, merely stand still."

The young man frowned slightly. Did he, like some men, prefer women who were ignorant?

"I am a farmer." He pointed to the east. "I have a farm just beyond the Vanzuyders'."

"Are they the people you were talking with?"

"Yes."

"Then that pretty woman is not your wife?"

"No. I have been farming here for three years without a wife."

"That must be very difficult."

His eyebrows, light and thick, drew together over eyes as blue as Delftware. "Difficult, yes. And lonely. But not so difficult and lonely that I would take just any woman into my home simply to have a wife."

She had no answer for that. He looked at her as if he wanted to say something more. She wanted to invite him to call, but felt it would be improper. The man must take the lead; the woman must wait. But she could smile, and smile she did, until he said the words she wanted to hear.

"May I see you again sometime?"

"Yes. I am free on Sunday afternoons and often at other times during the week. And evenings."

"Then we could walk somewhere this afternoon?"

As she said yes, she wondered whether it was wise to acquiesce so quickly, but she sensed a shyness in him, a pride that might be wounded by refusal.

"Then I will return perhaps an hour after church."

As she watched him walk away, she wondered whether he, like herself, was speculating about their possible future together. Or was she being too precipitate? No, she thought. He *was* different from the other young men she had observed: more respectful, more responsible, and with that square-faced chin and strong body, far more attractive.

He returned a few minutes after dinner. She had changed from her high-waisted flowered muslin dress to the brown linsey-woolsey she had worn on the sloop. Earlier she had told Judith she was going walking with a young man.

"The one who came over and spoke to you before church?"

"Yes."

"What does he do?"

"He's a farmer."

"I see." Judith looked uncomfortable, hesitated, then half-smiled. "Well, be careful about getting involved too quickly. You hardly know this young man."

"I realize that. We are only going for a walk."

"Yes. Very well. Take some of the little cakes Alicia made. But do not pretend you made them yourself."

"I can cook, kindle a fire, and simmer meats. My grandmother taught me such things along with lace making."

"And your father taught you the skills of the mind. With all that and your pretty features and dark gold hair, you will indeed be a fine prize for the right man. Just be sure he is worthy. And mind you wear your sunbonnet, or that fair skin will burn. Men like white-skinned women."

Margretta smiled at her reflection in the mirror as she tied on her bonnet. Never mind her skills and knowledge: no matter what a young man said about choosing a proper helpmate, the choice was usually based less on wifely skills than on beauty and warmth. If she had been toad-faced and warty, would he have crossed the church-yard to speak to her? Of course not.

Looking through her window, she saw him coming down the lane, sitting straight on his horse. This golden September afternoon was like a smile of approval from heaven. She carried a small bag with her as she went out: cakes, bread and cheese, and a bottle of cider.

He greeted her with a smile so serious that it was hardly a smile at all, reminding her of a student before an examination. They walked along the lane and down the long, steep bank to the river. Although she had done this many times, she allowed him to help her over the rough places, mostly because he seemed to find helping so pleasant.

They went downstream and sat on one of the benches the Van Badens used for picnics. Even alone she had always enjoyed being by the river, watching the changing patterns of light and shadow on its surface as well as the varied traffic on it. Today they saw a huge log raft floating downstream. On it stood a small cabin. In front of it a woman sat spinning. Children were playing about the logs and a man was fishing.

"How much they seem to be enjoying themselves," Margretta said. "Free to do whatever they wish."

"Perhaps. But when they reach New York, the raft will be dismantled and the logs loaded on ships. Then they have to go back upriver and begin all over again. To work the land—that is a better way of life. To watch things grow."

"How large is your farm?"

"A hundred acres. About the right size for one man to farm by himself. In the three years I have been here, I have done much, but much more work needs to be done. Someday when I have sons to work with me, I hope to acquire more land." His smile had lost its earlier uneasiness. "I have many, many plans. But perhaps you do not admire ambition in a man."

In a steady voice, looking straight into the blue of his eyes, she said, "But I do. Probably because I, too, look forward to a better future."

She told him then something of her background, even telling him of the Indian ancestry on her mother's side: her mother's grandmother.

"That is where you get those dark eyes and high cheekbones."

"And my desire to be free. At the dominie's . . ."

"You are not well treated?"

"Oh, very well treated. But I feel obligated, not really independent. But tell me something of yourself."

"I came here from Philipsborough three years ago. That's south of

Cortlandt Manor. My older brother is still there on the land my father farmed. But I wanted to start out fresh on my own. The soil here is excellent." He held out his hand about three feet above the ground. "Black dirt as deep as this."

His father had been English, he told her, his mother Dutch. And the woman his father had taken as a second wife after Stephen's mother had died when he was two had also been Dutch.

"Was she good to you, this stepmother?"

He hesitated. "She kept me fed and clothed."

"I think you did not much like her."

"Perhaps I would have. But she preferred my brother. He was friendlier, easier to love, I guess. Then, as I grew older, I became aware of how poor a wife she was for my father. He had come from Connecticut and was a man of some education. She was completely ignorant. Quarrelsome, too."

Margretta asked no more questions, but she understood now some of the reasons for his reserve.

The sun as it headed for its resting place behind the blue mountains soon lost its summerlike warmth.

"Are you cold?" he asked.

"A little."

He edged closer to her, put his arm awkwardly across her shoulder. Suddenly ill at ease, wanting to move closer to him yet fearful of too much intimacy too soon, she slid away from him. Her life so far had largely been spent either with children or with people far older than herself. Eager as she was for new experience, she was unsure of exactly how to respond to the attentions of a man close to her own age.

"I brought food," she said. "Would you like some?"

"Yes, I would. I have had nothing since breakfast. It was too far to ride home. More than an hour each way."

"Why did you not say so earlier?" She reached up and touched his cheek. "I could have given you this long before."

He took the hand that had touched his cheek. "I felt no hunger. Being here with you, I thought only of . . ."

"Yes? You thought only of . . . ?"

"Never mind." He released her hand. "Just answer one question. Would you be willing to see me again? Willing, possibly, to think of sharing a future with me?"

She took a breath, felt it tremble in her throat. The sun, just before its final descent, cast a too-bright light on the water. She had to turn away.

"I know it is too soon," he said. "And I am not really asking it, only asking you to think about it."

"I would be happy to consider it," she said. Then she opened the bag she had brought, spread a linen napkin on the bench between them, and placed the food on it. "Here, take it all. I am not hungry."

"No. Let us share it." His face solemn, he broke a piece of bread into two pieces and handed one of them to her.

He did not again attempt to put an arm around her, nor did he try to kiss her that day or on any of the subsequent Sundays in September and October when they walked by the river or down the road past the manor house. Margretta, having by now lost her initial shyness with him, rather wished he would.

In the cold of November they were able to snatch only a few moments together before the service. Sitting in the church with her feet on the little stove Alicia had brought in for her before going up to the gallery, Margretta thought constantly of him, wishing she could invite him into the dominie's house, perhaps even into her room. But the last time she had put on a cloak to go walking with him, she had seen Judith frown. And once she had said, "Again? Still that same young farmer?"

One Sunday Stephen spoke briefly to her outside the church. "December 6 is Saint Nicolaus Day, you know."

"Of course." The slaves had been making frosted gingerbread shaped into figures of saints and warriors, horses and wagons, as well as Deventer cookies, rich in fruit and spices. And Margretta had been teaching the children poems and songs to recite during the family celebration.

"We have been invited to a party," he said. "Some friends of mine, Jan and Maria Harten, are giving it. The Vanzuyders are going. Would you like to go with me?"

"Very much. But I am not sure I will be able to take any cookies or cakes."

"No matter. I have given them a haunch of venison."

She spent the next few days in a state of excitement as she sewed lace just below the elbows and around the low neck of a full-skirted crimson dress: a holiday dress she had months ago made in hope.

The first heavy snowfall of the winter occurred early that week, unifying the gardens, pastures, and roads in whiteness. That same week Nicolaus Van Baden returned to the manor. No one had as yet seen him, but Mr. Wortheimer, the agent, had been around to announce that the new young lord would be accompanying his mother to church on Sunday and that it would behoove the villagers to greet him properly outside the church.

Beyond a moderate curiosity about his appearance, little of Margretta's time that week was spent speculating about Nicolaus Van Baden. Most of it was spent dreaming about the party she would be attending, her first real party.

Although the sun had set, its afterglow still lighted the sky and turned the surface of the snow a warm pink as, watching from her window, her hooded cape over her shoulders, Margretta saw a sleigh come down the lane. She recognized Stephen from the profile of his body. Surely no other man sat straighter or handled the reins with more ease.

With a quick good-bye to the dominie's family and a nod to Judith, who said, "Mind you're back early. Tomorrow is an important day for the dominie—remember?", she rushed out before Stephen could come to the door.

"What a lovely sleigh you have," she said as he tucked the bearskin robe around her.

"It isn't mine. It belongs to William Vanzuyder. He and Sara couldn't come tonight. One of the children is sick."

"I'm so sorry," she said. And she was. Yet at the same time she knew an exquisite pleasure in being alone with Stephen away from prying eyes and frowning windows. The heavy-legged workhorse stepped smartly along the icy ruts as if drawing the finest of carriages, the most patrician of people, while the harness bells tossed clear tones into the air.

At the end of the lane, Stephen turned right. After perhaps ten minutes he turned left. Here was farmland, level, with now and then a farmhouse keeping a lonely vigil in the midst of whiteness.

"Is your farm along here?"

"No. Farther along toward the Taconics. To get there, you continue eastward from the lane that runs in front of the dominie's. I live a half-hour ride past the Vanzuyders' place."

Then she would not see his house tonight.

The Hartens' square stone house was warmed by a huge fire and by the breath and laughter of nearly thirty people, most of them younger than their middle-aged hosts. A long table on one side of the room sagged with cakes, cookies, and roasted meats. In the center was a large punch bowl.

Many of the faces were already familiar, since Margretta had seen them at church. But it was good now to be able to put names to the faces and, sometimes, occupations. Most were farmers and, she judged from their clothing, less than affluent.

Stephen introduced her around, clearly pleased at the way people received and admired her. One older man said, "A schoolteacher? That is what Van Badenswyck needs."

"I teach the dominie's children."

"Only them?" At her nod, he pursed his lips, then said, "Well, that is his privilege, I suppose."

This man, who said he was from Massachusetts, spoke as she did, and as Stephen, the son of a man of some education, did, but she noticed that most others spoke with rude accents and made many errors. But they made up for their lack of cultivation with warmth and friendliness.

As the punch bowl lowered, the two Hanssen brothers picked up their fiddles and began to play. After the furniture had been pushed back, ten of the couples took formation for a dance, arranged in two rows of alternating men and women facing each other. Margretta smiled across the row at Stephen, noting how, broad-shouldered and strong and yet with a special quality of bearing, he stood out from the others.

With stately steps, the first couple started down between the two rows of dancers, bowing or curtsying, and alternately swinging each other and every other lady and gentleman in turn, their clasped hands held high. Each man danced with his left hand on his hip, his partner using her left hand to hold her petticoats up.

When at last Margretta and Stephen moved down between the dancers, each swinging another partner and then returning joyfully to each other, she felt as if they had been through an initiation ceremony that had, with the approval of the other participants, recognized them as a couple meant for each other.

The couples danced to a point of mixed exhaustion and exhilaration, varying their steps with many flourishes, changing partners, teasing, joking. When the fiddlers called a halt, more punch was served; then the feasting began, trenchers piled high, fingers soon greasy and sticky.

After eating, the crowd quieted. As they dipped their hands in a basin of water and dried them on a linen towel, some women signaled their men. Margretta looked at Stephen and he nodded. If only, she thought, they were going to their own home, rather than for a long, cold ride that would end with separation.

"Before you leave," Maria Harten said, "some hot spiced wine to warm you on your journey."

Margretta took hers, cupped her hands around it; then, looking at Stephen and he looking intently at her, they slowly sipped. To her that look communicated more than the words most people used in declaring their love.

It was probably after midnight, Margretta thought uneasily as she pulled the bearskin in the sleigh up close to her chin. All the houses they passed were darkened now. She prayed that the windows of the dominie's house would also be dark. Yet he often worked late on Saturday night. And tomorrow, with young Lord Van Baden in attendance, would be a special day requiring a sermon that combined words of consolation for his father's death with words of welcome and inspiration.

Even with the fur tucked around her, the cold penetrated. She felt let down, the evening's gaiety dissipated. Only coldness remained and the knowledge that months might pass before she would see Stephen again.

The stars poked through the black arch of the sky like tips of icicles, glittering with a radiance as promising as it was unattainable. Stephen sat straight beside her, silent as the sky. Was it boredom, shyness, or simply an innate reserve that made him so reluctant to expose his feelings?

Three months had passed since he had asked her to consider sharing a future with him. Why had he failed to mention it again? Had he changed his mind but held back telling her so, hoping that during the winter months ahead she would gradually forget him and his hint at a declaration?

Partly for warmth but mostly to rekindle the closeness generated between them at the party, she moved closer to him and slipped her arm through his.

"Stephen, when will you take me to see your house?"

"In the spring. It is too cold now."

"Surely you have a fire."

"Yes. But when I go to the village, I have to cover the coals and pray there will be some live ones when I return. After that it takes several hours to warm up the place. When you visit, I want you to come into a warm house."

"I do not mind. I shall wear warm clothing."

He shifted position. Moving away from her? "It is not just that. Something else. I cannot speak of it now."

She sensed she had been too bold in slipping her arm through his, too quick to accept his invitations. But if he thought she was bold, then it could not lessen his opinion of her if she asked the question that had haunted her for weeks.

"Stephen. I want to know how you feel about me."

There. Blunt. This he could not evade with a generality or with no words at all. Yet in the silence that spread out like a wake on the river after her words had cut through it, she realized how peremptory her voice had sounded. Like a teacher. *I want to know the answer to that question. Right now.* Was it her teacherish manner that had made him hesitate to commit himself further?

At last, leaning forward, he wrapped the reins around the whip in its socket. Slipping his arm away from hers and still looking straight ahead, he said, "How do I feel about you? Frightened."

"Of what?"

"Frightened that what I have to offer you will not be enough. Frightened that I am not good enough for you. Frightened that if I tell you how much I love you and want to marry you, you will refuse. That is why I say nothing."

"Is it I then who must boldly say I love you and want to marry you? It would be unbecoming for a woman to speak such words."

He turned to her quickly. "Then let me say them. But how can I say it right? How can I tell you—?"

She touched his lips with her fingers, stopping the uneasy flow of words. "If the words are hard to say, why not show me?" Oh, more boldness. But this man who had early learned to conceal his feelings clearly needed help.

He put his arms around her then, his lips on hers tasting faintly of spiced wine, rekindling the memory of the moving firelight and the rhythm of the music while sparking an even brighter glow within her.

While the horse's iron shoes clopped along the icy road, they remained fastened in a tight embrace, Stephen's mouth hard on hers.

"When will we marry?" he said finally.

"In June. I told the dominie I would stay a year."

When they came to the crossroad, the horse hesitated. Releasing her, Stephen took the reins again and guided the horse. Now the words he had held back for so long rushed out like beer foaming from a keg that has been shaken. He spoke of his house, of how he would add to it, build a barn perhaps so she could use the garret for whatever she wished, how he would clear more acres in order to increase the crops he could raise. He spoke of their happiness together, of the sons they would have.

The horse turned down the lane that led between the manor house where young Nicolaus awaited his welcome and the dominie's house where, she prayed fervently, the entire family would be sleeping soundly. The windows, however, reflected a brightness that darkened her hopes.

Stephen secured his horse, helped Margretta out of the sleigh, and walked with her to the door. There he took her in his arms again. She lifted her face for his kiss.

The top part of the door opened. The dominie stood there in his long nightshirt, his tasseled nightcap.

"Margretta, cease this immodest display at once. Come directly inside." As he unlatched the lower part of the door, she went humbly in. "And you, young man," he continued, "I want you to leave these premises at once. I do not know what other young women you consort with, but this one happens to be of good birth. She also happens to be under my protection. Young ladies of her class do not stay out until after midnight."

With dignity Stephen said, "Reverend sir, I apologize for the lateness of the hour. My intentions toward your charge are of the highest. May I come in and speak to you of them?"

"You may not. They would be presumptuous at any time. But they are far more so at this hour. I asked you to leave. Now do so at once."

Closing the heavy door, the dominie bolted both top and bottom before turning to face Margretta. "I am ashamed of you, the daughter of my closest friend. When I asked you here to teach my children, I presumed you were of good moral character. You have behaved well enough these past months to allay my original suspicions, but this wanton behavior tonight—"

"It was not wanton. He has asked me to marry him, to share all his worldly goods with him."

"That illiterate peasant—"

"He is not an illiterate peasant. His father was an educated man."

"That may be, but he is still a serf. As for worldly goods"—he placed a hand on her shoulder—"the poor fellow has nothing."

"Dominie Hardenbroeck—"

He lifted his hand as he did in church. If a whole congregation fell silent at such a gesture, could she do less?

"We will discuss it later. If not tomorrow, then Monday. This Sunday is a big day for me, as you should surely have been aware. Already I have been forced to remain up far later than is my wont. Now, go quickly to bed. And quietly."

Her room had no fire in it, yet she hesitated to make the noise of shoveling the last coals from the parlor fire into a warming pan.

She undressed and got quickly into bed. Her feet were chilled numb. She rubbed first one, then the other, even put her face under the coverlet so that her breath would create warmth. In her own home no one would ever go to bed this cold. Her own home. Would she ever have one?

She was unable to erase the dominie's words from her mind: *the poor fellow has nothing.* Would the dominie lie to her? But his very profession precluded such immorality. She lay awake hearing the clock in the parlor strike two, then three, her body curled into as small a package as she could make of it, her thoughts leaping from the anger of the dominie's words to the sweetness of Stephen's. She refused to believe that Stephen had been lying to her. Why should he? Certainly not for those few kisses that she herself had invited. Yet why was he so reluctant to take her to his house? And what about that other reason, that secret he was so unwilling to divulge? Was it perhaps that there was no house, no farm at all?

Chapter 5

Margretta awakened to a lowering sky. A few desultory snowflakes fluttered in the air like moths uncertain of their destination. Her sleep had been light and intermittent, and the mirror reflected her tiredness in the paleness of her skin and the shadows under her eyes. If men liked pale complexions, then today she would certainly attract admiration.

But today she wanted not admiration but answers—from the dominie and from Stephen. When she saw Stephen, she would apologize for the dominie's brusqueness, explaining his concern about the service today with the new lord of Van Badenswyck in attendance. "And," she would add lightly, "he worries about my future. Apparently he is quite unaware of your holdings."

When she went out for breakfast, the dominie, leaving the table, greeted her with a frown. Judith evaded her glance, but Antonia said, "You're late. Did you have a good time at the party? You look terribly tired. Are you?"

She smiled at the child. "Yes to both questions."

She turned to Judith. "If I am late, I do not need to have breakfast."

"No, no. Have some. You will need something in your stomach if you are to wait in the cold for his lordship."

Margretta poked at the suppone, mixing the buttermilk and molasses more thoroughly with the cornmeal. Though cold, it tasted good. She had always enjoyed food and felt a special need for it when

47

her sleep had been short. By the time she had drunk two cups of tea, she felt ready to face talking with both Stephen and the dominie. By evening all her questions ought to have been answered.

When the bell sounded, she went out to the churchyard with Judith—a still quiet Judith who had as yet asked no questions about the night before.

Despite the cold and the thickening snowfall, a crowd had gathered to see how the new lord looked after his sojourn abroad and to assess how effective he was likely to be.

Margretta scanned the crowd, looking up the lane over and over. Knowing how much she would need to be reassured, Stephen would surely come today.

Hearing a sleigh, she turned joyfully. It was the two Van Badens, swathed in beaver. Jupiter, turbaned now in beaver, helped Lady Van Baden, heavily veiled, out of the sleigh and picked up her stove. Nicolaus Van Baden, a man with a narrow handsome face, a proud lift of nose, and black eyebrows arched like the spread wings of a bird, stepped down and held out his arm for his mother. They advanced through the waiting crowd, people bowing and murmuring, "My Lord Patroon."

His coat swung open revealing black waistcoat and breeches, relieved only by the shining knee buckles. He looked this way and that, acknowledging the obeisance with a nod. His gaze lingered on Margretta, perhaps because she neither bowed nor murmured the traditional words. Or was it her pallor that had caught his eye, or the combination of dark eyes and what the sailor on the sloop had called her honey-colored hair? It was she who turned away first, disturbed by his gaze.

At the doorway the dominie in his three-cornered hat bowed and greeted them. The people then filed into the church, tomblike in its chill, made bearable only by the small stoves or heated wrapped bricks underfoot.

Nicolaus and his mother sat in their thronelike chairs on either side of the tall wineglass-shaped pulpit, curtains drawn so that only their feet were visible.

Upon entering, the dominie doffed his hat and went to the front of the church, where he stood at the foot of the stairs leading up to his pulpit and faced the congregation. He raised his hand, invoking a moment of silent prayer. After mounting his pulpit and sitting down, he gave the fore-reader the scriptural selection. Following the scripture reading and the singing of a psalm, the dominie rose to speak. At the same time, the two Van Badens opened the curtains that had hidden them from view.

The first half of the sermon eulogized the deceased lord, welcomed the new one. After that the collection basket was passed twice, once for the church and once for the poor.

The second and longer part of the sermon dealt with morality and the attention that must be given to avoiding the appearance of evil, for that could corrupt others even as it ruined one's own reputation. Had he, Margretta wondered, meant this exclusively for her? It went on endlessly; her stove cooled, her patience dwindled. How could she manage to wait until next week to see Stephen, or if not then, the week after?

At dinner Judith complimented the dominie on his sermon. Frederic said, "The second part was too long."

"That is because you do not listen with care. If you did, your mind would be occupied with the wisdom imparted and the time would go quickly. Is that not so, Margretta?"

"Yes, indeed. One may even be rewarded by hearing words of wisdom meant especially for himself."

The dominie smiled. "Well put. Nicely said."

After dinner he retired to his study, did not send for Margretta. That evening he and Judith went to the manor house for a supper of oysters brought up by one of the last sloops to get through before the river froze. Margretta played games with the children, waited again in vain. At last she sent the children to bed, asked for a fire in her room.

She stood a moment by the window, though she could see nothing outside but blackness—that and snowflakes building up on the windowsill, every additional inch of snow making it more difficult for her and Stephen to meet.

She was filled with despair. It pressed against her heart, lay heavily in her stomach. "Oh, Stephen," she whispered. "Where are you tonight? What are your thoughts?"

The next morning Alicia interrupted her class to say that the "Reverend Master" wished to see her. She was relieved. Once apprised of the truth, she need no longer dread it.

"Sit down, child," the dominie said, smiling at her. "Now, let us discuss this penniless young man you seem to fancy."

"It is not just a fancy. I happen to love him and he me. And he is *not* penniless. As I tried to tell you Saturday night, he has a home and one hundred acres of land. He is planning to add onto his house and later to buy more land."

"Buy *more* land?"

"Yes."

"How can he buy more when he owns none now?"

Patiently, as if explaining to a child, she said, "As I told you, he has one hundred acres."

He shook his head slowly, his patience matching hers. "You do not understand. He is a *tenant* farmer. He may live in a house he calls his, he may farm acreage he calls his, but it is all part of the Van Baden estate. He is no more than a serf. The house and the land are not and never will be his."

"All the other farms—"

"All the other farms are the same. Owned by the Van Badens. All the farmers pay rent."

She stared at him, her mouth and lips dry.

"Where did you think the Van Badens got their money?"

"I thought they came from Holland with money, then were given land grants in return for bringing in settlers. Actually, I guess I never gave it much thought. I just saw them as wealthy titled people."

He came around his desk and clasped her shoulder. "Then you should start thinking about it," he said, as usual sounding the most kind when he was being the most cruel. "Ask yourself whether you want to live in a place that is not yours and whether you want to spend your life with a man who has deceived you into thinking he is a man of property."

"Yes, I shall. But I want to talk with Stephen about it. He may have bought his land. It's an hour's ride to the east, perhaps beyond the Van Badenswyck boundaries."

"My dear, in the seventy or eighty years that the Van Badens have been here, they have sold no land. Why should they, when they can collect rents on it forever, and when land prices are constantly increasing? If this farm you speak of is only an hour's ride to the east, then it must be part of the Van Baden acres, for they go all the way to the Connecticut border—or in fact beyond what Connecticut *thinks* is its border."

Moving slowly, she stood up. This must be what it was like to be old, this heaviness of body. "I'm still determined to talk with him."

"By all means. You should do so."

That afternoon, walking in tracks that had been made by sleighs, she went to the village, hopeful of seeing someone who might take a message to Stephen. She had no luck.

It snowed again the next two days, keeping her in. By then it was so late in the week she decided to wait until Sunday. But what if he stayed away from church altogether in the future? Could she then summon the boldness to go to his neighbors the Vanzuyders or perhaps even to his house to confront him?

Why, if he loved her, did he not send her a message by someone? Was it because he knew his deceit had been revealed? But she would not judge him yet.

On Sunday she stood by the parlor window, her cape over her shoulder. Behind her the slaves were taking coals from the fire and putting them in the foot stoves. Fine ashes filtered into the air and were caught in the shafts of sunlight that slanted through the windows. If he failed to appear, she would say she felt suddenly unwell and would stay home.

She waited. He came. He was in a sleigh with the Vanzuyders. As soon as she caught sight of him, she flipped her hood up over her head and hurried out the door. She had reached the sleigh before they were all completely out of it.

"Stephen, I need to see you. Do you suppose we could go for a walk after church?"

His blue eyes were grave. "It is a poor day for walking. The snow is too deep."

"But I must talk with you."

Turning then, he introduced her to the Vanzuyders, Sara and William. Sara said, "Why not come home with us for dinner? We got beans and salt pork. Been cooking since yesterday. Plenty for all of us. Then Stephen can take you home later and you can talk. I got to warn you, though, my house ain't too clean. I wasn't expecting no company."

"Perhaps the dominie will not allow it," Stephen said.

Aware of how much his pride had been wounded, she said, "The dominie was very tired that night. And nervous about the special service the next day. And we *were* at fault, Stephen. It was very late. But I am free to come and go as I wish."

"Then please come," Sara said. "My beans are sweetened with maple syrup from trees that Stephen tapped. There ain't nothing sweeter. Except perhaps his talk."

"You will come?" Stephen said.

"Yes." Oh, why did he not ask her to his house, where they could really talk? Or did he have a house? Did he perhaps live with, work for the Vanzuyders? She must find out.

The Van Baden sleigh, elegantly scrolled and decorated with brass, appeared then, and last week's processional into the church was repeated.

Lady Van Baden nodded this week to the waiting people, but her eyes, seen dimly through her veil, looked as always at a point above their heads, abjuring any suggestion of intimacy.

Nicolaus—Judith, who had watched him grow to manhood, had referred to him by his first name so often that Margretta rarely thought of him by his title—did nearly the same, except that, as they had last week, his eyes under the winged brows met Margretta's for a few seconds before she turned uneasily away and began speaking with Judith.

"The Vanzuyders, friends of Stephen, have invited me to their home for dinner."

"Did you accept?"

"Yes."

"Supper, too?"

"I'm not sure. Probably."

"What a shame. The dominie and I have decided it is time to introduce you to some suitable men. I've invited Gustavus Sulzer to come for supper tonight. He saw you one day and admired you. His wife died in the late spring."

"And he is already looking for another?"

"He has three children."

How flattering, Margretta thought. They had entered the church now and were seated in their pew before she whispered, "How old is he?"

"Around forty. Maybe a little more."

"Too old for me," she said, remembering Stephen's lean, strong body and the firmness of his features.

Judith frowned. "He is the same age as Oloff was when he and I were married. And I was only a bit past twenty."

And how happy are you? Margretta thought. She would rather comb St. Catherine's hair than endure that kind of marriage.

The dominie took his place in front of the pulpit in his black silken gown with the immaculate white linen neck band and the two falling bands which, in the old Dutch way, he referred to as his *befje*. He lifted his hand for the silent prayer. All murmuring ceased except for Judith's soft whisper into the quiet: "Try to come back early enough to meet this man."

Margretta nodded. She would try, yes, but not hard.

After church she left immediately with the Vanzuyders.

"Us women will ride in the back with the children," Sara said. "It will keep the gossips quiet. When Stephen takes you home, you can sit close to him as you want. He'd like that for sure. He don't talk of anything but you."

The Vanzuyders' home, a one-room stone cottage, was a clutter of poorly made furniture. The remains of breakfast still sat on the table, along with the unwashed trenchers.

"Don't them beans make a good smell?" Sara said.

Margretta nodded. But overwhelming it was the acrid odor of soiled diapers. While the men built up the fire, then went outside to take care of the animals, she helped Sara clean off the table and set out the food.

No silver spoons decorated this table, no pewter cups, no napery of any kind. The beans, which had cooked in a footed iron pot set in the coals at the back of the fireplace, were good, though far different from the roast loin of pork that had been in preparation when she had left the dominie's.

Later Sara sat by the fire and nursed Jeremias. She appeared so completely at ease that Margretta, beset by inner turmoil and questions, felt envious.

Sara, William, and Stephen did most of the talking. Margretta listened for comments that might answer some of her questions. At the party she had attended, the talk had been light and flirtatious. Today it was sometimes light, more often serious. What she dis-

covered as she listened was that these people had no love in their
hearts for the Van Badens.

"His lordship," William said. He bowed low and murmured "My
Lord Patroon" in an exaggerated imitation of those greeting Nicolaus.
"Lord and lady. It ain't a hereditary title. Did you know that? But
they figure nobody knows the difference."

"Where did you find that out?" Sara asked.

"At the tavern when I took the corn to be ground."

"Aha. So now they're grinding corn at the tavern."

"Now, listen, my girlie. When you've heaved ten sacks of corn
from the garret down a ladder and outside and into a wagon and then
out again at the grist mill, and then heaved the sacks of meal back
into the wagon again, you deserve at least one drink at the tavern.
Especially when you've had to leave one of the sacks of meal for his
lordship."

"Why one for his lordship?" Margretta asked.

"His privilege. It's part of our contract."

"What I hate most," Sara said, "is waiting outside the church for
them, when I could be inside getting my feet warm."

"I hate the bowing," William said. "In fact, I don't do it. Maybe
one of these days Mr. Wortheimer will take me aside and tell me
where I've been lacking. Lacking, but no lackey. How's that for a
joke?"

Stephen said, "The young lord has not been back long. Perhaps
he'll make some changes."

"Might be. Changes for the worse."

"Now, Will, you don't know. Stephen could be right."

"How do you feel?" William asked Margretta. "I just remembered
you been staying with the dominie. Maybe you're on their side, not
ours."

"I'm only just now learning there *are* two sides. I've only been here
since June, and I spend most of the time with the children. But
whatever my opinion, you can be sure I will never speak of what has
been said here today."

"I was sure of that," Sara said. "Somehow just by the look of you,
I knew you could be trusted. By the way, did you know that we are
going to have another child?"

Stephen said, "I've always heard a woman could not conceive
when she was nursing."

William snapped his fingers. "So much for old wives' tales."

Remembering her grandmother's talk, Margretta said, "Maybe a young husband's tale—a husband who does not want to postpone his enjoyment."

William turned to Stephen. "I fear you will have trouble with this Margretta Van Dyck."

"If he does," Sara said, "it will be good trouble."

They spoke as if a marriage would unquestionably take place, evidently unaware of the dominie's outburst. This might be the last time she would be with these people. She was sorry, especially about Sara. She liked her guilelessness and her outspoken way of talking.

Sara put Jeremias down on the mattress in the alcove next to the fireplace where she had said she and William slept. As she changed the baby, she said, "You want a little brother, Jeremias, don't you? Sure you do."

She turned to Margretta, who had come close, seeking warmth from the fire. "I don't mind. I had easy birthings with them all. It ain't no real trouble except for the diapers. With no water in the house and the pond frozen, it ain't easy. I soak them in this washtub here, but I don't have the water to rinse them good. If I didn't have lots of bear fat to put on the poor little fellow's ass, he'd probably be covered with sores. But"—she smiled now—"it will be warm when the next one comes. And perhaps soon William will figure out how to get me the water I need."

"I already know *how*," William said.

"Then you should take a chance." Speaking again to Margretta, she added, "Will's afraid they'll raise the rent if he does something about the water."

William's brows drew together. "I'm sure Miss Van Dyck isn't interested in our water problems, Sara."

But she was—very much so.

Darkness came early on these short December days. "We should leave soon," she said to Stephen.

"Wait for the moon to rise," William said.

Sara pulled a reed from a stack in the corner, dipped it in bear fat, lighted it, and placed it in the reed holder on the table, where it smoked and sputtered but gave a little light. They had more beans and some mulled cider, and with Jeremias asleep now and the girls in their alcove, the four adults sat at the table and talked awhile longer.

It was peaceful talk that looked ahead to spring sugaring, plowing, and planting. As she sipped the hot cider, Margretta looked around. How poor the furnishings were. No cradle for the baby—just a rude box. A piece of cornhusk protruded from the mattress in the alcove. Not even a feather bed. And William had obviously made the stools on which they sat. Hers wobbled on the bare, uneven, and unswept floor.

Was this the way she wanted to live?

At the door Sara said, "Sure was nice having you here, Margretta. It ain't too often I have a woman to talk to."

"To complain to," William said. Margretta noticed, though, that at the same time he put his arm around his wife. But if he loved her, why did he let her live in such squalor?

Stephen tucked the bearskin robe around her in the sleigh and placed a heated brick under her feet. He got in, snapped the reins, and the horse moved forward.

"So. You needed to see me?"

"Yes. I wanted to ask you . . . some questions."

He waited. In the face of such reticence, directness came reluctantly. "You told me, Stephen, that you had one hundred acres. Do you own that land or does it belong to the Van Badens?"

"I rent it from the Van Badens."

"And your house?"

"It goes with the acreage."

"Then you own nothing?"

"Tools. Farming equipment. Some animals. A little furniture. Why do you ask?"

"Because you led me to believe you owned it all. You spoke of *my* land, *my* house, as if they were really yours."

"I think of them as mine." Again he was silent, measuring his words before he spoke. "Why are you surprised? No one in Van Badenswyck owns land except the Van Badens."

"But I did not know that, not until . . ."

"Not until the dominie told you. Is that it?"

"Yes."

"And he feels that because I am not a man of property I am not good enough for you?"

Her silence was her answer.

"Just believe this. In no way did I attempt to deceive you. I thought everyone understood how manors are run."

"Everyone except me, I guess."

The moon had come up now, its light brighter than usual as its shine was reflected from the crystals on the surface of the snow. Stephen continued to look straight ahead, his profile proudly etched against the moonlit landscape. Finally he said, "But it does make a difference to you."

"Oh, Stephen, I do not know. The trouble is that after you talked about your farm and your plans for expansion, I built dreams around it for the kind of place we could leave to our children. It gave our future a purpose."

"I, too, had the same purpose. That is why I moved up here from Philipsborough. Here when you buy a leasehold, your sons can take it over simply by continuing to pay the rent. And the land is very good: rich soil, few stones."

"Then you do own something?"

"As I said, the animals, the—"

"No. I mean you do own your leasehold?"

"Yes."

"Is it something you can sell?"

"That's right. And if I improve the land and the house, I can sell it for more than I paid. But there is one problem. The landlord gets one-third of the profit."

"Would there be enough to buy some land elsewhere?"

"With savings added . . . but it is not easy to save. Profits are slim and have to be shared."

She fell silent now. Their ride, punctuated as it had been by silences and gropings for words, was nearly over now. She had hoped for a quick denial of what the dominie had said, solid reassurances of their future together. Oh, maybe it was wrong to think of comforts for her family, but she could not bear to think of bringing up children in a home like Sara and William's.

Most of all, she had hoped that once the matter had been settled, Stephen would again wrap the reins around the whip socket, leaving both his hands free to hold her while his lips sought hers, but he made no move to do so.

The sleigh reached the crossroads. Stephen guided the horse down

the lane toward the dominie's, turned in the drive, and stopped behind another sleigh, its brasses glowing in the moonlight. Through
the windows of the house Margretta could see the flicker of candlelight. The guest was still there.

Stephen helped her down, looked at her.

"Stephen, I need time to think."

"Yes." His voice was cool, withdrawn.

"Can you help me in any way?"

"The decision is yours." He accompanied her to the porch. "The
next Sunday that the weather is good, I'll come to church. You can
tell me then how you feel."

He turned quickly away, his face like a mask; nor did he look back
as he hurried to the sleigh—a big man dressed in deerskin and heavy
wool that needed mending, a man who clearly needed and wanted
her but was too proud to say so. She wanted to call out to him, but
he had spoken to the horse, flicked the reins lightly on its back, and
was off before she could find her voice.

Chapter 6

Flames crackled high in the fireplace, sending waves of brightness around the room. Candles made pools of light on tables or around wall sconces. Margretta could not avoid comparing this shining room with its scrubbed floors and polished furniture with the one she had recently left.

Judith was playing the melodeon. A man stood close by, watching her. The dominie took Margretta's cape, led her to the fire. "You must be cold, my dear."

The man came toward them, his velvet breeches and waistcoat whispering as he walked, the buckles of his shoes catching the firelight.

"Margretta," the dominie said, "may I present Mr. Gustavus Sulzer. Mr. Sulzer, this is that educated young lady I described to you—Margretta Van Dyck. Her nose is a bit red from the cold at the moment, but when the color fades, you will find she is as pretty as I have said."

So now he was saying she was pretty, emphasizing good points as if trying to impress a buyer.

Mr. Sulzer bowed, took her hand, and lifted it to his lips—dry and chapped. His hair, heavily powdered and thinning near the back, had a stale sweetish smell. But what had he smelled when he had lifted her hand? Soiled diapers? Rancid bear fat?

The dominie poured wine, handed a cup to Margretta, a silver cup at that. Judith, her eyes unusually bright, her cheeks pink, left the melodeon now and joined the others, who had drawn their chairs into a semicircle before the fire.

"I'll have more wine too, dear."

The dominie hesitated only a few seconds before getting up to pour it for her.

"Thank you *very* much," she said.

The conversation here differed greatly from the one at the Van-zuyders'. Mr. Sulzer had recently returned from Holland and England. It had been a bad trip, bitterly cold, the ship encrusted with ice when it sailed into New York harbor. He spoke of gatherings in both countries attended by highly placed people. Yet though he appeared absorbed by the people and incidents he was describing, his gaze kept straying to Margretta: her hair, her face, her figure.

A woman of eighteen, no matter how inexperienced, knows certain things intuitively. Margretta knew, just by the quality of his gaze, that this man had assessed her and found her pleasing. Perhaps she did, as the dominie had so reluctantly admitted on the first day, have a quality—something beyond mere prettiness—that men found attractive.

It soon became clear that Sulzer had been in Holland to handle business interests of his clients and in England to deal with some of the unreasonable, so he said, restrictions placed on Hudson River landlords by the crown.

"New York City would be nothing without us," he said. "Where else would they get their lumber and their grain for bolting into flour?"

"And the furs," added the dominie.

"The furs, of course. There is more stability here where the manorial system prevails than anywhere else in America. It's a great boon for the British. Even though they won't admit it, they must know how large a part of their revenues have their origins right here in our Hudson Valley."

"Yet still they bring pressure on us. Hamper us with legalities," the dominie said.

"Yes, indeed. The landlords are always in the middle. Royal demands on one side, tenants' complaints on the other. A difficult position. The wisest course, it seems to me, is to work on convincing the tenants that the landlords' main function is to protect them from royal encroachment."

The dominie said, "Miss Van Dyck—or perhaps she would not object if you thought of her as Margretta—has recently become acquainted with some of the younger tenants."

"Oh?" Sulzer's eyebrows rose. "And have you heard many complaints? What do they speak of?"

"Of what concerns most young farm people. Planting and crops. Babies."

"Indeed." Turning, he shared a supercilious smile with the dominie. "Most of them are illiterate and thus are largely taken up with their daily routines. I doubt that there will be any discontent here. Even the few little problems that have emerged on some of the other manors have been quickly resolved. Still, I am glad that young Nicolaus has returned."

"The older Lord Van Baden was a fine person, it is true," the dominie said, "but—"

"He pinched me once," Judith said suddenly. She put her empty cup down, her cheeks more deeply pink than before.

"My dear—"

"But he did. It was the year I came here. We were standing in a group talking. Suddenly he reached around behind me and pinched me. No, as I think of it now, it was more of a squeeze than a pinch." ·

As if deaf to the exchange, Mr. Sulzer said, "Young Nicolaus will doubtless promote some new progressive ideas."

"I can think of one," Margretta said.

"You can? What is it?" His smile now was pleasantly indulgent, as if saying: Let this charming child interpose her little suggestion before we return to serious conversation.

"Start a school in the village. Teach people so they can manage their affairs better and become more independent."

"But, my dear young lady, that is exactly what we want to avoid: independence. With education come ideas, some of them dangerous. Soon you would have rabble-rousers like those in New England. Future leaders should be privately taught. As for our tenants, what they want is to raise crops and children. And that is as it should be. Certainly a worthy purpose."

Persisting, Margretta said, "I would be willing to teach in such a school without a salary."

His gaze rested on her with even more warmth than before. "A generous offer, but I am sure you do not wish to remain a teacher indefinitely. So charming a young lady will surely want to ally herself with a responsible protector."

"Ally myself?"

"To marry, that is." His florid face had a sheen of sweat on it now.

Unwilling to reply to this, she lifted her cup, swirled its amber contents. After a moment she heard him say, "Taking their own courts away from the landlords was the biggest error perpetrated by the crown. Unjust, foolish, and expensive. All that unnecessary travel to Poughkeepsie and Albany."

"Ah, well," the dominie said. "It is always possible to find ways to work within a system."

"Indeed. But so much more cumbersome."

Margretta drank the rest of her wine, put her cup down. She would say nothing more. As she listened, however, she realized that Sulzer was not expressing opinions just to share them with the dominie. His glance kept straying to her as if to be sure she was listening. He was trying to impress her with the idea that he was an important and responsible person.

She noted the richness of his clothing, the satin lining of his waistcoat gleaming in the firelight. His wife, too, would dress in satins and velvets; her skirts would be panniered in the latest fashion. But at night she would get into bed with this man whose belly even now strained against the buttons of his passementerie-trimmed vest. She stopped short, unable to project her imaginings beyond that point without remembering what her grandmother had told her about the unceasing demands men made on women. Or was this man too old for such things? She had no idea when such desires subsided.

Strange—the thought had never entered her mind when she was with Stephen. She had enjoyed having his arms around her, the feel of his mouth on hers, had even agreed to marry him without considering that aspect of the future.

When at last Sulzer heaved up out of his chair, Margretta rose also along with the others. Mr. Sulzer took her hand, again bent his face over it. The same dry, powdery smell rose from his hair . . . so unlike Stephen's simple man-smell.

"Oloff," he said, "this young lady is all that you said she was: pretty, charming, and intelligent."

The dominie clasped his hands over his stomach, inclined his head, and smiled as if modestly accepting the credit for her charms, for her very existence.

"If it is within your power to grant it," Mr. Sulzer continued, "I should like permission to call on the young lady."

"She has no one but us. You may certainly call, provided the young lady is willing."

What could she say? "I am not especially eager"? She smiled and said nothing.

Still holding her hand and speaking now directly to her, Mr. Sulzer said, "It would merely be for the purpose of getting better acquainted. Would you object to that?"

She shook her head.

As soon as Sulzer had left, the dominie turned to Judith. "You should not have said that about Lord Van Baden."

"But it was the truth."

"Even so, he was an old man. He probably didn't know what he was doing."

"He knew what he was doing. He was exercising one of the prerogatives of the lord of the manor."

"Judith, you know that no hint of that kind of immorality has ever touched any of the manor lords."

"Perhaps not. Most have been more interested in acquiring new property. But old Lord Van Baden wanted both. Everybody knows that he had an interest in more than one of the young dark-skinned women around the manor."

"Those are only idle rumors."

"Then why are some of them so light-skinned? Alicia, for example. Did you ever notice her eyebrows?"

"Rumors, rumors. Perhaps it would be best if you retired now. I should like to speak with Margretta."

As his wife, accepting her dismissal, left the room, he said to Margretta, "Sit down, my dear. Tell me, did you confront that young man with the information I gave you?"

"Yes."

"And was I right?"

"Yes. But he had no intention to deceive. He thought I understood the status of the farmers around here."

"How do you feel about his offer now?"

"Dominie Hardenbroeck, I have had no time to think."

"That is true, I suppose. Well, then, were you impressed by Gustavus Sulzer? Could you bring yourself to entertain a proposal of marriage from him?"

"I have had no time to think about that either. He did seem a substantial and intelligent person, but I . . ."

"You are tired. I can see that. Go to bed, my dear. But remember this. If I seemed to interfere last week when you came in so late, or tonight by introducing you to someone I feel is eminently suitable, it is only because I desire the best for you. I owe that to your father. And remember this, too: a young man's kisses can set your blood on fire; an older man will ask for fewer kisses and give far more in return."

Surprisingly, she went right to sleep that night and awakened with no sense of having any problems. She spent the morning listening to the children read—something they were all doing quite creditably these days. Her concentration was complete, her mind avoiding all thought of decision.

At the end of the noon meal, when everyone except Judith and herself had left the table, Judith said, "Have you given any thought to Gustavus?"

"No. You may find it hard to understand, but I cannot think about him. Not yet. To me he is a stranger."

"And the young man?"

"I cannot think about him either. If I try, the thoughts lead nowhere. Does this seem strange?"

Judith, her elbow on the table, rested her cheek against her hand. "No. Sometimes too much weighing of all the good and bad in a situation leads to confusion. I think when you finally decide, it will be sudden. All at once you will know that you must do one thing, cannot do the other."

"I hope it will be that simple."

"Don't misunderstand me. The decision you come to in this way may be the wrong one. You may live to regret it."

"Judith, if I asked you a personal question, would you answer it? Or would it make you angry?"

"I wouldn't be angry. I'd answer it, but maybe not with complete honesty." She smiled. "You want to ask, don't you, what it's like to be married to an older man?"

"Something like that. Or what led you to do it."

Now Judith put her other elbow on the table so that both hands were supporting her head. She looked past Margretta out through the window to her snow-covered garden.

"The dominie can be very charming. And I had always looked up to him as my pastor. Besides, I had few suitors. I'm old enough now to admit that without embarrassment."

"You are happy, though—aren't you?"

Judith turned back from the window. "Let's say I'm not unhappy. Isn't that practically the same thing? I have my garden. And of course I have my children." She stood up and stretched. "We are all different, Margretta. We all make different compromises. I cannot help you with your decision."

For a few days Margretta succeeded in persuading herself she had no immediate need to make a decision. Then on Thursday afternoon she was in her room brushing her hair after dinner when Alicia knocked. "You have a caller. Mr. Sulzer."

"Tell him I shall be out in a few moments."

Alicia nodded pleasantly. Margretta was struck as always by her beauty, especially by the golden skin and luminous eyes. But today she also noted the curve of her eyebrows, very much, she realized, like the bird-wing brows she had noted on Nicolaus. Had Judith been right about old Lord Van Baden?

"Was there anything else? You looked as if you were about to say something else."

"No. Just tell him to wait. Thank you, Alicia."

She decided to wear her brown linsey-woolsey. Though simple, it set off the dark gold of her hair and was an effective background for the creamy lace at wrists and throat.

He stood by the fire, his hands behind his back. No one else was in the parlor—quite deliberately, she was sure. Crossing the room to greet him, she was aware of his eyes on her, of the swirl of her skirts around her ankles, of a sudden feeling of timidity.

As he had before, he took her hand and kissed it, but this time he also turned it over and placed a lingering kiss on the palm. Was that the tip of his tongue she felt against her skin? It made her feel shivery and uncomfortable. He looked at her intently as she drew her hand away.

"Come, let us sit and converse awhile," he said.

She followed him obediently. They sat by the fire facing each other. What followed was less a conversation than an inquisition. On Sunday he had observed her appearance, her manners, her charm; now he questioned her about people she had known in New York as well as the Van Dyck family. "A good name, Van Dyck," he said. "Many are people of property."

"Yes, but our branch of the family preferred scholarship to the acquisition of—even to the effort of holding on to—property."

"I see. And your father is dead?"

"Shipwrecked on his way to Holland."

"And your mother?"

"She died in childbirth. I was the only child. My mother, by the way, was English rather than Dutch."

"Indeed? Well . . . some of my best friends are English. An interesting mixture, Dutch and English. Clearly you are a combination of the best of each nationality."

"One more thing, Mr. Sulzer—"

"Please, if we are to be . . . well, if we are to be friends and possibly more than that, you must begin right now to call me Gustavus."

"Very well, Gustavus." And in just a moment, she thought, you will doubtless regret you encouraged some informality. "My mother was not of pure English blood. Her grandmother was an Indian woman."

The interest on his face faded into a mask that covered his feelings. After a moment he said, "You are part *Wilden?*"

"Yes."

He clasped and unclasped his hands several times; then quite suddenly the mask dropped and he smiled. "Ah, well, it is only a small amount of blood."

"Gustavus, I am proud of that blood. If you find me at all interesting, it is probably because of, rather than in spite of, my Indian blood."

That was unlikely to be true, she realized as soon as she had spoken, for her adventurous spirit and love of freedom were qualities a man like Gustavus would least prize in a woman.

"You may be right," he said. "At any rate, it is only . . ." He checked himself.

"Only what?"

"A formality, this inquiry about your ancestry. Only a part of my desire to know you better."

He spoke then of his own ancestry, pure Dutch on both sides, landowners and professional people in the Netherlands.

She nodded, uncaring, unimpressed.

Abruptly he said, "Do you have a dowry of any kind?"

How strange. Stephen, who owned so little, had never thought to ask her what she could bring to the marriage.

"Nothing except a few possessions," she said.

He rose to leave shortly after that. Judith came in, and the three had a brief impersonal conversation. Margretta handed him his greatcoat and cocked hat, then folded her hands behind her so that without grasping her arm and shaking her hand free he could not again plant one of those moist kisses on the sensitive skin of her palm.

After he had left, Judith said, "Well? Do you know him better now?"

"I know his ancestors better."

"What a strange child you are. Many women, here and in Albany, have vied for his attention since he was widowed. No doubt it is your indifference he finds so intriguing."

"I didn't think I was indifferent. I was polite."

"He'd be busy a great deal of the time, just as the dominie is. It would be a nice life, Margretta: travel, a lovely home, enough slaves so you would have little to do but direct them. You'd have time for reading and fancywork and visits with friends. Think about it."

During the next week she spent much time trying to imagine how she would feel as mistress of Sulzer's home. Yet marriage involved more than that. And why this pressure from everyone to decide? She must resist the efforts of the dominie and Judith, even though well meant, to rush her into a quick acceptance she might later regret.

On Thursday, a bitterly cold and windy day, Gustavus appeared again. He came in with his coat and muffler up around his ears and his hat pulled down to meet them.

Both Judith and the dominie were present. Margretta had been playing chess with Frederic, a game formerly of the taverns that the dominie had only recently permitted in his home.

The family quickly disappeared. Again Margretta and Gustavus faced each other, closer to the hearth today because of a cold draft across the floor.

Today the examination related to health, with Gustavus first informing her of his splendid physical condition, his freedom from ailments that plagued some men over thirty, his possession of all his front teeth. He then proceeded to question her: Had she ever had smallpox? Was she subject to colds? Did she have the ague? How many teeth had she lost so far?

Only one tooth lost, she told him. As for the rest, she was in fine health, with few illnesses in the past.

"Good, good," he said. Rising, he held out his hand. "Come. I should like to show you my home."

"It's not the best of days for walking."

"We won't be walking. My man is waiting outside with a sleigh and plenty of furs to wrap around you."

Waiting outside in this bitter weather?

"He's shivering. He must be very cold," she whispered to Gustavus as they approached the sleigh.

"Nonsense. They do not feel things as we do."

Giving them a frozen smile, the Negro helped them into the sleigh, tucked the furs around them. Beaver. No warmer than bearskin, but wonderfully soft and silky.

During the short ride he spoke of the weather, how cold it had been, how cold it probably would be in January and February, how it impeded travel. She said nothing.

A Negro woman opened the door, took their outer clothing. Immediately Gustavus took Margretta on a tour of the house. Everywhere, Margretta saw evidences of wealth: a turkey carpet of warm reds and blues draped over a table in the parlor, a leather-covered chair with brass studs, a Dutch cupboard painted with Apocryphal scenes and birds and flowers.

Upstairs, after a tour of the children's rooms and the attic weaving and workroom, he propelled her, his hand on her back, to a large bedroom, dominated by a huge four-poster bed.

"This is the room my wife and I shared. The one my future wife and I will share."

She glanced at the bed. From beneath it peeped the moon face of a large white chamber pot. She had a sudden vision of herself sitting on it while Gustavus lay in bed watching her. How could she ever do it?

Gustavus, having been married before, would probably feel no embarrassment, would stand casually over it, or sit on it red-faced and grunting.

"I see you are looking at the bed," he said. "Is it not beautifully carved? And it is very comfortable." He pressed his hand down into it. "Only the finest of goose feathers here." Smiling with confidence, he moved on to treasures that would impress her further.

"Now let me show you our *kas*." Opening the wide doors, he revealed an array of gowns, skirts, and petticoats spread out full length on shelves. "My wife's," he said. "My first wife's, that is. Fine materials." He pinched some velvet between his fingers. "Here, feel this."

She did, but with the sensation of touching something illegitimately, something not her own.

"They would be too large for you, of course," he said. "But they could be made over. It would be a shame to waste such fine materials—would it not?"

"I suppose so."

He rubbed his hands together. "Let us go downstairs and have some tea. One of the few English customs worth imitating. Oh, sorry. I forgot that you were part English."

"It does not matter. I agree that afternoon tea is a pleasant custom."

His hand on her elbow, they walked downstairs. He was always touching her. Not in an intimate way, but still . . .

They sat at a table in front of the wainscoted fireplace in the sitting room. The same woman who had opened the door for them brought in the tea on a tray. More Delft. More pewter. Some silver spoons.

Margretta poured the tea, put in the amount of sugar he requested, and handed it to him.

"You do that with great charm," he said.

So she had passed another test.

His children came in then and stood quietly waiting to be introduced. When Gustavus presented them, the boy bowed, the girls curtsied. The boy said they were all very pleased to meet her and they hoped she liked their home. Then, at a gesture from Gustavus, they said good-bye and left.

"Well, what do you think?" Leaning across the table, he took both her hands, a large smile on his heavy-featured face.

"They are nice children. Polite, well-spoken."

"Indeed. I am proud of them. And they liked you. But that is not what I meant when I asked what you thought."

"Oh?" She drew her hands away.

"I meant, what would you think of becoming mistress of this house?"

His words came as a shock. Despite knowing his intentions, she had felt he would engage in a decent interval of acquaintance and courtship before speaking of marriage.

The house *was* lovely, comfortable in every way. She could easily imagine herself sitting by this fire working on lace, reading, holding a baby. And if a baby, she need have no worry about diapers. Someone would take them to the washhouse and bring them back later, dry and sweet-smelling. Someone else would clean the house, make the candles, carry out the myriad details of housekeeping. And her adventure-loving nature could find pleasure in traveling to Albany, New York, or even Europe.

"Gustavus, I do not yet know you well enough to be able to answer that question."

"Then let me tell you more about my background. Or ask me anything you want to know."

"It is not your background that I am interested in. It is how companionable we might be." There's love to consider, she wanted to say. Love. He had not even mentioned it. Was it something that happened after marriage? How could she, so young and inexperienced, identify it and be certain of her feelings? Finally she said, "Gustavus, it is too soon for us to think of marrying. You don't really know me."

His face was serious now. "I know all I wish to know about you. Tell me, is it that I am too old? I assure you that I am in full possession of all my faculties and physically able to match what any younger man can do."

Did he mean what she thought he meant? Was she blushing? "I need more time, Gustavus."

"Very well. I shall give you more time. But let me say that I am very eager to remarry. I am lonely. And my children need a mother. How long will you need?"

"I'm not sure. Meanwhile, perhaps you should look elsewhere."

"No, no. I'll give you a few weeks. Well, a month."

He pulled a cord, and when the servant appeared, asked for their coats and ordered that the sleigh be brought to the side of the house by the entrance to the office.

"I'd like to show you my office," he said.

Carrying their coats, he led her to a smaller room. "Is this not a beautiful writing table?" he said. "And look at the carvings on this chair. As an educated person you will surely appreciate the number of books I have."

She nodded, tried to look impressed.

Again a self-satisfied look crossed his face. He took her cape from the chair, and, facing her, slipped it over her shoulders. His hands lingered there a few seconds; then suddenly he was holding her and pressing his mouth on hers. His hands slipped down her back below her waist, and grasping her tightly, he drew the lower part of her body sharply against the long, hard length of his. At the same time, the firm tip of his tongue began to pry its way between her lips.

Appalled, she tried to wriggle away.

"Don't be alarmed," he whispered as he continued to press his body against hers. "No one can see us. And no one will come in. I have given strict orders that I must never be interrupted when I am in my law office."

Again he sought her mouth. "No, no," she said, turning her head. "Please, Gustavus. You will lose all the ground you have gained. I cannot be won by such rough tactics."

Immediately he dropped his arms. His florid face was redder than usual. "Forgive me. I was carried away. You are so very attractive. It is hard for a man of vigor to be alone with you for long without giving way to impetuousness." He put his coat on. "At least you can be sure of one thing: my physical powers are quite undiminished."

She said nothing.

"Are you offended?"

"To be truthful, Gustavus, I am. I gave you no reason to think you could take such liberties."

"Please forgive me. I have been very lonely. And from the moment I first saw you on the dock, I have been captivated by you. Please, Margretta, do not look at me so reproachfully. I assure you that I will not touch you again until you have given me your promise of marriage."

He looked so foolishly beseeching, like a big dog who knows he has made an error, that her anger evaporated.

"Very well. Let us forget the whole thing."

"Indeed. Yes. That is the best way."

He took her home then. She went directly to her room to change, still annoyed by what Gustavus called his impetuousness and what she called his boldness.

At supper, the dominie said, "Where did Gustavus take you today?"

"To see his house."

"Ah. A most serious move. Excellent. It will not be long before he states his intentions."

Margretta poured more maple syrup on her corn cake. "He already has. He asked me today whether I would like to be mistress of his house."

"He did? Why did you not say so? I'll call for some wine."

"No, please. I gave him no answer."

He arched an eyebrow. "Still? Still undecided?"

"It has only been two weeks."

Judith said, "Don't rush her, Oloff. This is not a decision a woman can make quickly."

"If she is too slow," he said with irritation, "she may ruin her chances of making a good marriage."

"I don't want her to get married," Frederic said. "I want her to stay here and teach us and play with us forever."

"We do too," both girls said. "We want her to stay."

"Soon you will no longer need instruction," the dominie said to them. Then, turning to Margretta, he said, "You should consider his offer a compliment as well as an opportunity to step upward . . . rather than downward."

Much as she resented his statement, she realized it was true. She was, in effect, a servant here, lifted above the actual servant class only by the knowledge she had. Though now a dependent in a household, she could be mistress of an even finer one. Certainly by marrying Gustavus she would be rising from her present dependent position, but she refused to admit that marrying Stephen would be a step downward. To do so would be to admit he had no future.

But more important than the circumstances was the man himself and how she would feel about spending a lifetime with him. She prayed that the sun would shine on Sunday, that Stephen would come to church, and that he would come alone in the Vanzuyders' sleigh. She needed to spend more time with him, she realized, before she could come to a decision.

Chapter 7

Just as a warming sun had followed her bidding, so also did Stephen. He came to church, and he came alone in the Vanzuyders' sleigh.

"Can you take me for a ride after church?" she asked. "So we can talk? I have brought a little food with me."

"Yes. That was why I borrowed the sleigh."

At the end of the service, she spoke briefly to Judith, who nodded stiffly. Perhaps she could not be blamed. She and Oloff had made an effort to engineer a suitable match for her with a man far more desirable in their eyes than the man who would publicly accompany her away from church. Someone else was also displeased by the spectacle: Gustavus Sulzer. His disapproval was implicit in his formal, unsmiling nod.

The reins slapped lightly on the horse's back; the sleigh moved forward. At the end of the lane, Stephen turned to the right. Why didn't he go straight ahead to his house? They could stir up the fire, hold each other close to its warmth.

After a period of silence, broken only by the squeak of the horse's hooves on the hardened snow, Stephen said, "That man who was looking at us—is he the one?"

"The one what?"

"The one whose house you visited on Thursday."

"Who told you that?"

"A friend who was at the St. Nicolaus party. I told him the man was widowed and that you might have given some lessons to his children. Was I right?"

"No. He was . . . showing me his home."

Stephen turned toward her. "Ah. When a man shows a woman his home, his intentions are surely serious."

"Then yours cannot be."

"But—don't you understand?—I am trying to make it pleasing for you. When I have finished—"

"You could let me see it now and at the same time tell me of your plans."

"No." He sounded discouraged. "As I worked, I thought only of making it better than William's house. Now I fear that when you see it, you will compare it with Mr. Sulzer's."

No doubt she would. Yet when her thoughts turned to Sulzer's home, they did so in terms of the man himself: pointing out his bed, commenting on the clothes of his first wife, sliding his hands boldly down her back, trying for too much intimacy too soon. And the dry, powdery smell that always surrounded him clung to her memory as much as it had clung to him.

Stephen had the smell of a man who worked on the land and who spent time with animals. Yet his hands, even his wrists when they poked out of his sleeves, were always clean. She liked it, the honest man-smell, more appealing than the womanish smell of scented powder and soap that emanated from men who never lifted anything heavier than a quill pen.

The afternoon sun grew warmer. She set aside her muff, loosened her cape, threw back her hood.

"Stephen, one thing you must remember. When I marry, I shall marry a man, not a house. What is a house, actually, but a place to shelter people who love each other?"

Fastening the reins, he shifted his position so that he was facing her. The horse, with no one to urge it, proceeded at a slower and slower pace.

"That is what I have always thought. When I work in the house after chores, I think of what it would be like to be there with you. Loving you. . . ."

She smiled gently at his admission. "Now I'll tell you something. When I was at Gustavus Sulzer's, he tried to kiss me. I refused to allow it. I told myself it was because I did not know him well enough. Now, however, I know the real reason. It was because I was remembering how I felt the night you kissed me." She looked down at her folded hands. "It was as if when you kissed me, you put your personal seal on me." After a pause she added, "Perhaps I should not be saying such bold things."

"They are not bold."

"But my next words will be. Would you kiss me again, Stephen? Kiss me the way you'd really like to?"

He hesitated, looking at her. Then he moved close, slipped his hands inside her cape. Her mouth under his was like an opening flower. The kiss lasted until not just her lips but her whole body blossomed with a honeyed sweetness.

Abruptly he moved away.

"What is wrong?"

"Nothing. Everything is so right my body could easily be fooled into thinking we are already married."

She sat still, waiting for the turbulence within her to subside. Finally she said, "I told you I would give you my answer today. I think I already have. But I can put it into words if you want me to."

"I want you to."

"I want to spend my life with you, Stephen."

His was the slow smile of a reticent man. "Even to be just the wife of a poor tenant farmer?"

"To be your wife, yes. But not to spend my life with a poor tenant farmer. You will be more than that. We can go west or up to the Hampshire Grants. Any place where we can be free. I will help." She took his hand, held it close to her cheek.

"How beautiful your hair is when the sun shines on it," he said. "Like the dark honey the bees make from buckwheat and goldenrods in the fall." He kissed her again, but with more restraint.

"Are you hungry?" she asked.

"Very."

They had bread and cheese then, and Christmas cookies. Stephen took some oats from the back of the sleigh and put the feed bag on the horse. "She's a good horse," he said. "She's been very patient with us. I thought she might want to celebrate with us, so I brought some oats along for her."

"What if we had nothing to celebrate?"

"Then I would have given them to her to console her. I know she will be happy about this, for she likes it when I am happy and speak cheerfully to her."

They talked, dreamed out loud, stopped their conversation now and then to renew their intimacy with kiss and touch, every moment drawing them closer still.

But soon the sun lost its warmth, its brief pretense that it would give them the gift of spring along with the gift of love. Shivering, Margretta fastened her cape, covered her head, threw a crust of bread onto the snow for the birds. "I guess we should go back . . . unless you want to take me to your house."

"No. Not until spring. After the mud season is over." He turned the sleigh around, headed back.

As they rode, they made plans to marry in June, in the dominie's home if he would allow it.

It was growing dark when he left her. "I may not see you for quite some time," he said. "Perhaps not until spring. I have much to do this winter. And as soon as it is warm enough, I must begin plowing and harrowing."

She felt let down. At least four months of loneliness ahead. "But I should tell the dominie, shouldn't I? So he can get our license?"

"Oh, yes."

"I will be very lonely," she said.

He took her face in his hands. "It will be lonely for me, too. But spring is such a busy time. That is when I tap the trees. I also take the grain in to be ground once the streams are full enough so the grist mill begins running. Until you live on a farm, you cannot realize how much has to be done in the spring. And in addition I must get things ready for you."

"I can help with that."

Firmly he said, "I must get the house ready."

Happy that she had finally made a decision, though the happiness was tempered by the knowledge that she must wait through the long winter months, Margretta went into the house. Alicia and the dominie were drawing the dining table from its place by the window over to the fire. Judith was sitting even closer to the fire reading Gerard's *Herball*.

Looking up and smiling, she said, "Well, our little traveler returns. Come over here. You must be half-frozen."

Margretta went close to the fire. She was cold, colder than she had been at any time that afternoon.

"And have you made a choice?" Judith asked.

"Yes." She saw the dominie watching her, his face pleasantly expectant. Surely an intelligent woman would not disdain Gustavus Sulzer's proposal in favor of that of a poor tenant farmer. "We are to be married in June. Stephen and I. Will you get us a license, Dominie Hardenbroeck? And would you be kind enough to marry us?"

Moving from the table, he brushed his hands together, waited until Alicia had left the room, then said, "This is your final decision?"

"Yes."

Turning to Judith, he said, "That is gratitude for you. We have taken in a penniless young woman. We have provided her the opportunity to meet and receive an offer from one of the finest and most prosperous of men. And what does she do? She chooses, despite our warnings, a young man who can offer her nothing but a lifetime of fruitless labor."

"It is her choice, Oloff."

"Imagine how Gustavus will react. I led him to think she would be receptive to, even grateful for, any interest he might show in her."

With the humility she felt was required of her at this moment, Margretta said, "Please do not think I am ungrateful. What you did was very kind. But when a woman marries, it must be to a man she has a genuine feeling for."

"Such feelings can develop and grow within a marriage. Is that not true, Judith?"

Judith nodded, looked away.

"Surely you can see, child, that the difference in our ages has made no difference in our marriage. We have three fine children, a good life. Happiness. Is that not true, Judith?"

"Yes, Oloff."

"But," Margretta said, "that does not mean that any two people of disparate ages will necessarily be happy. I have not chosen Stephen for his youth; it is for personal qualities, certain things we both want and are willing to work for."

"Is it not his kisses that have inflamed you? Can you stand there and tell me in all honesty that you have not exchanged such kisses?"

The fire was burning high. Let him think her closeness to it was creating the warmth in her cheeks, for she was remembering how she had felt during those moments of closeness: the stirrings within her, the sure knowledge that her place was within this man's arms.

"Your refusal to speak is my answer," he said.

"Oloff," Judith said, suddenly rising, "this is useless. She has made her decision. She was not required to ask your permission. She knows her own heart."

"I only wanted her to think twice before making such a foolish move. It is for her own good. More than one man here has found her attractive. Even young Nicolaus made a reference to it. She need not marry so low."

Marry so low. It was as if he had struck her. Yet before Margretta could speak in defense, Judith said, "I told you, Oloff, she has made her decision. All she asks of you now is a license. And whether you will perform the marriage."

"Very well. I cannot refuse. I will see to it that you are at least properly married."

"I want only the simplest of weddings."

"That is all you will have."

"You will not give me your blessing?"

He gave her a cool smile. "As a man of the cloth, how can I refuse? I suppose I will. But do not expect it until I have had time to adjust to this . . . this new situation."

Alicia brought the food in then and called the children. They sat down to a quiet meal. Afterward, Margretta wrote a note to Gustavus. She told him she was greatly honored by his offer but that she loved someone else. One of the slaves delivered it the next morning, returned without an answer.

In the weeks that followed, she saw Gustavus a few times at church. He either pretended not to see her or nodded coldly or, if she happened to be with Judith and the dominie, asked her politely how she was, then ignored her.

Christmas passed, and the *Nieuw-Jaar,* the grandest festival of the year, celebrated here at the beginning of January as the Dutch had done since 1582. Early in the day the dominie and Judith dressed in their finest clothes and made a brief call on the Van Badens. After their return they sat in the parlor with a tray of cordials nearby and greeted a constant stream of guests. Margretta, not quite a part of the family, asked for a fire in her room and spent much of the day there reading, making lace, and hearing over and over the toast *Creden-*

cense! Someday, she thought, she would stand beside her husband entertaining in this way, enjoying the warmth of friendship along with the spirits contained within the cups.

Yet that day dallied all too far in the distance. How could she stand it, how could she wait? Her loneliness as she listened to the gaiety coming from the parlor was more acute than it had been at any time since her arrival.

What was Stephen doing right now? Was he alone thinking of her, or was he celebrating with Sara and William? She shook her head. It was best to shut him out of her mind, to put off planning until later, because to plan was to dream, and to dream was to long with painful intensity for the reality.

Chapter 8

Winter passed with the dragging steps of a dying animal. As one storm followed another, travel became more difficult. Sometimes Dominie Hardenbroeck preached on Sundays to no more than a dozen people. Stephen was never among them.

Distressing thoughts haunted Margretta. Perhaps he no longer loved her; perhaps he had changed his mind. She reminded herself that he was busy, told herself it was disloyal even to entertain such thoughts but could do little to dispel them.

Distracted by feelings of melancholy, she became less strict. The children wriggled restlessly, often hopping up from their seats in the midst of lessons to run to watch the falling snow, or pleading with her to take them sliding. Even Gertrude, the passive middle child, giggled and whispered. Margretta tried to be more stern, but her thoughts constantly drifted to Stephen and their future together, and her efforts lacked the firmness of her earlier days of teaching.

As soon as it was safely frozen, men from the village cleared an area on the river for skating. Margretta took her students there afternoons as a reward for work well done. They had fine imported, iron-runnered skates with protruding front ends curled up into large circles; others from the village skated on oxbones chopped off, filed flat, then strapped to their shoes. Often Margretta joined them, executing wide, graceful circles on her own iron skates, and was rewarded by an exhilaration that stirred her blood and made her tired enough to sleep well.

As the winter stretched slowly toward spring, the dominie's sermons dealt mostly with the blackness of sin, the uncertainty of redemption, and the fieriness of hell. Judith spent hours working with the mortar and pestle grinding her carefully dried herbs as if bent on their destruction; other times she frowned motionless over one of her tomes.

On February 2, Candlemas Day, the sun shone brightly, ensuring that if a groundhog came out he would be so frightened by his shadow that he would retreat to his lair for the sure six weeks of winter that would follow. Everyone sighed.

On this day also, the Hardenbroecks made a call on the Van Badens. Like the evening candlelight procession in the church, it was part of the ritual of the day. They returned with the news that Nicolaus was to be married in May.

"Her name is Cornelia Romeyn," Judith said. "They have known each other since they were children."

"What does she look like?" Margretta asked. "Did you see her?"

"Not today. I saw her when she was visiting two years ago. What does she look like? Like one of those delicate wildflowers of spring that will bend and fall with one sweep of wind. How would you describe her, Oloff?"

"Oh . . . she has real Dutch beauty. Lovely coloring. But very delicate. Her brother died of some lung disease before he even finished his house upriver. Not a strong family. I think Nicolaus ought to have chosen someone more sturdy, someone likely to give him a number of sons. It's important that there be a Van Baden to carry on the name."

But men and women do not, Margretta wanted to say, make their choices on the basis of sturdiness or any of the other qualities the dominie cherished.

She saw Cornelia at church in March. She had, as Judith had said, a look of delicacy that accentuated her blond beauty. Nicolaus, his handsome face aglow with proprietorship, walked close to her. His gaze, however, was not limited to her, and once again, as she had on the day of his arrival, Margretta was the first to turn away from its disturbing intensity.

March dragged on interminably, one day pretending to be spring, the next winter. So also did Margretta's hopes and fears alternate from day to day. The ground stayed hard until mid-April, when, after a week of sunshine, the warmth finally coaxed the frost from the ground and turned it to mud.

Sunday came and Stephen came too. She went to him before he had finished tethering his horse. Nothing had changed; they might have parted the day before.

"It was such a long winter," she said.

"Yes. I found it so. But I kept busy."

"Stephen, will you take me today to see your house?"

"It is too muddy. Hard enough for my mare to pick her way along with one rider. Two would be too much for her."

"Then next week?"

"Perhaps, if the sun and wind have dried enough of the mud. I am as eager as you are. I want you to see the place before you make your final decision."

"I *have* made it. Remember what I told you. I am marrying a man, not a place."

"Yes, but the place comes with the man and is like a mirror of what he is. I want you to be very sure, because"—his look was like a caress—"once I have you for my own, I am never going to let you go."

They saw each other only for those few moments. She felt deprived, but less so than during the winter. Now as the days passed and the world grew greener, her heart lifted.

Also, she had the wedding of Nicolaus and Cornelia to look forward to. It was to be one of the few weddings held in the church, something the local people could enjoy.

"It will be a royal performance," Judith said, her smile so enigmatic it was impossible to tell how she felt.

As the day of the wedding approached, friends and relatives came from upriver and downriver. Finely dressed men and women strolled the grounds of the manor house and went down the steps to the river. Parties abounded, with the dominie and Judith attending two of them.

Some of the villagers gossiped about the festivities, feeling it would have been more appropriate for Nicolaus to have waited a full year after the death of the old lord. Others, however, felt the young couple were entitled to happiness and that the family needed an heir.

The wedding indeed resembled a royal performance—or what the local people imagined a royal performance might be. The bride on that bright day in early May wore a fawn-colored gown of silk over a blue damask petticoat with hooped panniers at the side. Her hair was rolled and powdered. Nicolaus was resplendent in a peachbloom waistcoat and breeches with pearl buttons. He wore a powdered wig that accentuated the sharpness of his features and his dark, winged brows.

Their attendants were also dressed with color and attention to style: the young men in cocked hats, the young women with powdered hair trimmed with gauze and feathers, their feet stepping lightly in high-heeled red silk shoes.

After the service the bride walked slowly by the line of waiting people, taking time to smile and, with captivating shyness and charm, say a few words to each one. In the weeks that followed, however, young Lord Van Baden—the dominie said that they must stop referring to him as Nicolaus, for after all he was twenty-five years old now, a married man, and the owner of nearly 300,000 acres—and his beautiful wife made no more local appearances. They were busy visiting and being entertained by friends and relatives up and down the Hudson.

Margretta was enough inspired by the wedding to begin a dress of rose-colored linen with panniers at the side, lifted and shirred to expose a petticoat of darker rose beneath. It would resemble Cornelia's gown but would be less elaborate. Though extravagant for the prospective wife of a tenant farmer, it would make her wedding memorable.

Two weeks after the Van Baden wedding, Stephen again appeared at church.

"The roads are much more dry now, are they not?" she said. "Today, then?"

"Yes. Today."

After church she tied a dark blue riding skirt over her gown. Although he had said the ride would take nearly an hour, it seemed less long, every moment of it a pleasure as she sat with her body close to his, her arms around his waist. They passed some nearby houses, wooded areas, a few newly plowed fields, and finally a house which she recognized as the Vanzuyders', then more woods and after a while the beginning of some cleared land, much of it studded with tree stumps.

He slowed the horse. "Here is where my land begins."

The pride, the depth of feeling in his voice reached her. Our land, she thought as the horse began to move forward again with more spirit, as if, like her master, she found joy in touching her hooves onto land that was familiar.

A few chickens scattered as they came into a clearing. The mare stopped; Stephen dismounted and lifted Margretta down. They stood still, his arm light around her waist, facing a small stone house. Close to it a dark rectangle had already been plowed for a garden, and a hundred feet beyond that stood a smaller rectangle of posts and beams.

"That will be a barn," Stephen said. "I've been keeping grains in the house, mostly in the garret, but I thought you might not like that. I have a cow, as you can see, so there will be plenty of milk for cheese, and I'm fattening a pig for slaughter in the fall. He's in a pen over beyond those bushes. And I've two sheep for wool." He turned. "But it is the house you are interested in. I can see that."

It looked to be about the size of the dominie's parlor. Her domain. She had seen houses as small as this in the village and had wondered how people managed to raise families in them. Yet she smiled, praying her disappointment was well hidden.

"I know it does not look like much. Where I lived mattered little. But I have been working on the inside since meeting you, and will make more changes. Once the barn has been finished, we can use the loft for sleeping rooms for our children and for household storage."

Our children. She tried to envision children playing in the dooryard, found it difficult. She continued staring at the house. It could be made neater with curtains that hung straight, with a *stoep* scrubbed clean enough to be used for sitting on summer evenings. No one would be passing by, eager for gossip, but they would have each other's company.

"The previous tenants left a few things," he said. "As we replace them, we'll either sell them or burn them. I have already cut some pine for new stools." He placed his hands on her shoulders. "One thing . . . I have made one thing for you. For us. I began working on it the day I met you. I finished it three days ago."

That, then, was why he had refused to bring her here sooner. She could tell from the glow in his eyes, the vibrant touch of his fingers, how excited he was about his creation. She prayed she would feel as he did about it, or that if she did not, it would be small enough so that most of the time she could keep it hidden away—for safekeeping, she would say. But, no. She refused to be devious. She would not pretend to love it. She *would* love it. She would love it because it had been made by him and made with love.

At last she spoke. "Please take me inside. I cannot wait to see it."

He pushed open the door. One of its hinges loose, it creaked badly. Straight ahead, between her and the fireplace wall, she saw a square table and four stools, rough-hewn and poorly made. On her right were tools and piles of wood.

But looking to the left, she saw against the end wall, taking up more room than really could be spared for it, and in its elegance making the rest of the furniture even worse than it was, a four-poster bed, graceful and tall, a reflection of the craftsmanship of a skilled worker.

"Where did that beautiful bed come from? Surely no tenant left that here."

"No." He tried unsuccessfully to hide his pleasure in her words. Almost shyly he said, "I made it for you. It is what I was telling you about. It is our marriage bed."

Their marriage bed. Her heartbeat accelerated. Only three more weeks and they would be lying on it together. No doubt he was thinking the same thing.

Unexpectedly he said, "Would you like to try it?"

"Try what?"

"The bed."

She drew away startled, aware suddenly of how far they were from any other habitation, of all that her grandmother had told her about men and the horror and power of their desires.

"What do you mean?"

"To lie on it. To see whether it is comfortable."

"You must know whether it is comfortable."

"No. I wanted you to be the first to try it."

Timidly she went to the bed, lay flat on her back. "It is a wonderful bed. But what is that smell? It's like sassafras, but I do not see any bag hanging on the bedpost."

"It is sassafras. I rubbed the bedposts with oil from the bark. *My* wife will not have to suffer the bite of the bedbug."

Pulling up a stool, he sat by the bed. "All the time I was building it, I thought of you lying on it like this. Lying here waiting for me to come to bed at night. Lying here thinking about me. Lying here"— he placed the flat of his hand on her body just below the waist— "lying here someday with our child growing inside you."

The heat from his fingers burned through her riding skirt. She wanted to take his hand and press it deeper. But she must not be too forward, too impulsive. Even though they were betrothed, it was well to be modest.

"You speak almost like a poet," she said.

"No." His voice was soft. "Only like a man who has found the right woman to share his life. You do not know what it has been like alone here, working all day in the fields, coming in to a house where there was no warmth, no love. A man can be happy working his land, but the feeling is deepest if he is making it better for those he loves. Then the work becomes part of a dream of the future."

"You are poet enough for me."

"But I never talk like this. It is just that, having you here in this place where I have so long dreamed of being alone with you, I find myself saying words that have passed through my mind as I worked. Besides, there is something about you, about the way you listen, that makes it easy to talk."

"Talk, talk," she said with a smile. "As you worked, did not other thoughts pass through your mind?" Lifting her arms to him, she said, "I thought you had perhaps brought me here to kiss me."

He bent down, his lips sweet on hers. She put her hands on the back of his neck, holding his face close to hers a moment. Then his lips moved to her throat. When he began to loosen her bodice so his lips could find their way to the curve of her breasts, she whispered, "Why not lie down beside me, my dear?" She had never been so stirred before, not even on the afternoon in the sleigh when his kiss had helped her decide which direction her future would take. Perhaps it was that her awareness of him had grown during the winter of their separation; or perhaps she had grown more mature, her body more ready for the union of marriage.

She moved over to make room. "Here. Lie right here."

Abruptly he drew away. "No. Please forgive me. I forgot myself. This is a marriage bed."

"So? We are practically married, Stephen. The dominie already has our license. Certainly no one exists who would be likely to offer an impediment to our marriage."

"Even so." Taking her hands, he lifted her to a sitting position. "I want our marriage to be perfect in every way. This is a marriage bed, made for all that marriage means. The love between man and wife. The making and bearing of children. Come, let me show you what else I am making."

Her body found it hard to obey. She wanted to lie back again, to feel his hands and lips on her body, to feel again that spark that needed only a touch to make it leap into flame. Was she no better than those courtesans down by the main battery at the fort in Manhattan? Nice women, according to her grandmother, found no pleasure in intimacy with a man. She must be careful to suppress any behavior that gave the impression of immodesty or forwardness. It was man's role to demand, woman's to acquiesce. She must also avoid letting the authority she had developed when teaching touch this still-fragile relationship.

She sat a moment with her head against his chest. "I am sorry," she said. "I was wrong to suggest that."

"It is all right. You did not understand how difficult it would have been for me there, so close to you."

She was on her feet now. He held her, his body firm against hers. She pressed her face against his shoulder, reluctant to let him see the desire that must show in her eyes, to know the strength of her feelings.

"Come," he said again, releasing her, but still holding her hand. "I want to show you more things."

In the corner were two stacks of lumber cut in various lengths and shapes, some straight, some curved. "This," he said, "is going to be your rocker. I have already soaked and bent the rockers. See? How high do you want the back?"

"High enough so that you, too, can sit in it."

"But it is yours. For rocking our babies."

"Sometimes, Stephen, *you* will have to rock the babies. Make it high enough."

"You are right. But it will still be yours. Now, this"—he moved to the next stack—"will be the cradle. When you cannot sit down to rock him, you can touch your foot to it and keep him moving."

Him. She smiled inwardly. Already he dreamed of a son. Please, God, she thought, let the first one be a boy.

"Now come outside," he said, "and I will show you the stream."

At the doorway she hesitated, looking back at the room. She would rub the furniture with oil. She would place her *kas* in the corner to the left, facing the bed. She would put the pewter porringer and the clock on the mantel, make curtains for the bed, put a linen runner on the table when it was not in use.

Suddenly she said, "Where are your books?"

"My brother wanted them. I took tools instead. They were what I needed to get started here."

"It does not matter. I have my father's books. You can put a shelf on the wall between the bed and the fireplace for them."

In her imagination the room was already transformed. What had seemed no more than a hovel when she had entered now had the appearance and warmth of a home.

Outside, he showed her the soil, pushed a sharp stick down and pulled it up with the dark, rich dirt clinging to it. Behind the house he pointed to the stream that came down from a ridge to the east and never ran dry, even in August, and the small pond he had created by damming the stream, making a place where the animals could drink, where ducks could be raised, where children could skate in winter.

He took her back to the dominie's then. Now, as daylight faded and they were less conspicuous, she rode in front of him, feeling closer to him this way with one of his arms curved around her most of the time. On the way she told him he would have to produce two witnesses before the dominie could officially issue them their license. "They must be of good reputation and must be willing to testify they know of no obstacles to our marriage. And you must appear also for a private meeting with the dominie."

"I never knew getting married was so complicated."

She questioned him about what he would wear for the ceremony. He had some things of his father's, he said.

Later in the week he returned with William Vanzuyder and Jan Harten, who testified for him and signed the certificate of responsibility. He also brought for her inspection a long, full-skirted waistcoat and knee breeches, both of gray wool, and a yellowed linen shirt. She shortened the coat to the current style, removing some of the fullness, and bought buckles for the breeches. She made a ruffle for the shirt, washed it, and laid it over the top of a juniper bush to bleach it white.

The following Sunday Stephen remained after church to pick up the clothing and to have his private meeting with the dominie. They were closeted together for over an hour, during which time Margretta paced and fidgeted.

"He seemed satisfied with my answers to his questions," Stephen said when he came out.

Later that evening when she and Judith were talking in the parlor, the dominie, joining them, said, "Your young man seems an honest fellow. He also appears to have a deep feeling for you. That will likely make up for other things."

"Other things?"

"I am not speaking of qualities. Merely of the things you might enjoy were you to marry a man of another class."

He spoke kindly now, and she could see that despite his sometimes domineering ways, he had hoped to do well by her.

"I'm sorry I could not find it in my heart to love Gustavus. I realize you were acting in my best interests."

"Ah, well, child, I just hope this love you find so exciting now will continue as strong. A simple feeling of companionship can often be more rewarding and can lead to more permanent fulfillment than the passions the young choose to call by the name of love. Is that not true, Judith?"

"Yes, dear."

The days that led up to June 10 sped by now, busy as Margretta was with her sewing and other wedding preparations. She also spent her final hours with the children, outlining a study program for them and assuring Judith she would help at any time the need arose.

The night before her marriage, she slept little. A thunderstorm, the first of the season, rolled down from the Catskills and roared angrily through the valley. She lay still, frightened, wishing strong arms were already encircling and protecting her.

Still wakeful afterward, she let her thoughts skip from past to future. She thought of her father, wished he could be present to place her hand in Stephen's, wondered what he would think of this man she had chosen. She thought of her grandmother. Would she think any young man was worth having? Probably not. Yet Margretta missed her, missed having someone of her own family with her to share her joy.

Tomorrow was her wedding day. She sighed happily. She was not, after all, fated to comb St. Catherine's hair.

And tomorrow night was her wedding night. At the thought she was seized with a *frisson* of delight mixed with apprehension. The delight was for the kisses, the closeness; the apprehension was for what would come later. But she loved Stephen and he loved her. However bad it was, she would endure it and never let him know how unpleasant she found it. Besides, it would lead to the birth of children, to a family. Always in the future she would—they would—have others of their own blood with whom they could share their moments of joy.

Chapter 9

June 10, 1744, her wedding day. A year ago she had sailed up the Hudson her heart full of hope. It had been the first stage of her journey into adventure and discovery.

Now, in the early afternoon, as she laid out her clothes in preparation for the second stage of her journey, terror seized her. It was one thing to feel the warmth of a man's lips on yours and to decide that this particular warmth must be yours forever; it was quite another to realize that you were committing yourself, not just to the passions of love, but also to a different way of life with a man who in many ways was still a stranger.

Did Stephen, too, feel this same terror? Perhaps he had already loaded his tools and clothing into his wagon and headed back for Philipsborough.

Judith knocked, came in. "Can I help with buttons or anything? Are you as terrified, my dear, as you look?"

"Yes. What's wrong with me?"

"Nothing. Most brides feel the same way."

"What about afterward? Do the feelings change? Will everything be all right then?"

Judith gave her a compassionate look as she smoothed the folds of the rose-colored skirt. "Stop worrying. Everything will be fine."

"What if he doesn't come?"

"He'll come. Now, let me help you get ready."

Judith rolled and powdered the dark gold of her hair, helped her into her dress, brought her roses to hold.

Smiling into her mirror, Margretta saw that the rosiness of her dress had lit up her face, and excitement had brightened the darkness of her eyes. Any doubts Stephen might have would surely disappear when he saw her. If he came. . . .

She waited by her window, at last saw his wagon coming. Behind it were the Vanzuyders and behind them the Hartens.

She sighed. The last time. Never again would she stand by this window waiting for the future to come down the lane and gather her up into its mysteries. The future was here.

When everyone had assembled in the parlor—the three Hardenbroeck children, the Hartens and the Vanzuyders, the household's slaves—Judith invited her to leave her room.

The dominie in his robe and *befje* was standing with his back to the fireplace. Stephen, nearby, looked almost to the manor born, his sun-bleached hair tied back with a black velvet ribbon, his remodeled clothes fitting him as a gentleman's should.

As Margretta and Stephen stood side by side in front of him, the dominie spoke of the comforts and consolations of marriage, of the doubling of joys and sorrows. He read from Genesis, repeating the story of the garden of Eden.

"In this way," he said, "the Almighty Father who gave Eve to Adam to be his wife witnesses thereby that he doth yet, as with his hand, bring unto every man his wife."

He told Stephen to lead, instruct, comfort, protect, and love his wife and to maintain his household honestly and likewise have something to give to the poor. He told Margretta she must fulfill all the duties of a wife, and warned her against exercising dominion over her husband.

At last came the words "Do you, Margretta, take Stephen . . . ? And do you, Stephen, take Margretta . . . ?" and the joined hands and the blessing. As she felt the strength of Stephen's fingers and heard the blessing, Margretta looked up at Stephen and smiled, all her doubts gone.

Afterward, the dominie served several rounds of sack-posset, and Judith passed pieces of wedding cake rich with sweetmeats. Two collections were taken, one for the church and one for the poor.

When at last they moved to leave, the dominie gave them two bottles of wine and one of rum, gifts that moved Margretta, for she knew his store of spirits was small.

"You will have callers during the next few days and will wish to offer them something," he said.

"And the cake, too," Judith said. She wrapped the remainder in cheesecloth and gave it to Margretta, along with herb and flower seeds and slips.

The sun was setting as the men loaded Margretta's belongings in the two wagons and they set off, with the Vanzuyders and Hartens in the wagons behind them, ringing bells as they went up the lane and again at each house they passed.

The ride seemed endless. Margretta longed now to be alone with this man who had become her husband. When Stephen at last helped her down from the wagon, the sky had darkened. She whispered, "Will they leave soon?"

"I don't know." He held her a moment.

The men carried the *kas* in, placed it against the wall opposite the bed, and piled the remainder of her things on the floor next to it.

William produced a bottle. "We will drink to your health . . . and ours."

"We have wine to serve."

"Save that for your other guests. This is my wedding gift to you." He held it high.

Stephen set out bread and cheese. Margretta cut more wedding cake. The guests ate, drank, talked, sang, made jokes about the newly married. Hours went by. Sitting on a stool with nothing to support her back—she had given the rocker to Sara, who was close to her confinement—all the tensions, worries, and joys of the day converging in a sweep of exhaustion, Margretta, who never cried, suddenly found herself fighting back tears. She was unused to wine, had already had more spirits than she needed at the dominie's. Now, as she continued to sip—William insisted on filling their cups as often as his—she felt numbness creeping over her. When she smiled politely at his jokes, her cheeks felt stiff as bread dough. If they would only leave. All thoughts of a wedding night, joyous, terrifying, or painful, had left her, leaving only a desire for sleep.

They stayed. And stayed. And stayed.

She looked toward the window; it had turned gray. Dawn. Another day. The last thing she remembered before she put her head down on the table was William saying, "Well, we have accomplished one thing tonight. We have seen to it that no child will be born in this house exactly nine months from the wedding. It will have to be at least nine months and one day." He laughed hugely. "Unless you, my friend, have already found your way in under the bearskin in my sleigh."

She was too sleepy to be angry.

When she awakened, she was lying on the marriage bed, still clothed except for her shoes. Her head pounded. Stephen was sitting at the table, his head in his hands.

"Where did you sleep?" she asked.

He pointed to the alcove next to the chimney. "There, where I've been sleeping. I didn't want to disturb you."

"When did they leave?"

"Not long after you fell asleep."

"What time is it?"

"Nearly noon. I hate to say this, but you had best quickly prepare for guests. Don't take time to change your clothes. The women will want to see your wedding dress."

She looked around. Dirty cups, bread crumbs on the table and floor, spilled wine, ashes from the men's pipes on the trenchers. Flies. And in the corner, her pile of belongings.

"Would you get me some water? I must make this place presentable. And heat some water for tea, please."

He smiled as he rose. "Have you forgotten that you are not to exercise dominion over your husband?"

"But you are to comfort me. Please get me some water for my comfort."

Quickly he built up the fire, went out for a pail of water. By the time he had returned, she had fixed her hair, smoothed the rumpled beds.

While Stephen fixed some tea for them, she moved about wiping up spills, washing cups and trenchers, finding places for her belongings: the porringer and a linen runner on the table, a coverlet on the marriage bed, her clock and books on the mantel. As she stood back and surveyed the room with a feeling of pleasure, she heard the pound of horses' hooves.

They came all day, all week—farmers and people from the village. They came to look at the bride and her things and to partake of the wine and cake. How much better it would have been if they had waited until she was settled, she thought, yet she was grateful for their attention and pleased by the admiration the women showed for her *kas*. The first thing, however, that most callers noticed was the marriage bed. One woman even said it was really too nice for the house.

Margretta, who was herself aware that its size and beauty made it more appropriate for the upstairs room of a fine home, said quietly, "It was Stephen's wedding gift to me. Someday we'll have a better, larger home to put it in."

"Just try building something bigger and better," the woman said, "and see what happens."

"It probably won't be here," Margretta said. "We plan to sell the leasehold when we can make a profit on it and move on to new land that we can buy outright."

The woman smiled as she might have smiled at a little son who said he was going to marry her when he grew up. Then she said, "And your pewter. Lovely. Best to hide it, though, when the agent comes about the rent."

When the men slapped Stephen on the back and praised his good taste, or, as many did, poked him in the ribs while looking knowingly at the large and accommodating marriage bed, she turned away, certain that they saw her flush of embarrassment. How surprised they would be if they knew how little the bed could as yet tell them of love.

Although she had seen some of the people at the party at the Hartens', she knew few of the others. Some of them spoke only Dutch; others spoke English, but with the rude constructions of the uneducated. These were the people that Gustavus Sulzer had said were best kept in a state of ignorance. But, uneducated or not, they all displayed the same awareness when the talk turned to their lives as tenants.

"I had to put in four days workin' on his roads right at plantin' time," one complained. Another said, "It cost me a whole sack of grain to have ten ground. When I offered the rest for sale, it was Mr. Wortheimer who set the price, not me. I know I could have got more elsewhere. But I had no choice."

Everyone had a grievance. And one woman said, "It was us'n who paid for that fancy weddin'. And that carriage they ride around in like they was kings and queens."

Margretta was to hear more of that kind of talk during the even more exhausting second week of their marriage when she was obliged to climb up onto the horse with Stephen each day to return the visits. She might have enjoyed going out to call later on, but tradition demanded that it be done immediately; otherwise, people would feel she scorned the friendship they had proffered. It was an effective way of making her a part of the community of tenant farmers, for as each day passed, she felt removed by far more than an hour's ride from the dominie's house and the residence of the Van Badens themselves.

Every caller during the first week of marriage had been an intrusion, every one she returned was an abandonment of the home she wanted to begin improving. Once evening came, however, they could count on sitting alone on the *stoep*, her head on his shoulder, waiting for the fireflies that ushered in the darkness.

They had sat like that on the evening of the day after their wedding, free now to do whatever they wished. Margretta tried to think dispassionately of the coming night. It was impossible. She kept remembering the afternoon Stephen had brought her here, how she had lain on the bed and asked him to lie down beside her. Was he remembering? Was he expecting the same eagerness from her tonight? Strange . . . she felt no eagerness now, only a paralyzing shyness.

"I think it is time we went to bed," Stephen said. "Do you want to go in first?"

How sensitive he was. "Yes. That would be good."

Perhaps it was just change that she dreaded, she thought as she went inside, undressed and washed, for never after tonight would she be the same again.

At last she slipped into bed and moved over to the side close to the wall. She lay waiting, smelling the sassafras on the wood, aware of her body and all her senses as she never had been before. She told herself that millions of women all over the world had been married, had endured their first unions with their husbands, and many more after that, no doubt. Why was she so tense? On that afternoon when she had visited him she would willingly have yielded herself to him. It had seemed completely natural and right on that day. Now, in its strangeness and mystery and above all in its necessity, it was terrifying.

I won't think about it anymore, she said to herself, but, smoothing the linen sheet that covered her, aware of the empty place beside her, hearing Stephen as he opened the door and came in, she could think of nothing else.

Except for the faint glow of banked coals from the cooking fire, the room was dark. Her eyes, however, had grown accustomed to it. She watched him remove his clothing: shirt, shoes, stockings, breeches. As he came toward the bed, she whispered, "Stephen, where is your nightshirt?"

He sat on the edge of the bed. "I do not wear one in summer. Would it please you if I wore one?"

She took a moment to consider. She had thought that all men wore nightshirts; therefore, it was the right thing to do. But what difference did it make? He had a sheet to cover him. And why did he even need to be covered? He had, she noticed, a lovely back; broad at the shoulder, tapering to the waist. She sat up then, and wriggling a little, pulled off her chemise, folded it, and put it under her pillow.

"There now," she said. "We are both as God made us."

"Like Adam and Eve." He moved into the bed, pulled the sheet up over him. "I'm glad you did that."

"You want me to be naked?"

"No. Well, yes. But that is not why I am glad. It is just that I hate to do things simply because everyone has always done them that way. Do you feel the same?"

"I never thought much about it. Perhaps women care more about appearances than men do. Certainly, I wanted us to do all things properly for our wedding. But I did come up the Hudson by myself. And I married the man of my choice instead of the one the dominie expected me to marry."

Lying on their backs at least a foot away from each other, they were talking like two people still groping to know each other. Was this how they were going to spend the night, or would he, differing from other eager bridegrooms, simply close his eyes after a while and begin snoring? After all, he had slept little the night before.

"Are you afraid?" he asked suddenly.

"Yes. I know it is silly."

"No, not silly at all. I am afraid too."

"You? What could you possibly be afraid of?"

"That I might not please you."

"Is a man supposed to please a woman?"

"I want to make you glad you married me. And also I do not want to hurt you. You are so small, so delicate. When I take your hand, it is like holding a bird. I feel as though the slightest pressure might crush your bones."

"I am not so fragile." She slipped her hand into his. He held it, kissed the fingertips, the palm of her hand, and then her arm up to the inside of the elbow. "Your skin is so soft," he said. Moving closer, he kissed her mouth.

The fear left her. This was as it had been when she had visited here. No, it was better, for this time he was lying close to her, and now their bodies were touching, his muscular and hard with the power of manhood, hers soft, compliant.

But despite her receptivity, three nights passed before their marriage was consummated. It might have occurred sooner had it not been for his gentleness and consideration. Yet those nights cemented their marriage more effectively than a hurried, explosive union might have done, for as they explored each other with lips and hands, they also revealed their thoughts and feelings in ways impossible to do when the outside world or even their daily routine interfered. It gave him time to overcome his reserve, gave her time to shut out the image implanted by her grandmother of the lustful, importunate, overbearing male.

On the morning of the fourth day, she slipped out of bed unembarrassed as he lay looking at her; she stood at the foot of the bed, her hand on one of the tall posts.

"This is truly a marriage bed, Stephen, this magnificent bed you built for us."

His face bore the look of a man who cannot quite believe his happiness.

"Come, now," she said. "You must get up. Soon the callers will begin coming. We do not want them to know how much time we spend in this bed."

She dressed and went about her tasks then, opening the door first to look out at the day. Bluebirds had built in the apple tree on the opposite side of the clearing and sang out a welcoming *chir, chir, chir*. Already they had begun to feed nestlings, flashing by the door, their breasts like a sunrise, their backs like an October day.

She felt like joining them in song, expressing her happiness in this her own nesting time. Was her grandmother different from her, or had the ashes of passion choked out the memory of what it is like for the body to forget all its mundane uses in a flight of joy? But perhaps no one else had ever felt exactly as she and Stephen did, for in their discovery of love they were as untutored and as full of delight in each other as Adam and Eve must once have been.

The delight continued through the time of the calls from neighbors near and far and the return calls. Even when they settled down at last to the serious business of farm and household duties, they took no less pleasure in each other.

Stephen had already planted a garden. Now he spaded a larger area for her so she could plant the seeds that Judith had given her. She also put the lilac slips on one side of the door, the roses on the other.

Stephen was full of plans. Now and until the end of September he was too busy for working on household improvements beyond putting up a shelf for her books. He had hay to cut, corn to hill, hoeing and cultivating to do. She had butter to churn, cheese to make, bread to bake . . . and more. Each day she became more aware of all that had to be done. When the wild strawberries ripened, she gathered them. What they did not eat immediately, she put down in crocks.

So much that she had once taken for granted now became her responsibility. In the city her grandmother had bought soap. At the dominie's it had miraculously appeared in a dish on her washstand. Here Stephen stored the wood ashes in a barrel placed on a large flat rock and poured boiling water into it twice a day. The lye that formed ran out in a channel he had chiseled in the rock and collected in a kettle. This she boiled along with household fats until it turned into a brown marbled jelly that, placed in pans, was cut into cakes of soap after it hardened. She made enough that summer to last all winter.

Stephen had reed holders to use for lighting, but she preferred the brighter and less smoky light from candles. Thus another part of her summer was taken up with the melting of tallow and the dipping of candles.

As she worked, her arms aching from lifting, stirring, kneading, carrying, her mind wandered to the house of Gustavus Sulzer, where slaves did all such work, usually in outbuildings so that no unpleasant odors spoiled the air in the house. This, however, was her choice. She had not expected it to be easy. But she had also not expected it to be quite so hard.

Sometimes during the heat of July, when noon came and Stephen had not yet returned from the fields, she put bread, cheese, and cider into a basket and, an old blanket over her arm, set out to join him. They sat under an oak tree at the edge of the cornfield and talked of the future.

"In the fall," Stephen said, "I'll begin the cradle."

The week before, when her courses had begun, she had each day washed the linen squares she wore and spread them over the tops of bushes to dry and bleach. At night she had stretched out, straight and alone, on her side of the bed.

"One thing we know," she said now. "It will not be so early as March. Perhaps not even April."

"I know that. We're young. We have lots of time. William has said several times he and Sara had too little time to enjoy each other before the babies came."

She lay back on the soft grass. "It's so beautiful out here. At the dominie's, someone was always chattering. Here it is quiet and lovely. Our little world."

"Yes. Our own world."

He bent to kiss her, began to loosen her clothing.

"Oh, Stephen. Outdoors?"

"Why not? You are my wife. This is my land."

Not his land, she thought, but the thought flitted off in a rush of passion as his hands warmed her body, and they created another, smaller but more joyous world within the circle of each other's arms.

Chapter 10

The summer hours, most of them occupied with preparations for the winter, passed quickly. Margretta became more aware each day of the many tasks that had to be performed on a rural farm. The hours, the days, the summer months were too short for all that had to be done.

If a storm threatened that might spoil hay lying in the field to cure, she drove the wagon so Stephen could pitch hay up onto it. She helped him find the cow when it wandered off, even helped him build the barn, holding one end of each board up level while he hammered the other. When one of them fell against her arm, leaving a dark bruise that lasted for several days and that upset Stephen every time he looked at it, she assured him—quite honestly—that her light skin bruised easily and that it hardly hurt at all. And once again she reminded him that improving the property was as important to her as it was to him. It was their stepping-stone to something better, was it not?

They often worked until dark. After a light supper they went directly to bed without taking time to sit outside. Most of the time, no matter how tired, they made love before going to sleep, each moment of intimacy binding them closer.

Sometimes she glanced at her books. What a luxury it would be to take one out to the *stoep* and sit with the sun soothing her fatigued muscles and the wisdom within the books stirring her thoughts. But an urgent task always awaited, usually something that had to be picked, washed, boiled, chopped, pickled, dried, sugared, or salted before it spoiled.

In August, when Sara gave birth to another son, Margretta was with her.

"I'm naming him Oloff," Sara said. "After the dominie. Maybe it will bring us luck."

"You already have luck," Margretta said, holding the tiny bundle in her arms. Would she ever hold a baby of her own? Nearly three months had passed now with no sign.

"Be grateful you are not so lucky. When babies come too soon, they get in the way of things between a man and a woman. I'm too big beforehand and too sore afterward. Then I get busy with the baby I'm nursing and William gets jealous."

When Stephen came over later, he looked at the baby, his expression revealing nothing of his thoughts.

"Another boy," he said finally to William.

"You'll have a fine one yourself one of these days."

"Not one. Half a dozen."

"But first," William said, "you're going to have to fatten this young woman up." He was nearly able to span Margretta's waist with his hands. "See? She's getting smaller where she ought to be getting bigger. I'm afraid you been spending too much time in the fields and not enough in that fancy bed of yours. Say, maybe that's your problem—that great big bed. Maybe you can't find her in it."

"You talk too much," Sara said. "Nice people don't talk about such things. Stephen don't."

"Maybe he don't have anything to talk about."

Stephen made no answer. Margretta wished he would come up with a joking retort, but she had learned already that he dealt with his problems in silence. Sometimes she wondered whether she was a disappointment to him. Although she did all that was required of her, inexperience slowed her pace. Often her bread turned sour from overrising or came out heavy and flat because she had let the leaven get too damp. More than once she had put too long a trammel on a kettle and let the food, too close to the fire, scorch. She still had much to learn.

But far more serious was her apparent lack of fertility. She tried to make up for it in other ways. In the fall she helped shock up the corn, gather squash and pumpkins into piles for loading onto the wagon, stack firewood by the house, place spoiled hay and leaves around the foundation to help keep out the winter cold.

Stephen butchered the pig and one of William's cows, which they divided. Then they prepared sausage links, barrels of salt pork and corned beef, cured ham and bacon. Later Stephen and William went hunting, returning with a bear and two deer which also had to be processed for the winter.

Margretta was so tired much of the time that she barely glanced to the east, where the Taconic Mountains blazed with reds and golds. The previous winter had stretched out endlessly; the hope that sustained her now was that this one would last as long, give her time to rock, sew, make lace, or just sit by the fire and dream.

Her last big job before winter was the washing that all good Dutch housewives never failed to do quarterly. Fortunately, her dowry of linens, in preparation since her childhood and augmented by what was left of her grandmother's, was large enough to last for several months.

Every day for a week Stephen brought in water from the brook, which she heated in a huge kettle over the fire. He strung ropes of hemp from tree to tree on which she hung most of the clothing and linens. Smaller pieces she draped over the bushes. Although the work made her arms ache, it was satisfying when the week was over to have every last clean and sweet-smelling piece folded away in the *kas*. She would use them sparingly, for a hard winter could make it difficult to get enough water for another washing before spring.

When winter came, the outside work lightened. Stephen went to the barn twice a day. He took care of the fire, constantly refilled the wood box. And when the snows came, he shoveled paths to the barn, the outhouse, the brook, and the woodpile.

Even though confined when snows were so deep that even the mare could not get through them, Margretta enjoyed the winter. Like an animal that curls up in hibernation, she lived snug and happy in their little home, enjoying the warmth of the fire, the ladling of already prepared fruits from the stone jars, the slicing off of meat that needed only to be cooked, the baking or boiling of vegetables that required neither weeding nor immediate use. She still made cheese and bread and churned butter, but often Stephen helped her with these.

They had hot food often: pork slowly roasted on a spit, soups sim-

mered in a footed iron pot set inside the fireplace, corn cakes baked
in the ashes, and beans, apple and mince pies laced with hard cider,
all baked in the oven at the side of the fireplace.

When they went to bed, Stephen banked the fire, but before it
died completely down, they lay for a while watching the reflection of
the firelight move on wall and ceiling. They were growing and
changing in love, different people from the two groping neophytes of
the previous June. A touch, a look, and they turned to each other
and moved together with a sureness as familiar as it was, each time,
completely new. Sara had been right. These childless months had
brought them close together. Surely no two people had ever been
happier.

One December afternoon when she was standing at the table peel-
ing and cutting apples, he came up behind her, put his arms around
her, kissed the back of her neck. She turned so their mouths could
meet. Without a word, he lifted her and carried her to the bed. What
did it matter if the cut sides of the apples discolored? After love everything tasted sweeter.

"Do you mind?" he said. "I interrupted your work."

"I was just preparing food for you."

"I want you so often. It may be too much for you."

She touched his face. "Stephen, we must always be honest with
each other. Let me know when you feel that way. If it is not the right
time, I'll say so. And just remember this. Our six months of marriage
have been the happiest of my life."

Only forty-eight hours later, however, she foolishly made a casual
remark, one that rippled the smooth surface of their relationship in
ever-widening and disturbing circles.

She never, even in good weather, had enough water. Now she had
only water melted from ice chopped from the pond.

"At the dominie's," she said, "we had a well. Even I could use the
well sweep to lower a bucket and bring up water whenever I needed
it."

"I bring in water whenever you ask me to. I bring in far more than
I ever did when I was a bachelor."

"Perhaps you washed the trenchers with less care. Or used fewer
pots for cooking." When he did not answer, she added, "I was not
being critical. I just wondered whether we could dig a well somewhere, perhaps even figure a way to bring the water inside. At one

place where I taught in the city, they had an iron pump in the kitchen sink. You worked the handle up and down and the water poured out the spout. It was like a miracle."

He gave her a tight-lipped smile. "I am afraid I can manage no such miracles. As for digging a well—I could spend a week of good spring plowing time digging a hole and have it be a dry one."

"Let us say no more about it."

He did say no more about it; in fact, for the rest of the afternoon he said nothing at all, retreating to a secret place within himself to which she had never been invited.

After he went out to milk, she looked out the window at the barren landscape: the snow-covered ground shadowed with gray, the trees of darker gray lifting skeletal arms to a sky heavy with low-hanging clouds that nearly obscured the gray line of the Taconics. Far to the north and east of the range lay the Hampshire Grants, land as yet untouched by the greed of speculators, land open to settlers who wanted space and freedom. For a long time she stared thoughtfully in that direction. Some snowflakes appeared. She stood still, watching the snowfall gradually thicken, dropping a curtain between house and barn.

Stephen had been gone longer than usual. She felt abandoned. Why had she made that thoughtless remark about the water? And why, especially, had she made comparisons that emphasized the conveniences she had formerly enjoyed?

He came finally with the milk, lifted the trapdoor, and carried it to the cellar. When he came up, he stood staring out the window until she called him for supper.

"Is it still snowing?" she asked.

"Yes."

"Do you think this will be a real storm?"

"Perhaps."

They ate in silence for several minutes before she said, "Will you be working on the cradle tonight?"

"Probably."

"It will be a fine cradle."

He gave no answer.

Later, after she had washed the trenchers and cups and spoons, she sat in her rocker at one side of the fireplace and began a length of lace. The day before, she had finished knitting a pair of warm stockings for Stephen; now she felt free to indulge herself in exercise of a skill she enjoyed.

Stephen threw a piece of pine among the slower-burning oak logs, increasing the amount of light, and drew his workbench close to the fire on the opposite side. He spread out the pieces he had cut for the cradle, and slowly, mutely sanded them.

When he had begun a few weeks before, she had said, "It might be unlucky to make a cradle when there is no child."

"There will be a child. Besides, when the warm weather comes again, I will have no time."

After an hour he put his work away, dusted off the bench, and threw the sawdust onto the logs. Pulling the stool closer to the hearth, he sat and stared morosely at the fire.

Margretta continued working, deftly moving first one bobbin, then another, then still another, around the pins, over, under, across, and back. Watching the design grow satisfied an aesthetic urge she seldom acknowledged. It was accompanied by a yearning to read the prose and poetry of writers her father had loved. She glanced at her books. Perhaps next year she would be able to do her work faster and could now and then take a book down and lose herself in its contents.

Stephen, who rarely smoked, got his pipe, scraped it, and filled it with tobacco. Still silent, he lighted it and sat down again. Soon she could smell the smoke, the first whiff always the richest. The fire crackled and hissed, a log shifted and thudded to the hearth. Stephen poked it back.

Outside, the wind increased, blowing around the house like an animal howling to come in. Now it was trying to enter through the chimney, the sudden downdraft sending smoke and coals to the outer perimeter of the hearth. Stephen, with a broom made of leaves from cornstalks tied together, swept the cherry-colored coals back into the fire.

Earlier when heavy snows had kept them from attending holiday festivities, Margretta had felt no deprivation. It had been enough to be alone with her husband . . . but not when he smoked on and on, islanding her in uncertainty. If his behavior was caused by a feeling of inadequacy at being unable to provide her with the material comforts she had once known, then he was now making it worse, for he was giving her time for thoughts about her lack of intellectual pleasure.

To let such a silence continue was unnatural. "Stephen," she said, "would you do something for me?"

He took the pipe out of his mouth. "What is it you want now?"

"Would you read me some Shakespeare? Perhaps from A *Midsummer Night's Dream*. It might make us forget we are in the midst of winter."

"I do not enjoy reading Shakespeare."

"Then read me the Bible." Before he could move, she said: "'I opened to my well-beloved, but my well-beloved was gone and past. I sought him but I could not find him. I called him but he answered me not.'"

Seeing him frown, she said, "That's from the *Song of Solomon*. I may have forgotten a little of it."

"It sounds as though you remember it well enough so you need no one to read it to you." He emptied the half-burned tobacco from his pipe and swept it into the fire. "I am very tired and tomorrow I will have much shoveling to do."

He was deliberately ignoring her overture of reconciliation. Quietly she prepared for bed while he shoveled ashes over the flames and carefully covered the embers. He put a milk pail and snow shovel by the door for use in the morning. By the time he had finished, she was in bed, facing the wall.

She listened to him undressing, the rustle of leather and wool. At last he came to bed, bringing with him the odor of tobacco and wood ashes. Tensely she waited for him to draw her close. He had never failed at least to hold her for a while before going to sleep, but tonight he lay unmoving.

The wind blew louder now, shaking the house with savage gusts. She turned over. Stephen was lying on his back. Did he feel as chilled and lonely as she? They had never gone to sleep separated by such icy silence. She tried to recall exactly how she had worded her remark about the water but could not. Or had she said something else that had caused him to question her love? She must make things right between them again.

"Stephen, may I move close to you?"

"You are cold?"

"Cold, yes. But I want to be close to you because I love you. Stephen"—oh, the humble words came hard—"if I have done something to offend you, I am sorry." She eased close until her body curved against his.

He said, "You have done nothing to offend me. You have merely reminded me of some things I have chosen to forget. Especially am I reminded of the advantages you have had."

"I have had few advantages, Stephen. My father's family lost most of its money in unfortunate trading ventures long before he was grown. I know how people of wealth live only because I have taught children in their homes."

As if he had failed to hear her words, he said, "I have been thinking. When the roads are passable, you may wish to see the dominie or that rich lawyer friend of yours about having this marriage annulled. After all, there are no children."

She was shaken as if by one of those savage gusts of wind. Yet the wind itself was silent now, holding its breath while it waited for further disclosures.

"You want to be rid of me because I have not become pregnant? You hate me because of that?"

"I don't hate you. I love you. You must know that."

"Then forget this talk about ending our marriage."

"I cannot. I have taken what I had no right to take. I married you under false pretenses. I should have known the day would come when I would have to tell you."

False pretenses? Her heart began a slow pounding. She knew everything about his life here. It must be something that had happened in Philipsborough. Another woman? In her imagination she saw her. And perhaps a child. William Vanzuyder and Jan Harten had testified they knew of no hindrance to his marriage. But how would they know of a woman in Philipsborough?

She wanted to know, ached to know, but dreaded the pain of knowing. If she never heard him say the words, it would be as if it were not true.

"Don't tell me about it," she said. "I don't want to hear. Besides, it's all in the past. Isn't it?"

"It's in the past, yes. But it's affecting the present. I'm tired of trying to cover it up. It's best to tell you now before we become any more deeply involved."

Chapter 11

Some of the things he told her that night she had heard before, especially about the mother who had died when he was two.

"From what I was told, my mother was much like you," he said. "She did beautiful fancywork, loved books. She was not so strong, though. Always getting fevers. But she did teach my brother to read and write. She began when he was three. By the time he was six he could read everything."

Although Margretta wanted to know the guilty secret of his manhood rather than the details of his childhood, she listened patiently.

"My father remarried only three months after being widowed. How could a man take care of a child of two and one of six? He must have had little choice. She was ignorant and vulgar. He stayed away from the house as much as possible, drank too much. They quarreled all the time."

"Stephen, I hate to interrupt. But what does this woman have to do with our marriage?"

"Everything. You see, she never taught me to read."

"Then it was your father who taught you?"

"No. He was never home enough."

"Your brother, then?"

"No. He was my stepmother's pet. We never spent much time together."

"Then how did you learn?"

"I do not know how. That is why I refused to read to you tonight. I

110

could not do so." He paused, the silence heavy with his pain and humiliation. "So, that is what you have for a husband, Margretta. A man who cannot read except for a few words he has seen stenciled on barrels like 'flour' or 'rye' or 'wheat,' and who cannot write anything but his name. A man so dishonest he withheld this knowledge from you, so eager was he to win you."

For a long time there was no sound except for a rattling of sleet against the window. She was remembering the dominie's words: *He is nothing but an illiterate peasant.*

"You are silent. This news bothers you very much."

The silence lengthened as she sought the right words. "Yes, it does bother me," she said at last. "It bothers me that you could have thought it would make a difference in my love after I have shown you in so many ways how deep it is. Your secret could have been so many things: a woman somewhere, a child. I would have been helpless to do anything about either of those. But this I can easily correct." She slipped her hand under his shoulder. "This marriage will not be dissolved. But there will be some changes. Tomorrow I'll put my fancywork away and you'll put the cradle away. We are going to spend every spare moment we have teaching you to read."

"I'm too old."

"Nonsense. You are very intelligent. You've already shown that by marrying a teacher." He had turned over now and had tentatively curled his arm around her shoulder. "Come even closer, Stephen. Show me how glad you are that you married a teacher."

In the morning it was still snowing. It was bitterly cold and the wind was blowing hard. She awakened to see Stephen pulling on his coat.

"Stay in bed until the fire comes up," he said. "This is a real blizzard. I'll just push my way through to the barn."

Hating to have him return to a cold house after struggling through drifts, she hurriedly dressed and began fixing sausages, eggs, crisp corn cakes, and tea for him.

Every few minutes she went to the window and looked out. The wind had carved the snow into an unfamiliar landscape of mountainous drifts; the barn was barely discernible.

At last she saw him coming, an indistinct figure, some of the time walking backward, his body bent against the wind. Watching him, she felt a surge of love. Sometimes his stubbornness and his withdrawal angered her, for it was her nature to speak out about things that bothered her. When he withdrew, she must remember that step-mother whose love went to the older child. And she must remember that this too was part of his strength: the behavior of a proud man, often isolated, who had resolved to find his own way.

He came in shivering, stamping his feet, frosted with snow like a giant gingerbread man.

"I feel sorry for the animals," he said. "It is cold in the barn. I gave them extra rations and put blankets over the horse and the cow." He looked at the fire and the food she had prepared. "You did not stay in bed as I suggested."

"How could I lie there with you out in the storm? And I knew you would need a hot breakfast."

"What a lucky man I am."

"What a lucky woman I am."

Did other married couples act like this? Stop in the midst of their work to kiss and caress each other, sometimes so lost in their affec-tions that their work went undone, their food grew cold? She broke away from him. "Come now, we must eat quickly so we can begin the lessons."

During breakfast she caught him looking at her several times, his blue eyes glowing. Again she reminded herself that no matter how distant he sometimes seemed, his love was as strong beneath the withdrawal as the life in the bulbs and plants lying now beneath a coverlet of snow.

She soon found that the hardest part about teaching Stephen to read and write lay in overcoming his humiliation over his ignorance. At first he despaired of every error.

"I suppose I'll be spending weeks just reciting my ABC's," he said after she had shown him the chart, each letter followed by a picture of an object that began with that letter.

"We won't bother with that. But you must learn their names and sounds."

"But I want to be able to recite the alphabet."

"Why?"

"Because when our children are learning, I want to be able to help them, to know when they're doing it right."

"We'll begin doing five letters a day."

"Only five? Can't we do ten?"

His eagerness to learn was a revelation. She gave him one of the notebooks she had brought from Manhattan, had him print a letter of the alphabet on each of twenty-six pages. Then, concentrating on the letter A, she had him think of other words beginning with it. As he said them, she wrote them on her slate and he copied them into his notebook.

When he said "average," she said, "It would be easier for you if you dealt with shorter words."

Serious, determined, he said "I do not expect this to be easy. I want to learn as much as I can as fast as I can."

After he had listed ten words, ranging from "and" to "alabaster," she stopped him, had him read them back to her. "Now read them again," she said. "Read them very slowly and think about how the other letters in the words sound."

The snowy hours sped by. The weather cleared the next day and he shoveled paths, then returned to his slate and notebook. After he had learned the alphabet, she showed him how to transmute the printed letters into handwriting, had him practice on the slate, then write them in his notebook next to the printed words.

While he did this, she took another notebook and began a careful printing. She had decided to write a story for him, the story of their meeting and of their life together.

It began: In the year 1740, Stephen Warner, twenty years old, left Philipsborough, journeyed north to Van Badenswyck, and took possession of a farmhouse and one hundred acres of land. He worked hard clearing new land, plowing, cultivating, planting, with help from no one. He also began preparing the house for the family he would someday have.

She hesitated over some of the words with several syllables. But they were, she told herself, words that he commonly used. She was counting on his familiarity with the story to help him figure out the harder words.

By the end of the week he could recognize most of the words in the list under each letter. She had him read them to her at intervals during the day until he made no errors. The second week she tested him by picking out words from different lists, dictating them to him and having him write them on the slate. The third week she presented him with new words and was surprised at the speed with which he sounded them out. No doubt the years he had spent trying to figure out words stenciled on barrels and in the village store had sharpened his insight.

"I have taught many students," she told him, "and it took them six months to a year to learn what you have learned in less than a month."

"Perhaps they had not spent twenty years wishing to learn." Picking up his chalk, he wrote the word "when" on the slate.

"When?"

"When am I going to begin reading?"

"You are already reading."

"Just words. I want to read words that say something."

She handed him the notebook she had begun. Too proud to read haltingly to her, he went over each word in silence. He pointed to one. "Is that 'journeyed'?"

"Yes. The *ou* there has a different sound. These inconsistencies are what make English such a difficult language to read and write."

"I will master them all." After silently sounding out the words of the next sentence he looked up. "Is that really how you felt when you first saw me?"

"That despite your clothing I knew you were a gentleman? Yes."

"You do not record what I thought."

"I do not know what you thought."

He put down the notebook. "I thought: there is the woman I want for my wife."

And so they continued working through the long, cold winter months, the snow too high this year for travel. It was not until late March that William rode into the yard.

"What?" he said the minute he looked at her. "No sign of a little one yet?" He turned to Stephen. "Don't you know, my friend, what winter is for?"

"You're offending Margretta."

"Sorry, Margretta. Sometimes I forget that you're . . ."

"I'm what?"

"Different."

"You must remember, William, that no two human beings are alike. You shouldn't throw people together into a class and expect them to be alike."

"Well, I can tell you one group that's all alike. The landlords. Every one of them a thief."

"Then you ought to leave Van Badenswyck and buy yourself some land somewhere else. Be free. Be your own man."

"You don't understand what's involved. Leaseholds and such. Oh, by the way, I rode into the village yesterday. Couldn't stand the squalling of brats any longer. Had a drink or two at the tavern."

"What's the news in the village?" Stephen asked.

"Not much. It's just beginning to wake up after a long winter's sleep. The ice is breaking up on the river. The sawmill and the grist mill will be operating in another week or so." He turned to Margretta. "This will interest you. Gustavus Sulzer has taken him a new wife. He married her last summer in Albany, but just brought her here a couple of weeks ago."

"I do not see why that should interest me."

"Didn't you have something to do with him?"

"Nothing really. He was looking for a wife. I was single so he considered me. But I was considering someone else." She rolled up the breeches she was sewing for Stephen. "What is the new wife like? Young? Pretty?"

William burst out with a hearty laugh. "Not interested, eh? You sound pretty curious to me. Well, I ain't seen her. I did hear, though, that she has warts on her face but a nice pocketful of money."

Turning to Stephen, he said, "Have you begun sugaring?"

"No. I've been waiting for the mud to dry before I take the wagon into the woods. The sap is late this year. Such a long winter."

Before he left, Margretta said, "How's Sara?"

"Sticking out to here." He placed his hand a foot out from his stomach. "And complaining all the time. Too many diapers. Too many babies. Not enough water. Too tired for this, too tired for that. You know how women are."

She was as glad to see him go as she had been to see him come.

Two weeks later, when the roadway had dried enough so the wagon could be driven on it without being mired, Stephen loaded the back of it with sacks of grain to take to the grist mill. Margretta rode with him and went to the dominie's.

Her welcome was warm. Judith hugged her, then held her off and looked at her. "Still the same slim young woman. Sit down. I'll ask Alicia for some refreshments." She left the room, came back in a few moments followed by Alicia, who put down a tray with cider and some of her small cakes.

How pleasant it was to be waited on, to see Alicia again with her lovely golden skin and winglike brows. Standing up, Margretta gave Alicia a hug as warm as the one Judith had given her. "How good it is to see all of you," she said. "By the way, where are the children?"

Judith shrugged. "Off in the woods somewhere."

"And have they been well? I missed them, missed all of you. We went from December to the end of March without seeing another living creature, except two deer and some birds."

"How dreadful," Judith said. Then, when Alicia had left, she said, "I thought you might be bringing me a child to admire."

Margretta sipped some of the cider. It tingled on her tongue, agreeably hard. "Unfortunately not. It makes me sad. I know how much Stephen wants a son."

"You have plenty of time. Try not to worry about it. I've noticed that when people are too intent on having children, they are often unsuccessful."

"We . . ." Margretta looked away. "When we . . . are together, I'm afraid we are not thinking about having children. It is only afterward that I ask myself: Did it happen this time?"

Judith gave her an understanding smile. "That is as it should be. At least you are better off than Nelia."

"Nelia?"

"Cornelia Van Baden. They call her Nelia. Let's see . . . she's been married how long?"

"A month or so longer than I have."

"That's right. And she has already had two miscarriages. The second time she became pregnant, she went right to bed and stayed for two months, then lost the child."

Margretta thought of how joyful she and Stephen would have been if she had discovered she was pregnant. How horrible it would be after your hopes had been raised to have them bleed away to nothing. "I feel sorry for her. Perhaps I am better off than I thought."

"Nicolaus, too, is to be pitied. What is the use of being the scion of Van Badenswyck if you cannot pass along such vast holdings to someone of your own blood? I think he would even be happy to have a daughter. After all, he could marry her to a proper young man who could manage the estate."

Judith also told her that Gustavus Sulzer's wife had presented him with a daughter. "He says he married her last summer. Maybe so."

Or maybe, Margretta thought, he had been as eager to demonstrate his youthful vigor to this woman as he had to herself. She was glad she had chosen Stephen, yet when she witnessed the baptism of the Sulzer baby, she felt envious.

The Sunday after that she saw Nicolaus and his wife. The fragility that had been a component of Cornelia's beauty was emphasized now. She was thin, her skin as translucent as a piece of porcelain, and she leaned heavily on her husband's arm.

Nicolaus had grown more mature, and this maturity and the assurance that went with it added a new quality to his dark good looks. Margretta wished them well, this handsome young couple, and when she found his gaze had strayed to and lingered on her, she smiled in acknowledgment of the attention.

Now that warm weather had come, they discontinued Stephen's regular lessons. The concentrated work of the winter, however, had produced results. By June he was reading as well as any of the Hardenbroeck children. Margretta suggested he try some poetry, but he said, "Not now." One day she saw him studying his contract with the Van Badens and realized that his main interest lay in facts that applied to his life.

Still, she was proud of him, and the next time she visited Judith, she asked if she could spare one of the newspapers the dominie had already read. Judith gave her a copy of *The Weekly Post-Boy* and *The New York Gazette*.

"Never mind returning them. More will come on the next sloop. So you've turned into a newspaper reader?"

"It is Stephen who is really interested."

Judith's eyebrows tilted, but all she said was, "That's nice. I like a man who keeps up with things."

Stephen was delighted to get the papers. Sometimes in the evening when he was too tired for physical work, he sat on the *stoep* smoking and slowly reading them.

"Try not to move your lips," she said. "People might think you just learned to read."

"I'll try," he said.

That summer Stephen planted flax. He also expanded the cornfield by twenty feet, cutting logs and dragging them to a spot behind the house. William came over with his oxen and helped him pull out the stumps. In return, Stephen helped him rebuild the crumbling end of his house. Later Stephen took the trees to the sawmill, where he had them cut into clapboards. After the wood had seasoned, he would add a lean-to at the back of the house.

When the men exchanged work, the women often went along, taking handwork with them. When she came to Margretta's, Sara brought all four of her children. Anna and Maria played their own mysterious games while Jeremias, walking now, followed his father worshipfully around in return for an occasional pat on the head, or when his father was busy, climbed up onto Stephen's leg. Oloff was still at the breast, his feet resting on the protrusion that would soon be another visible family member.

"You can tell Stephen is taken with Jeremias," Sara said when they were alone. "What a wonderful father he'll be."

Margretta paused in the act of threading a needle. "If he ever does become a father."

"What a silly thing to say. Of course he'll be a father. Don't be so impatient."

"I can't help it. I keep feeling I've failed him. Sometimes I wonder whether he's sorry he married me."

"Now, *that's* silly. If you could see how he looks at you, you'd never wonder. Maybe he thinks *he's* failed *you.*"

That summer she helped him as much as her strength would allow. When he demurred, she said, "And is this your place or ours?"

"Ours."

"Then do not begrudge me the chance to help make it a better one."

She looked across to the ridge of hills: good land, a beautiful place. She had begun, she realized, to think of it as Stephen did, as theirs. She stood still as chickens do when they see the shadow of a hawk flying overhead.

"We must not let ourselves become too attached to this place, Stephen. It will make it hard to leave."

"We'll grow attached to another soon enough."

One day when they were at the Vanzuyders', Stephen mentioned the fertility of land in the Mohawk Valley to the north and west. "There's a lot of available farmland there."

"Ah," William said. "You've been listening to some of those fellows at the tavern."

"No. I read it in *The New York Gazette*."

"You *read* it?"

"Yes."

"Read it yourself?"

"Of course."

"I didn't know you could read. You never said."

"Now, Will," Sara said. "Just because he never told you don't mean he ain't able. Probably he can do lots of things he ain't talked about. Besides, who gets a chance to talk about anything when you're around?"

"Well, maybe there's a thing or two *I* can do that he can't do." Passing his wife on his way to refill his cup of cider at the barrel, he patted Sara's swollen belly.

"That takes little skill," Sara said. "Be still now."

Stephen fell silent. Margretta bent over her sewing, reminding herself that William was a good friend, always willing to lend his equipment or give his time.

"I know one thing," Sara said. "When the boys are old enough, I want Margretta to teach them to read. Would you?"

"I'd like to."

"We may not be able to pay you—"

"Of course we can pay," William said. "We'll pay in corn. Or I'll shoot an extra deer and give them the hide."

"Ah. So you *do* think it's important."

"Sure it's important. If only to have someone in the house to figure out them papers the landlords serve us with."

The previous fall Mr. Wortheimer had come to collect the rent, he had complimented Stephen on building a barn. This year he noted the newly cleared area and the pile of lumber behind the house. "You're a good worker," he said. "Every time I come here, the place looks better. We need more tenants like you." He collected the five pounds for rent, took a percentage of the sacks of wheat.

"He took more of your wheat than of William's," Margretta said afterward.

"I raised more."

"It isn't fair. You're penalized for working harder."

"I still have more left than William does. Besides, Wortheimer didn't raise the rent or charge for the lumber. Up on Livingston Manor a farmer was fined not long ago for cutting lumber without permission."

"He noted everything in his ledger."

"That's what a manager is supposed to do. Keep track of what's happening on each farm."

True, true, she thought. But who was to say that the manager was not waiting for him to more than double the value of the property before his attitude of commendation changed to one of manipulation?

"This is a good place, Margretta." He came close to her. She felt his touch. "You are happy here, are you not?"

"Yes. I'm happy."

But . . .

Chapter 12

In September Sara gave birth to her fifth child, Sophia. "Only twenty-four years old and already I have five children," she said to Margretta. "How many will I have by the time I'm thirty-four or forty-four? Where will we put them?" Tears rolled down the side of her face. "Babies, babies. I'm tired of them."

"Hush, now. You're just tired." The tiny creature fitted so well in Margretta's arms that she hated to put it down next to Sara. "She's beautiful. Hold her and you'll love her."

"Oloff still in diapers. Now this one. At night sometimes I dream about them. The diapers, I mean. Probably because I'm smelling them. William can't hardly stand them either. He leaves me alone lots of times just because of the children and the mess and the smell."

"Talk to him sometime about how you feel."

"He won't listen. William don't like to waste time talking when we're alone."

Margretta pitied her at the same time that she envied her. How long would it be before she held a baby of her own? But at least she would not this year be having a child in cold weather when the care was so much more difficult. As it was, she looked forward to their second winter despite the dread of cold, welcoming it for its easier routine.

"Will you finish the cradle this winter?" she asked Stephen.

"We do not need it yet. I will make you a spinning wheel out of red maple. Also, I want to learn to cipher."

So this winter she showed him how to calculate the areas of fields
and the distance around them. He had figured out how to add and
subtract, was delighted to learn about multiplication and division,
fractions and percentages.

While he worked on ciphering problems, she carded wool they had
sheared in the fall. And because his arms were stronger, he hackled
the flax, separating the coarse part from the fibrous parts. She saved
the wool and linen fibers in a large basket for the day when he had
finished her spinning wheel.

They had a St. Nicolaus Day celebration this year. When she told
guests Stephen had cut lumber for a lean-to or perhaps an additional
room, one woman shook her head. "We know a family did that. The
agent raised their rent so much they couldn't pay. They was evicted."
When pressed, however, the woman was unable to give the name of
the family.

Stephen went ahead with his plans anyway, having decided to extend the roof at the back down to within six feet of the ground and
make a room about half the width of the house, with the remaining
area a lean-to where wood could be stored.

After the party, winter set in hard. Even when they sat a few feet
from a roaring fire, their backs were cold. On nights of high winds
their bed curtains blew about like gauze, and Stephen often had to sit
up to keep the fire going. Even when he banked it well, he was in
and out of bed at intervals, fearful that a sudden gust might blow a
spark out into the room, and even more fearful that the embers might
die out completely.

"You worry too much about losing your fire," she said sleepily one
night when he came shivering back to bed.

"You say that because you were brought up in the city. If a fire
goes out there, all you have to do is look out the window and see
which of your neighbors has smoke coming out of the chimney.
Then you run over with a shovel or a foot stove for a few hot coals.
Do you realize how long it would take me to get to the Vanzuyders'?"

"We have our tinderbox."

"Yes. But many times I have spent nearly an hour striking flint
against steel, trying to catch the spark with a bit of tinder or cloth.
When you need a fire the most, that's when the little box is always
the most obstinate."

"Come close to me and get warm," she said.

It was no trouble, she reflected, to create a spark between them or to ignite that spark into an enveloping warmth. How wonderful it was to be young, to know the feeling of oneness with the man whose body was made to fit yours.

The winter slipped speedily into spring with its renewal of outdoor work and the onset once again of preparation of food for the next winter, beginning with the sugaring.

That summer, Stephen, in addition to working the fields and cutting more trees, also took time to build the room at the back of the house. In the fall when the rental agent came, he noted the improvements, took his percentage of the crop, charged the same five pounds rent, and with a compliment to Stephen and Margretta, left.

He did the same the next year when Stephen put an addition on the barn, and the next when Stephen installed the pump logs, bringing water into a trough in the back room. He had cut medium-sized trees in four-foot lengths, had laboriously bored a hole in each end with an auger until the holes met in the middle, then had placed them end to end from the brook to the house.

Now if I have a baby, Margretta thought as she wrote about this in the record of their marriage, I won't have to ask for water. I can dipper it into the washtub myself. *If I have a baby.* She had stopped thinking *When I have a baby.*

Surprisingly, Sara had stopped breeding. No baby had appeared since Sophia. Cornelia Van Baden so far had carried only one baby to full term and that one had been stillborn. But at least she conceived. I can't even do that, Margretta thought.

An itinerant weaver came that fall. He and Margretta bargained while Stephen sat by smiling. The man looked at her store of yarn and of linen thread, examined with great care the eight pieces of lace she brought out for him.

"You can get a pound for these two, I know," she said. "And for this long, wide piece. The rest a little less."

He was a small man with an impish grin that belied his shrewdness and skill. They came to an agreement, however, and he stayed for two weeks, accepting his bed—the alcove where Stephen had once slept—and board plus the lace in return for weaving her accumulated spinnings into cloth. She had already dyed some of it: some serviceable brown wool from alder bark and some of the linen a dark blue, using the bark from the same red maple that Stephen had used for her spinning wheel.

"Don't you have any black?" he asked. "You might need some for mourning sometime."

"We have no family, no one to mourn."

"Just married recently?"

"No. Five years now."

"No little ones?"

Stephen got up and left. "No little ones," she said.

He said no more about that. Instead, he gossiped about other places where he had been in the homes of both the rich and the poor. He told them of problems down on the Philipse Patent, where squatters from Connecticut were refusing to move off land that Philipse insisted was his. "There'll be trouble there," he said. "Mark my words." He spoke of the young Lady Van Baden and said her mind appeared unsettled and that sometimes her screams at night kept him awake, and of manor houses where he had been relegated to the attic to use the elaborate looms they had there, working through the heat of the day with poor light.

His news interested Margretta more than the news in *The New York Gazette*, for he knew who had married, who had given birth, who had died.

When he left, they missed the friendly clatter of his loom, missed his cheerful talk. Yet it was good to be able to touch each other again, to speak of their feelings with ease. During his stay they had made love only once, and that on a night when, after wine, he had snored so loudly they were sure he was asleep; even so, they had felt furtive and inhibited.

It was good, too, to have a supply of cloth in the *kas*, enough, probably, to last several years. Unless we have children, Margretta thought. Should she take some of this, cut it into squares for diapers? No, time enough to plan and make what she would need for a child after she knew it was on its way.

Meanwhile, she kept busy. She replenished her supply of lace. She spun, she sewed, she cooked; the winter passed. In the summer she helped Stephen with as much time as she could spare from her household tasks, for with enlarged fields he had more work than ever before.

The fifth year ended, then the sixth.

June 10, 1751. Seven years. The rosebush by the door was in full blossom. When Stephen came back from the barn, he brought her seven roses. She arranged them in the pewter porringer, put it in the center of the table where she could look at it all day long.

Seven years. Seven years of fruitful work; seven years of barren hope. Ahead were more years of household and outdoor tasks, more barren years stretching out to a point beyond the brook where the previous tenants had begun a small graveyard.

"Seven years," she said to Stephen when they sat down for breakfast. "A long time. We have accomplished much."

"Yes. More than I thought we would."

"But it's time now for a change."

He put down his spoon. "What kind of change?"

"It's time for us to move on. Leave this place."

"Why?"

"Because that was our original plan. To fix the place up, sell the leasehold at a profit."

"But I have more to do."

"You will always find more to do here. I married you thinking you wanted to push into the future—no, to *create* the future. Instead, you follow a routine season after season, letting the future happen instead of molding it yourself."

"Anywhere we lived it would be the same. That's what life is, Margretta. Wherever you go, you make a home and take care of it. You grow food. If you're lucky, you have children and take care of them until they are grown."

"Not everyone lives like this. Some people explore new lands, live every day with new experiences."

He poured more maple syrup on his suppone, cut off a piece of cheese. Without looking directly at her, he said, "Your problem is that you have no children. If you did, your mind would have no time for dwelling on imaginary adventures."

He was partly right. Yet there was more: a pioneering spirit inherited from her Dutch and English ancestors, and from that bit of Indian blood the belief that to move freely, to make your home where you chose, was a natural right. Here they lived in the shadow of the Van Badenswyck agent, whose dictates always had to be considered before their own desires.

"Furthermore," he said, "did we not want to have our own place so we could pass it on to our children?"

That was also true. But when they had first spoken of moving on, when he had described his own move northward, she had assumed he was as eager for change as she was.

"You are silent," he said. "Are you so very disappointed with our marriage?"

Quickly she moved around the table and placed her cheek against his. "I'm happy in our marriage. It's just that it's so easy to say that sometime we'll do something, and then let that time remain always in the future."

"We'll talk of it again," he said. "We must get ready now to go to William's. I promised I'd help him with his plowing. He fell behind this spring. If he doesn't get the wheat in soon, he'll have no flour for bread next winter."

Fell behind because he spent too much time at the tavern, she thought. But she said nothing. Stephen knew William's faults as well as she did but liked him anyway.

Sara that day was oddly reserved, saying little until William and Stephen had left for the field. Oloff and Jeremias went along with them to help. After suggesting the girls go hunting for strawberries, Sara said to Margretta, "Come. Let's sit outside. I love the summer."

"Yes. But soon the heavy work will start."

"The big girls help me now. It ain't so bad as it used to be." She looked unhappy, though, her shoulders hunched forward, her hands tensely clasped.

"Is everything all right, Sara?"

Sara gave her a bitter smile. "Oh, yes. All right it is. Everything's in good working order."

"I don't know what you mean."

"I mean I've begun breeding again."

Margretta felt the sourness of envy rise in her throat. Why did Sara have such a surplus of riches while she had none? Just one child, that was all she asked. Why did it never come? She knew it was too late now even to hope.

"I am very happy for you," she said. Sitting on the *stoep*, facing west, their faces shaded from the morning sun, she could see the outlines of the Catskills. Someone's future lay beyond those mountains, but obviously not hers. "No," she said. "I am lying. I sit here saying I'm happy for you, and all I can do is envy you and wish I were in your shoes."

Sara laughed. "I sure love your honesty. Now I'll tell *you* something. During those years when I had a baby every year, I kept wishing I was in *your* shoes. Always thin, never having no trouble getting around. Never struggling to keep babies clean. You can't imagine how wonderful these last few years have been. When we was first married, everything was so exciting. I used to think all day about what it was going to be like at night. I could hardly wait. Then after the babies begun to come, all I could think of was what it was going to be like with another one. The only time I could take any pleasure with William was when I was already pregnant. But only for a while." She bent farther forward, her head in her hands. "Now it's going to start over again."

"I thought when you went so long without a baby you were perhaps all through with childbearing."

"I sort of thought so too. But it was something else. You used to talk about the dominie's wife and how much she knew. One day I worked up my courage and went to see her. She told me how she managed to stop having children after Frederic. It was easy. Well, no, not too easy. I had to count days after my courses. Real careful. How I did it was, I put a pebble on the mantel every day, and after I had so many of them, I kept William away from me for a few days. It worked fine. Then one day when I was dressing a hen, I looked at the little string of eggs and thought: maybe I don't need to go to all this trouble. Maybe my eggs have run out. Well, they hadn't."

The girls returned then with a basket half full of strawberries. Sara patted her daughters and said to Margretta, "They *are* good children." Then later, after they had eaten the berries and cream, she suddenly said, "Maybe *you* should go to see Mrs. Hardenbroeck."

"Why? I don't need that kind of advice."

"But if she knows that much, maybe she can tell you something that would work the opposite. Or give you a herbal."

Margretta thought about it, felt hope rising again. If a remedy existed, Judith would know about it. She would go, she decided. Somehow, she would overcome her shyness about discussing such an intimate subject, a shyness that had increased with her sense of failure.

But when she did go, it was in the fall, and after only a brief visit with Judith, she headed for the manor house for an entirely different purpose.

Chapter 13

In that fall of 1751 a new agent appeared, a Mr. Frost, a man who exuded briskness with every gesture, every clipped statement. Like Mr. Wortheimer, he checked over the farm, noting each improvement. But he smiled less and offered no compliments.

In the house afterward as the men discussed the portion of the crop due to the manor, Margretta worked quietly on a complex piece of lace.

Stephen had his five pounds ready. When he laid it on the table, however, Mr. Frost said, "Ten pounds, please."

"But it has always been five. I realize the place has increased in value, but this results in a larger crop percentage for the landlord. That has always been enough for him."

"But your ten years are up. Tenants are given ten years to get on their feet. This place was worth five pounds a year when you came. Now, with a larger house, piped-in water, a barn, and more tillable land, the value has doubled."

Stephen sat silent, his hand covering his money. Mr. Frost glanced toward Margretta. Though angry, she remained composed, her fingers never faltering.

"If you are unwilling to pay, I know of another man who would be glad to pay it for such a fine place."

"If it is fine, it is because I have made it so."

Mr. Frost shrugged. "Even so."

"I have put ten years of my life into this place."

Again the indifferent shrug. "You must realize that I am merely doing my job, seeing to it that the estate does not run at a loss. If you refuse to pay, we can always exercise the power of distraint. It is your choice."

"It is not a matter of choice. My problem is that five pounds is all I planned on, all I have at this time."

"I see." The agent leaned back, looked again at Margretta. "What is that you're making?"

"Lace. To trim clothing."

"It looks like fine stuff."

"It is."

"Interesting. Have you any for sale?"

"Only two small pieces suitable for the wrists."

When she brought them, he looked them over. "I will take these for five shillings each." To Stephen he said, "I will give you until next week to pay the remainder."

Margretta looked at Stephen. The time had come—he must surely realize it now—to leave.

Stephen sat in silence until the sound of the agent's horse had died away. "The farm is well worth ten pounds a year," he said. "We will find a way to pay."

Margretta bent her head over her work until he left for the barn. When he returned, she had supper on the table.

He had an account book she had ruled for him. After supper he got it out and worked on figures.

"I suppose I could sell the sheep," he said.

She nodded, quietly prepared herself for bed.

After a while he closed the account book, banked the fire, and joined her in bed. They both lay listening to the katydids chanting their repetitive and never resolved argument: Katy did, Katy didn't.

"You're angry," he said. "You think we should leave."

In the darkness she pressed her lips together.

"I thought we agreed," he said, "that with no children, we do not need a place we can pass on to anyone."

We did not agree. You decided.

"And there are no children."

She could not dispute that.

"We have been happy here—haven't we?"

"Yes, we have been happy." *But I would have been happier in my own place. Our own place.*

Early the next afternoon, they heard someone riding down the lane.

"That must be William," Stephen said. "Probably here to complain about the new agent."

Rather than William, however, it was Mr. Frost himself. Today he was less brisk, more affable, and he addressed Margretta rather than Stephen.

"Lady Van Baden was very taken with that piece of bobbin lace I took her. She wants you to come to the manor house for two weeks and look at some of her laces, see whether you can repair them. Can you do that?"

"Yes. I can repair lace."

"Then you are to return with me this afternoon. Your work there, plus the finishing of what you bring back here with you at the end of the two weeks—just a few months' work, I'm sure—will take care of the remainder due for the rent. Is that agreeable?"

She looked at Stephen until he looked away. Finally she said, "I'll go. But not until tomorrow. I need time to prepare myself and my materials."

"Very well. I'll tell her to expect you then."

After Mr. Frost had left, Stephen went outside, no doubt to admire the land that meant so much to him. Supper was a quiet meal. He spoke of getting the place ready for winter; Margretta said nothing at all.

It was not until they were in bed that he referred to her leaving. "I dislike having my wife work at the manor house. Like one of the slaves."

And are you just realizing there is no difference?

After another moment he said, "But you do enjoy working on lace. You have often said so."

Yes, as a quiet way to shake off the day's cares. Choosing my own design. Making something beautiful. Stopping when I wish.

She had moved closer to the wall, turned her back to him. Her anger had dissipated, replaced now by disillusionment. She slept fitfully, awakening with a bitter taste in her mouth.

When they parted in the morning, he said, "At least you will see the inside of the manor house. You have always been curious about it."

"Yes, that's true. Good-bye, Stephen." She stood stiffly while he kissed her, then got on the horse and rode into the mildness of the September morning without looking back.

Within an hour she had reached the dominie's house. Judith was in the garden covering some of her delicate plants with leaves and dried grass.

"How nice to see you. You work so hard. I'm glad you took some time off."

"Not really. I'm going to the manor house to work on their laces. But I wanted to see you first." After an awkward silence during which Judith waited patiently, Margretta said, "I have a problem."

"And you think I can help?"

"I hope so. You helped Sara Vanzuyder."

"You hardly have the same problem."

"No. Mine is that I want a child very much."

"I see. I'm not sure I can help. But I can try. Come inside with me." She led the way into the back room, where she kept her dried herbs and decoctions, took a bottle down from a shelf. It contained a brown liquid.

"This is a decoction from the ginseng root. Supposedly it promotes fertility."

"In a man or a woman?"

"Either, I guess. I'd suggest you both try it. Even if it doesn't work, it should serve as a good tonic."

The bottle felt warm in Margretta's hands as if imbued with magic. She took a swallow. "I feel its heat in my stomach already. It must be working."

Judith smiled. "That's the alcohol base."

"I'll bring you some lace later in the winter."

"Never mind payment. I'll be repaid well enough if it works. Stay for dinner, won't you? We're having duck. They've already begun to congregate on the river."

Margretta stayed, saw the children again. Antonia and Gertrude were polite young ladies now, glad to see her. Frederic, nearly fifteen, had grown long-limbed and awkward; otherwise, he had changed little, though now he spoke of muskets rather than of bows and arrows. Yet he too appeared glad to see her. Even the dominie shook hands with her and inquired about Stephen. They were almost like her family, she reflected.

In the early afternoon, she went through the woods and knocked on the front door of the manor house. Jupiter came, recognized her immediately, and, smiling, said she was expected.

After indicating an oak armchair, he left her in the parlor. Instead of taking it, she walked around. The furnishings here resembled those she had seen in better homes in the city: a finely colored Oriental—much finer than Gustavus Sulzer's—draped over a gateleg table with a rosewood inlay. On it stood brass candlesticks and a sweetmeat box. She noted also a chandelier of polished brass, brass wall sconces, and a heavily carved mantel clock.

She waited nearly half an hour before she heard footseps. It gave her time to examine the biblical scenes on the tiles that framed the fireplace opening: one of Lazarus emerging from his tomb waving the flag of the Netherlands; one of Jonah, in Dutch costume, bursting out of the whale.

She stood up, prepared to greet the lady of the manor; instead she saw Nicolaus.

"This is a pleasant surprise. Have you come here with some petition?" His eyes held hers as they had so many times outside the church.

"I have come to work on some lace for your mother." She hesitated, finally said, "But, yes. I do have something to discuss with you."

"Sit down. I'll be happy to listen."

Just then another of the slaves, a young black woman, appeared. "Lady Van Baden will see you upstairs."

The straight-backed young woman led her up a narrow stairway and down a short hall to Lady Van Baden's room. The doors to her *kas* were open. She was laying out pieces of lace on her bed, her keys and Bible swinging from the chain at her waist each time she bent forward.

On the walls were two large portraits: one of Lady Van Baden holding a baby, the other of a boy around twelve, probably Nicolaus. Paintings interested Margretta. Perhaps later in her stay she would have a chance to examine them more carefully.

"I'm Mrs. Warner," she said. "Margretta Warner."

Lady Van Baden nodded. "Oh, yes, Margretta. I remember seeing you outside the church with Mrs. Hardenbroeck."

"I taught her children."

"I see. And then you married one of our tenants. Well, it is good that you have this little skill. Here, look over these laces."

Some were in fair condition. Many, especially those that had adorned the wrists of garments, were badly torn. Margretta arranged them in two piles. "These I can probably rework so they will at least be whole. This group is too badly torn to fix. It would take more time than to make new ones."

Lady Van Baden took out two of the badly damaged laces. "Could you copy these designs? I especially like these."

"I believe so."

"Well, first we will see how the repairs come out." Turning to the servant and indicating the pile of badly torn laces, she said, "Would you like these, Belle?"

"Thank you, madam." Belle's face was impassive.

"Take Margretta to the weaving room. She can work and have her meals there. Give her the west bedroom. Unfortunately, the small one is full of heavy clothing I am sorting."

"Yes, madam."

Lady Van Baden closed the door of her *kas*, revealing the painted Oriental designs on the front of it.

"You may go now," she said to Margretta.

Dismissed like a servant. But what else was she here? And what was Stephen but a servant of the Van Badens, tilling their soil, receiving shelter and enough of the crop to sustain his family? She had chosen to be the wife of a tenant farmer. Why did she feel so demeaned? Perhaps it was because she remembered learning that back in the sixteenth century Holland, free at last from Spain and now a republic, had proclaimed the doctrine that subjects are not created for the prince but the prince for the subjects. But that apparently had not applied to the colonies, nor to those the British had seized.

Belle opened a door at the other end of the hall. "This is where you will sleep. Miss Cornelia used to stay in this room when she came here before the wedding."

"Where is she now?"

"Downstairs. This is too high off the ground."

"May I go in and hang up my things?"

"Yes. But I must warn you, Lady Van Baden expects people to work when she hires them."

Margretta put her canvas bag on the chair, took out her other dress, and hung it on a peg. Next to it she put her riding skirt, a light cape, and her nightdress.

Then Belle took her up a narrow stairway. The entire third floor was one large room filled with looms, spinning wheels, and work-tables. The ceiling slanted on either side to within two feet of the floor. Large windows on either end provided light. Although Belle opened them, it did little to dissipate the heat that had accumulated.

Margretta sat at a table near the north window and spread out the laces. Selecting one with few holes, she laid it out and pinned it to her pillow. This kind of work was about as pleasurable as mending a pair of old stockings.

As her fingers moved, almost without her guidance, her thoughts wandered. Eight years ago, sailing upriver, she had looked up at this roofline that now imprisoned her and imagined herself a part of the life here. Now she *was* a part of the life here, she thought—struck by the irony of it.

Her hands perspired in the increasing heat and stuck to the threads. Lace making, like knitting, was most comfortably done in cool weather. She loosened her dress at the neckline, pushed up the sleeves, lifted her petticoats.

At last Belle came with her supper. Bread and cheese, a small amount of cold sturgeon, a sweetmeat. Tea. She ate hungrily, then picked up her tray and went down to her room. On the wall was a pewter lavabo. She turned the spigot. Cool water ran into the basin below.

After washing her hands and face, she lifted the bowl and emptied it into the covered pot under the bed. She descended a stairway at the back of the house. A second one took her to the ground level, lower at the back of the house than at the front. She found herself in the summer kitchen, where six slaves sat around a long table eating and talking. Nearby on the stone floor stood various-sized footed iron kettles, each with a pile of red coals under it.

Belle stood up. "I would have come for the tray."

"I wanted to go for a walk. It was no trouble."

"Thank you. It *is* hot climbing those stairs." Belle smiled, making Margretta feel she had made a friend.

Outside it was warm, but not oppressively so. She walked out through the pines at the back of the house and down the stone steps to the river. She sat on one of the benches there, her hands quiet at last. The river was quiet in the early-evening stillness, its flow to the south indiscernible. Perhaps at this moment the tide was forcing a part of it backward into a northward flow. Watching a piece of wood move slowly upstream, she was struck by the incongruity of it. A river should move steadily toward the sea rather than constantly turning back on itself. And a country, she thought, should move forward into freedom rather than backward into feudalism and slavery.

This was the river she had come up, her mind simmering with questions about the role she would play here. There, a few hundred yards up the shore, was the bench where she had sat with Stephen on their first afternoon together: laughing together, dreaming together, breaking bread together. Balanced on the threshold of a new life, she had felt nothing but joy and wonder.

Where was the wonder? What had happened to the joy? Now she was like a ship becalmed by an ebbing tide and a dying wind.

While she watched the sun draw closer to the blue peaks over which it hovered, an Indian paddled up the river close to the shore, his canoe gliding forward at least three times its length with each dip of the paddle.

When she had left Manhattan, she had wondered about Indians in these sparsely settled lands along the Hudson. Had not Schenectady once been attacked, with sixty people massacred? But that had been in the previous century, and the attackers had been Indians from the north spurred on by their French allies. So far as she knew, the local Indians were friendly.

The Indian lifted a hand in a wave. Standing up, she waved back, held out both arms after he had passed. Take me with you, she wanted to call out. Let me glide up the river with you, free and independent.

She sank back to the bench. How absurd. She was twenty-six years old, a mature married woman. She should not be thinking such thoughts. A married woman, yes, but a woman married to a man who cared more for the piece of ground he farmed than he did for her. The land—his mistress. And didn't a man always give his deepest love to his mistress? If he really loved me, she thought, he would have refused to let me come here.

She put her hands over her face. She would not cry. She would *not* cry. She never cried.

"What is wrong, Margretta?"

She looked up at Nicolaus standing tall and handsome in front of her, his dark-eyed gaze so intense it must surely be penetrating the turmoil of her thoughts.

"Nothing. Nothing at all." His gaze stirred her in a discomforting way. "Were you here when the Indian went by?"

"Yes, standing on the stairs eavesdropping quite shamelessly on your thoughts."

"I happened to be stretching at the time."

"Naturally. I too often feel an urge to stretch when I see an Indian paddle by. They are so lithe and make such wonderful use of their bodies." He sat down beside her, put his arm across the back of the bench. "Why the tears, Margretta?"

"I'm not crying. I never cry." Yet when she reached up, she felt a wetness on her cheeks.

"You are lonely?"

"Yes. Somewhat."

"You miss your husband."

"In a way."

"Shouldn't you be missing him a great deal?"

"Maybe. But aren't there times in all marriages when things aren't right between a man and a woman? They don't agree on something, perhaps, or one has one kind of dream, the other another."

His hand slipped down to her shoulder. She did not object. It made her feel less alone. "What is your dream, Margretta? Or am I asking too personal a question?"

She glanced at him, saw nothing but a friendly concern on his face. "To have our own land somewhere."

"And your husband's dream?"

"When we married, I thought our dreams were the same. Even now he says he wants to leave. But never this fall, never this spring, never this summer. Always an excuse. I think he does not want to leave the Hudson Valley. He loves it too much."

"And you do not have the same love for the land?"

"Not if I don't own it." She was quiet now, feeling a certain guilt in having confided something so personal to someone practically a stranger. At the same time, she felt a relief in having spoken of problems she had held within herself for too long. And the hand on her shoulder was comforting. It was comforting, but she was suddenly aware that it was a man's hand, and that the touch, even though casual, was reminding her that she was a woman.

"I think I understand how you feel. My own dreams have brought nothing but sadness and disappointment." His clasp tightened on her shoulder, then lifted as he rose. "My mother awaits me. Come up soon or it will be so dark you won't be able to find your way."

Margretta waited until he was out of sight, then climbed the stairs to the manor house. Opening the wrong door, she found herself in the sour-smelling cheese room with its brass milk cans, hanging baskets, and wooden press. Through a door at the side, she reached the kitchen, empty now, the fire banked, the floor cleared of kettles and coals.

Three candles lay on the table. She took one and held its tip against a coal at the back of the fireplace until it caught fire. After covering the coal, she went to her room and placed the candle on the stand by her bed.

As she undressed, she heard voices downstairs: the voice of Nicolaus, deep and low; his mother's voice, cool, measured; then another woman's, shrill yet sweet, subsiding, then gathering all its shrillness into a scream; Nicolaus speaking again as if quieting a child. Then silence.

The lavabo held warmish water now. A clean linen towel hung nearby. The receptacle beneath her bed had been emptied and her bed turned down. She blew out the candle and slipped tiredly between the fine linen sheets as soon as she had washed. Before she fell asleep, she heard another scream from the floor below. Twice during the night she awakened and reached out for Stephen. How strange it was to be sleeping alone—strange and cool. It made her feel like a girl again, young and virginal and cool.

She awakened to a morning already warm. Glad she had brought the lightweight linen dress and the thinnest of muslin petticoats, she dressed quickly and went down the back stairs to the summer kitchen.

Belle was there. Jupiter too. "I took one of your candles last night," Margretta said.

Belle smiled at her. "We left them for you. I was afraid it might be dark when you came in. Would you like some breakfast? I have some sausage cooked, and water heated for tea."

"May I eat it here with you?"

Belle exchanged looks with Jupiter. "If you wish to."

"You would not mind?"

"No."

They spoke mostly of the weather while they ate. Jupiter said he had looked out early and had seen clouds hovering over the mountains across the river. "We'll be having a thunderstorm before this day is over."

Belle nodded. "The breaking up of summer. It takes one good storm to end it."

Margretta liked listening to them talk. Like Alicia, they spoke slowly, as if they had more time than most people. Perhaps they did, for they had no need to hurry, to plan for the future. They had only to do what they were told.

How simple. And how terrible.

But she had work to do and a need to do it quickly. She finished her breakfast and hurried to the attic room, where yesterday's warmth still lingered. As the hours went by, the heat increased and her fingers grew more sticky and awkward. Late in the morning, she heard steps on the stairs.

Lady Van Baden entered. "Ah, you are working. How much have you done?"

People who did no fancywork, especially work that required much skill and attention, had no idea of the time involved. Margretta pointed to three completed laces. "Even small holes take time to repair. That is, if you want them to look as if they had never been torn."

"I see. Well, if that is all you can do . . ." Picking one up, she took it to the window and examined it. "I must say you do quite nice work."

"Thank you." I could do better, she wanted to say, in a cooler place.

"Well . . . I'll look in on you again."

Belle brought her dinner at midday but left quickly without conversation, saying Lady Van Baden needed her. Margretta continued working, eating as she worked. She hated it here, hated the heat, the monotony of the work, the isolation. At home, although often alone all day, she was rarely lonely.

When in midafternoon she again heard footsteps on the stairs, she was relieved. Even to listen to Lady Van Baden again, despite the critical attitude and impatience she took no pains to conceal, would be a relief.

It was Nicolaus. "How can you work in this heat?"

"It is not easy. The thread gets sticky."

"I'm not surprised. Why not work downstairs?"

"Because Lady Van Baden told me to work here."

"What do you need for your work?"

"Just this padded board and the bobbins and thread."

"Then come downstairs."

She shook her head. "That's very kind of you, but this is where your mother told me to work."

"I am the head of this house and I say you are to work in the parlor." He smiled. "Besides, my mother just left in her carriage for Clermont and will not be back for a week or more. Come on. The servants won't tell."

Carrying her workbag, she followed him down the stairs. He left her in the parlor, where the casement windows facing the river let in a cool breeze. Her work progressed more rapidly now; her thoughts lightened. The clock said six when he returned.

"Belle will serve us supper in the upper kitchen."

"I had planned to go downstairs to—"

"You will have supper with me."

She was reluctant, mostly because she felt Lady Van Baden would violently disapprove of her eating as a family member rather than as one who served the family.

"Hurry," he said. "Go upstairs and freshen up. Then come to the upper kitchen. It's at the back of the house to the right of the stairs."

Again he was commanding her. What choice did she have? And furthermore, what difference did it make? Clearly he just wanted company during his meal.

Chapter 14

The upper kitchen bore little resemblance to the lower kitchen. Here the floors were of sanded wood. Pieces of pewter, Delft, and English glass decorated the shelves of the cupboard, and a pewter chandelier hung over the table.

Lord Van Baden pulled a chair back from the table for her. Margretta recognized the Queen Anne design from the turnings, though, unlike those she had seen in New York, these were painted the gray-blue favored in the Hudson Valley. She saw silver spoons, and mugs and candlesticks of shining brass. Yet despite her enjoyment of these, she felt uncomfortable. She had no right to be eating with the lord of the manor. She belonged in the kitchen below. Nor had he invited her, she was sure, out of kindness. Bored, he probably would have as happily asked the weaver to dine with him in the hope of change and entertainment.

Belle served them. Margretta wanted to stop her as she walked by and say: Look, I had no choice but to eat with him. It is not that I am pretending to be any better than you.

The sturgeon was delicate and flavorful. Margretta was also pleased to see a purple-wrapped, cone-shaped loaf from which they could scrape off sugar for their tea, a welcome change from the maple syrup she had been limited to since her marriage.

Beyond asking her how she had happened to come to Van Badenswyck, Nicolaus asked few questions. He spoke of his sojourn in Europe and especially in Paris, telling her about Versailles and about the art treasures of the Louvre.

140

His behavior had changed from that of the man whom she had seen walking into the church, looking over the women as if he had the right of choice among them. At the moment his arrogance, if it were that, remained hidden. She found herself enjoying his company, wishing the meal might last longer.

Afterward he suggested a walk by the cool of the river. They went along the shore to the place where she had sat with Stephen that first afternoon, then back to sit awhile on the bench where they had sat the night before.

"How long have you been married?" he asked.

"Seven years."

"And how many children do you have?"

Her breath sharp in her throat, she said, "None."

"Oh, like Nelia. No doubt you have heard about her."

"Yes." This was a subject she disliked discussing. She stood up. "I think I'll go back now. Perhaps I can get some more work done before it is time to go to bed."

The sun sank through masses of anvil-shaped clouds, startling in their beauty even as their brightness faded.

"Will we have a storm tonight?" she asked.

"I wouldn't be surprised."

She sighed.

"You do not like storms?"

"Not especially."

"I feel just the opposite. I love them. I love the violence and excitement of them. Here at Van Badenswyck every day is like the one before, until a storm comes along and stirs things up. But come, we had best get back to the house and get some candles lighted before it darkens."

In the ground-floor kitchen, he lighted a candle in the embers and preceded her up the shadowy stairway and down the hall to the parlor. "I'll light the candles in the parlor for you," he said, "and then I'll visit Nelia." In the parlor he lighted the candles in the chandelier and the sconces, his movements swift, restless. "No, first we'll have some rum."

"None for me, please. I might lose track of my design."

"Don't be silly. It will improve your skill. Besides"—he lifted his finger, alerting her to the low rumbling reverberating across the hills—"it will give you courage to face the storm and me the courage to visit Nelia."

He handed her a glass with too much rum in it, lifted his own, and drank it quickly. After sipping a little of hers, she put it down and picked up her bag.

"No, wait," he said. "Come with me. You met Nelia on the day of our wedding, didn't you? Come in and say hello."

She had no desire to see Cornelia in her pitiful state, while she herself flaunted such good health. But she had little choice.

Cornelia lay dwarfed by the hugeness of her bed, her once-beautiful blond hair resting in lifeless strands on the pillow. Her skin, nearly pierced by the bones of cheek and chin, was like a piece of yellowed silk, her eyes deep sunk in their sockets. Her elbows and wrists were larger than the rest of her arms, bared now in the heat. Little trace remained of the lovely young woman who had once asked her polite questions about children she had taught in Manhattan.

"Have you heard about my baby?" she asked Margretta.

Unsure of which baby she meant, Margretta nodded.

"I lost the last one," Cornelia said. "But this time everything will be all right—if I take care of myself. It's going to be a boy. We're quite sure. Aren't we, Nicolaus?"

"Yes, my dear. That is all we need to make our happiness complete."

"I wish you much luck," Margretta said.

"Thank you. But everything is going to be all right."

"We'll let you rest now, my dear," Nicolaus said. He leaned downward to kiss her.

"No, no," she said, her voice shrill. "We must do nothing to endanger the baby. Nothing."

"I meant only to kiss you good night. Good night, Cornelia."

"Good night," Margretta said.

Cornelia appeared to hear neither of them.

Margretta followed Nicolaus back to the parlor. As he reopened the rum, she noticed a nervous tic in his right cheek.

"More for you?" he asked.

"No, thank you. I still have some."

His glass filled, he sat down, crossed his silk-clad legs. "So, what do you think?"

"Only that it is very, very sad. Will she be able to carry this one to full term?"

"There is no child. She lost it a year ago. For the moment she has forgotten that. Sometimes she remembers, relives it. If you hear any screams in the night, you will know it is one of those times."

"Is there no hope for her?"

"Who knows? She has had spells like this before. They pass after a while and her thoughts become clear again. But each bad time lasts longer then the previous one." He emptied his glass in one swallow, got up to refill it. "You're sure you won't have some more?"

"No. I still have some."

"You're not drinking it."

Obediently she finished her drink, put the glass down. Taking the pillow from her bag with the lace fastened on it, she arranged the bobbins in the proper order.

After watching her awhile, he said, "I remember seeing you the first time I went to church after I returned from Europe. You have a look about you that a man remembers."

This kind of talk made her uneasy. "I was eight years younger then. What you saw was the freshness of youth. All young women have it."

"No. Yours was a wistful quality, a look that said you were waiting for wonderful things to happen to you. It made a man wish he could make those things happen."

More uneasy now, she bent her head over her work.

"And did any of those wonderful things happen?"

Her reluctance to answer bothered her conscience. Finally she said, "A few did. But last week something less wonderful happened. Something unexpected and unjust." Now she looked up at him, her gaze steady. "And I believe it happened as a result of your orders."

"I can think of no orders I gave concerning you. I'm not even sure of your last name. I do remember your first name. Margretta. Lovely. It suits you very well."

"Lord Van Baden, did you not send a new agent to Stephen Warner's home to double the rent?"

His expression changed as the dark, winged brows lifted. "I have hired a new agent, yes. Mr. Wortheimer kept good records, but he was not making enough money to run the manor properly. If the new agent evaluated your farm and decided it warranted a higher rent, I am sure he was justified."

"But he did not raise our neighbors' rent."

"Is your farm better than theirs?"

"Yes, but only because r ιy husband has made it so. When others sat on their *stoeps* smoking their pipes and gossiping, he was always working. Year after year he has produced larger crops, cleared more new land than anyone else in the area."

"No doubt he has an exceptionally good piece of land."

"No better than the others. He produced more because he fertilized with care, spent more time cultivating. I often worked with him and know how much effort he put into it. I think it is unfair to penalize him for his labor."

He looked at her for a long time; she looked unblinkingly back. "It is like this, Margretta. When I hired Mr. Frost, I gave him free rein to handle my affairs, and in such a way that he makes a profit. I do not interfere."

"You would not even if you learned he was treating a man—an honest, hardworking man—unjustly?"

"I trust the men I hire."

"This one may indeed be trustworthy in looking after your interests but unfair when it comes to ours."

"His decision does not sound unfair to me. The farm is worth more; ergo, the charge for its use is higher. Your return is larger; our return must then also be larger."

"In other words, you reward sloth rather than industry."

"Well said. But clearly you do not understand how estates like this are managed." He got up and went to the window. "Did you see that lightning?"

"No. Only a brightness here in the room."

"I think we're going to have a really good storm."

As he turned, she gave him a steady look accompanied by a faint smile. "Will you not speak to him, intercede for us?"

Now he smiled, though the tic appeared again in his cheek. "I suppose so. What did you say your last name was?"

"Warner." She paused. "Mrs. Stephen Warner."

"Warner. I'll remember that. I'll bring up the subject the next time I see him."

Encouraged, she persisted. "One more thing. When we objected to the increase, he threatened us with distraint. He said you could legally take over the farm, including our personal effects. Even furniture I brought with me from New York. Is that true?"

"Is the word 'distraint' in your contract?"

"Yes, but it isn't defined."

"Why worry? All you have to do is comply with the terms of the rental. It sounds quite simple to me."

Just like the slaves, she thought. If they behave themselves, they won't be sent to the West Indies. Aloud she said, "Not when the terms are unfair."

"Now we are back where we started." On his way to his chair, he stopped and poured a little more rum in his glass. As he sat down, he said, "You plead very well. And I admire your spirit in fighting for your husband's rights. If he could see you now with that wistful smile on your face and your eyes all bright and eager, I'm sure he'd appreciate your performance. My suggestion, however, is that you leave such matters to him. Women are unlikely to understand such things. They are made to raise children and take care of a household."

"You must remember that I have no children. My mind is quite free to consider other things. Nor is it untrained."

"True, quite true. Tell me, how do you feel about not having children? Do you grieve?"

"I have little time for grieving." She concentrated on the bobbins, on moving them around and over and down, crossing one over the other. He was making concentration difficult. And the air was growing heavier, as if it held a weight of water that pressed against her skin. She wanted to be away from here, away from him, away from a disquieting unease in her body that was surely caused by the approaching storm.

"I presume that, like Nelia, you have lost babies?"

"No." Abruptly she stood up. Granted he was lonely, granted he was upset about his wife, granted even that he had drunk too much rum—he still had no right to invade her personal life in this way.

Seeing her putting things in her workbag, he said, "You're not leaving?"

"Yes. I'm very tired. It has been a long, hot day."

"You won't sit here and talk with me?"

"I do not think we have much to say to each other. You must remember also that I am merely a servant in your home."

"But I like talking with you. You have a good mind."

"Thank you. But I wish to retire."

"Very well." He took a candle from the chandelier. Such a waste, she thought—all those candles burning at once. "I'll light your way to your room."

"It is quite unnecessary." She held out her hand for the candle, noticed that her fingers were trembling.

For a few seconds before relinquishing it, he stood still looking at her. "You have so much vitality, Margretta. A man feels more alive when he is around you, more a man. And you are very beautiful. I noticed it the first time I saw you. Your eyes especially. Such a rich, warm color. They seem to hold all kinds of dreams and promises."

She took the candle. "My eyes are simply what I see with, Lord Van Baden. Good night, and thank you for your company. It has been a pleasant evening." She hurried out of the room and up the stairs.

After putting the candle in the sconce, she went to the window. It was black outside. Then a flash lit up the landscape so that through the trees she could see the sheen of the river and the irregular outline of the hills beyond. Slowly, as her father had taught her to do, she counted. One hundred . . . two hundred . . . three hundred . . . If you could count to five hundred before the thunder came, the storm was still a mile away.

At seven hundred she heard thunder, loud but not frightening. She drew the curtains. If she could not see the lightning, she would wait with less anxiety each time for the thunder. Besides, this house had stood here undamaged for several generations. Why should she be suddenly so anxious? She was used to these Hudson Valley storms.

Hot and sticky, she removed her clothing and washed her body carefully. The water, if it had been brought warm, had now cooled. It left her skin pleasantly refreshed. The soap, she noticed, had a faint scent. Her body was like that of an unmarried woman, her stomach flat, her breasts firm, her hips slim. She would have preferred the thickened waist and sagging breasts that were the badges of motherhood.

As she wiped herself dry, she noticed a tenderness in her breasts. Before her monthly courses they were often like this. She could not recall whether it was close to that time. How wonderful it would be if this time no flow began, if her breasts grew larger and her belly swelled. Would it ever happen? Some people went childless for years; then suddenly they were blessed. She had even heard of a childless woman in Manhattan who had given birth to her own child a year after adopting one.

The ginseng Judith had given her—would it work? Her heart filled with hope, imbued with a sense of impending change.

A flash bright enough to shine through the heavy curtains sent her scurrying toward the bed. Although the room was hot, she feared opening the window. This time the thunder came before she had time to begin counting. Quickly she slipped into her nightdress and got into bed.

The rain began not with scattered droplets but with a pounding downpour that sounded like a regiment of soldiers marching up the slanted roof. She gripped the edge of the sheet when lightning flashed again, buried her face in the pillow as if it would protect her from the ensuing crash of thunder. No storm had ever frightened her this much, not even on her first night in Van Badenswyck. Something about the atmosphere in this house had heightened her apprehension.

After a seemingly endless time that might have been no more than ten minutes, the rain stopped and the storm moved silently away. She waited. Was it really over? She tried to relax, had nearly succeeded when once again thunder shook the house. A second storm was moving in. Sometimes it went on like this for hours as one fast-moving storm chased another across the Hudson Valley.

Oh, Stephen, Stephen, why did you let me come here? Why are you not here to protect me and comfort me?

A flash, a deafening clap of thunder . . . and then another sound, a crash—perhaps a falling tree—and a scream. Had lightning struck the house? A person?

Moments passed. The rumbling grew fainter as this storm moved even faster toward New England. Then, just as her heartbeat returned to normal, she saw a moving brightness around her door. Oh, God, the house was on fire. Throwing off the sheet, she sat up. She must run somewhere, seek safety. Her room, though in the second story, was actually three floors up from the ground. She would die if she tried to jump.

Slowly her door opened. The brightness she had seen came from a candle held by a man. Had he come to lead her to safety? He was silent, however, coming close to her bed and standing there, the candle throwing his shadow on the wall behind him, black and menacing. She waited, mute with terror, then was relieved to see it was Nicolaus Van Baden. He was wearing a silken dressing gown that caught the shine of candlelight in its folds.

"Are you afraid?" he asked.

"A little. More than a little, to be truthful. I've closed the curtains so I can't see it. It's been very bad. I think it struck a tree outside my window."

"Yes. It was then that you screamed. That's why I came. I thought you had been hurt."

"But I did not scream. Perhaps it was your wife."

He was staring at her. Following the path of his gaze, she realized that in her panic her breath was coming quick and hard and her breasts were rising and falling in the same rhythm. She drew the sheet up over her.

"You had best go see about your wife."

"I have already looked in on her. She is all right."

"But she screamed."

"She often screams in her sleep. It means nothing."

His voice had changed, grown deeper. When Stephen's voice did this, she knew what it meant. It was an accompaniment to desire, the voice moving lower in the throat, as if to make contact with a rising surge of passion.

"You had best leave me." She spoke with forced calmness. "I thank you for coming to check on me. But as you can see, I am quite all right." A third storm was moving in now, but in this new and greater fear she felt remote from it.

He put the candle on the stand. "What I can see is that you are quite possibly the most beautiful woman I have ever seen. In America or in Europe. I had to see you in a proper state of undress with your shining hair all loose to realize." Bending low, he kissed her on the lips, then straightened as lightning flashed and thunder rumbled on its tail. He crossed the room and drew the curtains back.

"You must learn to enjoy these storms, Margretta. Open yourself up to them and become aware of their energy and beauty. It's part of life, and you do not appear to be the kind of woman likely to turn your back on any aspect of life."

From her bed now as he moved back toward her she saw lightning split the sky, edge the mountainous piles of clouds with silver. She covered her face with her hands to blot out the image, waited a moment for the monstrous clap of thunder that followed. Then she heard a rustle of silk as Nicolaus shed his robe, felt the bed sag as he sat down on it, felt him take her hands by the wrists and hold them away from her face back against the pillow. When she tried to wrench them away, he held them even more tightly.

He bent again to kiss her, this time more warmly, more searchingly. She turned her face to the side, only to feel his lips burning against her cheek, her throat.

He said, "I think we have both known ever since supper how this evening would end."

"Maybe *you* knew. But I . . . Oh, please, please leave me. I have never been with any man but my husband."

A headiness—from the touch of his lips? the storm? the ginseng? the unaccustomed drink of rum?—was making her thinking fuzzy. She must do something, get away from him somehow. Run away. But where? Out into the storm? Through the woods where trees were falling?

Perhaps she could go to the cellar and ask the slaves to shelter her. But as she tried to wriggle away, his hold tightened. She would have to wait for a moment of inattention while she continued to try to hold him off with words. If only the dreadful thunder and lightning would stop so she could think clearly. All she could say over and over was, "Please leave me. I don't want this. I don't want this."

"Margretta, when I saw you last night by the river with your arms stretched out toward that Indian as he paddled along the shore, I saw a woman full of yearning. Every line in your body cried out with passion and longing. You cannot deny what you were feeling then."

"Only a desire to be away from here. To be free as he was free. Free to move on to some new adventure."

"*This* is the adventure. Listen to the storm. It's like an orchestra playing just for us."

Against her will she listened: to the sweep of wind across the river and up through the trees, to the sound of them swaying, to the staccato of rain on the roof. The energy from the storm charged the air in the room, rippled along her skin, mingled with her hurried breathing.

Nicolaus began to caress her. Oh, unfair. Unfair. She was too vulnerable now, her nerves leaping at his touch. When he began tugging at her nightdress, she made one last effort to frighten him off.

"Nicolaus"—how could she call him Lord Van Baden now?—"I am going to scream. The servants will come. It will be very embarrassing for you."

"They won't come. They are used to hearing screams in the night."

Now as she struggled to move away, he held her by her upper arms—a not unpleasant feeling, this tight grip of passion, and so strong that it was useless to resist.

It was not her fault. It was not her fault. She told herself that over and over as she felt his weight on her, felt his mouth move from eyes to cheeks to lips, felt his body uniting with hers, her feet curled curiously around his ankles. The storm was directly overhead now, the rain lashing against the roof. She lay still, a part of herself wanting to die, but another part conscious of just how alive she was, and during every heartbeat her body, that womanly body made for love and procreation, grew increasingly aware. Out of its heightened awareness and its habit and memory of couplings made in love and hope came a shallow tremor of feeling. As the tremor deepened and warmed and spread, she felt a shame so intense she wanted to cry out not against him but at the faithlessness of flesh that would permit a man other than her husband to bring forth such a powerful response.

Above them the storm reached its peak. Lightning and thunder occurred simultaneously, the lightning so close she could actually hear it—as if God had snapped his fingers. Terrified, she moaned, "Nicolaus . . . oh, Nicolaus," and wound her arms around his neck. Then, holding him close, she abandoned herself completely to the tumult he had generated within her.

The storm gradually subsided, rumbling across the ridges to the Taconics. Quiet at last, Nicolaus lay beside her, still holding her, the moist warmth of his skin giving off a faintly salty odor. Now and then a tremor shook her body.

He touched her cheek. "You're crying. I thought you said you never cried."

"I never do. But tonight I . . ."

"I've loved you and wanted you for years, Margretta," he said. "But until tonight I never knew how strong my feelings were."

Nor did I.

"I wish it were possible for us to marry right now," he said. "There is so much I'd like to do for you, so many things I'd like to give you."

She could not speak. When she moved away from him now and slid out of the bed, he did not try to hold her. She lifted the window and took deep, ragged breaths of the cool fresh air. Rain still fell gently, or it may have been dripping from the trees, but no more storms were coming. Far across the Hudson and above the Catskills a few stars peered timidly through the darkness.

In the east the storm grumbled more like a thwarted child than an angry god. The world had returned to normal. But she had not. Between her and the rest of the world, and especially between her and Stephen, this incident—oh, how could she call such a violation an incident?—would always hang like a dark and heavy cloud.

Behind her Nicolaus moved about. Silk rustled as he put on his robe. He would go now. She waited numbly. Why was he taking so long? Suddenly she felt him behind her. Lifting her mass of hair, he pressed his lips against her neck.

She wheeled around and faced him. "Have you not defiled me enough?"

"Defiled you? I have not defiled you. I have only made love to you, made love to you very naturally and tenderly and passionately." He put his hands on her shoulders. "You cannot say you did not respond in the same way. A woman can simulate passion when she feels nothing, but there is no way she can hide it when it takes complete possession of her."

She felt more exhausted than after a long hot day of helping Stephen with the haying. She had to struggle to remain standing, struggle to put words together so that they made sense. Finally, in an emotionless recital of facts, she said, "I am a married woman. I have always taken my marriage vows seriously. I love my husband."

Moving to the row of pegs on the wall, he lifted her dark red dress off. "Linsey-woolsey. This is all he can give you. Someday when I am free to marry you—and it may not be long—"

"Don't say anything more, please. I cannot bear it. Just leave me. Please, please leave me." As he stared quietly at her, measuring the truth in her words, she said again with even more determination, "I am a married woman. I want only what my husband can give me."

On his way to the door, he flung the linsey-woolsey dress toward one of the bedposts. It missed and fell in a heap on the floor. "Your husband? Why, he cannot even give you a child. At least my pitiful wife has had three miscarriages and one stillbirth. It is not my fault she is unable to carry a child to full term."

For a few chilling moments after he had left, she remained motionless. Then she forced herself to cross the room. She picked up her dress, shook it out, and hung it up. It was a lovely dress, this dark red linsey-woolsey with the fine lace at wrist and throat. She had always felt like a queen in it.

Earlier she had used most of the water in the lavabo. With what little was left she washed herself, washed the odor and moisture of his body from hers. But not the memory or the shame.

After that she lay on the bed until dawn touched the sky with gray, then stained it with red. Reaching up, she touched the elaborate carving on the headboard of the bed. It was an ugly bed. She hated every heavy, ugly line of it, hated most of all the heavy posts that rose prisonlike around her, each one a reminder of the power of the Van Baden male and of her own ineradicable guilt.

Chapter 15

Soon after dawn she heard stirrings below: a door opening, ashes being shoveled, the clatter of utensils. The smell of wood smoke and of sausage cooking drifted upward. She went to the window. A huge pine, split from top to root, lay on the ground, its heartwood exposed, sap bleeding into the ground.

Quickly she dressed, the fibers of her clothing an affront to tender flesh. After a visit to the attic room, where she left her completed work, she hurried down the back stairs.

Belle was in the lower kitchen alone, stirring some suppone. "Are you looking for breakfast?"

"No. I am looking for writing materials."

When Belle brought them to her, Margretta sat at the long, refectory table and wrote:

> Lady Van Baden:
>   A sudden illness has overtaken me and I must return to my home. You will find the completed laces in the workroom. I am taking the remainder with me and will send them when finished. As for copying and making new laces, I would also prefer to do that in my own home.

She ended simply by signing her name. Her hands shaking, she folded the note and handed it to Belle. "Would you see that Lady Van Baden gets this on her return?"

"Yes." Belle scrutinized her face, the trembling of her hands. "You do not look well."

"I am not. I'm going to the dominie's."

"You have a bruise on your wrist."

"Yes. I fell last night trying to get to the window to close it during the storm."

She looked away. Nicolaus had further corrupted her by forcing her now to lie. How many more lies would she tell before this memory faded? But it probably would never fade, would haunt her until she did her final recoiling from it on her deathbed.

Hurrying out the door, she went around to the side of the house and found the rough path that led to the lane. Saturated from last night's storm, the ground squished under her feet and sent up a smell of moist dirt and vegetation. Every breeze sent a shower of droplets down on her.

Early morning sunlight caught the mist rising from the forest floor and illuminated it in golden shafts slanting between the trees like light coming through a stained-glass window into a church. All the green plants, all the rocks, all the shining tree trunks were washed clean. In this world where everything was pure, clean, and fresh, she felt like a trespasser.

She found Judith on her knees in the garden, her hair still braided, filling a basket with aromatic leaves.

"What is wrong?"

"I do not feel well. I think it may have been the decoction you gave me." She sank down beside Judith.

"Get up. You will get your dress all wet."

"It is already."

"You should not have come over here so early. Soon the sun will dry everything off." She stood up, held out her hand to Margretta to help her up. "You look terrible, as though you've had no sleep. And look at your arms. Did you fall?"

"Yes . . . I fell. Trying to get to the window during the storm. You know how confused you can be in a strange place."

"Yes. Well, let us go in. Have you had breakfast?"

"No. But I want nothing."

"Some peppermint tea, then; it will settle your stomach. After that I want you to lie down so I can put compresses on those bruises. We

will soon have you in fine shape." Judith propelled her inside. "Wait
here."

As Margretta, her head light and strange, waited at the table,
shame engulfed her again, but this time it flamed into anger. Nicolaus had no right to do what he had done. Her grandmother had
taught her how to protect herself on the streets of Manhattan, but
you do not use your knee or teeth or fingernails on a manor lord.
Secure in his position, Nicolaus had taken advantage of her fear of
the storm, of her vulnerability. Despite his calling it an act of love
and despite her ultimate response to it, she had been unwilling—had
she not said so over and over? Thus it was actually an assault, and
was not sexual assault a criminal offense in the province of New
York?

Judith returned with a cup of steaming greenish liquid.

"What is it? Hemlock?"

Smiling, Judith sat down across from her. "Just peppermint tea
with a little syrup of violets to help you relax. You should have come
here last night. Then you would not have been alone during the
storm." Her gaze was speculative. "You are sure that is all that happened—a fall during the storm? They were not unpleasant to you?"

"Lady Van Baden was pleasant enough, I guess. But it was brutally
hot working in that attic. Sometimes I felt as though I could hardly
breathe. I was wakeful the first night. It seemed so strange to be
alone. Also Cornelia sometimes screams. Then the second night the
storm went on and on for hours. It struck a tree right outside my
window. It was terrifying. I didn't sleep at all."

"I believe I saw Lady Van Baden go off in her carriage yesterday.
Oloff said she was going to visit the Livingstons."

"Yes." Margretta closed her eyes.

"Would you like to lie down?"

"I think so. Yes. And perhaps have some water to wash with. I
used up all of mine last night."

"None was brought to you this morning?"

"I left before it could be done."

"I see. I'll get Alicia."

Margretta went into what she still thought of as her room, took off
her dress, hung it on a peg, and was sitting on a chair looking out the

window when Alicia came, a pitcher of water in her hand, clean linens over her arm.

"So, you are to be our guest. For how long?"

"Not long." She watched Alicia make up the bed. "A few hours of rest will cure me. I did not sleep at all last night." She stood up, felt dizzy, swayed a little.

Alicia came quickly to her. "You really do not feel well. Come, lie down right now. If you are dizzy, you should not try to stand." She took her by the elbow, suddenly stopped, lifted the arm, and looked at it. "You must have taken a fall."

"Yes." She offered no resistance when Alicia removed her clothing, gently bathed her. After Alicia had left, Judith came in carrying a bowl, a bottle, and a clean nightdress.

"First we will attend to those bruises." Her face expressionless, she examined Margretta's arms and body. "We must see to it that they have faded before you go back."

"I am not going back."

"You will not finish the work?"

"I will do it at home."

Judith soaked a compress in a bowl. "You picked a good time. Just yesterday I finished making this iris-root decoction. It will help any soreness and take the darkness out of the bruises."

"They really do not hurt," Margretta told Judith. "They look much worse than they feel. I always did bruise easily."

Judith put cool compresses on the wrists, the upper arms, then wrapped dry linen over them. When she had finished, she had Margretta sit up while she slipped a sweet-smelling nightdress over her head.

"Now, drink this," Judith said. "A little bit of syrup of violets was hardly enough. You need sleep. Don't be afraid of it. It's nothing but tea made from the shells of poppy heads." As she watched her sipping it, Judith said, "Would you feel better if you talked about it, Margretta?"

"I don't think so."

Judith pulled up a chair close to the *slaabauck*. "Try to sleep now. You are welcome to stay here as long as you wish."

"I want to go back. Back to Stephen, that is."

"You cannot go until those bruises have faded. Stephen is no fool.

Like Alicia and me, he would readily conclude that they did not come from a fall."

After that Margretta slept. Whenever she awakened, she saw someone sitting by her side: sometimes Judith, sometimes Alicia, sometimes Antonia or Gertrude. Usually they sponged her face with cool, scented water, gave her broth or tea, then held her hand until she went back to sleep. For two days she was cared for and fed as if she were a baby, surrounded by love as healing as the medications Judith applied. The teas, she suspected, were what kept her in such a somnolent state. But she enjoyed it; it was better than being awake, her mind seething.

"You look much better," Judith said on the third morning. "How do you feel?"

"Like a human being again. I'd like to get up."

"Good. But don't do much. Read, walk around a little, come out and watch me in the garden."

She did all of those things, although she found it hard to concentrate when reading, mostly because a plan was taking shape in her mind. Near the end of the week as she knelt in the garden with Judith helping her pot some plants to take inside for the winter, she said, "How is Gustavus?"

"Well enough. He has two more children by Helena. You must have seen them in church. All girls."

"Do you like Helena?"

"Well enough. As the dominie's wife it is my place to be gracious to everyone. Probably she cannot help being a rich woman who thinks she is better than anyone else."

"No doubt she is well received at the manor house."

"No doubt." Judith looked up at her. "Do you sometimes wish you had made a different choice?"

"Never. But it angers me that a difference in position can bring forth different treatment. I am still me, and I deserve to be treated with justice." She lifted some borage into a pot, patted the dirt around it. "I am thinking of seeing a lawyer. What do you think of that?"

"What lawyer?"

"I know only one."

"I think it would be most foolish. If you sue for mistreatment, you will find it very hard to prove."

"But you and Alicia saw the bruises. You would tell the truth if you were asked, wouldn't you?"

Judith stood up, brushed loose soil and leaves from her hands. "My husband's position here is dependent on the whim of Lord Van Baden. I am willing to treat your ailments, Margretta, and offer you kindness and refuge. But I could not testify on such a matter. I could only tell what I know: that you came here bruised and told me that you had fallen. Anything more I might say would be pure speculation."

"I see."

"Forget the whole thing. I can understand your motives. But you have little chance of success."

"I plan to see him anyway. I need some legal advice, need to have some legal terms explained."

"Well, go then if you need to. But as for the other matter, be discreet. And fix yourself up a little. Give your hair a good brushing. That honey-colored hair alone is enough to make a man receptive to any importuning."

Margretta went the following week, dressed in her cool blue linen, her hair brushed to a shine and formed in the old way into curls that fell forward over her shoulder. The weather had come off clear, warm but not humid, with no storms in sight. She knew she looked well; her mind was as clear as the air that surrounded her, sharpened for argument and convincing statements. Her mirror before she left had told her that seven years of marriage and hard work, and even one night of devastating disillusionment, had done little to disturb the girlishness of her face.

She walked straight to Sulzer's house, oblivious of passersby, remembering the side door that opened directly to his private office. He opened it almost immediately, appeared genuinely glad to see her.

"Margretta, my pretty one." Taking both her hands, he drew her in. "What brings you here? If it is to accept my offer of marriage, you are seven years too late. I have a whole new family."

"I have heard that, and I am happy for you, Gustavus. As for your offer of marriage, I was flattered, as you must surely know. But I had already met Stephen, and our interest in each other had grown strong before I met you."

"Ah, well, it was a long time ago. I was quite taken with you, though." He still held her hands.

"It was only that—"

"Never mind trying to explain. It's all in the past. What brings you here now?"

"I am here on business, Gustavus. I wish to engage your services. May I sit down?" Without waiting for a reply, she drew her hands from his and sank into a chair. "I need some legal advice on a business matter. I also wish to sue someone. I have six silver spoons that I can pay you with if you will take the case. One thing, though—I want the assurance that whatever I say to you will be kept in confidence."

"But of course. Nothing you say will ever go beyond these four walls, will ever be repeated by these lips, except in court and at your bidding."

She smiled, her confidence growing. "First, would you explain what is meant by the word 'distraint'? Or perhaps I should say the term 'exercising the right of distraint.'"

"Used where?"

"Used in a contract between landlord and tenant."

"It means that the landlord has the right to confiscate the tenant's personal property if the tenant fails to live up to the terms of the agreement."

"But what if the landlord changes the terms? Raises the rent, for example."

"That is his right. It is his land. He has the right to sell or rent it to anyone else, to raise the rent, to evict. Nowhere in any of the contracts I am familiar with does it say the amount of rent will never be changed."

"But what if the tenant has made improvements? Paid for them out of his own earnings?"

"He paid for them out of what he earned from the landlord's acreage. If he did things to make himself more comfortable while renting, that is his prerogative."

Her arguments were dissolving. "It is unjust."

He spread his hands in a casual gesture. "No tenant is kept here against his will. It is his decision to come, his to leave if he dislikes the terms of the contract."

It occurred to her that Gustavus himself might have drawn up some of the leasehold contracts. If so, he knew well how they were weighted against the tenants, had seen to it that the legal terms were beyond the understanding even of those with some degree of literacy.

"Any more questions on that?"

She shook her head.

"Well, then. What is this lawsuit you mentioned? What kind of case is it?"

"A case of assault."

"What kind of assault?"

She looked down at her tightly folded hands. "Assault against a woman."

"Be clear. Are you speaking of rape?"

She nodded, hating to say the word, unsure it was even the right word. "I was most unwilling," she said. Looking up, she saw how much the admission had disturbed him.

He sighed. "When I think that I hardly dared to kiss you. Do you remember the day I showed you my house? When I showed you my bedroom, my bed? It took great strength for me not to lead you to it. But I was afraid of frightening you, that in your innocence you might refuse to marry me once you had been exposed to the strength of my passion. Afterward, I often thought I should have been bolder, that I might have stirred you to the point where you would have felt about me as I did about you." He gave her an unbusinesslike smile. "What do you think?"

She said, "I think we should forget the past. We are both married to other people. Your wife is probably no more than a dozen feet away from here right at this moment."

He hitched his chair closer to hers, so close their knees were almost touching. "My wife and the children set sail for Albany this morning. We are quite alone. The servants do not disturb me in my place of business. We may speak freely."

"I want to speak only of the case I am hoping you will take. Are you willing to bring suit for me?"

Hitching his chair an inch closer, he let his hand drop casually to her knee. "Of course I am willing. But there are problems. You can sue and you might even win. But you'd end up with little satisfaction. They are never able to pay. What you would gain is a loss of reputation, for there would always be those who would say the assault was a result of your allurement."

His hand moved on her leg. She shifted it off. Without changing her tone of voice, she said, "It was not a tenant farmer. This man can pay. And he ought to be exposed."

"Perhaps you should tell me his name."

"I'd prefer not to."

His smile was condescending. "My dear, you cannot sue a Mr. Blank."

"I thought you could prepare the case. Then when it was to be heard in court, I would tell you the name."

"This man—is he highly placed?"

"Yes."

"How high?"

"Very high."

"Here in this community?"

"Yes."

He gave her a thoughtful look. "I may have spoken too hastily when I said I would take the case. I might find myself preparing a case against a friend."

"Do you have among your friends men who would force their attentions on unwilling women?"

"Certainly not. But some women say no with their lips at the same time that they say yes with their eyes. You, for example, have been sending me all kinds of messages, all kinds of invitations with your eyes ever since you got here."

Only her need for help made it possible for her to control her anger. "If my eyes conveyed any message, it was to implore you to listen to me and to help me."

He stood up, moved to his desk. He was all lawyer now, a man of a different class. "That I cannot do."

"You said you would. Is your word worth so little?"

"It was a misunderstanding. You led me to believe you had been raped by some ignorant farmer."

"I did no such thing. You jumped to that conclusion."

"It was a natural assumption."

"Gustavus, it was Nicolaus Van Baden. He should not go unpunished."

His face showed no astonishment. "I had already guessed you had selected him for your accusation."

"Will you represent me, Gustavus?"

"It is quite impossible." Without asking her permission, he got out his pipe and made a long business of lighting it. "In the first place, I doubt you have a case. Without a witness, it would simply be your word against his."

"Such things are not likely to occur in front of witnesses."

"So?" He shrugged. "Wherever you were, you could not have been far from people. Why did you not scream?"

"If I had, no one could have heard me. It happened during that storm last week."

He sucked on his pipe, blew out a stream of smoke. "For all I or the judge who heard the case might know, this may be something you and your husband have concocted to get money from Lord Van Baden. After all, what basis do I have for trust in what you say? Did you not once lead me to believe you were seriously entertaining my proposal? Then within a week you informed me you were marrying someone else."

She rose and moved closer to him, her voice pleading. "Gustavus, forget the past, can't you? Please help me now. My husband knows nothing of this. But it did happen."

"There you go again—sending me signals with your eyes and the movement of your body as you ask for favors. Did you by any chance ask Lord Van Baden for a favor?"

"I did, but—"

"Then I can only conclude that if what you say did happen, it was hardly the fault of Lord Van Baden." In a genial voice, he added, "I'm sorry, Margretta, but I cannot fulfill your request. Any other favor now or in the future, yes. But surely you must realize that I am Lord Van Baden's personal attorney in addition to being his representative at the Assembly. If you were to bring suit, I would be the one who defended him."

She went to the door, her head up. "I will send you some of my silver for the time I have taken of yours today."

"That won't be necessary. After all, I did not take your case."

Her hand on the doorknob, she said, "Fortunately, you are not my last resort." Before he had a chance to exchange his look of surprise for one of urbanity, and before he had a chance to question her and discover how little foundation existed for her bold statement, she hurried out.

Judith gave her a questioning look when she returned.

"You were right," Margretta said. "He won't help."

"Perhaps that's understandable. In a way, I'm glad. A lawsuit would have hurt your reputation even if you had won, which is very doubtful. Think of how it would have hurt Stephen. How much of this, by the way, are you going to tell him?"

"None. I'll just say I was unwell and went to your house for care. Or something like that. I'm afraid I'm not a very good liar."

"The way to lie successfully," Judith said, "is not to lie at all. Tell the truth about what can be told and leave out the rest."

Margretta nodded, but she dreaded the moment of confidence no less.

Chapter 16

The September day glowed with the warmth of summer, yet the haze over the Taconics and the changing of colors spoke of fall. Along the roadside as Margretta rode toward her home, clusters of white asters were spread out like pieces of handwork placed on the grass to bleach in the sun.

How we women strive for whiteness, purity, she thought. Is it because men work so hard to divest us of it?

Earlier that day when she was in her room preparing to leave, Judith had knocked. "Someone is here to see you, Margretta." She came in. "It is Lord Van Baden. Do you want to see him? I can tell him that you are unwell."

"No. I'll see him. I'll be out in a moment."

She combed her hair around her finger, let the curls fall to the front of her right shoulder, pinched her cheeks to brighten them, and went out to the parlor.

"You may leave us alone, Judith," Nicolaus said.

After Judith had left, Margretta motioned toward a chair. They sat facing each other as she and Gustavus had once done. But she had been indifferent then. Now as she waited for Nicolaus to speak, she was acutely aware of him and of herself. His expression was serious, even brooding, but his eyes under the winged brows had the capacity to see within her, to search out the conflicting emotions, to stir her with the power of touch.

"I understand you visited my attorney last week."

164

"Yes."

"That was rather foolish of you."

"What is foolish about seeking redress for a wrong? It is common practice in civilized countries."

"You will receive redress. But first you must understand the state I was in that night. You can't know how upsetting my wife's condition had been for me. Then, being alone in the house with you. And you so appealing, especially when you were pleading with me."

"You're implying I invited your assault?"

"Don't use that word. It has a criminal sound."

"It was a crime."

"Please let me go on. You are very hotheaded."

"And you are always cool and in control?"

"If you would stop accusing me for the moment—"

"All right."

"Whether or not you were inviting my attentions, the spirits I had been drinking made it appear—"

"A gentleman, no matter how much he drinks—"

He held up his hand. *"Please.* Will you give me a chance? I'm trying, though with poor success, to say I'm sorry. Also I have told Mr. Frost a revision has been made in your contract. He is not to raise your rent again."

She hardly knew how to respond. Finally she said, "I suppose I should be grateful and say it is very generous of you. But what might my husband think if our rent is never raised again? Might he not become suspicious?"

"I didn't think of that."

"It might be best to raise it, but only a small amount each year that we remain. A *fair* amount."

"Yes. Perhaps that would be wiser." He got to his feet. "So . . . so we have an agreement, then?"

"An agreement?"

"Yes. Your silence in return for my concessions."

"My silence." She was turning possibilities over in her mind like rocks liable to have slimy grubs under them. At the same time, she was considering how weak her position was. "I have always hated this kind of promise. Circumstances have a way of changing. Let me say this: I will remain silent as long as your agent treats us with fairness."

Because she had not risen with him, he stood looking down at her. "A few moments ago I said I was sorry. You said nothing in return."

She too now rose, proud of her control. "What else can I do but accept your apology? It is the mannerly thing to do." His hands were on her shoulders now. Her control was forsaking her. "Please, Nicolaus. Please do not touch me."

"I want only to say one more thing. I am married. You are married. Because of that I feel great guilt. But as I stand here with you in the coolness of this room with no storms brewing outside, with no spirits inside me, I find I am just as stirred as I was that night. Maybe more, because now I know what it is like to be with you. What I want to tell you is that I wish we could be together forever."

The hands on her shoulders drew her closer. His lips met hers. It was less a kiss of passion than of renunciation.

He left then without saying good-bye, and within an hour she was on her way.

Now as she rode, she brushed the back of her hand across her eyes. She must stop thinking about Nicolaus. She must banish the entire episode from her mind; otherwise, how could she greet Stephen without giving away her secret?

Or would he look at her and immediately sense her infidelity, however unwilling it had been? How could she, so different now, present to him the face of a woman unchanged?

When she came to the beginning of their land, she started to tremble. He was raking the dooryard. Immediately he stopped and lifted her down from the horse.

"You feel so good," he said. "I've missed you so." Holding her away from him, he said, "So beautiful. I was afraid you might have changed."

"Changed? In what way in only two weeks?"

"I guess I feared that after the luxury of the manor house, you would be less satisfied here, might love me less."

She looked up at his face, the skin roughened by sun and wind. Here was no effeteness, none of the polish that glossed over self-indulgence. Here was an earthiness, a solidity that a woman could lean on, depend on, trust.

"I could never love you less," she said. "Being away from you only made me appreciate you more."

After he had watered the horse and left her to graze, they went into the house. From the trough in the back room he brought a jug of cool cider, poured some for each of them. Instead of sitting across from her at the table, he sat next to her. She sipped the cider slowly, prolonging the moment before . . . before what? He kept touching her, brushing his fingers along her arms, stroking her hair. She wished he would stop. Did men think of nothing but women's bodies?

"Why not lie down for a while? You must be tired."

"No. I am not at all tired."

"Then let us lie down anyway."

"No, no, I cannot."

"Oh, I see. I had forgotten. It is that time."

She stared at him. Deep inside her she felt a queasy turning such as she had felt in childhood when she had twisted too long on a rope swing and stepped off, dizzy, disoriented, her body beyond her own control. And she remembered the night at the manor house when she had noticed the soreness of her breasts.

"No. It happened while I was away. It is over."

So. Her first lie to Stephen. An unavoidable one.

"Then why . . . ?"

"I was just thinking I had to unpack, do some things here in the house." His eyes looked hurt. "Oh, Stephen, I will tell you the truth. I have not been well. I am only just now beginning to feel better."

"What made you unwell?"

"Working at the manor house. I had to work in the garret. It was very hot and uncomfortable. Then I fell the night of the thunderstorm crossing the room to close the window. I went to Judith's the next day and she gave me some herbals."

As she stood up, the queasy turning in her stomach came again, stunning her with the possibility it uncovered. That kind of feeling never came so soon, but still . . .

She gave Stephen a smile sugared over with falseness. "I have changed my mind. The work can wait. Lock the door in case William decides to come over."

"You are sure you feel well enough?"

"Yes." She went to the *kas*, removed her clothing.

As he came toward her, she said, "Wait. I just remembered something. I asked Judith whether she knew of any remedies for infertility. She gave me a decoction from the ginseng plant. She does not guarantee it but says we both should take it. If nothing else, it will serve as a tonic."

They lifted their teaspoons with the solemnity of a wedding toast. Then he carried her to the bed.

He was eager, anxious, quick. Not like . . . No, she must not think of *him*. But it was impossible to banish the memory, impossible to lose herself in this lovemaking.

"You seem different," he said afterward. "As if you held yourself away from me."

"We've never been separated before, Stephen. I have to get used to you all over again."

He made love to her again that night. In the darkness it was easier to feign pleasure.

"I'm happy to be back here with you."

"I'm happy too. I have a feeling, Margretta, that tonight, this time . . ."

"Don't hope too much, Stephen. We have done too much of that. It just leads to disappointment."

By the next day she was established in her old routine while reserving part of each day for Lady Van Baden's laces. Eager to rid her home of every reminder of her stay at the manor house, she completed the work at the end of October.

The next day, while Stephen was doing morning chores in the barn, she experienced the early-morning nausea that Sara had so often described. She told him when he came in.

"I thought so," he said with quiet pride. "I've been counting. Are you happy? You look strange."

"When the queasiness passes, then I'll be happy."

"No more horseback riding for you. I'll deliver your work to the manor house."

"All right."

"Shall I stop and tell the dominie's wife that her decoction worked?"

"Shouldn't we wait until we're absolutely sure?"

"I could say we had reason to hope."

She laughed at his exuberance, his pride. "All right. Tell her. And tell her I'm fine."

After he had gone, she sat outside on the *stoep* awhile and gazed at the mountains to the east. A few golds and deep reds remained to mark the end of the season. The blue jays had taken on their raucous fall voices. Now at this time of seasonal change, she felt a resignation. She could do nothing, she realized, to alter what had happened. And the possibility of her pregnancy had brought a look of pride to Stephen's face that she had despaired of seeing. She must now look to the future.

"Did you go to Judith's?" she asked when he returned.

"Yes. She sent you this." He held out a small bottle. "She said it will help your morning sickness."

It did. It helped so much that it was hard to believe she was pregnant. But as the winter progressed, her body showed other signs. First the enlarging of the breasts and finally the unmistakable swelling at the waist.

The winter months that accompanied the increasing swell of her body were the happiest she and Stephen had known. The harvest had been good; their supply of food was plentiful. Though the winter was harsh, their bed and hearthside were warm with a love that was full of hope for the future. She spent much time sewing necessities for the baby. In addition, she made a long, pale yellow, lace-trimmed christening shirt, more beautiful than any she had seen in Manhattan.

Often now Stephen did read to her, usually from Locke. "I like the way he thinks," he said.

In early February William strutted into the house to announce that Sara had borne another son for him whom they had named Pieter. "Let's hope you're as lucky."

"We already feel lucky," Stephen said. "A daughter, a son—who cares as long as it is a healthy child?"

In late February the redwings returned to the swamp and the pussywillows unsheathed their soft gray catkins. In March the bluebirds came, in April the robins. Near the end of April Stephen went fishing and returned with a dozen brook trout as well as the first arbutus, tiny fragrant flowers that grow in hidden places.

And then it was May. Spring in the Hudson Valley is all gentleness and beauty, but no month is lovelier than May. It is a virgin month: the leaves are tender, the flowers fragile, the air and sunlight soft.

Into this ephemeral world of May, Paulus chose to make his entrance. It began late in the afternoon of May 6 and continued through too many hours of struggle while Stephen remained awake and alert, leaving her only for a few intervals in the barn to milk or feed. He fixed a rope for her to pull on; he wiped her forehead with a cool, damp cloth; he held her hands between contractions. And when she screamed, sweat appeared on his forehead as well as hers.

"If I had known it would be this bad," he said, "I would have gladly gone without children."

She could imagine now how frightened her mother must have been. Her mother. Now, in this shared sisterhood of pain, she felt suddenly close to her. Part of Margretta's terror, as the night went by and daylight came, lay in sensing that this labor might go on until her exhausted body could, like her mother's, handle no more. As midday approached, the pains became continuous. She was too weak now even to hold on to a rope.

"Stephen, something is terribly wrong. I should have let you go earlier for Sara or Judith. Go now, please."

"I cannot leave you."

"Then I shall die." Too tired now to care, she almost welcomed the relief of death.

"No." His voice was calm, reassuring. "I will not allow it. I have delivered calves, even at problem births. I think I can save both of you. Will you trust me?"

"I always have."

He left her, returned with a cup. "Drink this."

She tasted it. "It's the brandy Judith gave us to celebrate the birth of the child. It's too soon to drink it."

"Drink it. It will help you to relax. I am going to try to turn the baby."

She drank the rest of it, let him turn her so that her legs dangled off the bed. Then he reached up inside her with both hands. She tried not to scream, tried not to fight him off.

"Push," he said. "That is good. Push. Push hard."

She was pushing not because he commanded her to do so but to push him away. One last surge of straining effort and the hands were drawn from her body. The pain lessened, became bearable. She heard a cry, thought it was her own, then looked up and saw Stephen holding a small red object.

"Foolish little man," Stephen said. "Did you not know you were supposed to come into this world headfirst?"

She watched him wipe the baby off and put it down on her belly. "Hold him while I ease you back onto the bed."

She put her hand on the small, slippery form. It was warm but still.

"Is he dead, Stephen?"

"No. I think he will live, though he has had quite a battle for one his size." He cut the cord and moved the baby to her breast. "There will be no milk yet, but if he begins to suck, it will come soon. As soon as the afterbirth comes, I will make you comfortable and clean."

She could feel the baby's mouth on her breast, his body joined to hers in a new way. And now, even as her body convulsed again to rid itself of its remaining burden, she screamed no more but passively followed Stephen's instructions.

It was over. Lifting her, Stephen rolled down the sheet, slipped out the towels placed under her to protect the feather bed, washed her, and put clean linen on the bed.

The baby began to suck. It brought her pleasure, a dreamy, sensual relaxation. How strange and lovely to be quiet and without pain, to be aware of nothing but the rhythm of the small sucking mouth. One of the primal rhythms of life. Life. So close to death. And now, not one life here on the bed, but two. No, three, for now Stephen was lying beside her.

"I thought I was going to die. The baby too."

"I thought so too. That was why I had to take the chance of hurting you terribly . . . and lying to you."

"You lied to me?"

"Yes. I never delivered a calf, though I have seen others do it. But I hoped to give you confidence."

She slept while he went to the barn. When he returned, he asked whether she was hungry.

"No."

"Shall I put the baby in the cradle for a while?"

"No. I want him here close to me."

Again Stephen lay down on the bed. She knew he must be exhausted. "Here we are again," she said, "in bed in broad daylight. No wonder we have such a huge family. Oh, look, Stephen, he is sucking again. And more strongly."

She drifted off into dreams of sybaritic pleasure. When she awakened, it was dark. Stephen was in her rocker, holding the baby, humming a melody in a minor key.

"Is he all right?"

He nodded. "He just woke up a moment ago. I think he is hungry."

"Bring him to me."

He brought the baby to her, placed a candle on the stand next to the bed, pulled up a stool, looked at her as if he hated to miss a moment of this miracle.

"Stephen, I want to say one thing to you before I forget what yesterday and today were like. They say the pain fades from the memory. They say it is a woman who brings forth a child in suffering. I want to say that I know your suffering was as great as mine. More than that, I know there would have been no baby had it not been for what you did."

"You might have made a final effort."

"No. I had no more strength."

He smoothed her hair. "Whoever did it—you, me, or God—I am glad that it is behind us. That chicken you put in the pot yesterday morning. It is still simmering and smells very good. Can you eat some now?"

"You eat some. I will have some of the broth."

Moving to a sitting position, she held the baby up so she could see his face. Such tiny features, giving no indication of what he would look like later on. Stephen opened and closed the outside door. In the draft the candle flame bent, and in the temporary brightness she saw the baby's eyebrows and followed their line with her finger— straight, then bending like the spread wing of a bird. A coincidence. It had to be a coincidence. The shape would change as he grew older.

They named him Paulus after her father.

"The next boy we'll call Jonas. After *my* father," Stephen said.

She nodded sleepily, drifted off again. When she awakened, Stephen picked Paulus up. Cradling the baby in his arms, he looked down at him and said, *"Tabula rasa."*

"Tabula rasa?" She gave him a puzzled look.

"I read about it in Locke. It means a blank slate. That's what his mind is right now: a blank slate."

Again she smiled, so warmed was she by the gentleness in his voice. "An hour ago that may have been true. But I think that already marks have been made on it about a father's love. He can tell this from the way you hold him, from the sound of your voice. With a father like you, his slate will record only good things. He will grow up to be as fine a man as you."

"Better. Because he has you for a mother."

Sara had said that having babies came between a man and a woman. But Paulus only drew them closer together. Stephen worshiped the boy, worshiped her for bearing him. During the first ten days after her confinement, he made her stay in bed while he prepared the food and took care of the diapers, shaking them out in the outhouse, then washing them in the brook.

"Don't ever let William see you doing these things."

"Why not?"

"He would laugh at you. Women's work."

"He is our son, not just yours."

The day after Paulus was born, she had Stephen bring her the book of their marriage. She read through the skimpy contents: their meeting, their wedding, Stephen learning to read, and then little more but a record of additions to or improvements in the house or barn, the buying of new farm animals.

Now she wrote: "Yesterday, on May 7, 1752, a child was born to us. We have named him Paulus. He shows every sign of becoming a fine, strong man."

Stephen picked it up and read it. "You should have said our *first* child."

Our *first* child. The word struck her with terror. What if no more ever came? What assurance did she have that more could be conceived here in this bed?

"And you should have said how proud we are."

"When we read it in our old age, we'll remember how proud we were."

Yet as she said the words, she too felt how much had been left unsaid. Who on reading this account would be able to sense the sadness and yet the closeness of those barren years, her despair and guilt after her stay at the manor house, the pain of Paulus' birth, the quiet joy she now felt? What words could ever convey the extremes of joy and pain the human heart can accommodate, the hopes and terrors about the future?

Chapter 17

When Paulus was a week old, Stephen went to the woods and returned with a pine tree a foot high. He planted it near the corner of the house.

"This will be Paulus' tree," he said. "He can watch it grow. I picked a white pine because they grow faster than other pines. My father planted one for my brother. He was so proud of it he wouldn't even let me sit under it."

She smiled at him. "So did you refuse to let him sit under yours?"

"I had no tree," he said.

Perhaps this tree would bring him joy, she thought, would smooth the roughness of his own childhood memories.

As soon as she was strong enough, the three of them went to church so that Paulus could be christened and his name made public. He wore the christening shirt she had made and a bearing robe of fine wool from Sara.

Margretta had dreaded going, fearful of seeing Nicolaus and of having him see the child. But Stephen, who had waited so long for fatherhood, was eager to have his friends see the baby, to hear his name pronounced. Go now, she told herself, and put it behind you. If nothing happened this time, then nothing would happen later, for on subsequent visits the child would be inconspicuous.

She delayed so that they arrived just before the service. Judith had to leave afterward, but they spoke long enough for her to admire the baby and to invite Margretta to bring him in soon for a longer visit.

Margretta felt blessed in that neither Nicolaus nor any other Van Baden was present. Standing by the altar with the baby in her arms, she would have been all too close to the thrones where the landlord and his family sat.

The ceremony went well, with Paulus making no cry when she turned him over to the dominie.

Two weeks later, when Stephen had some errands in the village, she rode in the wagon with him holding Paulus.

"Do not hurry," she said to him when he left her at the dominie's. "Have a drink at the tavern if you wish."

"You would not mind?"

"Stephen, you were alone with me for months before Paulus was born. It's time you talked with some men."

"And you with another woman." He smiled at her, gave Paulus a look so full of worship that it filled her with apprehension. What if something should happen? Many an infant never made it to maturity. It would break her heart, but it would more than break Stephen's: it would subdue his spirit. And no other child might grace their home. Thus Paulus, perhaps their only stake in the future, was doubly precious.

Judith greeted her with tea and some of Alicia's tiny spice cakes, spoke of the winter's activities. After a while she said casually, "Stephen—how does he feel about Paulus?"

"He adores him."

"He had no questions, then?"

Margretta was nursing him now. "Only a great pride."

"Aren't you glad now that you did not sue Nicolaus? Think of how your life would be if the affair had been made public. You're far better off."

Margretta had to admit she was right.

"Let me hold him," Judith said when Margretta had finished nursing. She held him up in front of her. "He is a handsome child. Very well-formed." After a moment she said, "I suppose you've noticed the eyebrows."

"I tell myself they are not especially unusual."

"Perhaps not. Besides, no one but you and I would be likely to notice."

"Can you give me a tonic to improve my milk? I want him to be strong and healthy."

"I can. But I think he looks healthy enough."

"I worry. We waited so long. . . ."

"First babies always seem more precious."

The sound of wheels on loose gravel came in through the open windows. Still holding Paulus, Judith went to the door. "It's Lady Van Baden. She's been in New York since Christmas."

Margretta rose when Lady Van Baden entered, less for her title than for her age. Lady Van Baden nodded.

"You have a new baby, Judith? I did not know."

"No, oh no. This is Margretta's. You must remember Margretta Warner. She went to the manor house early last fall to do some lace work for you."

Lady Van Baden gave Margretta a cool smile now. "And left abruptly without finishing your work."

"I finished it at home and sent it to you."

"The repairs, yes. I intended for you to copy some laces also. Don't you remember that?"

"She was not at all well when she left," Judith said.

"Perhaps you would be willing to do it now that your health has improved."

"I am not unwilling, but the baby does keep me very busy. I would not be able to work so quickly."

"Please sit down," Judith said. "I'll get you some tea." As she started to hand the baby to Margretta, Lady Van Baden said, "No. Give him to me. It has been forever since I've held a baby." She sat down in a rocker. "I thought I'd be holding a grandchild long before this."

Margretta said, "How is young Lady Van Baden?"

"A little better. But we have quite given up hope that she will ever have a child. I think she is too highly bred for childbearing. You don't know how fortunate you are. How many children do you have?"

"Just this one."

"Oh? You have not been married long, then."

"Long enough," Margretta said abruptly.

"Yes, of course." Lady Van Baden pulled back the blanket that obscured part of Paulus' face and looked searchingly at him. "What a handsome child he is. He reminds me of Nicolaus when he was a baby."

Judith, returning with tea, overheard the remark. "You said that when you first saw Frederic. Remember?"

"Did I? Perhaps I did." Her manner more pleasant now, she turned to Margretta. "I bought some lovely lace in New York. Several pieces. Very unusual. I'd like to have them copied. When can you come to the manor house?"

"I am sorry, but I am unable to leave my child."

The older woman smiled with the graciousness of one for whom all minor problems are quickly resolved. "Bring him with you. One of the slaves will care for him."

"I am a farmer's wife, Lady Van Baden. At this time of year, except for a rare visit like this one, I am seldom able to spend any time away from home. Gardening and preserving food for the winter keep me very busy. Such work cannot be postponed."

Looking past her, Margretta saw Stephen drive in, his wagon in sharp contrast to the shiny brass-trimmed carriage. "I must leave now. My husband is here to take me home." She attempted to draw Paulus from the older woman's arms. For only a few seconds, but long enough to impress itself on her memory, Lady Van Baden held on to him. They were like the two harlots standing before Solomon, each claiming the child. Then she felt Lady Van Baden's hold loosen, and with a quick smile she lifted Paulus from the arms that held him so possessively.

Outside, Stephen helped her into the wagon. "Whose carriage is that? Lady Van Baden's?"

"Yes."

"Did she see Paulus?"

"Yes, and she admired him greatly. Envious, I think, since her daughter-in-law has produced no heir."

"Perhaps Lord Van Baden did so much carousing in Europe he caught the pox and cannot father a healthy child."

"That might well be." She held Paulus close.

"Did she say anything about the laces you sent?"

"She implied I had not done all I had agreed to do."

"Had you?"

"I think so." She waited a moment. "She wants me to copy some new patterns she bought in the city. I told her I could not leave my baby. Would you object if I did some at home?"

"I don't mind if you enjoy doing it. But I have often regretted allowing you to do it to pay the rent. The farm should produce enough to cover the rent and make us a profit as well."

"It can't if the rent is unfairly high."

She held even more tightly to Paulus as the wagon tossed them this way and that on the bumpy road. Would Nicolaus keep his promise? Was it even a promise?

Gathering courage, she said, "This would be a good time to leave, Stephen. You ought to inquire about selling the leasehold. Start planning. Have everything arranged before Mr. Frost comes in the fall."

"Maybe he won't raise the rent this year. I've made no improvements. Too busy being a father, I guess."

"You'd be an even better father if you left now and found a place of your own that you could leave to him—wholly his own." *Pleading. Always pleading.*

Her ears picked up his sigh even before it escaped his lips. "We cannot travel northward with a new baby, find land, and build a house. You are not strong enough yet."

"I know my strength better than you do."

"No you don't. You are always too ready to do things. I have seen you come out to the fields eager to help me. Then later I'd see how exhausted you were."

"I wish I could be sure . . ." she said, then stopped.

"Sure of what?"

"Sure you were saying this only for my sake, rather than simply because you don't want to move."

"I want to . . . when the time is right."

It was useless to continue pleading. She must wait. Meanwhile, she would live with the fear that Nicolaus might someday see Paulus, might jump to a conclusion, and might leap beyond it to claim the child for his. With his desire for an heir so strong, the possibility was within reason.

They stopped briefly at the Vanzuyders'. Sara brought Pieter out to the wagon and they compared their sons, Sara's two months older. "Ain't it great they're so close of an age?" Sara said. "They'll be good friends."

While the men talked together, Margretta said to Sara, "You seem happier than when you first knew. Are you?"

"Oh, yes. Pieter is such a good baby."

"Paulus, too."

"And him being born near the end of winter, washing ain't been such a care. Besides, the girls help a lot. How about you? Ain't your whole life different?"

"Yes. And better. I would be happy to have more children. But as you may have noticed, I do not easily conceive."

Stephen put his arm around her shoulders. "You will. If you did it once, you can do it again."

As she got into the wagon, she heard William's aside to Stephen: "She'll settle down now, be less trouble."

That evening she said to Stephen, "Do you enjoy going to church?"

"Why do you ask?"

"You always went before we were married. I thought it meant something special to you."

With a laugh he said, "I went mainly in the hope of seeing you. Now I go to find out the latest news."

"But we don't need to go so often. Do we?"

"We don't need to go at all if you don't want to."

How quick he was to sense and accede to her wishes. In every matter but one. But even this concession gave her relief, for it meant that she no longer need fear each Sunday that Nicolaus might see the child. Her optimism rose. Perhaps by spring Stephen might decide, with no urging from her, that it was at last time to move on.

She felt, in fact, so sanguine about the future that she completely forgot Lady Van Baden's remark about new lace, forgot it until on one of the hottest of July afternoons she saw Lady Van Baden's carriage roll into the yard, saw Jupiter getting out and coming to the stoep.

"Lady Van Baden would like to know if you are home. If the answer is yes, she would like to call."

"Tell her she is welcome to come in." About as welcome as a rattlesnake slid down from the Taconics in search of water. What did she want? And why had she lowered herself to visit the wife of a tenant farmer?

Jupiter opened the door of the carriage and helped the older woman down. Margretta, holding the door to the house open, tried to put warmth into her greeting.

Lady Van Baden went directly to the table and put down a box she had carried in. "These are the laces I mentioned when I saw you. Are they not beautiful?"

"Yes, very beautiful. True Valenciennes lace. I love the diamond-shape mesh and the floral patterns they create."

"Can you copy these patterns?"

"Yes. But it is not quickly or easily done." She thought of how long it would take to trace the pattern onto parchment, then, after fastening the parchment to her pillow, to insert pins through the paper along the lines of the design. And then the process of manipulating the bobbins, interweaving and twisting the threads.

"You will do it?"

"Yes."

"Very well. Do a copy of each of these five, and I will then consider you have fulfilled our agreement."

Remembering her hours of meticulous work on the repairs, Margretta was stunned.

"I am even supplying the materials," Lady Van Baden continued. "You will find some sheets of parchment and fine linen thread in the box. Even extra bobbins."

"Thank you." Then she hospitably offered Lady Van Baden a glass of cider and invited her to sit down. Lady Van Baden, however, walked past the chair Margretta had indicated and took the rocker next to the cradle.

In the back room, Margretta poured the cider. When she returned, she saw Lady Van Baden gently rocking the cradle. Paulus was gurgling and waving his arms.

Taking the cup and looking around, Lady Van Baden said, "You have two nice pieces of furniture." She nodded toward the bed and the *kas*.

"And the cradle."

"Yes. Also the cradle." She continued rocking it back and forth. Was that why she had come—to rock that cradle?

"How many rooms do you have here?"

"Just one. Well, two. This and the room in back where we store things. And the loft."

"I suppose one grows accustomed to living in such . . ."

"Squalor?"

"I was going to say 'limited space.'" Lady Van Baden put her cider cup down on the floor. "You are probably wondering why I am here."

"Not at all. You came about the lace."

"Only partly. I came because of the child. After I saw him last month, I had a talk with my son."

Margretta sat up straighter as fear uncoiled inside her and lifted a wary head.

"It was a rather lengthy talk we had. I mentioned I had always been puzzled by the abrupt way you had left the manor. In the end he confessed that you and he had enjoyed a brief interlude together."

Margretta's heartbeat quickened. "Enjoyed? When a man forces a woman to submit to him, it can hardly be called an enjoyable interlude."

"Force? My son said nothing about force."

"Perhaps not. But I was most unwilling."

"And do not women often pretend unwillingness to add spice to the game of love?"

Calm. Be calm, Margretta told herself; otherwise you will be unable to think clearly. "I have never thought of love as a game, Lady Van Baden. My husband and I take love very seriously. For each other . . . and for our son."

"Does your husband know. . . ?"

"That I was assaulted and I resisted? No."

"You say you resisted, but here in this cradle is the evidence. This child—Paulus, is that his name?—is the very image of Nicolaus when he was a baby. I could show you a painting of me holding him when he was two months old, and it might as well be this child here."

"And Stephen says Paulus looks like *his* father. I think he looks like mine. When it comes to babies, most of us see in their faces what we want to see."

"I know what my eyes tell me. This is my grandchild. May I hold him?"

"No!"

"Why not?"

"Because he is fearful of strangers. Because it is time to nurse him."

Smiling thinly, Lady Van Baden said, "If he is afraid, why does he not cry when I bend over the cradle? If he is hungry, why does he not cry to be nursed?"

"Because he is a good baby. He rarely cries."

"Yes. Nicolaus was like that also. He cried only when he was alone and hungry. It was as if he knew how much we loved him, how long we had waited for him. Our only child."

Seeing her look at the baby, the sharp lines of her face softened, Margretta felt a momentary kinship with this woman she had every reason to dislike. Finally she said, "Lady Van Baden, what is it you want? Are you hoping to visit here occasionally so you can see my baby, who you fancy bears a resemblance to your family?"

Lady Van Baden frowned and shook her head. "No, that would not be enough. I want to adopt the child. You would, of course, be adequately remunerated."

"Paulus is not for sale."

"Then let us not call it a sale. Let us barter something. I have not yet told Nicolaus about the child. I wanted first to discover how you felt about enriching our lives by providing us with the heir we have longed for. But I feel sure that if I told him, he would be more than willing to turn over this house and land to you and your husband, free and clear. Certainly you could not expect a more generous offer."

Margretta stood up, her body rigid. In a voice so soft that Lady Van Baden had to lean close, her head cocked, birdlike, to listen, she said, "Thank you for what you consider to be a generous offer. But no. And no again. If you offered us all of Van Badenswyck, we would not give up Paulus."

"But you farm women—your houses are full of children. You can always have more."

"Lady Van Baden, even if I were willing to give up Paulus, I would not give him to your son. I want him to grow up with a father who sets the right kind of example for him—someone moral and upright. Someone who would never take advantage of anyone weaker than himself."

Rising, pulling on her gloves and buttoning them at the wrists, Lady Van Baden said, "You must not blame Nicolaus for that one little episode. You cannot imagine what it is like for him to be married to Nelia. You cannot imagine the grief he feels every time she loses another child."

"I am surprised that he does not find a way to divorce her and look for someone who is better at breeding."

"That would be quite impossible. Her mother is one of my dearest friends." After a brief hesitation she added, "Perhaps you would like more time to think it over. My offer, I mean. Talk it over with your husband."

"Lady Van Baden, my husband is capable of great love. But he is also capable of great anger." She looked up at Stephen's musket resting on the brackets along the side of the rafter over her head. "If he knew what happened to me, I would fear for the life of your son."

The older woman's hand flew to her mouth. Then, after a moment, she said, "Well, I think I will at least take advantage of your offer to see the child now and then."

"I made no such offer. I merely asked whether that was what you had in mind. You will not see Paulus again, except by accident."

The thin smile now took an ugly twist. "We'll see about that."

"Yes, we will. If you attempt to do anything more about this, you will find I can also do some things. I am not without influence in New York. My father had many friends in government. I, in my teaching, met many of the leading families. I can go all the way to the governor if I need to. And everywhere I go I will tell about your son's behavior."

"You would risk having your name besmirched?"

"Lady Van Baden"—Margretta felt in control now, sure of her ground—"I have far less to lose than your family does. When I came here, I knew nothing about the manor system. Now I know a great deal. And one thing I know is that the crown is not happy with the way it is being operated. England wants to see this land settled, developed. The landlords are, with their tactics, discouraging settlement. A story like the one I have to tell might be enough to cause the crown to initiate further moves, and more drastic ones, against the whole manorial system."

Lady Van Baden stared at her. Margretta stared back until the older woman turned and went out the door.

Resisting the urge to bolt the door, Margretta picked up Paulus and held him close. The child. The child. Lady Van Baden had spoken of him as if he were an object, an object to be sold or bartered. As if sensing her turmoil, Paulus began to howl. Sitting down in the rocker, she opened her bodice. As he began to nurse, she felt calmness descend on her.

Stephen came in. "I saw tracks outside, and fresh horse droppings. Who was here—William?"

"Lady Van Baden." She stroked the silk of the baby's hair. "She wants me to do some more work for her."

"And will you?"

"I have little choice. I cannot prove I fulfilled our agreement."

"Well, do them and be done with it."

Kneeling down beside her, Stephen kissed her. "When the little fellow has had all he wishes, bring him outside so we can show him how much his tree has grown."

After Stephen had gone out, she continued nursing Paulus and thinking about Lady Van Baden. Despite her anger, she felt a certain sympathy for the older woman, knowing what it was to long for a baby to hold, a baby of your own blood. Still, that did not excuse her arrogance, condone her assumption that a mother would willingly give up her child.

You farm women, you can always have more.

She rocked more vigorously. Can always have more? Could she? Would she? And if she did not, would Stephen begin to think, to wonder . . . to count?

Chapter 18

For years Margretta's marriage had differed from those of other young wives she had met. During their childless years, she had felt free to go berry picking whenever she wished, to join Stephen in the fields, to get in the wagon with him when he went to the village, to ride to Sara's on a moment's impulse.

Now their life changed as if, newly married, they were just developing a routine. Instead of Stephen getting up at night to check the fire, it was she who, getting up to attend to Paulus, did it. Instead of speaking directly to her when he came into the house, it was to Paulus that Stephen turned first, and it was Paulus' needs rather than Stephen's that she took care of first.

And the washing. What had once been a quarterly event became in the first months a weekly one. Over and over she had to remind Stephen to hang the huge kettle over the fire so she could heat water for the baby's clothing. She had been determined that her house would never smell like Sara's, but sometimes when she came in from the outside the odor assailed her. How hard it was, she thought. No wonder Sara's children had so often been dirty. How could you keep them clean and still see to it they were properly fed and clothed? And for weeks she was tired and uncomfortable while the slow healing from the tearing of the birth took place.

For nearly six weeks after Paulus was born, Stephen had merely kissed her good night with affection. On the night when he finally approached her, she was ready for him, slipping her arms around his neck. His lovemaking this night was less importunate yet more satisfying. Afterward, he continued to hold her in his arms.

"It was different tonight. Did you notice?"

"Yes. Better."

"Do you know why?"

"The long wait perhaps. Our delight in Paulus."

"Yes, all that. But something more. In the past I was divided. Part of me was making love to you and part of me was trying to father a child. I was always asking myself why. Or: what is wrong with me? Or: will a child result from this union? Now, with no need for questions, I thought only of expressing my love with tenderness."

She tangled her fingers in his hair. "Stephen, I love you very much. Are you aware of that?"

"I used to think you were too good for me."

"No. Far from it." Far, *far* from it.

"When I met you I could not even read."

"And now you read more, understand more, than I do. You have only one fault, Stephen. Sometimes when you are upset, you withdraw from me. You withdraw so far that my words, even my love, cannot reach you. Why can't you share your thoughts with me at such times and let me help?"

"I don't know." He was silent a long time. "My stepmother used to call me sullen. But it wasn't that. I can't explain what it was. What it is."

"Will you try to change a little?" she asked.

"Yes. I'll try."

"And now tell me what faults I have that you would like me to change."

"None. You are perfect. Honest, loving, faithful. And a good helpmeet. What more could a man want?"

What more? A woman, perhaps, who never lied to him. A woman who had never felt her blood warm at another man's touch. A woman who had never, however reluctantly, allowed herself to be seduced and lifted to a new level of feeling. A woman who did not walk always with a secret burden of guilt.

That moment of reassurance when Stephen expressed his faith in her became one of the significant memories of that year. Some years overlapped each other, indistinguishable in their sameness; others stood out or were remembered in detail. The year of 1752 was one of those, a year of happiness and change, a year of sorrow and change.

Late in the fall after Lady Van Baden's visit, Margretta awakened one morning with a queasy feeling. Was it possible? Reluctant to raise Stephen's hopes, she remained silent for five weeks. Then, sure, she told him.

He was jubilant. Sara said, "So soon? It's going to be hard. Two in diapers at the same time."

William grinned and slapped Stephen on the back. "Once you get the knack of it . . ." he said with a lewd link. Stephen smiled back, trying to disguise his pride.

Margretta awaited this child with much joy, though she felt less well than she had the first time. And Stephen, even happier, made plans now to put dormers in the loft so that sleeping quarters could eventually be built there.

Then on a raw day in January she lost the baby. Stephen had gone to the village; she had stayed home to watch the fire and to rest quietly. It hadn't helped. If you are going to lose a baby, you do so, she thought, no matter how careful you are. And you lose not just a baby but a dream.

She was more devastated than she had thought possible. All afternoon she rocked Paulus, getting up only to put more wood on the fire—rocking, thinking, holding back tears. She had thought she understood how Cornelia Van Baden felt; now she realized with sharp identification how great Cornelia's sorrow and disappointment must have been, especially when the experience was repeated again and again.

"Acceptance is all," her grandmother used to say. But acceptance came slowly, for she had imagined this second child with such clarity that it had become a familiar creature already held and known.

Even Stephen was far less affected than she. For him this child had clearly as yet been unreal. "We will have another," he said. "And more after that."

Sara too viewed the loss with little concern. "You'll be glad later you didn't have them so close. It's hard. But you must get pregnant again soon's you can."

"What if I turn out to be like my mother? Or Cornelia Van Baden? I don't know how many babies she's lost."

"There's something real wrong with her. She ain't never had a healthy child like you. Anyways, once you're pregnant again, you'll forget all about this."

Surprisingly, Sara was right. Before the buds on the trees began to swell in the spring, she knew that a new life had begun within her.

The year 1752 was also the year England and its colonies adopted the Gregorian calendar that Holland had been using for 170 years. From now on the new year would officially begin on January 1 instead of March 25, and this year, the day following September 2 would become September 14.

"It's crazy," William said one Sunday. "Why drop them days from September just like they never happened? I bet our lord patroon won't cut the rent by them eleven days."

Stephen, who had read about it, explained that since the old system had a leap year every four years, extra minutes and hours had accumulated into days over the centuries, but that the new calendar would call for leap years only when the year could be divided by four, except for centuries which must be divisible by four hundred.

William listened to Stephen with respect these days, Margretta noticed, and made fewer crude jokes about him.

Margretta also noticed as the months went by that other men displayed a growing respect as they listened to Stephen. It was not just that he could read, but that he understood what he read and explained things clearly. More and more people were finding their way down the lane to talk with him about various events and to discover what his opinion was.

Her gift to him after he had learned to read was an almanac. Each year thereafter he had bought one. He pored over it, studying the weather forecasts, absorbing the advice on when to sow, when to reap, and how to care for livestock. He became an authority on astronomical data, often stepping outside on nights when stars filled the sky with brightness to study his findings.

Other farmers stopped by to ask about the almanac's forecasts or its homeopathic remedies. Or to talk about the troubles surfacing on other manors. While Margretta, showing signs of her pregnancy now, sat on one side of the room with Sara and the other women, talking of housekeeping problems and watching Paulus and Pieter creep about, she also listened to the men, often with a chill of apprehension.

Up on Livingston Manor some farmers whose land was claimed by both New York and Massachusetts had accepted Massachusetts titles and were refusing to pay their rent to the Livingstons.

William said, "Livingston claims Massachusetts is grabbing his tenants. I say, why not? Half these landlords got their land for practically nothing just because they was in a position to get favors from the governor."

"Or bought tracts of land from the Indians," Stephen said, "and then deliberately misunderstood boundaries. Instead of recognizing a particular stand of pines or a waterfall, they found another miles away."

"For all we know, we may be breaking our backs to pay rent for land the Van Badens themselves never paid a shilling for," William said.

"Maybe," Jan Harten said thoughtfully, "we should try to get titles from Connecticut. Or from the Indians."

"Why not?" William said. "It would be legal. And what could Van Baden do about it? My Lord Patroon."

Sara stood up, arms akimbo. "I'll tell you what he could do. He could arm a bunch of men and march them over here. They'd either burn you out or throw you out."

"But that would be illegal," Stephen said. "We are under English law here, a common law that protects us all. In such a case, we would hire lawyers."

Margretta gave her husband a look half-loving, half-fearful. Although she admired both his intelligence and his idealism, she feared the latter sometimes got in the way of the former. Remembering Gustavus Sulzer's flat refusal to take her case, she wondered how much success anyone who hoped to fight the Van Baden rental system would have.

And while at one time she would have welcomed the challenge of taking sides in such a conflict, Sara's words had frightened her. With one child creeping trustfully along the floor and another growing inside you, you had no desire to face a group of armed men. You wanted only to shield your children.

That night in bed she said, "Do you realize, Stephen, that we have been married nearly nine years?"

"Yes. And we'll be married many more."

"And will we spend all of them here on Van Baden land?" Hearing his sigh, she said quickly, "I know you think I bring this up too often."

"The talk today frightened you. Those actions on Livingston Manor have nothing to do with us. Besides, we can't leave now. You're expecting a child."

"Other women have moved when they were with child."

"But you have had one difficult birth, and you have lost a child. We can't risk either of those."

"After the child is born?"

"We'll see what happens in the summer."

What happened in the summer was that an armed band of Livingston's men retaliated against some of the farmers who had taken Massachusetts titles, burning the home of one and confiscating another's wheat. Others were jailed but escaped when sympathetic jailers turned their heads. At intervals rumors filtered southward of more confrontations, more arrests.

"They're foolish, those farmers," Margretta said to Stephen. "Don't they know they can't win against people as wealthy and influential as the Livingstons? They would be wiser to leave, to start over somewhere else. Stephen . . . ?"

Ignoring her implied question, he said, "I don't like what's going on at Livingston Manor either, Margretta, but it may quiet down. Let us wait and see."

So she waited. And as she waited, a newly ominous bank of clouds appeared on the western horizon. The storm it heralded extended as far north as the St. Lawrence, as far south as the confluence of the Monongahela and the Allegheny rivers that formed the Ohio, and as far west as the Mississippi. It had been gathering for years, and like most of those that threatened the Hudson Valley and New England, it originated in the western lands claimed by both the French and the English.

Margretta, who mainly worried about violence between landlords and tenants, at first refused to believe it when Stephen warned that far more serious confrontations were liable to take place between the French and the English. Hadn't they fought each other periodically, both here and in Europe, and hadn't they resolved their differences with the treaty of Aix-la-Chapelle in 1748?

"But they weren't resolved," Stephen said. "And when two countries want the same land and neither will compromise, war is inevitable." He also pointed out that the French had increased their strength through alliances with the Hurons and Algonquins to the north, as well as the Ottawas, all traditional enemies of the English-allied Iroquois Nations.

Margretta sighed. It must be as important as Stephen said. But the countries of Europe had always had wars. That France and England might fight in remote areas of this continent was hardly surprising. Yet as the weeks went by, she was more interested in her pregnancy as she sailed from summer into fall like a sloop propelled by a gentle wind, successfully maneuvering past the danger points. And when, in the midst of a howling December storm, Catherine was born, the birthing was easy.

A boy and a girl. If I have no more children, she thought as she admired the daintiness and perfection of her little daughter, this will be enough.

Catherine was christened on such a bitterly cold day that Dominie Hardenbroeck was forced to break a sheen of ice on the baptismal bowl in order to sprinkle water on her head. She shrieked with indignation, as if Margretta, in handing her over to such cold hands and icy sprinkling, had violated a sacred trust between mother and child.

If Catherine had been born first, Margretta might never have wanted another child, so fussy and difficult was she. Margretta was so busy now she could only dimly recall what it was like before she had children. Catherine gave her little chance to sleep at night; Paulus kept her running all day. And then, the following summer, before she had grown used to her new responsibilities, she found herself pregnant again.

That was the same summer that the twenty-two-year-old George Washington surrendered Fort Necessity to the French after earlier failing to convince them of the legitimacy of Virginia's claims to trade and settlement along the Ohio.

For Margretta, the incident, occurring so far to the south, had little significance. But to Stephen it was a sign that the French, with troops at the headwaters of the Ohio, and a line of forts from the St. Lawrence to the Mississippi, were less likely than ever to give up their claims to America.

But when five hundred Indians swept down on Hoosick, killing the town's inhabitants, Margretta could no longer close her eyes to reality. Even though France and England were still at peace, other forays were made, closer and more frightening. A boy was killed and two were captured in Petersburg. The following year a man in Kinderhook was scalped.

As she lay in childbed awaiting the birth of her third child, Margretta wondered whether she was bringing him into a world too dangerous for survival. She felt trapped by Stephen's intransigence, trapped by their contract, trapped by the French who instigated the Indian attacks. And now, in 1755, the French had a fort at Crown Point on Lake Champlain. Rumor said they were moving on down to Ticonderoga.

Jonas arrived in March on a springlike day, his birth easy; even so—as Margretta recorded in her notebook—he came into the world with an aggrieved cry.

Elated, Stephen once again spoke of having bedrooms in the loft by the time the children were old enough to notice things at night.

Margretta listened in silence. The more he improved the house, the more of himself he poured into the land, the more he felt a part of it. *My house. My cornfield. My pasture.* How could she ever persuade him to leave a place that had become almost an extension of himself?

Perhaps she should give up. Perhaps she should instead indoctrinate her children in the philosophy of freedom and let them move away if they wished to when they were older. But Stephen was still young. Surely one day he would of his own accord decide to make the move. Meanwhile, she would try to ignore what was going on beyond the borders of Van Badenswyck and bring up her children in an atmosphere of peacefulness and love.

Chapter 19

Catherine differed from Paulus in every way: quick, mercurial, moving as she grew into childhood from one activity to another, quick to cry, quick to laugh, and quick to resent any prohibition placed upon her.

Jonas, light-haired and square-chinned like Stephen, lacked Catherine's energy, Paulus' interest in his surroundings. But he was complaisant, studious, and always eager to please.

Margretta told herself that she and Stephen loved each of the children equally, yet to them Paulus was special, partly because he had been so long awaited and partly because of his own joy in life, in people, and in everything that grew. Each year he eagerly watched his white pine send out new growth, five fingers that stood up at first like miniature candles, then extended themselves horizontally into new stems, each with its packet of five needles. Squatting next to her, he helped Margretta weed her garden. By the time he was four, he had his own garden, laying out the rows with care, kneeling to examine the seedlings when they were so small the adult eye could barely perceive them.

As soon as he could walk, he had begun accompanying Stephen to the barn. Whatever he saw Stephen do, he wanted to try, and in whatever he did he imitated Stephen's every motion and gesture.

"If I met him in the village," William said one day, "I'd know right off he was yours, Stephen. Walks just like you, even swings his arms like you."

The words pleased Stephen, but they pleased Margretta far more. They gave her a confidence that helped to smother the fear she felt as Paulus' features matured, the curve of the eyebrows more noticeable, the sharpness of the nose. As long as they remained in Van Badens- wyck, the possibility remained that someone might see and know.

During the summer after Jonas' birth, Margretta was disturbed by reports of continuing troubles at Livingston Manor. More arrests on one side, more defiance on the other. Then rebellion spread north- ward to Rensselaerswyck. In February, New York constables had gone to Nobletown, near Claverack, to arrest Robert Noble; instead of the constables taking Noble to a New York jail, Noble's men car- ried them to jail in Springfield.

In April the frustrated landlord sent a larger force. This time they captured Noble, but only after a battle with his followers. One man was killed, others arrested.

Arrests were one thing, Margretta thought as she went about her work, but killing was something else. It proved how determined the landlords were to keep their lands and their control intact. And they had everything on their side: the law, the political power, and the money to buy arms and men.

"What everyone should do," she said to Stephen, "is leave. Go off to the Grants or to the West."

He shook his head. "Leaving is not the answer. Those who left would find their homes quickly inhabited by new settlers. Everyone wants land now, and there is none better than right here in the Hud- son Valley."

She felt despair. "For thirteen years, Stephen, you've been pouring your life's blood into land that is not and never will be yours. When, *when* are you going to wake up?"

He gave her a long look. "When are you going to stop hounding me? You're free to take care of the children and prepare the food as you wish. Let *me* plan the rest."

"We used to talk easily about such things."

"We have already talked too much about this."

He was gone, off to his retreat in the barn. He was a good man, better than most: faithful, loving, a hard worker. Why did he have this one fault? Why did he shut her out, making her feel useless, unloved, powerless to promote the changes she knew must be made in their lives?

Yet until he had made up his mind, she must live here in a home that was not her own. Perhaps it's just avarice, she told herself—the desire to possess. Someday when she and Stephen were dead, someone else would live here. Would it make any difference that she and Stephen had not owned it? Yes, it would, for it meant that the children they now had would also be tenants . . . and their children after them.

As if he already sensed the bleakness of his future, Jonas began to cry. She picked him up, rocked him. He kept on crying. Catherine came over, wanting to be held also, wanting to get in the cradle, wanting attention.

How tired I am, Margretta thought.

Coolness prevailed between Stephen and herself for a while as he held himself quietly away from her. Although it finally dissipated, a little of it remained following each unresolved argument, like the additional accumulation of ice on the Hudson after each freeze.

When he silently made love to her, she imagined herself standing away from the bed looking down on herself lying there submissively, unable, without words of love and caresses of significance, to arouse herself to respond. In the past she had been like a fire banked under the ashes for the night, ready, if stirred, to burst into flame. But all too often now the embers barely brightened before dying into grayness.

When she looked at their marriage bed, she often thought of the secret love Stephen had put into its making. The first time she had lain on it, back before their marriage, was still precious in her memory. So many hours they had spent there since, even being drawn to it during the day before the children came and before people had taken to dropping in at odd hours with news or questions.

But these days they tucked no new secrets between the covers. Why did it upset her? Change was inevitable. A woman could not remain young and tremulous forever, nor a husband eager to explore her mysteries and demonstrate his prowess. When no mysteries remained to be explored, when children demanded time and energy, when tasks multiplied, how could a relationship between two people remain the same?

Yet she found it hard to accept. Must change involve a moving away from each other? Why not a more intense moving toward each other? Or did intensity itself diminish with age? Was it natural to talk less of their personal feelings and hopes and more about larger events in the province, the country, and even the world?

After seeing how Stephen enjoyed the dominie's newspapers, Margretta had sent a subscription to New York for *The Weekly Post Boy*. It was worth the eight shillings she had received for a piece of lace from Madame Renault, the dressmaker, to see his expression when he received his first copy.

"How much you have done for me," he said that day. "Instead of depending on rumors, I feel now as though I really know what is going on in the world."

He saved all of the four-page papers, many with passages he had marked, often referring to them. Although the paper arrived anywhere from a week to two months late, for him the news had the authenticity that can be lent only by black printer's ink on white paper. For Stephen, so long denied access to it, the printed word had flung open a doorway to a new world, and now as conflicts from that world intruded on their rural existence, it became even more important.

He shared information with friends, quoting from periodicals and supporting their democratic beliefs with statements from Locke; thus they sought and respected his opinions.

Identifying the British army with the ruling landlords, and having heard that British generals considered American soldiers inferior, the tenants were not altogether disturbed when in 1755 news came that Braddock and all but five hundred of his men had been routed and killed near Virginia on their way to take Fort Duquesne, surprised by a company largely composed of Indians who opened fire from behind trees and stones.

The following year, when Britain declared war on France, and local men joined the army, their safety became a source of worry. But the real fear was of a British defeat, with the entire area overrun by vengeful French and Indians. Already, though, the British were building forts at the southern end of Lake George to prevent the French from crossing the pass from there to the Hudson.

And if the French attacked those forts . . . and succeeded, what then? Margretta held her babies closer as she thought of raids, of scalpings, of torches destroying their home, a home suddenly important to her. For a time she abandoned her dream of independence just as most of the men channeled their belligerence against a larger and more fearful enemy.

"What about it, Stephen?" William said. "Why don't you and me join up? They're paying a good bounty just for joining, I hear. Three pounds in addition to salary."

"If my boys were older, I might. But who would harvest my crops and cut wood for winter? I can't leave."

"Me neither. Jeremias is going, though."

"And Frederic Hardenbroeck," Margretta said, "though he still seems like a child to me."

"Jeremias is fifteen, big enough to carry a gun."

Almost overnight Albany became a huge army camp with maneuvers constantly going on, the men eager to move northward.

It was a time of waiting, a time marked by one British defeat after another. Although the colonies supplied their quotas of men and arms, campaigns to take Fort Niagara and Crown Point failed. And on the sea Admiral Boscawen failed in his attempt to blockade Canada.

As the French and Indians made further incursions, setting up Fort Ticonderoga, destroying settlements along the Mohawk, Margretta remembered the times she had urged Stephen to move there. Now on sleepness nights she thought of the massacres there, shuddered and crept close to Stephen.

"Don't ever take him away from me, Lord," she said in one of her rare moments of supplication.

Soon the British issued orders for more regiments and increased enlistment bounties. A sizable regiment marched up the King's Highway from New York, with volunteers joining all along the way.

Watching it straggle by, William said, "I used to think this was England's war. Or the landlords'. But when it gets this close, it begins to feel like our war."

At night Margretta often heard noises, usually made by raccoons nosing about the woodpile or deer looking for apples. Indians would be more quiet. Still, she was fearful. Her nervousness increased when she saw Stephen at the table cleaning his gun, loading the muzzle with the round bullets, each wrapped in a patch of greased linen, and saw the avid way the boys watched him.

"Papa, why do you wrap the bullet like that?"

"To make it fit better, Paulus."

"Will it kill a man?"

"Yes. But I will use it for that only if . . ."

"Yes, Papa?" Paulus' eyes were bright.

"Only if my family is endangered."

That night in bed she said, "I hate it when you talk to the boys about war and killing."

"Why? They are men. Someday they will have families. Women have always shied away from war the way a skittery horse leaps back when a few leaves tumble across its path."

"And men leap forward to embrace it. Why?"

Easing away from her, he said, "Discussions like this lead nowhere. Besides, I'm quite tired tonight."

Soon she heard his regular breathing. Feeling shut out and unloved, Margretta remained wakeful. All too often now when she spoke to Stephen of things close to her heart, he responded reasonably, then turned away. Perhaps she sought closeness to avoid thinking about a war that grew increasingly frightening as it edged closer. Fear for the safety of her children lurked always in the back of her mind. She worried also about Jeremias and Frederic, who had marched off too excited to be able to imagine the horrors of war. Men in battle had always been required to dispense with compassion, but here in America a new dimension had been added by the Indians, who, urged on by their French suppliers of weapons, killed with savagery and whoops of delight.

The most harrowing of these attacks occurred in 1757, when the colonel in charge of Fort William Henry, besieged by the French, asked for reinforcements. Instead, British General Webb sent word for him to surrender.

Jeremias, one of those lucky enough to escape, came home wounded, his leg dragging. William took him to Judith, who attended him with decoctions from St. Johnswort and with leaves of adder's tongue stamped and boiled in olive oil. She also gave him the juice of pippins to ease his melancholy. Under her ministrations the wounds healed, but the melancholy remained and the boyish look of eyes and face never returned.

Weeks later, one night when William was dispensing spirits and talking about General Webb and the new expeditions he was planning, Jeremias stirred from his apathy.

"General Webb." He spit out the words. "*Traitor* Webb. He don't care about the frontier settlements. Why didn't he send help? Why did he tell us to surrender?"

They listened now as Jeremias, his face flushed and his tongue loosened by drink, spoke of the relief within the fort when the white flag was hoisted and they knew they would no longer have to wait in fear.

He paced back and forth, his limp especially pronounced, his gait uneven, his large hands waving in gestures that imitated the Indians' actions.

"They rushed in yelling. They make you crazy scared. They ain't like anything human. They come at the people with knives and swords and bayonets—anything that could kill. The ones they treated the worst was the Indians on our side, especially the Mohawks. They killed and killed, all the time screaming like they was opening presents they was crazy about. I saw them cut throats, rip bodies open, and yank out the bowels and throw them in a man's face. And babies." He stopped pacing, slumped to a stool, covered his face with his hands. "Children, little babies. They . . . Give me something more to drink, Pa."

William got up, filled the cup. "It's all over, son. You might as well forget it."

"I ain't ever going to forget it." He downed his drink, strode to the door, and went outside.

They sat quiet a few minutes. William sighed, kept looking at the door. "Why don't you go talk to him, Stephen?"

Stephen shook his head. "It wouldn't do any good. Just leave him alone. What do you think, Margretta?"

"I'd leave him alone for now, yes." She felt shaken, relieved only in that the children, outside playing, had been spared this tale of brutality.

A miasma of fear hung over the countryside. With Crown Point, Ticonderoga, and Fort William Henry in the hands of the enemy, it appeared certain that Montcalm would march to Albany. If he took it and commandeered the ships there, he could easily raid every settlement on either side of the river.

The British, instead of attacking the lakefronts and ensuring the safety of the Hudson Valley, suddenly began another campaign against Louisburg on Cape Breton Island in Nova Scotia. The campaign succeeded, and on July 26, 1758, Louisburg fell. France, having lost her Gibraltar in America and much of her navy, was unable now to communicate with Canada or to raid coastal New England.

After that victory and the transporting of the French sympathizers there to New Orleans, Fort Duquesne became the next goal. Captured, it was renamed in honor of Pitt, the British Prime Minister who had given precedence to the campaigns in America. When Frontenac finally fell, it opened the way to the St. Lawrence for the British.

1759—Britain's wonderful year. Victorious in America, in India, at Guadeloupe. Bells rang in London again and again as one victory after another was announced.

During this year Margretta went often to see Judith for news of Frederic, who had gone all the way to Canada in the campaign to win Quebec, writing letters as he went, and reenacting the roles of his childhood in Indian-like treks through forests and along waterways. Judith worried constantly about the fearlessness that might endanger him, and not until Quebec at last fell after the fearsome battle on the Plains of Abraham did she finally know relief.

A few weeks after that the letter came, the dreaded one addressed in someone else's handwriting. The first part had been written by Frederic.

> Dear Mama and Papa and Everybody,
>   It seems like this war has gone on forever. I miss you
> all but I will be coming back soon. I have volunteered
> for a special mission, one that ought to end the siege of
> Quebec. I am very excited and wish I could tell you
> what I am going to do. I think you will be proud of
> me. I'll finish this later and let you know what
> happened.

The letter's postscript said that Frederic had been one of the volunteers who had ascended through a rocky ravine to the top of the three-hundred-foot cliff that was part of Quebec's supposedly impregnable fortress, surprising the sentries into surrender and opening the way for the British army to assemble on the Plains of Abraham for the epic battle. The letter commended his bravery and his thoughtfulness of others. It said his death was quick.

The dominie held a service for him, a funeral without a casket. Although his voice quavered as he spoke, he remained rigidly upright.

Judith, too, was in control. Margretta, however, suspected that she was leaning heavily on an opiate of her own deriving. So much the better. Remembering the cheerful little boy who had wriggled through his lessons, learning his letters only because her will was stronger than his, she was deeply saddened. It haunted her for a long time, this death of a child she had known so well and loved more than she realized.

A year after Frederic's death, Montreal fell, and on September 8, 1760, Governor the Marquis de Vaudreuil surrendered all of Canada to the British.

When Stephen came home with the news, Margretta's first thought was that no obstacle now remained to their leaving Van Badenswyck forever. The children were old enough; all were in good health; they had produced a good harvest.

"Now . . ." Stephen said.

"Yes?" She gave him an eager smile.

"Now we no longer need fear surprise attacks. We can get back to the business of living."

And although she waited each day for him to say something more, he spoke of nothing that fall but of getting things ready for winter.

Chapter 20

Sometimes a forest fire rages along trunks and branches, crackles through treetops; other times it travels underground, smolders in roots and leaf mold, then flares up in unexpected places. The land-lord-tenant conflicts through the late 1750's had followed the latter pattern; a spread southward from Rensselaerswyck and Livingston Manor to the patents and manors in Dutchess and Westchester counties. The tenants in Van Badenswyck, which lay nearly midway along the course, had so far remained watchful, ready to talk but unready to act.

When callers stopped by, new terms fluttered around Margretta's head like burned papers rising from a fire: *fee simple, fee absolute, tenure at will*. The tenants wanted a *fee absolute*, one with no conditions or limitations. They rebelled against terms like *tenure at will* that gave landlords the freedom to terminate a tenancy whenever they wished.

Wappinger Indians were claiming that the eastern portions of Philipse and Van Cortlandt property had been taken illegally while they were fighting in the war on the side of the colonists. Now disgruntled farmers were accepting titles from them and refusing to honor their agreements with the landlords.

"The landlords won't stand for that," Stephen said.

"'Course not," a caller said. "First they send the sheriff to collect the rent. When that don't work, they send a posse. If the farmer still says no, out goes him and his whole family. Can't take things with them. Distraint, you know. And sometimes the man is arrested and carried off to jail."

"The landlords got all the power on their side."

"Maybe, maybe not. One farmer alone can't do much. But you take a bunch, and they can do a lot. Some of the new families already been burned out. Plenty of others got threats. Believe me, there's real trouble brewing. Take everything away from a man, and he ain't got a thing to lose. He ain't afraid to go roaming around making things hot for the farmers that's still kowtowing to the landlords."

Trouble, always trouble in the world, Margretta thought, and later she said to Stephen, "Is there a chance some of those marauding bands might come up here?"

"It's unlikely. They haven't anything against us. We aren't paying rent to a Philipse or a Van Cortlandt."

"But what if we start having the same trouble here?"

"That too is unlikely. They complain, but a lot of them are satisfied to have a home and a living for a minimum of work."

Like William, she thought.

She had to admit that the improvements Stephen had made in recent years had resulted in only minimal increases in rent, but she was unsure whether this was due to fairness on the part of Mr. Frost or to her long ago talk with Nicolaus. She had to admit also that they had made some real advances. The fifties, despite the war, had been good in many ways: years of nurturing, years of seeing Stephen grow in confidence and leadership. The war years had also brought higher prices for wheat.

By 1760 they had their own pair of oxen, three horses, a second and larger wagon. Paulus, at eight, and only a little impeded by a worshipful Jonas, was giving Stephen solid help in the barn and fields. Catherine was reluctantly learning how to run a household. All three of the children also, during the months before and after the growing season, spent a part of each day on reading, writing, and ciphering, with Catherine showing a special aptitude for the latter. Pieter joined them nearly every day, less to learn, Margretta suspected, than to be with Paulus. But she was glad that at least one of the Vanzuyders was acquiring some skills, for Sara had decided the girls didn't need it, and Jeremias and Oloff weren't smart enough.

Just as Paulus had once trailed after his father mimicking the swing of his step, the set of his shoulders, so also did Jonas now follow his brother, his five-year-old legs struggling to keep up with a brother now turned nine. Pieter Vanzuyder, only a few weeks older but already taller than his friend—a good-looking boy with light brown hair and gentle brown eyes—also spent as much time as possible with Paulus. Though their friendship was deep, they allowed Jonas to go along whenever he asked. They even taught him to bait a hook and praised him on the proud day when he came home with a fish he had caught without help.

Jonas' consuming passion was to be exactly like Paulus, to be able to do everything Paulus could do. It was difficult, for Paulus worked with Stephen's painstaking skill. Jonas tried. When the things he made at five failed to fit or hold together and he cried, Margretta reminded him that he was younger than Paulus, that no one expected him to work with such competence. But although he was soon reading with far more competence than other children, he brushed aside Margretta's praise. It was as if he felt he could win love only by excelling at what Paulus did.

Paulus' new interest this year was ships. Whenever he and Pieter went to the village, they headed immediately for the wharf, where they studied the ships passing by or badgered sailors for information on names of things and how they worked. At home afterward, they began carving. Their talk was of keels, foremasts and mainmasts, bowsprits and jibs. The first sloop that Paulus made floated successfully across the pond. Pieter succeeded on his second try. Jonas gave up before he had finished carving his first hull.

One night at supper he said to Stephen, "Where is my tree?"

"Your tree?"

"Yes. The tree I can call my own."

"Why, son, you can pick any tree on this farm and call it your own. Even carve your name in it if you wish."

"I mean *my* tree that was planted when I was born. Like the tree you planted for Paulus."

Speaking slowly, Stephen said, "It's like this, Jonas. When two people have their first child, it's important because it's the beginning of their family. Often they do something special that one time to mark the event. Do you understand?"

Jonas swallowed, nodded, yet his eyes mirrored the understanding that Paulus was more important than he.

Catherine lifted and moved her head so that her pale yellow hair swung over her shoulders. "Who cares about an old tree?" she said. "This place is full of trees. I wish we lived in Manhattan like Mama did, where we could see people all the time. All we see is that stupid Pieter."

"You're just saying that," Jonas said, "because he never pays any attention to you."

"That's because he has so many sisters," Paulus said. "He can't abide girls."

"Well, I can't abide boys." Again Catherine flung her hair around her shoulders.

A pretty one with promise of being hard to manage. How difficult it was as they grew more individual to deal with their foibles and pains. Margretta felt that she must constantly prop Jonas up, hold Catherine down. Yet though Paulus presented her with no problems, she worried far more about him and his future, for even greater than her burden of guilt was the fear of what Nicolaus, with all his vested power, might someday do.

Yet most of the time she felt blessed by the miracle that had given her three children after so many years of discouragement. Three were enough. After Jonas, she had successfully followed the counting method that Sara had learned from Judith.

Blessed as she was, she felt pity for Cornelia Van Baden, who, so Judith had said, had at last accepted that she would probably never bear a child.

Cornelia died on February 10, 1761, a date that, when word had crossed the water late in the spring, was also made memorable by the signing of the Treaty of Paris, which ended the Seven Years' War in Europe as well as the conflict in America. Her own struggles over, Cornelia was laid to rest in the Van Baden section of the graveyard behind the church, where the stones bore dates going back to the end of the previous century.

During the rest of the winter, Margretta, wary, fearful of meeting Nicolaus, rarely went to church. Stephen offered no resistance, nor did the children, who hated the enforced inactivity of the long service.

She also feared trouble at Van Badenswyck to match the increasing turbulence on other manors. New faces were appearing among their callers. Many had come from Europe to escape feudalism. Too poor to buy land outright, they had accepted the terms of tenancy as a temporary measure, only to discover that contracts and inability to get money ahead trapped them as effectively as they had been in Europe.

Others had come over from New England. These men, all with some education and born to freedom, were even more resentful. Listening to their complaints, Margretta sensed a new kind of discontent, one that was liable to erupt into action.

Stephen, as always, counseled moderation, reminding complainers of how little the rebels elsewhere had gained; many had, in fact, lost the investment of years of work in the farms they had rented.

As spring drifted into summer, Margretta remained full of unease. Where was the spice in living if you were not struggling toward a goal? More and more the old desire for adventure pervaded her thoughts.

Early one June evening when the two younger children were playing outside, she, pretending great preoccupation with the socks she was making, said casually, "I wonder what it is really like up in the Grants."

Stephen, busy at the table shaping a new ax handle, did not look up. "They have a few good river valleys, I guess. The rest is mountains."

"What are the Grants?" asked Paulus, who as usual was standing close to Stephen, watching and learning.

"It is land granted to New Hampshire from the east side of Lake Champlain to the Connecticut River. It's not good level land like ours. Hilly. Probably full of stones."

"We're lucky," Paulus said. "Our land is good."

"But," Margretta said, "this is not our land."

Paulus moved from Stephen. "This is not our land?"

"We work it," Stephen said, "and get our living from it. In that sense it is ours."

"But we do not own it? It is not really ours?"

"No."

"That's what Pieter said. I told him he was wrong. You always called it our land."

"It is owned by Lord Van Baden," Margretta said. "He allows us to work it and raises the rent each time we make an improvement, thus making it difficult for us to prosper as people up in the Grants can."

"What your mother does not realize is that ownership of the land called the Grants is in question. Although New Hampshire claims it, New York says that by virtue of the original grant to the Duke of York its land goes all the way to the Connecticut River."

"Well, then," said Paulus, "why do we not go to Connecticut or Massachusetts?"

"They are already crowded. That's why so many have moved over here." Stephen put his hand on the boy's shoulder. "You are young and eager for change, son. If we stay here, all this fine acreage can someday be yours."

"But I will not own it."

Margretta said, "It is nearly the same as owning, Paulus, except that the landlord is free at any time to exercise his rights. He can evict you at will."

"But, son, they do not evict tenants like us."

"No," Margretta said. "Not so long as the tenant makes no trouble." She gave Stephen a hard look. "What would happen if you sometime refused to pay the additional assessments? And how much do you suppose they would raise our rent if you added enough rooms onto the house so we could live in decency?"

Stephen's face whitened. After staring at her in silence for a few moments, he said, "I must attend to some things outside before dark."

"I'll go with you, Papa."

"No. Stay with your mother."

Margretta went to the door, called Jonas and Catherine in and told all three to get ready for bed. She put her work away in the *kas*, checked on food for breakfast, every movement slowed by the weight of guilt. She had said far too much.

Jonas had gone up to the garret, and Catherine was asleep in the alcove by the chimney when Stephen came in. Margretta in her chemise was turning down the coverlet on their bed. Paulus in his nightshirt lingered by the table, polishing a bow and arrow he had just completed.

"Papa, I've been thinking. I'm already quite big, and Jonas is getting bigger all the time. If we went to the Grants and got our own land, we both could help. Maybe Pieter would come too. It would be the labor of four men instead of just one. We could have a fine farm in no time."

Stephen's voice was soft. "Did your mother tell you to say that?"

"Mama? No. Except to tell us all to get ready for bed, she has not said a word since you left."

"I see. Well, then, if your mother told you to get ready for bed, I'd suggest you do so."

"I *am* ready."

"Then go."

Margretta slipped into bed, moved as usual over to the far side by the wall. She saw Paulus walking slowly toward the ladder, his shoulders slumped. It was rare for his father to dismiss him with such abruptness.

"Wait, son," Stephen said. "I just want to say this. You are only a boy and there is much you do not understand. When you are older, we'll speak of it again."

Paulus nodded, his moving shadow sharp and black on the wall as he climbed the ladder.

Stephen attended to the fire, put out the candle, undressed in the dark. He got into bed and lay on his back, his hands under his head.

"Stephen? I'm sorry if I hurt you."

"I am not hurt. Just surprised. I thought you had long since grown accustomed to our life here. I did not know you were so dissatisfied."

"I am not actually dissatisfied." Just restive, she thought, and eager for change, a change too long awaited.

"Then you are completely happy and want no more than we have?"

She was silent despite knowing how much her failure to speak hurt him. After a time she did say, "I do love you, Stephen. Very much."

He said nothing.

She reminded herself he had once told her he loved her even when he withdrew from her. You must always remember that, he had told her.

She did remember it. At times like this, however, it was hard to believe in it.

Chapter 21

Heat shimmered across the fields as Margretta and Paulus rode to the village. In her saddlebag she carried laces to deliver to the dressmaker. They should bring enough to buy Paulus the shoes he wanted. How pleasurable it was to be riding beside her son. How handsome he was with his sleek, dark hair, his curving eyebrows, his eyes shining with anticipation. How straight he sat in the saddle. He was almost regal-looking. More like a lord of the manor than . . . The thought had strayed in like a small wild creature that frightens even as it is itself frightened, a thought best sent scurrying back to the hidden place where the blackest of memories were concealed.

As she dismounted in front of the dressmaker's, the opening and closing of a door alerted her, and she glanced across the road at Gustavus Sulzer's home. Like a sudden wind that sets dry leaves to shaking and falling, a gust of feeling shook her. After all the careful years of rarely attending church, of leaving Paulus to play with Pieter when she knew Nicolaus was in residence—after all those years that had lulled her into a feeling of safety even though a part of her had known that it had to happen sometime—they were now to meet, for Nicolaus had seen her and was deliberately crossing in her direction. He stopped, faced her.

Smiling faintly, she nodded politely. "Lord Van Baden, this is my son Paulus."

"It is a pleasure to meet you, Paulus," Nicolaus said gravely. His eyes beneath the curving brows studied the boy's face.

Paulus looked uncertainly at Margretta, whispered, "Should I call him 'My Lord Patroon'?"

Margretta shook her head. "'Sir,'" she said softly.

"It is a pleasure to meet you too, sir." Paulus bowed slightly.

"How old are you, son?"

"Ten, sir."

"Are you making calls or are you here on errands?"

"My mother may wish to make a call, sir. I wish only to buy some shoes. Fine square-toed shoes with brass buckles. Like yours, sir." Again Paulus turned to his mother. "May I go in and look at the shoes?"

"Yes." She smiled and he ran quickly inside. "I must go with him," she said. "He cannot select shoes by himself."

"He is a fine, intelligent boy. I'm sure he knows what he wants in shoes and can tell whether they hurt him."

"He has never before selected shoes by himself." She did not add, as she moved to turn away from him, that until now Stephen had made moccasins for him from deerskin.

"Wait, Margretta. Don't go yet. Tell me, how long ago was it that you came to the manor house about the laces?"

Though agitated, she retained an outward calmness. "I'm not sure. About a dozen years, I think."

"That long? I would have said it was a bit less. More like eleven. It was on a day like this, I believe, that I found you upstairs working in all that heat."

"Nicolaus, I really must go." Even in her agitation she refused to honor him by using his title.

"In a minute. You heard about Cornelia?"

"Yes. I was sorry. Life was very sad for her."

"For all of us. All those years of marriage, and now nothing. No children. No wife. When she was herself, she was a sweet and lovely person. I miss her very much."

"Do you?"

"Yes. You look as though you don't believe me."

"I don't. When I think of that night . . ."

His face grave, he said, "Yes, that night. I don't think it will ever stop haunting me. The guilt. Guilt over her, guilt over you. I truly was not myself at the time, Margretta. And you. I don't think you had any idea of how beautiful you were, how seductive, as your hands fluttered like butterflies over your work. How appealing you were with the candlelight shimmering on your hair when you looked up at me with those dark eyes and asked a favor of me."

"I asked no favors. I asked only for justice."

Still regarding her steadily, he said, "I remember it as if it happened last night—the effect you had on me. I have spent many hours thinking of it, speculating about how I would feel if we met again. Now I know that what I felt then was no superficial emotion."

Her fingers twisted nervously. Shaken by the feelings his gaze stirred within her, she said, "I must attend to the boy."

"Ah, yes. The boy. I want to do something for him."

"If you want to do something, forget him."

Ignoring her statement, he continued: "Frost needs help running the manor. Why not let the boy go to work for him? We need someone to train in managing all aspects of the business."

He wanted to take Paulus away from her. She had always known he would want that. "That would be quite impossible. His father needs him on the farm." She turned to walk away.

"We will talk about this again sometime."

"No," she said. "No."

Inside the shop, Paulus was trying on boots, showing them to her, asking her opinion. She gave it automatically, her thoughts still in turmoil.

That night at supper Paulus said, "We saw Lord Van Baden in the village today. We even talked to him."

Stephen looked at them. "What did you talk about?"

"I told him about my shoes."

"I wish I had shoes like that," Jonas said.

"You'll have them when you're as old as Paulus."

"I have to wait for everything."

"We all have to wait, Jonas. For everything."

In the spring Margretta was relieved to hear that Nicolaus had gone to Europe. "To forget his grief," Judith told her, and then added, "or perhaps to find another wife, one who might be more successful at breeding."

"Like choosing a mare or a cow," Margretta said.

"Why not? If it makes sense to select an animal that will produce healthy offspring, why does it not make even more sense to select a mate that way?"

"But what about love?"

"What about it? A good breeder can go on for some time. How long does love last?" Tipping her head to one side, she said, "Can you honestly say you and Stephen feel exactly as you did when you were first married? Come on. Admit it's different. Admit your life is mostly work now, and you look forward to going to bed mostly because you're exhausted."

With her silence Margretta admitted it.

"The mating urge is the same with humans as it is with animals," Judith went on. "But we don't want to admit it, so we add poetry to it."

Margretta shook her head. "No. I refuse to accept that. It may be for some people, but for others the love is always there." Someday, she assured herself, Stephen would make the hard decision to break away from the Hudson Valley that he loved so much. Then, as they began a new life in a new place, their love would spring to life in a new way.

But Judith had been right about Nicolaus. He did come home in the fall with a new bride, Anna, a round-faced young woman with light curly hair and innocent blue eyes. Looking at those eyes as the new wife came into church clinging to Nicolaus' arm, Margretta, when she bent to pray, offered a few words for the new young mistress of Van Badenswyck, already, so Judith said, carrying a Van Baden heir within her. And she prayed that the child would be a boy, someone who would become the center of Nicolaus' thoughts.

More and more Stephen treated Paulus like an adult companion. Only one subject did he refuse to discuss with him, and that was a move away from the farm. Like herself, Paulus understood, at least to the point of refraining from urging a move, though he did sometimes preface remarks with phrases such as "When we own our own place . . ." or "When we go up to the Grants or out to the Mohawk Valley . . ." And sometimes when he was with Pieter and Stephen was not around, Margretta heard them speaking about moving away or even of sailing away to foreign lands. They had not yet lost interest in ships.

Pieter, perhaps because he had spent so much of his time with them, spoke and sounded more like a Warner than a Vanzuyder. Margretta was pleased now to learn that he had the same enterprising spirit Paulus had.

She heard them speaking too about the continuing trouble on the Philipse Highland Patent, where proprietors were bringing suits against farmers who had bought land from the Wappingers, and the Indians in turn were seeking redress in New York courts.

"What if the landlords win?" Pieter asked.

"The farmers will be put out of their homes."

Jonas, who had been lingering nearby, turned to Margretta. "Is Paulus just making that up?"

"No, Jonas."

He looked frightened. "Could they do that to us?"

She put her arms around him. Though eight years old, he was still her baby. "Not without a good reason."

"They will never put us out," Paulus said. "If they come here, Papa will pick up his musket and order them off the property. He told me so."

"There will be no violence here," Margretta said.

But when she told Stephen under the cover of darkness that Paulus was too young for that kind of talk, he replied, "He must be made aware of the problems a man has and how they are faced." He moved restlessly. "Besides, I think we will have trouble here at Van Badenswyck before long."

"Trouble? What kind?"

"I heard talk when I went to the mill the other day. Some think the Van Badens do not really own all the land they claim, maybe not even the land where we are."

The words portended more then they said. Finally she found the courage to ask, "Is that why you stay here? Do you think you may sometime make this place legally yours?"

"Is that all you think of—moving away? Has nothing I have done for you here pleased you?"

Refusing to let him make her feel ungrateful, guilty, she said, "You have not answered my question."

"All right, yes. It is one of the reasons. The other is that right now I am needed here. There is so much ignorance, so much hotheadedness. But fortunately the men will listen to me. I hope I can prevent needless bloodshed."

"Now I'll answer your question," she said. "Yes, the things you have done for me have pleased me. The back room, the work you have begun upstairs on the new rooms, the water that runs in, the shelves, the pegs, the furniture. And especially this beautiful bed."

He moved closer to her then and warmed her with his lips and his touch. Feeling loved, she gave herself up to a renewed closeness. Who knew how many years they had left together? Perhaps all the happiness they would ever have lay within these walls. Then she reminded herself that it was for a secure future for their children that she wanted to move. But she would wait a little longer, wait and remain silent.

In May of the next year Paulus proudly turned twelve. That summer Stephen gave him his own musket. In the fall they hunted together, often taking Pieter Vanzuyder with them. Although they went off together like three men, Margretta was aware of Paulus' as yet childishly sweet voice and silken skin. He was still far from being a man. But he did, late in the season, shoot his first bear, a big animal heavy with fat, enough for a whole winter for shortening and for making boots and moccasins waterproof as well as for preserving the wooden handles on tools. It also gave them meat to be salted and a fine piece of fur.

In May also the new young Lady Van Baden died in childbirth, leaving Nicolaus with a baby daughter, Alida. Margretta pitied him for the tragedies he had suffered. But now he had a child. She was happy for him, but beyond that she tried to put him out of her mind. All too often ever since the day she had met him in front of the dressmaker's, she had found herself reflecting on the words he had spoken, and her senses reawakening with the memory of the way he had looked at her.

But during that summer her thoughts were disturbed by an increasing rebelliousness she noticed in the talk of tenants who met together, and she feared that despite Stephen's efforts, the resentment so long suppressed might, like an inflamed boil, come to a head and spread its infection everywhere, especially since it was now rumored that the first Van Baden had been given the rights to his huge tract of land through friendship with an early governor for a token payment of only twenty-five pounds.

Yet, no matter how reluctantly, the tenants continued to abide by their contracts: to give their allotted days to the lord of the manor each year for work on fences and roads, to pay their rents even in seasons of drought or hardship. They might speak of change, but they spoke of it as if it might occur, like changes in the weather, without any help on their part. No one was ready to make the first move.

One sharply cool fall evening as they were about to begin supper, they heard a knock. Stephen opened the door to a wild-looking young man. Behind him stood a woman carrying a baby.

"We're in trouble. Could we come in?"

Stephen nodded, helped the young woman up the step. "What's wrong? Where are you from?"

The young man pointing to the east said, "From Sharon, over in Connecticut. My father didn't have land enough for all his sons, so we settled over here."

"I've never seen you in the village."

"We just came about six months ago. Bought our land from the Indians. My brothers and some friends raised our rooftree, helped build a log cabin."

"And now it's burned to the ground," the woman said.

"Oh, you've had a fire?"

"Stephen," Margretta said. "These people are in trouble. Ask them to sit down and have some hotcakes. We'll ask questions later."

The young couple sat down. Their feet were muddied, their faces scratched, their clothing torn—evidence of a trek through fields thick with brambles and through woods and streams. The man ate ravenously. The woman, still holding her baby in the crook of her arm, picked at her food. Now and then a dry sob shook her body.

"Catherine," Margretta said, "take the baby and rock it. And you, Paulus, give their horse some oats."

"Got no horse," the man said. "Had to leave everything." Finished now with his food, he told them his name, Ethan Forester, and introduced his wife, Elizabeth.

"You've had a hard time," Margretta said. "There's nothing worse than a fire. But you were lucky to get out. What if it had happened when you were asleep?"

Elizabeth stared uncomprehendingly at her, shook her head. Leaving the table, she took the baby from Catherine and sat down in the rocker. Turning it toward the warmth of the fire, she opened her bodice and nursed the baby. She had not spoken except for her one statement upon entering.

"It's hard to accept these things," Stephen said to Ethan. "But you can rebuild. If your brother and friends can't help you, I'll find people here who will."

"You don't understand," Ethan said. "This fire was no accident. Last week they came with papers, told us we had to leave. We refused. We had bought our land fair and square. Why should we leave? Today they came again—more of them."

"Just a minute," Stephen said. "Who came?"

"First the sheriff and some men. They said they represented Lord Van Baden. Today more men. They said they'd burn us out if we refused to leave. We locked the door and watched from the window. First they took the horse and the cow and tied them to two of their horses. Then they burned the barn. Next the Indian corn. All that corn that I plowed and harrowed for and set out one kernel at a time." He wrung his hands in despair. "They set torches to the hay I had piled around the foundation of the house. When the wood itself caught, we had no choice but to go outside."

Elizabeth, still rocking, began a soft moaning. Margretta put an arm around her. "Let me change the baby. Then we'll put him in our cradle. Somebody—you, Jonas—get the cradle from the back room." Paulus, she noticed, was sitting at the table with the two men.

"They wouldn't let us take any of our belongings," Ethan continued. "I wanted to go back in for our title, but they lifted their guns and held them on us."

"I wanted my grandmother's Bible," Elizabeth said.

"How could they do this if you have a title?"

"They said it was no good, that the land belonged to Lord Van Baden."

As she listened to the despair in their voices, Margretta looked around at the marriage bed, the cradle, the rocker, the *kas*. They were more than possessions: they were part of the fabric of her life. Deprived of them and the memories they held, her life would never be the same.

"What will you do now?" she asked. Then quickly added, "Why not stay here a few days? We have plenty of food."

"I thank you," Ethan said. "You are good people. For a while today I thought there were no good people left. We stopped at two farms before we got here. They wouldn't let us in. Afraid the sheriff or maybe his lordship would find out and they'd be turned out for being sympathizers."

"We have no such fears," Stephen said. "You are welcome here. Stay as long as you need to."

"Just until tomorrow," Ethan said. "Then I'll walk to Sharon and come back in a few days with a horse. Elizabeth could never walk over the mountains. She's too frail."

"No," Stephen said. "I have three horses. We'll ride over on two of them and I'll lead the other one back."

Before they went to bed they sat and talked. Elizabeth and Ethan were both nineteen. "When I came back from the campaign in Canada, I went through the Grants," Ethan said. "You never saw such beautiful green mountains and deep valleys, some with good land. I wanted to settle there, but when I told Elizabeth, she held back. Didn't want to go that far from her parents."

In his voice Margretta heard the all-too-familiar echoes of disagreement between husband and wife: the one who wanted to leave, the one who wanted to stay.

Margretta made up the marriage bed with clean linens for their guests. Then Stephen went upstairs with the boys and she squeezed into the alcove with Catherine.

The next day, starting out at dawn, Stephen rode off with them to Sharon, he on one horse, the Foresters on the other.

"A sad business," he said upon his return.

Margretta, worried, said, "This looks like the beginning of troubles here."

"Maybe. Maybe not. Who knows—maybe they had no title at all. We have only their word for it."

Later, when they were alone, she said, "Stephen, what *will* we do if there is trouble here? Where will we go?"

"We won't have that kind of trouble. I was talking to Ethan about that today. If he had come and talked with me earlier, I would have counseled him."

"Telling him what?"

"To get a lawyer. To offer to pay rent until the case was settled."

"Stephen, don't you know no farmer can win in a court here? No one sits in these courts except landlords and their friends."

With great calmness he said, "But people must try those channels

first. If they do not work, then you fight. But you do not fight by
yourself like Ethan."

Then you fight. The cold logic of his words pierced her heart like a
splinter of ice. First you fight, then you die. Didn't he know that?

"Stephen, this makes no sense. Have you thought of what would
happen to me if you died like some of the men at Rensselaerswyck
and on Livingston Manor? I have no parents to turn to. How would I
take care of the children? Stephen, please, for their sake if not for
mine, be reasonable."

"It is you who are being unreasonable." Slowly, as if closing a door
between them, he turned over.

She was not so easily silenced. "You refuse to discuss it?"

"You are forgetting how tired I am. I have ridden for two days over
very rough terrain. And the night before I left I slept on the floor in
the loft."

"Yes, I had forgotten." She eased herself down onto the bed and
lay staring into blackness. No matter what happened, he would inter-
pret it in such a way that it supported his desire to remain here. How
strange that a man who so loved the earth did not want a piece of it
that was truly his.

And now this new fear, not just of being deprived of the opportunity for freedom, but of possibly being deprived of a husband also.
Men. Men. Why were they always so willing—even eager—to fight?

Chapter 22

Bitter cold overspread Van Badenswyck during the winter of 1764–65. The tenants spent their time trying to keep warm rather than rebelling. Besides, news had spread about the Foresters. Mean as their possessions were, no one wanted to see them go up in flames.

Early in May Stephen went to the village one day to have the wheelwright put two new front wheels on his wagon. He returned with a black-bordered newspaper. Waving it, he said, "Look at what the British have done now. It's something called the Stamp Act. They're going to put stamps on everything from legal documents to playing cards, and the stamps will cost anywhere from twopence to six pounds. It's the death of liberty, the paper says. That's why the black border."

"But why are the British doing this?" Paulus asked.

"To raise money to defend us, they say. The French and Indian War was costly. Now they need 350,000 pounds for ships and troops to defend us in the future."

"Why is that the death of liberty?"

"Who's about to attack us? Certainly not the French or the Spanish. Can you think of any other reason the British might want troops here?"

Paulus shook his head.

"To control the colonists," Margretta said quietly.

"Of course," Stephen said. "There's something about settling here, battling the elements, clearing land, fighting or making peace with the Indians, dealing with wild animals, that makes people strong and independent. And that scares the British."

Yet though the tenant farmers found the Stamp Act mildly oppressing, they were used to paying tributes. Besides, their purchases were limited.

Not so with the upper class. Accustomed to levying rather than paying, they were incensed. And with their extensive purchases and legal work, they had far more to lose.

When a month after the Stamp Act Parliament passed the Quartering Act, resentment spread in even wider circles, for now colonists were required to billet British soldiers in barracks, public places, or even private homes.

"It's a bad business," Stephen told the family. "And New York will bear the brunt of it. What better place for ships to come in and land troops? And the Hudson provides easy access to the interior."

Hearing about riots in the big cities and about the rebellion of the Sons of Liberty, composed largely of the wealthy, excited the tenant farmers. They watched as the Sons of Liberty extended their activities to the villages—even to Van Badenswyck—hanging stamp collectors in effigy and forcing them to resign, tolling bells, flying flags at half-mast, all mourning the death of liberty. And when Lord Van Baden posted notices saying he was working to save his tenants from unjust taxation, the farmers, knowing how much more the British acts affected the wealthy, laughed behind their hands.

Here and there in Van Badenswyck during the summer of 1765 a recalcitrant farmer—usually a recent settler near the New England border—was ejected. If he left peacefully, he was allowed to take his things with him; if he resisted, he was deprived of his possessions, his grain seized. Sometimes a few friends organized to support him, but their skirmishes were brief and quickly defeated.

Even this much rebellion, Margretta felt, would not have occurred had it not been for the riotous examples set by the upper class, and she was relieved when this class turned to the colonial legislatures to denounce the two British acts, and in October met at the Stamp Act Congress in Boston to resolve that no freeborn Englishman could be taxed without his consent and that, since the colonists had no representation in Parliament, it was unconstitutional for Parliament to tax them.

Again the farmers learned. They began to hold formal meetings, most often in Stephen and Margretta's home. Margretta dreaded them—the resolutions and the hotheaded talk—and the effect it might have on the children, whom she often caught peering down from the loft above to listen.

Somehow, without any election, or without his having spoken of it to her, Stephen had become the leader of the local dissidents. He sat one Sunday at the head of the long table and read their contracts as they passed them to him.

"Yes," he'd say, "you've granted him the right of distraint."

"But I didn't know what it meant at the time."

"Nor did I," said Stephen. "We were all ignorant and they took advantage of our ignorance. Yes, this one also says 'tenure at will.' You could be ejected at any time."

"It's no way to live," one man said, carefully folding his contract. "How can you rest easy when you know you can be ejected anytime the landlord wishes—say, just when a fine crop is about ready to be harvested?"

"Or knowing he can send his men in anytime and take possession of anything he wants."

"Or raise the rent if you improve the place."

"Or insist on a percentage of the skins when you do any trapping."

One man said, "Let's march on the manor house. Make our own right of distraint. Take what we want of their fine things. Haven't we paid for them with our own sweat? Then set the torches to the place."

"Throw all the Van Badens out. Throw them in the river. They only paid twenty-five pounds for all this land. Now they collect a hundred times that for rentals alone."

Stephen rose. Putting his palms flat on the table, he leaned toward them. "Let us not get carried away. However little the first Van Baden paid for the land, he obtained it legally and has the papers to prove it."

"Not the land he got from the Indians. We all know he took far more than he contracted or paid for."

"If so, that is the Indians' problem, not ours. Aren't distraint and tenure at will our greatest grievances? Certainly no one objects to paying a fair rent."

Most of the men nodded.

"Then let us work on those two things."

Margretta felt a surge of pride. He was a good leader.

Five days before New Year's, Stephen, William, and two other men went to the manor house. Sara came over with Pieter. The two women sat at the table and sewed. The young people sat on the floor and played backgammon. Margretta in a casual sideways glance that froze into understanding saw Pieter smile at Catherine, saw her tip her head flirtatiously as she smiled back. Good heavens, she was only twelve, Pieter only thirteen.

This was what propinquity did. Although Margretta was fond of Pieter, she felt that Catherine could do better. No doubt her father would have felt the same about her marriage to Stephen. She soothed herself with the reminder that Catherine, flirtatious or not, was far from a marriageable age.

Darkness had fallen by the time the men returned. Hearing their voices outside, loud and boisterous, Margretta knew they had been to the tavern as well as to the manor house. Had they celebrated a victory? When they came in, the women hastily removed their sewing things from the table, making room for the men, quiet now, to eat supper. Had they got their way, they would have bragged enough. Afterward they stood outside for a long time. It was not until they had all gone that Stephen moved to the chair by the fire. "I suppose you want to know what happened," he said to Margretta.

"I think I already know."

"That we failed, yes. But you do not know how badly, how humiliating it was. They didn't hear us out and give reasonable arguments in response. Instead they laughed at us."

"They?"

"Mr. Frost and his assistants. They laughed mostly at our stupidity in thinking we could get any kind of concession. 'A contract is a contract,' Mr. Frost said. 'Don't you know what a contract is?' It was then he laughed at us. He also accused us of being levelers."

Unable to remain silent, Paulus said, "What are levelers?"

"It's a recently coined term, son. They began calling some of the rebels that down Westchester way. Levelers supposedly want to change the whole system. No more ruling classes and poor farmers. Everyone would be on the same level. I don't think that even down there the farmers ever wanted that much. All they want, like us, is justice."

A trip to Poughkeepsie a few days later by another group in search of a lawyer was just as fruitless. No one cared to represent tenants in litigation against a landlord.

A feeling of discouragement prevailed among those who had let themselves hope they could find a peaceable solution, and when they met on New Year's Day, the merriment was subdued. The lifting of their mugs with the traditional *Credencense!* and the bowing and wishes for a happy 1766 were accompanied by a lowering of the eyelids. It was like wishing many more happy birthdays to a person known to be near death.

If 1759 had been for the people of England that wonderful year with bells ringing constantly in celebration of victories, 1766 was for the tenants in the Hudson Valley that terrible year with nothing but despair following defeat.

It was the year when many of the tenants of Van Badenswyck roused themselves to join those on other manors in open conflict. Evictions multiplied and dissidents formed in angry groups. Fear, as during the French and Indian War, became the dominant emotion. Those who remained loyal to the manor lords lived in fear of marauding groups of evicted farmers. Those who sympathized with the rebels lived in fear of sheriffs' posses and troops hired by the proprietors. No one, least of all the women, felt safe, for it was the women who often remained alone at home with their children.

William Prendergast. Afterward Margretta tried to remember when she had first heard that name that later became so intertwined with her own sorrow. Had William Vanzuyder mentioned him, speaking in April of the proclamation issued for his arrest, or was it one of the strangers who came to confer with Stephen? Or was it Stephen himself? At first it was just another name: William Prendergast, a Dutchess County farmer who had become as strong a leader of the disaffected farmers on the Philipse patent to the south as Robert Noble was in the Claverack area to the north. A fiery-tempered Irishman, he advocated the direct group action that appealed to men long held back by fear of reprisals against them as individuals.

The action began in Westchester when evicted farmers, angered at seeing new tenants taking over land they had improved and the crops they had grown, united and seized the land for themselves, refusing to pay rent for it. When three of these men were arrested and held in a New York City jail, the group made plans to march on the city to rescue them. A large contingent of farmers, including many of those who had been meeting with Stephen, decided to join with them, bringing the number of men up over five hundred. The entire group was led by William Prendergast.

With dismay Margretta watched Stephen getting ready to leave. With even more dismay she listened to the questions Paulus asked, saw the glitter in his eyes as he followed Stephen's every move: the filling of the powder horn, the cleaning of the musket . . . the preparation for battle.

"You wanted no part of the French and Indian War," she said. "Why this? It isn't your concern."

"It is indeed my concern. Already there have been evictions right here at Van Badenswyck. You know that."

"But isn't it primitive to go out with guns to straighten out such problems?"

"We have no plans to use the guns. Not unless someone uses guns against us. I agree it is an uncivilized way to settle matters. But what choice do we farmers have when we can find no one to represent us? Anyway, all we plan to do is march to New York City. Show them we mean business."

"It is the end of April. You have crops to plant."

"The land is plowed and harrowed. The planting can be done when I return."

She sent the children out for eggs, then said, "Stephen, what if you should not return? What am I to do?"

He took her hand, squeezed it. "This is only to be a show of strength, not a battle. And remember, we will be welcomed in New York City. All the poor will join with us—you wait and see. We're calling ourselves the Rural Sons of Liberty. If the wealthy can organize Stamp Act riots protesting the actions of the crown, then are we not also entitled to our own demonstrations against injustice?"

"I asked what I was to do if you did not return."

Avoiding her gaze, he said, "Paulus is nearly a man. He can do anything I can do. I have taught him everything."

It was useless to say anything more. Committed to the cause of justice, he was unwilling to admit the campaign might fail.

The next day as he kissed her good-bye he said, "Remember, I'm doing this for you and the family."

Afterward she stretched out on the marriage bed. When he had

built it, he had been doing something for her and for the family he
hoped to have. This desertion, this courting of arrest or even of
death, she could in no way construe as something done for her. Yet
she could do nothing but wait. Wait and work. Work and worry. As
she went through her daily routine, her mind wandered in other di-
rections. What would it be like to be a widow? she wondered, and
she lived out the rest of her life in her imagination, trying first one
role, then another . . . liking none of them.

Word came at the end of a week. Pieter, just back from the village,
brought it. The five hundred had marched as far as Kingsbridge, then
sent a delegation of six to negotiate for the prisoners' release. Having
heard, however, that the marchers planned to burn the city, the governor sent out the militia against them. The Sons of Liberty in the
city would have nothing to do with these lower-class levelers. The
poor were either unconcerned or fearful. The marchers were forced
to retreat.

"Was anyone . . . lost?" Margretta asked.

Pieter was looking at Catherine. "What?"

"Were any of the men killed?"

"I didn't hear about any."

She continued to wait. The following week Stephen returned, exhausted but undefeated.

"The governor has issued a proclamation offering one hundred
pounds for the apprehension of William Prendergast," he told her.
"That shows how much they fear us. I guess it never occurred to
them that we would unite and become so strong."

"Strong? You were defeated."

"No. Dispersed. We weren't there to do battle. When the militia
appeared, we didn't resist. We had no quarrel with them. It is the
landlords we are against."

She had been hoping he would return with a realization of the
futility of his cause. Instead, he was full of eagerness to fight for it.
Success to the south would mean that success could also be achieved
at Van Badenswyck. He did do the planting with the help of the
boys, but the seedlings were never properly cultivated, the land
promising a better crop of weeds than of grain. Much of the time he
was away from the farm seeing people.

In early June he joined a mob of five hundred that rescued John
Way—a debtor unable to pay his rent—from the Poughkeepsie jail.

This act was followed on June 20 by a proclamation elevating the charges to high treason for William Prendergast and others who led the so-called levelers. Proving how seriously the government, prodded by the landlords, took this rebelliousness, the Twenty-eighth Regiment was sent down from Albany to Poughkeepsie.

Now the spirit of rebellion permeated the air, spread further by rumors. More armed clashes occurred at Rensselaerswyck and at Livingston Manor, where two hundred men marched on the manor. In Albany County one hundred men sent to carry out an eviction met an armed group of sixty. Three farmers were killed and many wounded, including Robert Noble, their longtime leader, who managed to escape.

Margretta helplessly watched Stephen change from a man who had once thought of nothing but his farm, who had later spoken of negotiation and conciliation, who now talked of nothing but the fight for justice.

He left again with the hay still standing, hay that needed to be cut for next winter's food for the animals. This time he did not pretend he was off on a mere demonstration of strength. This time he and the seventeen hundred angry men who headed for Poughkeepsie and the three hundred more who gathered near Prendergast's house to protect him planned, if necessary, to use their muskets and swords. They were ready to fight.

The children were a comfort. They helped her with her work and cheered her with their talk. Thus she got through the days. But at night she lay alone in the marriage bed and thought of what it would be like to bear such aloneness for the rest of her life. She struggled with the idea, gave in to it, gathering strength from resignation, for once resigned to it, she was absolved from worrying about the possibility. She grew stronger. Waiting, she told herself, either destroys people or makes them strong.

He came back. He came back filthy from days of hiding, his left arm bound with linen to cover his wound. Sitting at the table, he told about the fighting with the Twenty-eighth Regiment at Poughkeepsie, as skilled at arms as they were handsome in their bright red white-trimmed uniforms.

"We were no match for them," he said as she washed his wound and laid woolly leaves of lamb's ear over it. "Fighting in the woods, yes, but we lacked the training for face-to-face combat. They even had field pieces." He bowed his head. "They took eight prisoners before we were routed."

"Where did the men go? Where did you go?"

"Some to their homes, those that lived nearby. Some to Prendergast's to help him out. Some into hiding. I had to hide in a cave because of my wound. It bled profusely at first. A friend brought me food and water and the news. None of it good. The day after the rest of our men were routed on Quaker Hill, fifty or so of them came forward with a white flag of truce. They were immediately arrested and imprisoned."

"Oh, Papa," Paulus said. "What a traitorous thing to do, to surrender like that."

Stephen lifted his head tiredly. "We were all brave enough when it was our men against the men the landlords could hire. But it takes more than bravery for a little band of poorly equipped farmers to fight the British army. The more men we gather for our side, the larger the army contingents the landlords manage to have brought in to fight us."

"What about William Prendergast?" Margretta asked.

"He refused to accept defeat. The last I heard of him, he was brandishing a cutlass and swearing he would make light show through anyone who tried to capture him. His Quaker wife was trying to persuade him to surrender."

A knock came on the door. Stephen's already pale face turned the color of wood ashes.

"See who's there," he said to Paulus.

"Hide. Hide in the back room," Margretta said. She took him by the shoulder. "For God's sake, hide."

Stephen remained seated. The pounding began again. "It's a friend," a hoarse voice from the outside said.

Paulus opened the door. A rough-looking man with a matted beard and soiled buckskins came in. After nodding to Margretta and murmuring, "Ma'am," he said to Stephen, "Bad news. They got Prendergast."

"Where is he?"

"They took him to jail in New York along with a few others. Reckon they knew we'd go to Poughkeepsie and let him out if they put him there."

"Will you have some beer? Some bread and cheese?"

"Thank you, ma'am. But I have to be moving on."

To Margretta's relief, Stephen said nothing about going to New York to rescue Prendergast. Instead, for the rest of the month he did what chores he could manage with his wounded arm. By July, when it had healed, he had set to work like a man possessed: cultivating the fields, cutting wood for the winter, pulling stumps. Although rioting continued in Poughkeepsie, where rebels had made a fort of a large house, Stephen elected to remain on the farm. Perhaps, Margretta thought, he had learned the futility of rebellion.

Rioting also continued in Rensselaerswyck, but now the opposition had grown stronger. The Forty-sixth Regiment went to Poughkeepsie and the Nineteenth Infantry to that part of Rensselaerswyck where William Noble still held sway.

As they were speaking of this one evening at supper, Paulus suddenly said, "This would be a good time for us to move. Get away from all this trouble."

Stephen said firmly, "We are not yet defeated. And no matter what happens, I will not leave before finding out how Prendergast's trial comes out."

"You *know* what will happen," Margretta said. "The verdict will be *guilty*, the sentence will be death. How can it be anything else when he is accused of high treason? No stronger charge can be made against anyone."

"Perhaps, but I still like to think that justice will prevail. He's a good man. He had a fine farm and no debts. He went into this only to help others who were being treated unfairly. They're good people, he and Mehitabel, the kind of people who put the good of others before their own."

Paulus said, "Then we can move when the trial is over?"

"I did not say that. We have crops to harvest. You can't just plant things and leave them for someone else. Besides, we'd need to take food with us, enough grain and salted meat to last us until we raised a new crop."

So . . . now the time was stretching to fall. Would any time ever be right? Margretta forced herself to remain silent. Yet the next time Paulus mentioned moving, she said to Stephen, "There is something else we should keep in mind. If your participation in the march on New York and in the fighting in Poughkeepsie becomes known—or even your leadership here—you will be arrested and we will be ejected. We ought to go while we can do so safely and can take our best things with us undamaged."

"Margretta, if they arrested or ejected every man who had participated in this rebellion, they wouldn't have enough tenants left to provide the landlords with any income."

Yet even now on the Philipse patent, former rebels were being driven from their homes, watching, as they moved out, new tenants move in to take over their homes and look with favor on their maturing crops. It was not beyond imagining that revenge might be exacted here on those who had stood up for what they felt was right even though it was outside the borders of Van Badenswyck.

All remained quiet, however, through the stillness of the July heat, the suspension of variety in weather accompanied by a suspension in vagaries of behavior.

Chapter 23

At the end of July the Supreme Court tried the rebels who had surrendered and punished them with prison terms, fines, or hours in the pillory, depending on individual charges.

When on August 6 the more important trial of William Prendergast took place, Margretta, leaving the children with the Vanzuyders, attended it with Stephen, partly because she wanted to see William Prendergast, but more because, if the verdict should be unfavorable, she wanted to urge Stephen to go home with her. A rescue attempt could end only in failure and bloodshed.

Outside the courthouse a large crowd moved restlessly, controlled by a contingent of arrogant British soldiers. A few men spoke with Stephen as they edged through the crowd. Once inside and seated, Stephen whispered to her that George Henry of the Twenty-eighth Regiment, wounded in the fighting in June, had just died following the amputation of his leg.

"Very inopportune," he said.

Margretta had so often heard William Prendergast spoken of in terms of admiration and reverence that she was unprepared for the pale, rather small man who was led into the courtroom shackled at ankles and wrists. A woman clad in a blue-and-white linen sack—slim, brown-haired, serene-faced—rose from one of the seats and took a place beside him. His Quaker wife.

Chief Justice Daniel Horsmanden read the charges, every phrase falling like an ax stroke that cut off another of the poor man's chances for acquittal. The prosecuting attorney enlarged on each charge, then described the defendant's activities from the march to Manhattan to his capture.

Prendergast, who acted as his own attorney—for what lawyer would take his case?—refused to plead guilty. Instead, he responded to each charge as it was summarized:

Inciting men to riot. . . .

Mehitabel, standing next to him, whispered in his ear. After a moment he said, "I took the leadership because of my pity for poor people who were turned out of possession."

"Indeed, your Honor," Mehitabel said, "he is a man of great compassion, not given to violence. He wanted only to help those who had unjustly lost their homes and crops."

The prosecuting attorney said sharply, "I move that this woman be ousted, lest by her very looks she too much influence the jury."

The chief justice took a few moments to think. Finally he said, "Motion denied. You might as well move that the prisoner himself should be covered with a veil lest the distress painted on his countenance should too powerfully excite compassion."

A murmur like a sighing wind went through the court. If even the judge had been aroused to compassion, then surely the jury would be. Yet Margretta saw by their distinctive attire that every one was a man of wealth and position. How could anyone hope for justice with such a jury?

The second charge was read: *Breaking into the Poughkeepsie jail and releasing the prisoner John May. . . .*

Prendergast responded: "The prisoner was in jail for debt, and the debt was for rent. We did not approve of that rent, as he was on land illegally claimed to be part of the Philipse patent."

Murdering a British soldier. . . .

Again husband and wife conferred. Then Prendergast said, "I regret the death of this man. But when a soldier uses weapons against others, he surely knows that weapons may be used against him."

Insurrection. Crimes against the state which amount to high treason. . . .

Insurrection. High treason. These were the most serious of the charges. Though knowing that if adjudged guilty he was likely to lose his life, Prendergast said calmly, "Is it insurrection when the laws are unjust, when they are made for the wealthy rather than the poor?"

Then, turning toward the jury, he lifted his shackled hands and told them in a short but eloquent speech that his motives had been at all times humanitarian.

At last the jury retired. They were gone far too short a time, as if they had reached a verdict even before the trial had begun. The chairman stood, paused until all was quiet in the courtroom. In a steady voice he said, "Guilty. Guilty, but with a recommendation of the King's mercy."

Sentencing was deferred for a few days.

With saddened hearts, they went outside. Mehitabel was mounting her horse.

Stephen went to her. "Do not worry," he said. "If we cannot accept the sentence, we will rescue him."

Her head lifted, her eyes blazed with courage. "Thank you, but I am sure it will not be necessary. I am going to New York to see the governor right now."

"But," said Margretta, "it is seventy miles."

"That makes no difference. I have no time to lose."

People moved aside to open a way for her. Even the British soldiers' faces registered awe and respect.

Riding home with Stephen, Margretta pictured Mehitabel galloping down the King's Highway, counting the stone markers that would tell her how far she was from the city, urging her horse forward, yet praying it would not stumble on the sun-baked ruts made in the spring mud by the oak wheels of the wagons of the poor. And who knew what she might encounter at night? Wild animals? Hostile Indians? Highwaymen bent on robbery or worse? This Quaker's courage diminished all other acts of bravery.

When the day for sentencing came, Margretta remained at home. "Promise me," she said to Stephen, "you won't do anything dangerous if the sentence is unfair. Come right home."

"I promise," he said. "However bad the sentence is, it cannot be carried out immediately. I may stay a short time to talk with some people, but I'll be back, if not late tonight, then sometime tomorrow morning."

"Let me go with you," Paulus said.

"No. You have a job to do here. I'm counting on you as my lieutenant."

Throughout the long day, as Margretta went steadily about her work, she tried to put all thought of the sentencing out of her mind. An impossibility, of course. She thought of Mehitabel. How could Governor Moore resist her beauty, her sincerity, the cleverness of her arguments? Surely he would reduce the sentence to a token punishment.

When just before dawn Stephen's horse came slowly into the yard, even the hoofbeats had a despairing sound. Stephen went directly to the barn with the horse and stayed there for nearly an hour.

Paulus, who had waited up with her, finally looked at her. She nodded. He went out to the barn, returned to say, "He'll be right in. He wants no food."

Stephen came in, wreathed in silence, too full of terrible words to be able to speak. Perhaps, she thought, they had already executed Prendergast. One of the British soldiers might have been willing to do it. Still silent, Stephen sat down in the rocker by the fire.

After a while Margretta moved to his side and said, "Prendergast— what happened?"

"He was sentenced."

"And what was the sentence?"

He motioned toward Paulus. "Not now. Not yet."

Paulus said, "Papa, I want to know. I'm old enough."

"No one is old enough."

"I am old enough. I want to hear."

"Very well." Stephen withdrew a slip of paper from his pocket. "I wrote it down so I could get every word right." He read, his voice toneless, yet now and then breaking off as if searching for the breath to go on:

"'That the prisoner be led back to the place whence he came and from thence shall be drawn on a hurdle to the place for execution, and then shall be hanged by the neck, and then shall be cut down alive, and his entrails and privy members shall be cut from his body and shall be burned in his sight, and his head shall be cut off, and his body shall be divided into four parts, and shall be disposed of at the King's pleasure.'"

Paulus stumbled to the door, his body shaking with a spasm of nausea. He went outside. When Margretta started to follow him, Stephen called her back. "Leave him alone. He insisted on hearing. Let him learn about some of the evils in this world. It is part of becoming a man."

"But he is only fourteen."

"That may be, but he is manly in many ways. Let him fight through this without having his mother hold his hand."

"I'll hold yours, then." Kneeling by the rocker, she took Stephen's hand and held it against her cheek. "I thought the jury had recommended mercy. If that is mercy, what can cruelty be?"

Stephen shook his head.

"Did he say anything?"

"Prendergast? Yes. He said: 'I just want to say that if opposition to the government is deemed rebellion, then no member of this court is entitled to sit upon this trial.' You should have seen the justices then. Some I know are Sons of Liberty. Maybe all of them. I know for sure John Morin Scott stirred up a number of riots against the Stamp Act."

Paulus came back in, a sour smell clinging to him.

"What about his wife?" Margretta asked. "Didn't she ride to New York to get the verdict reversed?"

For a moment Stephen's eyes brightened. "That woman. She rode the 140 miles down and back in three days. She recounted all the details to the governor and begged for his mercy. He took it . . . 'under advisement,' I believe the term is. In other words, he'll think about it. What a woman she is."

His admiration for Mehitabel aroused an unease in Margretta. What did she herself do but manage a household? Yet how could anyone envy a woman who lived under the shadow of such horror? Bad enough to have your husband cleanly and quickly executed, but how terrible to think of the body of the man you love so cruelly mutilated. It was jealousy, not of Mehitabel but of the admiration she had seen in Stephen's eyes. How long had it been since they had brightened that much looking at her?

During the rest of August, heat shimmered in waves over the fields. The Hudson Valley was like a steaming caldron. Tempers flared. The children quarreled incessantly. Every household task became monumental. Stephen and the boys came in from the fields red-faced, sweating, itchy, and irritable from insect bites. Except for a few brief but violent thunderstorms that brought little relief, it never rained. Stephen sometimes went off to meetings, returning tight-lipped and concerned. Margretta felt too listless to inquire.

The storms accented the turmoil everywhere in the area. Clearly the landlords were disturbed at the interruptions in their normally satisfactory way of life. But if they were troubled and discommoded by the seeking for justice that had culminated in the rebellion and riots of 1766, they were at least powerful enough to demand well trained and well equipped troops to carry out their orders.

One contingent of these succeeded in dispossessing all tenants unfriendly to the Van Rensselaers and in capturing Robert Noble and taking him to jail. Others invaded the homes of rebels on the Philipse patent, burning and looting.

At Van Badenswyck the rebellion proceeded for the most part underground, its main object now to save William Prendergast and to help beleaguered tenants to the south.

And in Poughkeepsie, where Prendergast awaited his hideous death, the sheriff advertised for someone to help with the execution, but despite the offer of a good reward and the promise that the helper would be disguised and secured from insults, no one came forward.

The month ended. With September and the time for execution at hand, Stephen prepared for battle. His powder horn and bullets in a leather sack and his musket over his shoulder, he marched off in the name of justice.

In two days he was back. "The governor granted a reprieve. He is going to leave it to the King's pleasure."

"And will Prendergast be out on bail now?"

"No. He is considered too dangerous. We stormed the jail yesterday, Margretta. Fifty of us. We've been planning it for a long time."

Margretta drew in her breath. Fifty lives risked to save one. But Paulus could not contain his excitement. Like a child he clapped his hands together. "Oh, Papa—then you freed him? How wonderful."

"No, son. He refused to leave. If he did, he said, his property would be seized, his family would be left with no means of livelihood, and he would be a hunted man forever. He said he would rather await the King's decision."

"That seems wise," Margretta said.

"Wise only if the King decides in his favor."

Her heartbeat was heavy, slow. "If he doesn't?"

"Then we will go again."

"But they will be prepared for you."

"We will be even better prepared. More of us and better armed."

He looked at her, his gaze unwavering. "If we lose our lives, it will have been for a good cause."

"How brave you are," Paulus said.

How foolhardy you are, Margretta thought. To die for a good cause—oh, such glowing, heroic words. But what about the families left behind? The grief, the want, the danger. More than one wife had been driven with her children from her home after her husband had been carried off to jail. Could she expect any better treatment for her family? The miracle was that Stephen, whose leadership in Van Badenswyck must surely be suspected, had not yet been arrested or served with eviction papers.

If only he would decide to leave before his role became completely clear—leave while they could go safely with their possessions. Probably he would say she cared too much about things, not realizing how much of her grandmother was in the old *kas*, how much of her father was in her books, and how much of Stephen himself and of their whole marriage was in the bed and the other furniture he had made. Men did not understand how such possessions became an almost living part of a woman.

Paulus said the words she dared not say. "You told us, Papa, that we might leave here in the fall."

"I said we would talk about it."

"Then can we talk about it now, begin planning?"

"Talk about it? What is there to say? A man's life is at stake—one of the finest, bravest men I've known. What kind of man would I be if I deserted and left him to his fate, left the others who trust me to fight alone? No. I must wait to see what the King's pleasure is. It could take just a few weeks or several months. Who is to say he will decide immediately?"

Paulus' eyes gleamed. "If you attempt another rescue, may I go with you?"

"No!" The word exploded like a shot. It was a few seconds before Margretta realized the sound had erupted from her own throat.

Stephen looked at her as if he read all her subversive thoughts in that one word, then turned to Paulus.

"No, son. You are old enough, but it is for that reason that I leave you here to protect the family. I know it does not seem very exciting. But it is important work."

Margretta sighed. He was so sincere, so sure of the rightness of what he was doing. Was it possible that it was she who was unreasonable and he completely right?

Later that night she moved close to him in bed. Out of her need for reassurance, she said, "It has been a long time, my husband, since you have made love to me."

His sigh was like a mournful winter wind. "Make love? How can I think of pleasuring my body when I think of . . . ?" A moment passed before he spoke again. "That sentence. To have parts of your body cut off and destroyed before your eyes."

"I thought being close to me might help you forget."

"I would think of it all the more. Think of him. He did no wrong, Margretta. He got involved only to help those less fortunate than himself. If he were evil or cruel, then perhaps he might deserve such a sentence."

"*No one* deserves such a sentence. It is evil. Only an evil person could carry it out. If their aim is to rid the countryside of such a person, why not just hang him?"

"Because they want to strike the heart of every farmer with horror and fear. They want to make them so craven they will never again dare any kind of protest. They want to crush us." He stopped speaking. The moment stretched out. Then he said, "Have you ever thought of how Mehitabel must feel?"

Anger stirred her. "Have I ever thought of her? When have I thought of much else? And every time I think of her, I put myself in her place, put you in his place. Oh, Stephen, I don't want you to do anything foolhardy. The thought of your receiving such a dreadful sentence, dying so ignobly. . . ."

"And if I were the one imprisoned awaiting such a sentence—what then? Would you want my comrades to free me?"

"Who knows what I would want? Maybe I'd go out begging them to do something. The thought of losing you . . . Oh, Stephen, I cannot bear it. What would I do?"

Turning to face her, he took her hand and brought it to his lips. "You would be brave just as Mehitabel is being brave. You would manage. You would encourage the children to be strong. With their help you could run the farm. As they grew older, it would be easier. And you are beautiful and competent. You would probably remarry soon."

She felt as if he were giving her a marked-out plan for behavior after his death. A chill shook her. Then she felt his arms around her, felt his body coming to life against hers. She tilted her face so his lips met hers.

Life had to go on, she thought. Of all the cruelties imposed on the tenants during these past years—the killings, the taking of prisoners, the ejectments even of women with babies whose husbands had been imprisoned—Prendergast's proposed punishment was the most cruel. Yet life had to go on. Men and women still must live together as husbands and wives, must bring children into the world, must nurture and love them.

Passion blazed between them like a fire of papers and was as quickly consumed, as if they must hurry, as if they both knew their time of happiness together no longer stretched out to an indefinite old age.

Chapter 24

$\mathbf{M}$r. Frost came a few days later, looked over the farm, checked their crop, settled on the manor's portion, and announced a three-pound rise in the rent.

"That's the largest jump in a long time."

"The place is worth more than it was a year ago."

"But I have made no improvements this year."

"I noticed. It even appears that you have let some things go. Your pigpen needs repairing."

"I plan to do it this week."

"You did not extend your planting at all this year?"

"No. I have cleared as much land as I can take care of while my sons are this young."

Mr. Frost's small eyes searched his face. "You are satisfied with this farm? With your contract?"

"With the farm, yes; the contract, no. You may recall that I visited the manor house just before the new year to inquire about possible contract changes."

"I do. I thought you might have changed your mind."

"Not at all."

Later when they compared notes with William, they learned that he had said he was satisfied on both counts. Others had responded the same way.

Stephen said afterward to Margretta, "In a group they talk boldly enough, but alone with Mr. Frost, they lose their courage. I suppose they can't be blamed. The Prendergast verdict has frightened them. It's made them realize how very much power the landlords do have."

"I wish you had lied to Frost too. I didn't like the expression on his face when you said you weren't satisfied with your contract."

"I thought it was quite expressionless."

"Exactly. He carefully kept it so. But he's suspicious about what you've been doing with your time. I'm scared, Stephen. I think we should leave. Right now."

"I will not leave until William Prendergast has been set free . . . one way or another. By then I fear winter will have set in." He went to the fireplace, lighted his pipe, took a long, thoughtful draw on it. At last he said, "We will leave next spring when the weather warms."

So. He had finally set a definite time. But the decision had grown out of defeat rather than victory and hardly called for expressions of joy. Besides, like a horse dragging a stone slab across a field to level it, the decision dragged after it a heavily weighted *if*. *If* Prendergast is freed by the King . . . *if* Prendergast's freedom is denied and I return after the campaign to rescue him . . .

Yet she, like Mehitabel Prendergast, could do nothing now but wait. Men waited too, but as they waited, they plotted; they gathered ammunition; they drilled. Only Prendergast waited helpless as a woman, but even he, it was said, managed to send out messages of encouragement and hope to his followers.

Then it happened. In the midst of October's blaze of color, Mr. Frost returned with the sheriff. Their faces sober, they stood stiffly near the door, refusing to sit at the table. Margretta retired to her rocker to work on some lace.

"All right," Mr. Frost said to the sheriff.

The sheriff, who had known him for years, asked Stephen his name, then said, "The court at Van Badenswyck has empowered me to serve you with eviction papers. You are to vacate these premises as of December 30, 1766."

"For what reason?"

With the cold smile of an executioner, Frost said, "You are not satisfied with your contract. We have prospective tenants who understand the terms and find them fair. Dissatisfied tenants are often troublemakers." He narrowed his small eyes. "Furthermore, we have learned you gave assistance to a couple from Sharon. Involvement with such interlopers can only lead to the kind of trouble they are having with rabble-rousers on the other manors."

Margretta stood up so quickly that her pillow fell to the floor and the bobbins rolled in every direction. "It is unfair. Monstrously unfair. You know how difficult travel is in midwinter. What if there is a blizzard?"

Mr. Frost shrugged. "If God chooses to send some snowflakes your way, then certainly we cannot interfere with His will. It is of little concern to us. We feel we are being extremely lenient in allowing you as much time as we are."

The sheriff, who had spoken no words beyond the reading of the notice, gave them an embarrassed look, then followed Mr. Frost out.

Margretta bent down and one by one rolled the threads back onto each bobbin, put her work away. "We must leave right away," she said. "You realize that, don't you?"

"Not until I have heard the King's decision. I cannot desert this man who has sacrificed so much."

"You have always said it would be impossible to travel in the winter."

"We'll find a way. Take the wheels off the wagon, put runners on. We'll find people who will let us sleep in their barns. At least we have food. Perhaps food and household items enough to barter for shelter if need be."

She said no more. The determination on his square-jawed face silenced her even more than his words.

Autumn's blaze died to a sere brown. November's bare trees twisted toward the sky. Grass shriveled. One gray day followed another. And with each new day's dawning, Margretta's heart grew heavier. What she had longed for would soon come true, but it would not be a happy leaving, this forced exit in midwinter, a winter that the almanac had prophesied would be bitter and snowy. Sometimes she found herself standing by the hearth and running her fingers over the stones, memorizing the roughness of the texture, fixing in her mind the reality of what life was and had been in this house. The eviction enhanced what they had here. More and more, instead of looking forward with hope, she caught herself looking backward, reliving the good moments, the sweetness of the early days of their marriage, the joy in their children.

Stephen, as if no threat had been made, no deadline given, moved through the fall in his usual routine: storing grain, butchering animals, splitting wood, placing hay against the foundation of the house. Nor had he yet seen about the runners to convert the wagon to a sleigh. It was as if, hating to believe it, he had persuaded himself that life could not, would not change.

Sometimes he left the house without saying where he was going. Sometimes men rode into the yard and went out to the barn with him to talk.

The cold had come early in November. A wintry wind propelled them into an even colder December.

"We should be making preparations to leave," she said.

"After the message comes. It should not be long now."

"What if the river freezes and snow falls on top of it so no sloop of even a messenger on skates can get here before the end of the year? You know how slow a journey can be on the King's Highway in winter. It's often impassable."

"The message will come in time. It has to."

"But what if it does not?"

"It will come. Very likely he will be pardoned. If not, he will be rescued. Then I can leave with a clear conscience. I cannot desert my men now."

My men. Fear crowded against her heart, for it was on the leaders that the landlords exacted the most vengeance.

The next day she announced she was going to visit Judith. "It may be my last chance," she told Stephen. "I may even stay overnight."

Always a little awed by her close friendship with the dominie's wife, he offered no objections. "It will do you good to get away. You need to forget about all those imaginary dangers that fill your thoughts," he said.

Shooing everyone out of the house, she washed herself carefully and dressed in a brown wool gown she used for Sunday entertaining and calling. Stephen saddled one of the horses and brought it to the door for her. Protected by a warm riding skirt and a hooded cape, she rode off. Although the air was sharply cold, no snow had yet fallen. The horse stepped smartly over the already frozen ground.

She had been praying for snow, so much that it would prevent a march to Poughkeepsie and the almost certain death that would follow, for undoubtedly the authorities would have extra British soldiers—perhaps even another regiment—on hand, fully equipped and moved by none of the sympathy harbored by the local sheriffs and jailers. She prayed for enough snow to prevent the march to Pough-keepsie but not enough to prevent their travel northward.

As she rode, other worries passed through her mind. What about their other animals? Could they follow through the snow? Should they sell them? But if they kept the cow, they would at least have milk on their journey. They would, that is, if they were able to take along enough hay and grain for her as well as for the horses and oxen. All the way to the village, she worried, considered, planned.

Months had passed since she had last visited Judith. Was that why the atmosphere seemed so strained?

"How is everything here?" Margretta asked when they were seated by the fire with hot cups of tea.

"Not good. We feel almost in a state of siege. We never know when some of those hotheaded levelers will march in and start burning and pillaging. Or worse."

Hotheaded levelers? The muscles of her back tightened. "I'm sure they have no such intentions."

"Of course they do. They don't want to work. They want everything given to them—land, homes, rights to use the mills and cut the wood, rights to ship their produce from the Van Baden docks, all without paying."

"Judith, you've heard only one side of the story. It's the people on the farms who are fearful of being burned out. Some of them have already experienced it."

"Only those, I'm sure, who broke their oaths of fealty. Doesn't an oath mean anything anymore?"

"Many had no idea what they were promising. And you must be aware that some of the contracts are couched in legal terms that are incomprehensible even to people of some education." She hesitated, gathering courage. "I did not come to argue with you, Judith. I have never felt anything but fondness for you. In fact, I consider you my one real friend in Van Badenswyck." After another pause she added, "I thought perhaps you were fond of me, too."

Judith's face softened. "I am. You know that. You did so much for my children."

"They were good children—all of them." She stopped, seeing a shadow pass over Judith's face, knowing they were both thinking of

Frederic. After a moment she put her cup down as if she needed her hands free to support her next words. "I came here, Judith, to ask a favor of you."

"Well, of course. Anything I can do. What is it you want—some kind of herbal? Not pregnant, I hope."

"No, no. I just wish a simple herbal could solve my problem. But it's much more serious. We are threatened with eviction. We must be out by the end of the year."

"You want me to lend you money for rent?"

"Thank you, but no. It is not for nonpayment of rent. They say that since Stephen is dissatisfied with his contract, he is a likely troublemaker."

"But that hardly has anything to do with me."

"I thought you might persuade the dominie to intercede for us with Mr. Frost. We do not want much—just to be allowed to stay until spring. And we will gladly pay a fair rent for the extra time."

As she spoke, she saw the expression change and harden on Judith's face. Judith crossed the room and moved some of the books on the shelf over the table as if needing time to compose herself. Or to compose a statement.

At last, turning, her face cleared now of emotion, Judith said, "You must understand something, Margretta. As my children's teacher and as my companion and confidante, you have always been much loved. As Stephen Warner's wife, however—as the wife of one of the rabble-rousers who've been setting criminals free from jail and rambling the countryside terrorizing people with clubs and swords and torches—you are hardly my friend. You are, in fact, one of the enemy."

"Those are harsh words."

"These are harsh times. Tell me, do you approve of what your husband is doing?"

"My husband does not threaten or terrorize people. Never. He has helped a few men and women, sick or with new babies, who have been evicted. I cannot say I disapprove of that." She reached out beseechingly, then, seeing how her hands were trembling, drew them back. "If you could say a few words to the dominie and he in turn could speak to Mr. Frost—"

Judith shook her head quickly, emphatically. "That would be quite impossible. I could never go to the dominie with any such thing about you. Already he . . ."

"Disapproves of our friendship?"

"To be honest, yes. He was not happy when you married Stephen, but he accepted that. Once it was rumored that Stephen was involved with those levelers, he turned against him completely."

Margretta folded her hands loosely, with resignation. Judith had been her last hope. No, she had one other, but she preferred to resort to that only if no other choice existed. She did know some relief in that Judith had said nothing about William Prendergast. Perhaps Stephen's support for him was as yet unknown.

"Judith, I hardly know what to do. I want to leave right away. Stephen says it may be late December before he can be ready. I fear travel will be difficult then, but I cannot get him to change his mind. I even fear he may be thinking of resisting eviction. I don't know . . . I really don't know what to do."

"Leave him. If he wants to court death by stirring people up and making trouble, endangering you and the children in the process, then leave him to his craziness."

"Leave him? I have nowhere to go."

"Then come here."

"I would be welcome?"

"Alone. Alone or with your children you would be welcome. Considering the circumstances, a divorce might be arranged. You still are a woman of beauty, Margretta. You could live a normal life with the right sort of man, one who would not put you in such a dangerous position."

They spent another hour then in calmer talk of children and church and events in the village before Margretta went home to more days of waiting.

The days passed. No good news. No bad news. Then on the morning of December 11 an exhausted-looking man galloped into the yard. Stephen went outside and talked with him for no more than two minutes before the man left and Stephen came back in, his face tense.

"Was he from the sheriff's office?" Margretta asked.

"No. From Poughkeepsie. He's spreading the word. One of our men sailed up from New York with someone who had just got off a ship from London. The word is that the King's decision on Prendergast will be read in court tomorrow."

He took his musket down from the side of the rafter and got out his bag of shot.

"Stephen, you're not going there tomorrow?"

"Of course. We cannot allow them to torture and murder this man."

"Don't you suppose they'll be prepared for a rescue? God knows how many new regiments they'll have there."

"They haven't had time. They didn't know any more than we did when the message would come."

"But half of your men are gone."

"The cowards have gone. There will be none there tomorrow but brave men who will fight to the death."

The moon came up that night with a halo around it.

"Ice crystals," Stephen said. "It will snow soon."

Margretta was too concerned to respond. She could see them, the little ragtag army of rebels in moccasins and knitted hats with no equipment but their often ancient muskets, clubs, and knives—these pitted against the highly trained and fully equipped British soldiers. She felt pity for William Prendergast and his wife and family, and wanted him to be saved, but not at the expense of other men's lives. Not her own husband's. Sometimes you had to harden your heart and weigh the cost of one life against many. One life. So easy to dispense with when that life was not closely connected with yours.

That night Stephen made love to her: slowly, tenderly. But the ardor that had once aroused a response in her was missing, as if he were saving all his fire for the more important activity of the day to come.

Afterward, he slept poorly. She could tell, since she too was wakeful, lying quietly, trying to ignore his tossing. If it snowed tomorrow, she thought, and fighting occurred, it would be difficult for anyone to escape. Even if they succeeded in freeing Prendergast, where could they take him that their footsteps would not be traced?

She lay awake until the black of the windows turned gray. At the first sign of light, she got up, uncovered the embers, and put wood on the fire. The cold penetrated her clothing, but by moving quickly as she got breakfast, she maintained a semblance of comfort. Soon the smell of cooking sausages filled the air with their pungence, along with the milder smell of the boiling cornmeal.

Hearing her, Stephen too got up. Taking off his nightcap, he splashed his face with water from a basin she had brought in. At this moment, his face rosy from the cold water, his straw-colored hair still tousled from sleep, he looked curiously childish. She wanted to protect him, to tease him out of his foolishness, to say, "All right, now, forget those games you planned for today. Let's get on with living. Living, not dying." But she said nothing, knowing her speech would only antagonize, wanting to part on this day as lovingly as possible.

He dressed and ate quickly, went over his gear again. Outside, dawn introduced a gray day, the sky low and heavy.

The children appeared before he left, Paulus still hurt about being left behind, and Stephen said to him, "Remember, Paulus, you're the man of the house while I'm away. That means you see to it that the chores are done. With the help of your brother and sister, of course. You are to get the water and the wood your mother needs. It's no small thing I'm asking of you—to take over what I've always done."

Paulus looked somewhat mollified.

"It looks like snow," Catherine said as she pulled back the window curtain. "You picked a poor day, Papa."

"I did not pick it, but I am committed to it." He kissed the children, held Margretta and kissed her last of all. "Remember," he said, "I love you."

She stood still, frozen with unexpressed emotion, her arms limp at her sides. If she moved to hold him, she was sure she would cling so tenaciously he would have to remove her by force.

"I must hurry now. We're to meet at the crossroads south of the village."

He left. The sound of his horse's hooves on the frozen ground rang out in knells that echoed back in diminishing waves until they could be heard no more.

Chapter 25

The sky remained foreboding all morning and into the afternoon, threatening at every moment to drop its burden of snow. Margretta made samp porridge, adding salt pork, potatoes, and turnips to the beaten and boiled Indian corn and putting it in a kettle on a short trammel high over the fire, where it could simmer for hours, or days, always ready to provide a hearty meal for Stephen on his return. Soon after dinner she heard the sound of a trotting horse. Stephen? Or was it two horses she heard?

Opening the door, she saw the two horses. And two men: Mr. Frost and the sheriff. Reluctantly she let them in.

Mr. Frost said, "Where is your husband?"

"He is not here."

"Where is he?"

"I do not believe I am required to answer that."

Mr. Frost looked at the sheriff. "No," the sheriff said. "She is not required."

"When will he be back?"

"Perhaps tonight. Perhaps not for two or three days."

Mr. Frost's lips curved into the kind of smile that is the special property of those in power. "Then we can be fairly sure where he is." He turned to the sheriff. "Serve her with the papers. It concerns her as much as him."

"I'm not sure that's legal, but I'll tell you what's in them, ma'am. It's a notice of eviction."

"We've already received that."

"I know. This is a new one. You and your family are to be out of this house by noon tomorrow."

"But why has it been changed?"

"Because," Mr. Frost said, "we have just received intelligence regarding your husband. It confirms our suspicions about his involvement with those levelers to the south. Worse still, he's been turning Van Baden tenants against authority. He is to be arrested, his family evicted."

Paulus stepped forward, manly in demeanor, childish in voice. "How can we leave without my father to help us?"

Ignoring him, Mr. Frost said, "You will leave tomorrow of your own free will or you will be forcibly ejected."

Of your own free will!

"Thank you for informing us," Margretta said. "Now, if you will please leave . . ."

As soon as they had gone, Margretta went directly to the *kas*, unfolded the red wool dress she had made for holiday calls, and put it on. She unbraided her hair and combed it in the old way, winding curls around her fingers. She touched her fingertips to a bottle of scent, long unused. And from a secret drawer she took two silver coins.

"Where are you going?" Catherine asked. "You look as though you're going to a party."

"I'm going to the village."

"But you just went to the dominie's."

"I know, but I need to go again. Paulus, you take care of the chores. Jonas you help him. And, Catherine, you feed them some of the samp porridge if I am not back tonight."

Catherine nodded. Margretta left. They were good children, all of them capable. As she rode, she planned what she would do when she saw Nicolaus, how she would act as she asked her favor. Two favors, actually: freedom for Stephen and the deferment of their eviction until warm weather.

She tried to avoid thinking beyond that. Perhaps it would not be necessary to be seductive. Perhaps he felt he owed her a favor and would willingly grant it. But if not . . .

It was midafternoon when she rode to the main entrance of the manor house, tethered her horse, and knocked on the door.

Jupiter answered the knock, an older Jupiter who smiled less, and—a bad sign—wore no fancy livery.

"I'd like to see Lord Van Baden."

"I'm sorry, ma'am. He's not here."

"When do you expect him?"

He shrugged. "We've been expecting him for several days. He's coming up on a sloop, I think."

So braced had she been for an encounter with Nicolaus that she felt as let down as if a table of food had been magically moved away just as she pulled up a chair. After a moment she collected her thoughts and said, "Then may I see Lady Van Baden?" They, too, could reach an understanding in a different way. She was willing to promise anything now, even to saying she would bring Paulus in for a visit and a talk about possible work in the manor office.

"I'm sorry, ma'am. She also is away. She'll be in the city with Alida until there is no more fear that those violent farmers will break in and kill her."

"They would not do that."

"She fears they will. We all fear it."

"Are you afraid of me?"

"No." For the first time, he smiled.

"Then let me in, please, and bring me some writing materials. I must leave a note for Lord Van Baden."

He led her to the parlor where she had sat that night with Nicolaus, uneasy and afraid, but less so than now.

As soon as Jupiter had brought paper and pen, she sat down at the table. The words came slowly, for her message must be prepared with a certain ambiguity in case it fell into the hands of the wrong person.

> My dear Lord Van Baden,
>   You will perhaps remember me—Margretta Warner.
> We have spoken together on several occasions. At this
> time my family is very troubled. Because of rumors
> about my husband, he is now being sought for arrest.
> Worse still, we are threatened with immediate eviction.
> I am alone with my children. My husband is away. I
> do not see how we can move without his help.
>   This decision may have been yours. I do, however,
> beg of you to reconsider or to ask your manager to

reconsider. I do not ask to stay indefinitely, merely until spring or until my husband returns. It would be a great hardship to leave tomorrow.

You may remember our meeting in this house in September of 1751. I most humbly beg your kindness in the matter for the sake of my children—Paulus who will be fifteen next May, and Jonas and Catherine, his younger brother and sister.

Your humble servant,
Margretta Warner

She hated the closing. She was not humble, never would be, yet she felt she must write the words, even write the word "beg" twice. "For the sake of my children." Let him read that. Let him remember and count.

Beyond this, she had no more ideas. If Stephen returned tonight undetected, perhaps they could start out immediately. Even if he returned early in the morning, they might be able to do so.

Jupiter returned. She gave him the folded letter. "Would you see that Lord Van Baden gets this as soon as he returns?" She took the silver coins from her pocket and handed them to him. "You will not forget? It is *very* important."

"I will not forget. The minute he returns."

She did no more planning on her way home. The last half-hour of her journey was made in darkness. Margretta let the reins lie loosely on the mare's back and let her find the way and make the decisions.

Paulus came out of the barn. "I was beginning to worry."

"I'm all right."

"Did you go to ask the dominie for help?"

"I went to ask for help, Paulus, but was unable to see anyone who could help me." She handed him the reins, and, leaving him to unsaddle the horse, went inside.

Food was on the table. "We were waiting for you," Catherine said. She too looked concerned.

"You go ahead. I'll have a little bread and cheese while I'm working. I have much to do."

She stayed up all night arranging linens, putting her valuable pieces in the *kas*, waiting tensely for Stephen's return. As she worked, she thought of the letter she had written. Had it been a wise move?

At the time, she had been sure of herself, yet as the hours of darkness crept by, she grew less sure. What if Jupiter forgot to give it to Nicolaus? What if Nicolaus decided to stay longer in Manhattan? Worst of all, what if he returned and read the letter but was so angered by the problems the rebels had created that he threw it aside?

At daylight she opened the door and saw that a light snow had begun. Please, please, she prayed, let him be on his way home. Yet the morning was half over before she heard the sound of a galloping horse.

Joyfully she went to the door, then saw not one but seven horsemen trotting in, forming a semicircle in front of the house against a background of falling snow. Only two faces were familiar, those of Mr. Frost and of the sheriff. Five of the men were holding muskets. One of them held a lighted torch that flared sickly under the leaden sky. Hastily Margretta threw a cloak over her shoulders. "Stay inside," she said to the children. "Let me talk to them."

"But, Mama—"

Closing the door on Paulus' words, she went down the steps and out into the semicircle. Strange how you can smile, force a light comment out of a throat tightened by terror. "Not the best day for riding, is it, gentlemen?"

The sheriff nodded an acknowledgment of her greeting, then said, "Mrs. Warner, you have been properly served with papers. You are to be out of this house by noon. You are to take nothing with you but the clothing you are wearing."

Oh, Stephen, Stephen, where are you?

"It is impossible. We cannot leave before tomorrow."

"We are here to see that this eviction order is carried out, ma'am. If you refuse to leave, we set fire first to the barn, then to the house."

Never had she felt so weak and defenseless, yet she lifted her chin and said as if questioning a servant—hoping her show of confidence would diminish theirs—"Who gave these orders? Was it Lord Van Baden?"

Mr. Frost said, "I am empowered to act for him. I gave the order."

"But you will find, if you talk with him, that he has reason to countermand it. Surely he has given you this message."

Frost appeared pleased to be able to say, "His sloop docked just before I left. We had a few words there before I joined this group. He had no messages for me about any of the tenants on the manor."

Behind her she heard the door open. "But I left a letter for him, made a request he could not . . ." She broke off. The men were raising their muskets. Surely they did not intend to . . . "Wait!" she called out. "Wait! Stop! We will not resist."

Her words were shattered into unintelligible fragments as three shots rang out. A man in the center of the posse fell from his horse, fell to the other side. Gunsmoke, acrid in her nostrils, merged with the falling snow.

She turned. Paulus was standing at the foot of the steps, the musket he held still smoking, his face distorted by a smile like the hollow grin on an ancient skull. He stood like that for a few seconds, then slowly, as if let down by strings, slumped to the ground.

She thought he had been felled by the recoil from the musket, persuaded herself he had, or that he had fainted, for, manly as he thought he was, he was still a boy who could be frightened—all this she told herself as she walked the few steps to where he lay. As she bent over him, she heard more galloping. Dear God, how large an army did they need to conquer one defenseless woman and three children?

Putting her arms under his shoulders, she tried to lift him. He was too heavy. Some of the men had alighted. She looked up. "Here, help me. He's only a boy, only a child. You've frightened him with all your crazy shooting. I think he has fainted."

The sheriff helped her lift the limp body. As they did so, she saw blood crimson against the snow. More blood trickled now from the corner of his mouth, moved unevenly through the down of his cheek.

Her words came out in a terrible whisper. "You have shot him? You have shot this boy?"

"He shot first, ma'am. He got one of our men."

One of the posse came forward. "Hawkins is all right, sir. The shot just grazed his shoulder."

A horse galloped into the dooryard, slid to a stop. Just a single horse, and on its back a man in formal cloak and hat, gold-threaded waistcoat, and red stockings. Nicolaus.

At her side, he said, "I came as quickly as I could, without even changing. Jupiter gave me your message as soon as I entered the house. Frost had already left." Turning then to the men, he said, "What is going on here?"

Margretta answered. "They have shot Paulus."

"How serious is it?"

"I don't know."

"Let's get him inside." To Frost he said, "Leave here immediately. Send a surgeon out to take care of this child. If you cannot find one, ask the dominie's wife to come. She will know what is needed."

He carried Paulus in and laid him on the marriage bed. In silence Jonas and Catherine backed off. Nicolaus picked up one of the limp arms, held his finger on the wrist.

"Bring me a hand mirror," he said to Catherine.

He held it in front of Paulus' face. Margretta watched, saw how clear the glass remained. She put her head down on Paulus' chest, her ear over his heart. Nothing. She knelt down, pressed her face against the coverlet, feeling the cool darkness on her eyelids.

When at last a hand touched her shoulder, she raised her head. "Leave me," she said to Nicolaus.

"I cannot do that. Where is your husband?"

"In Poughkeepsie, I think. But I need no one. Just another woman to help. Catherine, Jonas, ride to the Vanzuyders' and tell Sara I will need her help tomorrow, early. Paulus must be laid out properly. Hurry. You can both go on one horse. Stay the night there; I shall sit up with Paulus."

Soon, bundled in heavy clothing, they rode off.

"They know the way?" Nicolaus asked.

"Yes, they can find it in the dark. Even in snow."

Still kneeling by the bed, she took Paulus' hand, held it against her cheek. "Leave me now to my grief."

Bending, he traced the curve of eyebrow and cheek with his finger, then knelt beside her. Again he put his hand on her shoulder. She shrank away.

"You're forgetting," he said. "It is my grief too."

"You gave the orders."

"Not this. Nothing like this. And I came as soon as I could to tell you that you may stay here until spring."

"It is no consolation. Oh, please, please leave me. Let me grieve alone."

She got up, began pacing back and forth. She stopped and automatically put a log on the fire, then commenced pacing again, sometimes wringing her hands, sometimes rubbing her cheeks, moving distractedly about picking up objects and putting them down again.

Nicolaus pulled a stool close to Paulus and sat looking at him. Once she thought she saw a shine of tears on his face. After a while she sat down in the rocker. Suddenly she laughed.

"Margretta, what is it?"

"I was just thinking: the lord giveth and the lord taketh away. The lord of the manor, that is."

"That's cruel. I did not take his life. I would give anything—"

"Oh, what difference does it make now? He's gone. It's as if he had never lived."

But the trouble was that he had lived. Memories marched through her mind, triggering the agitation again, the pacing, the senseless wringing of hands. She could not—how could she?—live without this boy. She could not stand the loss. She could not stand the pain of the loss.

It grew dark. Nicolaus put more wood on the fire, lighted a candle. "Are you hungry?" he asked.

"No. But there is bread and cheese there. Somewhere. And samp porridge. Eat some if you wish."

"No. I wish for only one thing."

"What is that?"

"That the clock could be turned back. Turned back to early this morning."

"Or fifteen years?"

"Yes. That, too."

Once when she stood still by the bed looking down at Paulus, Nicolaus came close and tentatively put his arm around her.

"Stop!" It was a cry.

"My only wish is to comfort you."

"You are of no comfort to me. I told you long ago to leave me. Hours ago."

"I will not leave you alone here."

He turned his head, listening. She listened too, heard the sound of a horse. Stephen? Or news of Stephen? If he had died . . . She was unable to react to the thought beyond realizing that it would mean she would not have to tell him about Paulus. Besides, her capacity for pain had been reached. Another death could not increase it.

Nicolaus went to the door. Margretta sank to the stool by the bed. From there, after the door opened and closed, she heard whispering, then, finally, footsteps behind her. She looked up. It was Judith.

"I brought a saddlebag full of herbals," she said. "Nicolaus tells me it is too late." She felt the boy's forehead, then laid her head on his chest as Margretta had done. She straightened, her eyes welling with tears.

Margretta looked up at her. "There is nothing you can do?"

"I can use the tansy I have brought to make his body sweet. Get me clean linens for the bed, please, and fresh clothing for the boy. But first I want you to drink this. Get me a cup, Nicolaus." She handed the cup to Margretta, watched her drink its bitter contents. "Sit down and let me take care of him. Nicolaus. I need your help, even though you've never done anything like this before. Then I want you to leave."

Margretta got the linens, the clothing, smoothed the shirt briefly with her fingers before she turned away. She sat down, moving her rocker so she could neither see them nor hear their whispers, soft as wind in pine trees. She thought of Paulus' tree and felt her throat swell, but a quietness that must have originated in the drink Judith had given her gradually stole over her. Like an old woman who has lost all other goals in life, she rocked gently back and forth.

Nicolaus was standing in front of her. "I am leaving now. Judith says it is best."

She just stared at him.

He took her hand. "Please believe me, I am sorry. Deeply sorry. And grieved. When I think of what might have been . . ."

Her hand lay limp in his. She could think of nothing to say.

When Nicolaus had gone, Judith said, "Do you want to see him now? He looks so much better."

Margretta got up slowly. He lay now in clean clothing on a fresh coverlet, the smear of blood gone from the corner of his mouth, his face as fresh as if he were awaiting morning.

"I'll sit with him now."

"No," Judith said. "You must—"

"Please. Please don't say I must eat or I must sleep. I can't. I won't. I don't want to."

"All right. Just sit down, then. Drink some more of this."

Obediently she drank. For the way it dissolved pain, for the way it dissolved time. "It must have been so hard for you, Judith. Frederic, I mean."

"Yes. In a way, I almost envy you. At least you have a body to sit with, to grieve over. And one that was laid out with loving hands."

And sweetened with the tansy you could not use on your own son, Margretta thought. For a while she was silent. Then she began to speak of Paulus, of his goodness, his skillfulness, his reliability, his love for growing things, his kindness to everyone. She talked on until she heard her voice trail off into incoherence, felt Judith putting a blanket over her legs.

And so the night passed with periods of drowsing, periods of pacing, periods of talking, periods of staring wordlessly at the face of her firstborn son.

In the morning Sara came. After they had hugged each other, Margretta led her to the bed. Sara looked down at Paulus, looked away, hugged Margretta again. "I cannot believe it."

"Nor can I." And it was true. She really did not believe it. The day, the night, were as unreal, as diffused as a nightmare. It was impossible now even to believe that Nicolaus had been here and had helped to wash and prepare the body of her son for burial.

Sara disengaged herself, said briskly, "Has the cow been milked, the animals fed?"

"No. I forgot. How could I have done such a thing? The poor things."

"I'll take care of them. Where's your milk pail?"

After Sara had gone outside, Judith put on her cloak. "You're in good hands. I'll leave now." From the bag she had brought she took some small cakes. "Eat these when you feel better. Or give them to the children. Alicia remembered your fondness for them. And this green bottle is to calm you down if you feel yourself losing control. Take a teaspoon every two or three hours. And this one is for Stephen. Brandy. It's a medicine, too, but more acceptable to men than decoctions in little bottles."

They were so busy talking, they did not hear the horse. What they did hear were shouts, a huge cry repeated several times: "Hooray for King George! Hooray for Georgie!"

Then Stephen was standing in the doorway, swaying drunkenly.

"Hooray for King George," he said. "He has pardoned my good friend William Prendergast. Hooray for Georgie." He looked at the stillness of their faces, looked at Judith, who had never before been in this house, and soberly said, "What's going on here? Where are my children?"

Chapter 26

Oblivious of the cold, Stephen worked in the back room, sawing, hammering, fitting, measuring—making a coffin for Paulus. All the time he worked, it snowed. He came in when he was called, ate meagerly, meagerly answered questions.

Jupiter rode in on the second day. Without speaking, he handed Margretta an envelope.

"Is an answer required?"

"He did not say so."

"Very well." She thanked him, went inside. Although the envelope—heavy paper marked with the Van Baden coat of arms—was addressed to Mr. and Mrs. Warner, she left it on the table unopened. When Stephen came in, he opened it, looked at it, put it back, and returned to his work.

After he had left, she read it. She had never seen Nicolaus' handwriting before, an even script with heavy down strokes, the kind of writing that might be expected from a man in a position to wield power. It was written in the third person—a shrinking away from involvement.

> Lord Van Baden deeply regrets the death of your son
> and wishes to state that you may remain in your home
> as long as you wish.

When Stephen came in again for supper, he said nothing about the letter. Nor did she. Although she appreciated the offer, she feared

Stephen might seize the opportunity to remain indefinitely. Now more than ever they should be making plans to leave this place that would always remind them of the most tragic event in their lives.

With the help of Jonas, Stephen dug a grave on the rise above the brook. After clearing the snow off, they hacked at the frozen ground with a pick until they broke through, then with shovels dug for hours, dug deeper, perhaps, than they needed to, until the bottom was a neat, flat rectangle. Jonas came in several times to warm himself, but Stephen rarely rested.

No one came from the village for the unannounced burial, but the Hartens and the Vanzuyders rode over and the three men carefully lowered the coffin into the grave. After the dirt had been replaced and smoothed to a mound, the small group stood around it with their hands linked and recited the Twenty-third Psalm and the Lord's Prayer. While their hands were still linked, William said, "He was like a son to me."

"And to me," Sara said. "I watched him grow up."

"We were like brothers," Pieter said.

Catherine lifted the gold of her hair away from the back of her neck. "I'll never forget him."

"He was a fine young man," Jan Harten said.

"And brave," his wife said.

Jonas, with a catch in his voice, said, "I didn't want him to die."

And Margretta, her cheeks numb, said, "God bless you, Paulus. You will always be a part of my life." She squeezed Stephen's hand, waited. He said nothing. At last he turned, the first to walk away, and headed for the barn.

Margretta served hot spiced wine—Sara had brought it—and the guests sipped it and talked, mostly about predictions for even more cold and snow in the months to come. Now and then they glanced toward the door.

"You must forgive him," Margretta said. "He is having a hard time. I know he appreciates your coming. But he cannot yet talk to anyone."

They nodded, got their things together, left. Sara and William and Pieter were the last. William squeezed her hands. "The trouble is, he feels it's his fault. If he hadn't stayed to celebrate Prendergast's freedom, Paulus might . . . well, you understand."

Sara hugged her. "It will be better soon. He'll come out of this, talk again, act like himself."

Margretta nodded. She was not so sure.

January was a bitter month: more snow, freezing temperatures, high winds. A path opened to the barn filled in almost as fast as it had been dug. Each day Stephen methodically did his chores. He got up early and went to the barn, returning a long time later with a pail of milk. Most of the hens had been killed in the fall, the surplus of eggs put down in crocks and covered with waterglass. The remaining hens laid few eggs.

When Stephen was in the house, he spent most of his time staring at the fire. Twice he took down Margretta's Bible and read it, but soon he closed it and put it back, then sat with his head in his hands.

"Is it all right if Catherine and I play backgammon?" Jonas asked him. It was Paulus' set.

"Yes."

At night when they might have lain close together sharing at least a physical warmth, Stephen remained rigidly separate, never offering solace even when Margretta sometimes shivered as the cold and despair seeped into her bones. At mealtimes he sat walled off in a private fortress, neither hearing nor seeing. He ate, but only enough to sustain him.

Noticing the children's hurt puzzlement when they looked at Stephen, Margretta forced herself to smile at them, to show them extra love, and discovered as the days went by that a smile that is at first forced gradually comes unbidden, that love becomes warmer each time it is demonstrated and easier to express each time it elicits a response. Perhaps, she thought also, women who have carried life within them are closer to both life and death, can accept either with more resilience than men.

Acceptance is all, her grandmother used to say. But her grandmother had never been forced to accept the death of a son who stood on the brink of manhood, who with his curiosity and intelligence appeared destined to be a part of all the brightness the future promised.

Late in January the weather cleared, the snow stopped blowing and settled enough so that horses and sleighs could traverse the roads. Margretta rode alone one day to the Vanzuyders' and sat awhile with them, speaking finally of her worry about Stephen. "It has been nearly two months," she said, "and he has never once spoken Paulus' name. He hardly speaks at all, just stares at the fire. It's dreadful."

"I'll think of something," William said. "It's terrible to lose a child, but even more terrible to forget you have other children. And a wife, too. I'll think of something. Don't you worry."

One afternoon the following week William came with three other men, strangers to Margretta. Sara came too and sat quietly near the fire with Margretta. The children lay on the floor, Catherine drawing a picture, Jonas reading. The men sat at the table and talked. Stephen merely listened.

The men wanted, as soon as the snow was gone, to march on the manor house. They were serious this time about looting and about killing all the white residents. "We'll let the slaves go free."

"Free as us," one man said with an ironic laugh.

"We'll all be free then—don't you understand? Our own land. No more rents to pay. What about it, Stephen? Do you like the idea?"

He finally spoke. "No. Besides, you won't succeed."

"We could do it."

"You might succeed in the assault. But it would be followed by a bloodbath all over the countryside."

"Maybe not. I hear the King is leaning toward our side. Maybe he'd refuse to send any more troops."

Stephen shook his head. "Even if he did sympathize, he surely would not countenance anarchy."

One man leaned close to him "Whatever happened, Stephen, it would be a fitting revenge."

Stephen's mouth tightened. At last he said, "I have no heart for revenge, gentlemen. And I have no wish to discuss this any longer."

Thus dismissed, the men got up, said good-bye to the women, shook hands with Stephen, and left. William stayed.

"They're fools," Stephen said. "Don't they realize our backs have been broken? Will they do it without me, do you think?"

"No," William said. "Not without your leadership. We—they— just wanted to do it for you. We thought it would be a fitting memorial to Paulus."

Stephen's face, no longer expressionless, turned a dull red. "There can be *no* fitting memorial to a child who has been murdered in cold blood."

"Perhaps not," Sara said. "And I may be risking our friendship to say this, Stephen, but"—William put his hand on her arm as if to hinder her from speech, but ignoring it, she continued—"but doing *anything* would be more fitting than sitting here brooding day after day, cruelly ignoring the needs of your wife and children."

"I have always provided for my wife and children and I shall continue to do so." He took his coat from the peg by the door. With his hand on the latch, he said, "You must excuse me. I have chores to do."

"You have already done them," Margretta said.

His look was colder than it ever had been, full of the knowledge that she had exposed details of their life to outsiders and asked for help. "I did not finish."

"Let me help you with them," William said.

"Thank you, but I need no help." He lifted the latch, opened the door. His last words, repeated, floated in on a rush of icy air. "I need no help."

"He forgot his lantern," Margretta said. "Shall I—?"

"No. He has the moonlight to guide him."

"But in the barn. . . ?"

"He will not need it. We all know he has no chores to do." William turned to Sara. "You said too much."

"I know it. I was only trying to help. Instead, I made it worse."

"Uncle William," Jonas said. "What is wrong with my father?"

"He is grieving for Paulus."

"I know that. But it's like Paulus was the only one he ever loved."

"No, my boy. If it had been you, his grief would have been the same."

"And he would have acted like Paulus didn't even exist?"

"Very likely."

"Sometimes I wish *I* was the one who was dead." He burst into tears. Margretta reached out to him, but, shaking his head, he stumbled past her and climbed up to the loft.

Catherine said softly, "Even before the accident, Jonas always felt that Papa loved Paulus best."

He did, Margretta thought. When you have waited seven years for a son, he means everything when he finally arrives. No other child can ever quite attain the place of one who has filled such an emptiness.

"With girls it is different," Catherine went on. "It's easier to love them even if they don't have the same qualities the father has."

"You're too wise," Sara said.

"But she's wrong," William said. "I love my girls just as much as my boys."

"She did not say that. She said the love was different."

They talked on about aspects of love. Part of Margretta's mind heard their words, but most of it was occupied with thoughts of Stephen. She pictured him out in the barn, probably huddled next to one of the horses for warmth, warmth he preferred to that from his wife, his children, his friends.

Often she too had an urge to run away, to huddle somewhere wrapped in a mantle of grief. But she resisted and, mostly for the sake of the children, smiled and stayed strong. Yet every day she and Stephen had grown farther apart. This day had been the worst since Paulus' death. Stephen's last statement, "I need no help," was like an ultimatum that plainly said: *Do not try to get close to me.*

When they left, Sara hugged her again. "I'm so sorry. I'm scared I made things worse."

"Don't be sorry. I went to you for help. I thought someone else could reach him better than I."

William patted her shoulder awkwardly. "It will take time. You must be patient with him."

After the crisp clip-clop of their trotting horses had faded and after she and the children had eaten and had warmed their beds and retired for the night, Margretta lay listening for the footsteps that were like the heartbeat of her life. They came at last, but instead of the brisk, light steps of a young man, they were the dragging steps of someone walking hopelessly toward his grave. Stephen was forty-seven years old. He had always been vigorous. He should still be walking with vigor. She wanted desperately to help him, to comfort him, but how could she when he refused to share his feelings with her, refused even to admit he had feelings?

She waited, her body tense, as he banked the fire and removed his clothing. He came quietly to bed, lay flat on his back. Moonlight brightened the room. She could see that his eyes were open. So also had Paulus lain until Nicolaus had gently touched the eyelids and closed them. She was tempted to do that to Stephen now, for in his mimicking of death, he conveyed the message that he was more comfortable with the dead than the living.

She understood. Paulus remained as much in her thoughts as if he still slept in the loft above instead of in his grave above the brook. When she thought of him, she did so with pain, yet she felt the pain as a thrumming pulse of life, the reverberation of a heart that refused to be still.

If only Stephen would turn over and press his body close to hers so that their pulses could mingle, hers giving new life to his. Impulsively she reached out and touched him. For a moment her hand lay on his body, a body so quiet and unresponsive as to be barely alive. Then, very deliberately, he lifted her hand by the wrist and placed it on the bed.

She had never been so rebuffed, so humiliated. Yet, trying to help him even though he had said he needed no help, she rose above her pride and said, "Stephen, you *must* stop grieving. You must begin to live again."

At first she thought he had not heard her. She waited. At last he said, "I am not grieving. I feel nothing at all. Absolutely nothing."

She understood then what he had done. Unable to bear the loss, he had closed his mind to it. That was why he never spoke of Paulus. He had shut off the memory of the boy's life as well as of his death. In the process of shutting off all feeling for Paulus, he had shut off all other feeling.

"Stephen, you must not turn away from me. I love you very much. If we could share what we feel about this tragedy, it would bring us even closer together. We can start over, Stephen. We can find—"

His interrupting voice was as cold and sharp as the crust on the snow outside. "You will not leave me alone, will you?"

"No, I will not. Because I love you."

This time he failed to respond with words; instead, he left their bed, crossed the room, and got into the alcove bed where he had slept before their marriage.

After a few minutes she slipped out of bed and went to his side. "Stephen," she whispered. No response. "Stephen," she whispered again. "Come back to our bed. I will not bother you in any way. But come back to our bed. It is wrong for husband and wife to sleep apart."

He had been facing her. Now he moved, turning his back to her.

With an ache in her throat that nearly made words impossible, she said, "Stephen, if you do not come back to our bed, if you will not answer me or give me any comfort in my own grief, then I can no longer consider us husband and wife."

He remained silent.

The floor was icy under her feet; a chill moved up through her body and settled around her heart.

"Very well," she said. "Then I shall leave in the morning. I'll be taking the children with me."

This, if nothing else, should have elicited a response. When it failed to, she knew complete defeat. Feeling as lost and alone as Jonas must have felt earlier when he had sought refuge in the loft, she crept back to their marriage bed. End-of-a-marriage bed. It had grown cold, and all night long, neither she nor the blankets contributed any warmth to each other. All night she lay wide awake and cold in the bed that had once been a place of warmth and delight.

Chapter 27

February 2, 1767. She thought of the date as she rode away with Jonas on the horse behind her. Catherine had flatly refused to go, but she would care for Stephen and give him a reason for continuing his daily routine. Even in her abandonment, Margretta was concerned about him.

February 2. Candlemas. Her shadow traveled ahead of her, sharp against the snow, a dark creature leading her away from home. How much she, like the Gentiles of old, needed a procession of candles to guide her and assure her she was moving in the right direction.

Jonas clasped her waist more tightly as the horse slipped on the crusted snow, then regained her footing.

"Mama, why are we going to the dominie's?"

"Because Mrs. Hardenbroeck invited us to come sometime. I felt this was a good time to go."

"Papa is . . ."

"Very troubled. But don't worry, Jonas. We will be welcomed at the dominie's. You will like it there."

She was right. Jonas soon found friends among the slave children and spent much time playing with them in their quarters or outdoors sliding or skating with them and with children from the village. He also delighted in all the books in the house.

As for Margretta, unused to having no responsibilities, she at first followed Judith around like a lost child as she ground, mixed, simmered, and strained the herbs she had dried. But after a while she settled down to lace making, sitting near Judith and waiting for her to look up from her reading and begin a conversation. She was hungry for talk, hungry for the warmth of human companionship.

Both Antonia and Gertrude were living in New York now. Judith spoke little of them except to express relief that they had found and married good men who were doing well in business. She did speak of Frederic and in their loss of sons they formed an even stronger bond than before.

Margretta told her about Stephen. "Will he ever get over it, do you think?"

"Who knows? He is very intense. He feels things deeply but is unable to let his feelings out. He might get worse rather than better. There's all the guilt working on him, too."

Margretta rubbed her cheeks. "I probably should not have left him."

"Again I can only say—who knows? Sometimes it's best to let your emotions guide you instead of trying to think things out. If he needs to work things out in silence, then you have given him the opportunity to do so." She turned her book upside down, folded her arms on the table, and looked directly at Margretta. "As for you—how are *you* feeling? You seem to be holding up well. Almost too well. I have yet to see you cry. Or do you do it when you're alone?"

"No. I have simply accepted it. It hurts, but I have accepted it and I manage to hold up. When you have other children, you have to be strong."

Judith frowned. "Are you sleeping well?"

"Sometimes."

"In other words, you're hardly sleeping at all. If I give you something to help, will you take it?"

"I'll try it."

"Take a half-teaspoon every night for a while, then try skipping every other night, then two nights. Get yourself into a sleeping pattern again."

"It's so good to be here with you. You're such a good friend."

Judith regarded her gravely as she glued a paper on a small brown bottle and wrote "For Sleep" on it. "You know better than that. But I'm as good as I can be. I play several roles. Some overlap, some don't."

Margretta was grateful, however, for all Judith did for her, grateful for the shelter and the counsel, grateful to be away from Stephen's coldness and the frustration she had felt in not being able to melt through to an understanding. She took the sleeping medicine one night, didn't like the way she felt in the morning, and put it away in her bag.

February, the shortest month of all, was a long winter in itself. March showed little change; more snow, more cold, more whistling wind.

She began reading some of the dominie's books, even some of Judith's, and found her ability to concentrate gradually improved. Alicia's cooking had begun to fill out a body grown thin. She was even more pleased to see Jonas growing in confidence as he mixed with new friends, both black and white. The dominie showed a special interest in him, talking to him, acting almost fatherly toward him.

When one evening at the supper table Jonas said, "I think I might like to be a dominie when I grow up," Margretta realized how much the relationship meant to him, this interest that was focused on him alone. She could also see how much his response delighted the dominie.

"Perhaps you will, son," he said. "If you still feel that way a few years from now, I'll help you all I can."

Gustavus called one afternoon. He took Margretta's hand but did not kiss it. "I am sorry about your son. Tragic. Very tragic. I understand he was a fine lad."

"Yes, he was. What about your son, Gustavus? What is he doing?"

"He's living in Holland. Running a trading company." He sighed. "I never see him."

Gustavus too took an interest in Jonas, including him in his conversation with the dominie about politics and about possible worsening relations with England as Pitt's power declined. He even invited him to his home to look at his books.

A few days later Margretta said to the dominie, "I've been thinking about trying to find a small house in the village, perhaps starting a school. What do you think?"

He considered his reply, folding his arms, looking thoughtfully upward. "A good idea, I think. It would keep you busy. I don't know how many pupils you would have."

"Would anyone disapprove, do you think?"

"Probably not. Many people mixed with the British during the French and Indian campaign. I think some felt ignorant enough to want something better for their children. I know of no empty houses right near, nor of anyone planning to leave. But you may stay here as long as you wish, Margretta. Judith and I have always been fond of you. You did so much for our children. Especially Frederic." As he looked away and rubbed at his eyes, he struck her as being more human than she had realized. As was Gustavus.

A thaw came near the end of March; then it turned cold again. Winter was reluctant to leave. Her despondency returned. Would she be able to carve out a new life for herself, one without Stephen? Stephen. Strange how rarely she thought of him. Paulus was real to her at almost every waking moment, but Stephen had faded into the background, a misty figure, a onetime husband.

One night she dreamed he was carrying her to the marriage bed, his face aglow with desire. Then he dropped her and vanished. She woke up with tears on her face.

She began to feel restless, closed in. One afternoon in early April she walked to the top of the ridge so she could look down on the frozen expanse of river.

Startled at hearing footsteps behind her, she turned quickly. It was Nicolaus.

"I thought you were in the city for the winter."

"I was. The winter is over."

She kicked at a frozen clod. "Hardly."

"Enough so that I rode up the King's Highway."

"A long ride." But not too long for Mehitabel Prendergast—both ways in three days.

"Very long. However, I stopped along the way and stayed with friends."

They had started walking. Toward the manor house, she suddenly realized. She pulled her cloak close to her throat.

"You're cold," he said. "Come in and have a warm drink."

"Oh, I don't think . . ."

But he was already guiding her up the steps.

"Bring us something warm to drink, Jupiter," Nicolaus said. "Some hot buttered rum would be fine."

He took Margretta's cloak, offered her a chair. Instead she went to the hearth and held out her hands to the fire.

"How long have you been at the dominie's?"

She stood stiffly now, her back to the fire. "About two months."

"Just you?"

"And my son Jonas."

"I remember him. But what about your husband?"

"He has remained at our home."

"Have you left him?"

"I am here; he is there. It must be clear that I have left him."

"Don't be sarcastic, Margretta. It doesn't become you. I'm asking whether you have left him permanently."

"I don't know."

"Do you love him? Did you ever really love him?"

"That, my dear Lord Van Baden, is no concern of yours. Just because you once forced your way into my body does not mean you can now force your way into my thoughts."

He closed his eyes a moment. "We had a child together, Margretta. Isn't that enough to dull the edge of your hatred?"

"When you were responsible for his death?" More hurtful words came pouring out. She was unable to stop them. "Never mind whether or not you fathered him. Just think about this: you were responsible for the death of a child who was guilty of nothing more than of trying to protect a woman who, for the second time in her life, needed help in defending herself against your lordly prerogatives."

"Not true, Margretta. Neither was a case of a lordly prerogative. That night, the night of the storm . . . I had never done anything like that before. Nor since. I don't know what kind of demon possessed me. As for the boy's death—when Frost met me at the wharf, he merely said he was about to take part in an ejectment. I had always trusted his judgment, left most decisions to him."

"A responsible lord of the manor would have known exactly what was going on."

"You're right, Margretta. I should have."

The rum came in then, in silver mugs. "You may leave us alone now, Jupiter," Nicolaus said. And to Margretta after Jupiter had left, "No need to be fearful. I promise not to touch you."

"If you did, you'd turn to stone." More sarcasm. Why could she not control her speech? She felt tense, strange, not at all herself, as if she were young and this the first time she had been alone with a man.

"Margretta, I have known grief too. Two wives. All those lost babies. And a son I spoke with only once."

"You have a daughter now."

"Yes. Alida. She is in New York with my mother. A lovely little girl. I am very proud of her."

"You don't wish she had been a boy?"

"Before she was born I did. I would not exchange her now for half a dozen boys."

She smiled, but without kindness. "Sometimes, Nicolaus, I am almost convinced you have a heart."

"I do. And I wish you could look into it." He lifted his mug. "To spring—if it ever comes."

"You have already said winter is over."

"But between it and spring is a black, cold void."

"I have thought that, too."

"I'm glad we agree on something. Drink some of your rum, Margretta. It helps. Temporarily."

She sipped some. It was strong and she felt its impact almost immediately, felt the nerve-loosening sensation curling and stretching inside her like a warm and lazy cat.

"Margretta, if I got down on my knees and begged your forgiveness, would you accept my apology?"

"Oh, please don't. I wouldn't want you to humble yourself like that." *Even though I have been trying to hurt and humble you from the moment I came in.*

"Then just let me tell you how sorry I am. Sorry for everything. Hardly a day has passed in all those years that I have not thought of that night and regretted what I did. And what happened in December . . ." He shook his head. "Let me tell you one other thing— whether you believe me or not: I love you. Deeply and totally."

She looked at him over the rim of her cup. His gaze held hers with a familiar force, so strong that she had nearly always turned away from it. But this time she kept her eyes steady. At last she put her cup down. "Nicolaus. I said that if you touched me, you would turn to stone."

He lifted one winged brow, put his cup down. Waited.

"You won't," she said.

He came hesitantly toward her.

"Do you love me enough just to hold me?" she said. "Just to let me rest my head on your shoulder and be comforted?"

His arms closed around her. "I love you enough."

Her face against his shoulder, she said, "I have never hated you, Nicolaus. I forgive you for everything. At neither time were you entirely at fault. Through the years, whenever you looked at me and that night by the river when you put your hand on my shoulder and later in the parlor as we waited for the storm to break—all those times I was half-aware of and very conscientiously suppressing all kinds of wild and unfamiliar feelings in myself." She took a deep breath. "Perhaps we should sit down somewhere. Or I should leave."

"Don't go yet. We have more talking to do." He led her to a chair, pulled another close beside it. For a while he just looked at her. Then he said, "I won't ask you again, Margretta, whether you have left your husband permanently or not. But I will say this. If you had left *me* two months ago, I would have come to get you."

"You are not Stephen."

"I wish I were. I wish I had been married to you all these years. I wish I were married to you right now. I wish you would agree to marry me tomorrow."

"I am already married."

"Would you marry me if you could get a divorce?"

"You must know that in this province divorces are practically impossible to get."

"Gustavus could get one for you. He knows people in Albany, in New York, even in England. We could arrange it somehow."

"Nicolaus, the very fact that you could do all that arranging would be reason enough for me to say no. I have lived too long under the shadow of your power. The mighty landlord who asks not only rent but also labor, whose restrictions make it impossible for people to save enough to become landowners themselves. And there's another reason. It isn't just that I am legally married. It's that I take my marriage vows seriously. Right now Stephen is too full of melancholy to be the husband he once was. In time, though, he may come out of his paralysis. When he does, if he does, he will need me. Perhaps then he will begin to think about leaving."

"I said in my letter you were free to stay as long as you wished."

She shook her head, smiled. "Nice of you, Nicolaus. But not the best thing to say to Stephen. He loves it too much here in the Hudson Valley as it is."

"Then it's you who wants to leave?"

"It has always been me. I want to be free. Own my own land."

"Would you stay in Van Badenswyck if I gave you the farm?"

She shook her head. "No. Too many memories there."

"But I want to do *something* for you, somehow assure your happiness." He took both her hands. "It has always been you, Margretta. The first time I saw you standing outside the church, I knew you were going to be important to my life. When I spoke to my mother, however, she reminded me that my marriage to Nelia had been long taken for granted. I was fond of Nelia. I loved her in many ways. She was charming and sweet and gentle. Any man would want to protect her. But as for being the great love of my life—the passion that every man dreams of—neither she nor Anna was. It was always you, Margretta."

The depth and extent of his feeling awed her. "Thank you, Nicolaus. That was a nice tribute. I'll remember it when I'm old and gray. Grayer than I am now."

"I don't see any gray."

"It mixes in with the rest and doesn't show."

"How old are you, Margretta?"

"I'm forty-two."

"Strange. You are even more beautiful than when you were young. Hardship and sorrow have made you even more womanly."

"Thank you again, Nicolaus. I think that perhaps you, too, have changed for the better." Gently now she drew her hands away. "It's time for me to leave."

He went to the door with her. "Will I see you again?"

"I don't know, Nicolaus. I just don't know what will happen in the next few weeks. Perhaps Stephen will come to see me. It may even be that I'll go to see him. I can't make any plans at the moment—for the future or even for tomorrow."

"I won't let this be good-bye," he said. When he smiled he looked just like Paulus. He kissed her on the cheek before opening the door to the April chill. "I'll walk with you to the dominie's."

"It isn't necessary. I know the way."

"It's growing dark."

"Thank you, but I want to be by myself."

As she walked through the trees, she thought of his proposal. It was pleasant to be desired, especially after Stephen's coldness. But she must stop thinking about Stephen's coldness, his complete repudiation of her and of their marriage. She must plan for the future. She thought again of the school. Or perhaps she should return to New York. Catherine would like the city. Jonas would learn to like it. What to do? She was unable to think. She was unable to think rationally because her mind had suddenly filled with a picture of Paulus. Her longing to see him again was so acute that, suddenly weak, she stopped and leaned against a tree, pressed her cheek against its bark, rough and kind as the hand of a workingman.

After a few minutes she took a deep breath, straightened her shoulders, and moved on, once again in complete control.

Acceptance is all.

Chapter 28

Early the next morning, Margretta walked down to the river's edge, and brushing the snow off one of the benches, sat down and stared at the ice-covered expanse.

Her thoughts drifted to Stephen, frozen in guilt and grief. What was he doing now? Milking the cow? Stirring the fire? Eating the breakfast Catherine had prepared? Or was he perhaps still lying in bed ignoring Catherine's call?

His daughter's voice would eventually arouse him to the point where he would get up and pursue his daily duties, but it would not be enough to stir him to life. Merely to move through the hours, to eat and sleep, was not living, any more than her mindless routine here at the dominie's was living. Living meant looking ahead; it meant planning; it meant above all else reaching out to those you loved, sharing your feelings with them.

Oh, Stephen, Stephen, she thought, why do you not come to me and tell me that you love and need me, that you want me to return with you?

Cold had crept inside her muff, numbing her fingers. It was time to go back. As she rose, she heard a cracking sound, like a gunshot. Moving out onto the dock, she felt a vibration beneath her feet. She looked down and saw a narrow crack in the ice, and beneath it the sparkle of moving water—as if a body laid out in death had stirred and pushed at the shroud that covered it. It had never been really dead, just waiting for a lessening of its burden, a lessening that only time could bring.

Oblivious now of the cold, she remained by the river all morning listening to the sounds of awakening life, to ice grinding against ice, to water sighing and moving as air and sunlight once again touched its surface. By noontime the river was no longer a still, flat expanse. Patches of water glimmered here and there amid humps of ice. Again she thought of Stephen. If only he had witnessed this with her, seen this awakening, this throwing off of burden, this need to expose oneself to the elements essential to life. But, oh, what good would it do? You cannot tell someone to stop grieving, she thought; you can't show them how it's done. We all have to reach acceptance in our own ways.

A hand touched her arm. Judith. "I've been worried about you. Come along. You look half-frozen."

"Do you see the river, Judith? It's like a live thing just beginning to stretch and move again."

"Yes, I see. But remember, underneath the ice it has been moving all the time. Just as your heart beats and your breast rises and falls beneath all that winter clothing. Come now, my dear. You have stood here grieving long enough."

"I have not been grieving."

Without answering, Judith took her arm and guided her up the path and over the ridge to the house. Inside, she fixed tea. "Let's sit here by the fire. I'm afraid you've taken a chill from such a long exposure."

"I'll be all right. I've always been healthy. But you mustn't sit here with me. You must have work to do."

Judith gave an amused laugh. "I never did do much housework. Not if I could think of anything more interesting to do. And I usually could. You know that. Today I've been drawing up a plan for my garden. Would you like to see it?"

As Margretta looked and listened, her thoughts wandered to her own plot of ground. She longed for the feel of damp earth in her fingers, the waiting for seeds to poke through the earth. Had Stephen plowed their garden space? She was filled with curiosity and with a desire to see it, to feel and smell the rich promise of its dampness.

"Judith? I think I'll ride out to the farm tomorrow. Stephen should be getting the ground ready for a garden. And poor Catherine. The work may be too much for her, there is so much to do in the spring."

"Will you take Jonas with you?"

"No. This is only a visit. Besides, ever since December, nothing has gone well when he and his father have been together. We will just speak quietly and calmly together. It's time we made some decisions about the future. I cannot continue to impose on you."

"It has not been an imposition. The winter would have been deadly without you. But I think you are right to go for a talk. If you are not going to live together, then you ought to start thinking about your future. You are a handsome woman. If you could get a dispensation to dissolve your marriage, I know more than one widower who would probably propose immediately. Including"—she jerked her elbow in the direction of the manor house—"that one. He's not a bad sort, Margretta. He's had enough sorrow to give him a compassion that he lacked before."

"Marriage to anyone other than Stephen is nothing I want to think about right now."

"Then go to your husband."

The next day she rose at dawn. Her throat was dry and sore and she sneezed at intervals, but otherwise she felt well and full of purpose. As she mounted her horse, she glanced toward the manor house. Within it waited a man eager to reach out to her, to comfort and to love her. But ahead lay all the binding ties of nearly twenty-three years of marriage.

Beneath her the horse moved to a trot as she crossed the road to the village: the landscape was still wintry, the trees bare, the fields a brown stubble patched with snow. But yellow coltsfoot, round and bright as miniature suns, grew along the roadside where the hooves of her horse left imprints in the softening earth.

The sun came up over the Taconics in a rosy softness that differed from the cold fire of winter sunrises. As it lifted higher, she saw across the swamp that the tips of the maples were red with swelling buds and the willows and birches were touched with greeny gold. And from the same swamp came the *konkaree* of a redwing blackbird. She remembered how a different, younger Stephen used to come rushing into the house, sometimes as early as the third week in February, and announce with as much enthusiasm as if the King himself had come on a state visit to Van Badenswyck, "The redwings have arrived." For them, whether or not the arrival was followed by a blizzard, spring always came with the redwings.

As she rode down the lane to the house, she felt as much a

stranger as she had the first time she had come here, and far less sure about her reception. Wisps of smoke came from the chimney. Not much of a fire. Perhaps they were still asleep. She shook her head. Such sloth. Dismounting, she led the horse to the barn and into her familiar stall. The cow lowed and moved restlessly, eager to be milked.

The door was bolted fast. She had to knock several times. Stephen opened it finally, his face puffy with sleep, his straw-colored hair hanging unkempt about his shoulders, his blue eyes registering neither happiness nor irritation.

"So you have come," he said.

The room was disordered, the bed unmade. The air smelled of stale wood smoke and sleep. She shivered. "It's very cold in here. Did I awaken you?"

"No. I was just getting up, had just started to stir up the fire." He went to it now, poked at a smoldering log, put another behind it, moved the kettle over it. "It will soon be warm in here. And we will have hot water."

"Catherine is still sleeping?"

"Yes. Pieter came over last night. They sat in front of the fire playing backgammon until very late. I went to bed, but I could not sleep for her giggling."

Margretta was horrified. "You mean Pieter is calling on her? Surely not as a suitor. She's not yet fourteen."

His shrug was noncommittal. "I suggested that to her. But Catherine does pretty much as she wishes."

What did he expect when he did nothing but sit around with his head in his hands? But she, too, had bowed to Catherine's pronouncement about remaining at the house. She should have insisted that Catherine go with her, should have realized that in some ways she was no longer a child.

While Stephen did his chores, she found buttermilk, dried-out cheese, and some stale bread and placed them on the table . . . after wiping off yesterday's crumbs. Again she shook her head. In the cellar below, the odor of mold and of rotting vegetables hung in the air. She carried some of the rotting potatoes up and threw them across the dooryard, then mixed cornmeal with warm water and put it on two trenchers, pressed down the centers, and filled them with buttermilk.

When he returned, she said, "I cannot find the maple sugar."

"There is none. It is gone."

"Last year's, yes. But where is this year's?"

"There is none."

"Surely the sap ran well. The weather was just right for a while—warm days, cold nights."

"Perhaps it was. I didn't do any sugaring."

"Why not?"

"I don't know." He sat down, put his elbows on the table and rested his head in his hands. "I kept planning to do it. But somehow the days passed. It may be that I can trade with someone. I have extra corn from last year."

"It was very improvident of you to neglect the sugaring. And everything else around here. The mold should have been trimmed from the meat, the rotten vegetables thrown out."

He dropped his hands, stirred the tea she set in front of him. "Yes, you're right."

She sat down across from him. He was even more spiritless than when she had left in February. Uncertain of how to approach him, she looked around and said, "This place needs a good sweeping."

His spoon clattered onto the table. "Is this all you returned for?"

"You mean to clean?"

"I mean to criticize."

It was a moment before she could answer calmly. "I came to see whether you and Catherine were all right. It is clear to me that you are not."

"Then you had not planned to stay?"

"No." Was that relief she saw on his face?

"Catherine and I are fine. We have enough to eat and neither of us objects to a little disorder."

She went over to the bed, pulled up the covers, smoothed the quilt she had made. Memories crowded her mind, moments of happiness and fulfillment. With difficulty she composed her face. She must not let him see how deeply hurt she was that he had failed to welcome her in any way, that he had now let her know she was neither needed nor wanted here—neither in this house, nor in this bed.

But what had she expected? Because she had been moved by the breaking up of the river's ice, was there any reason to suspect Stephen had been moved by something similar? It was as foolish as having a dream about someone and awakening with the certainty the person had shared your experience.

In silence she passed by his unrelenting back, picked up her cloak, and went outside. As she went down the steps, she felt slightly dizzy. Her cheeks felt hot, whether from anger, from disappointment, or from a fever associated with her sore throat, she could not tell.

Since he had neglected to greet her when she arrived, she had decided to forgo saying good-bye. Besides, her control, the acceptance she had so carefully nurtured, was slipping. She felt heady, completely unlike herself—unloved, unwanted, empty, lost. And although she sensed that Stephen felt the same way, she was unable to let him know that she understood.

As she stepped into the dooryard, a phoebe fluttered from under the eaves, nesting material in its beak. Here in the shelter of the house the sun was warm. Oh, go away, spring, she thought. Go away, spring, with all your false promises of new life. Leave us to live out these weeks on our island of winter. When summer came all dusty and brazen with heat, life would be more bearable. But spring was too tremulous, too full of hope and promise.

At the corner of the house the tree they had planted for Paulus still stood guard. Symmetrical, straight-spined, it reached nearly as high now as the chimney. She remembered showing it to Paulus, remembered how he had said wonderingly, "My tree?" and then, with the joy of ownership, "*My* tree."

Moving closer to it, she saw that five slender fingers of new growth had emerged and were standing upright on the tips of the branches.

"My tree has put out candles for me," Paulus used to say. His eagerness had been her joy. How he had loved every manifestation of life. Even last spring when he had begun concealing his feelings in his haste to take on manly qualities, he had shown the same excitement about the arbutus he had found on the hillside and planted under his tree.

Where, exactly, had he planted it? She poked at the needles under the tree with the toe of her shoe. No sign of any flower. It had died out completely. Well, it was appropriate. Stephen had been right when he had said such flowers rarely did well when transplanted. She had turned, given up lifting needles with her toe, when she suddenly saw the unmistakable gray-green wrinkled leaf of an old arbutus plant. She went down on her knees and gently lifted the pine needles from it. In the center of the plant amid new greener leaves, five starlike flowers lifted their delicate waxy heads.

In his faith Paulus had willed this plant to live. But no amount of faith or hope would bring Paulus himself back. Perfume from the flowers drifted toward her. It was almost too much sweetness, too heavenly a fragrance. She could not bear it.

Oh, Paulus, Paulus, Paulus. In her anguish she put her face down to the ground, the pine needles warm against her cheek. *Oh, Paulus, Paulus, Paulus.* The words came out in sobs. She rolled over on her stomach, sobbing into the pine needles, sobbing away the restraints that had made her think she had accepted his death and all the sadness and coldness and rejection that had followed it.

After a long time she heard Stephen's voice.

"Margretta, are you hurt? Did you fall?"

Unable to respond, she felt herself being lifted, carried into the house, and placed on the marriage bed. She lay there breathing heavily, now and then torn by a sob.

Stephen put his hand on her forehead, then her cheek.

Evidently Catherine had come down, for Margretta heard her saying, "What is wrong with her?"

"I cannot tell. She seems feverish. Perhaps she became dizzy and fell. Catherine"—his voice was sharp, commanding—"I want you to take a horse, not the one she rode here, and go to the dominie's. See what kind of herbals Mrs. Hardenbroeck has. Tell her I want something to calm your mother and something for fever."

"It will take a while. Maybe three or four hours."

"Come back as quickly as you can. Your mother is very sick. I have never seen her like this before. And, Catherine . . ."

"Yes, Papa?"

"No stopping at the Vanzuyders' to talk with Pieter."

"Not even for a few minutes?"

"Not even for a few seconds."

"Oh, *Papa.*"

He must have given her a look, for she said nothing more. The door opened and closed. Perhaps he had gone outside to see that the horse was properly saddled. Margretta rolled over on her stomach, buried her face in the pillow. Buried. Once again a spasm of sobs shook her.

"Where do you hurt, Margretta? What can I do?"

She moved her head back and forth. He pulled a stool to the bed-side, removed her shoes. Lifting her body, he undid her heavy riding skirt. She felt his hand on her shoulders, then on her back, as he began to massage all the places where the muscles were bunched painfully together. As she was soothed by his touch, the sobs came further and further apart.

Stephen moved away. When he came back, he placed an icy cloth on her cheeks, her eyes, dipping it in a pail, wringing it out, touch-ing her skin with coolness.

Without asking whether she wanted any, he fixed her a mug of tea. He stood up pillows behind her, handed her the tea. She sipped it slowly.

"Did you fall?"

"Not really."

"You will feel better when you have finished this."

"No, Stephen. I will not feel better. I will never feel better." She put the cup down, put her hands over her face. "I am sorry. I am sorry, but right at this moment I want only to die. I want to pull a carpet of pine needles over me and die."

"Don't say that." Suddenly his arms encircled her, his face pressed against her breast. "I could not live if I knew you were gone forever. I thought losing Paulus was more than I could bear. But when you left, everything ended. All those weeks you were gone, the house was always cold. It was as if the heart had been cut out of it. Last night I dreamed about you. When I awakened I was surprised you were not there . . . loving me still. Then I heard pounding on the door, and there you were—frowning, annoyed."

"Only because you were not glad to see me. Then, when I went outside, I found the arbutus that Paulus planted. It blossomed, Ste-phen. You said it would not, but it did. It lived and blossomed. And I could not bear it." Once again she covered her face with her hands. "Death is bad enough in the winter, but in the spring you think of resurrection. You see life returning everywhere, and you have to face the knowledge that the one life you want to have return will never do so. I cannot bear it, Stephen."

"Nor can I."

Moving her over on the bed, he lay down beside her and held her. For a long time they lay like that in quiet refuge, so close that even though they lay as if asleep, she was aware of every breath he took, every beat of his heart.

She opened her eyes. He was looking at her. He moved his head the imperceptible amount necessary for his lips to touch hers.

"I love you," he said. "I always have and I always will. Even when I could not talk to you, I still loved you. Didn't you know that?"

"I tried to tell myself it was so. But after a while I could no longer believe it. You could have said something."

"No. It is the way I am made, Margretta."

"I know. I think I understand."

They were silent. He kissed her again, very gently, as if he were beginning a courtship. Finally he said, "Do you mind if I ask you a question?"

"Of course not."

He waited.

"Go ahead," she said.

Again he hesitated. Then at last she heard him saying, "Was the lad mine?"

Can a heart actually lurch and then stop like a wagon drawn by a horse that suddenly shies? It seemed so. She stared at him stunned, unable to speak.

"You cannot answer?"

"It is because I am so shocked. I'm shocked that you should think I—"

"I do not want to think it. But it has always been there in the back of my mind. I thought of it sometimes during the first year of his life, but then I pushed it far back. After all, the child bore him no resemblance. But after you left, perhaps I had too much time for brooding. I have wondered whether you were seeing him again, wondered how he felt . . . if the child was his."

His long speech gave her time to compose herself. "What man are you speaking of?"

"Mr. Sulzer. The man you once considered marrying." He paused, then went on slowly. "Remember when you went to the manor house to repair laces for Lady Van Baden?"

"Yes, I remember it well." Her heart was beating faster now. How could he fail to notice?

"Before you returned, you were seen one day—Jan Harten saw you—coming out the side door of Mr. Sulzer's house. He said you looked flustered. He wasn't carrying tales. He thought I might have sent you there to get legal advice on our contracts."

She moistened her lips, swallowed. Her throat was raw from sobbing, but the feverish soreness was gone. "I did go there, Stephen, to find out whether 'distraint' meant what I thought it did. I found out that it did and that there was little hope of changing the contract."

"And. . . ?"

"Nothing happened between us. I will admit he made a gesture of . . . well, call it affection. I was able to parry it. It upset me. His wife was away."

"Yes, I heard that, too."

"But he did not—absolutely did not—father our son. You were more his father," she continued, "than most men are to their sons. And he was more your son even than mine. Except for his desire to move away from here and be free. He got that from me."

"We'll go in June."

"Go where?"

"Away from here. To our own land somewhere. But first I'll have to see Lord Van Baden about selling the leasehold. I will not deal with Mr. Frost."

"You really mean it?"

"I really mean it."

So. The dream had come true at last.

And the question she had always feared had finally been asked. Was he satisfied with her answer? Would his mind leap someday to other possibilities? True, he had seen Nicolaus many times at church, but he had never spent a lengthy time with him: time to observe the contours of his face, the lift of nose, the shape of eyebrow. As he talked with him about the leasehold, would the truth suddenly come to him? But sometimes the mind will refuse to accept what it does not want to believe. She would let that thought sustain her.

By the time Catherine returned, they were sitting at the table making plans.

"Jonas insisted on coming along," Catherine said, "even though I told him you hadn't had a really bad fall. Just a stumble. Mrs. Hardenbroeck sent this bottle. She said it would calm your nerves and ease any pain. And here is something to reduce a fever."

"Sit down, children," Stephen said. "And we will tell you about our plans for the future."

Chapter 29

When Margretta went back to the dominie's for her things, Catherine and Jonas, riding a second horse, went with her. "There's nothing to do here," Catherine said. "Besides, Pieter is out plowing with his father."

As they rode down the lane and tethered their horses in front of the dominie's, Margretta saw Nicolaus coming out of the graveyard behind the church.

"Margretta. I was not expecting to see you. And are these your children?"

"Yes." She introduced them and was proud of the way Jonas bowed. She was less proud of Catherine's flirtatious smile and the way she said, "I've always wanted to see the manor house."

"Then why not come over and see it right now? Would you like to see it too, Jonas?"

"I guess so, sir."

"And you?" He looked at Margretta.

"Thank you, but right now I have to do some packing."

While she gathered things together, she told Judith about Stephen's recovery and about their plans for leaving.

"Is he completely his old self?"

"I don't think he ever will be. Any more than I will. But things are all right between us again."

She was still packing and talking when the children returned. "Is there time for me to take Catherine to the village?" Jonas asked. "She'd like to meet some of the friends I made during the winter."

"Plenty of time." When they left, she said to Judith, "They've had little time for friends in their lives. No one nearby but the Vanzuyders." She put the last of Jonas' things in his saddlebag. "I have one other thing to do now. I want to see Nicolaus and tell him about Stephen and about our plans."

"He'll be sorry to see you go, Margretta. He's confided in me a little. Hasn't anyone else to talk with. I doubt that his mother will be back with Alida until she's sure all the turmoil here in the valley is over." She gave Margretta a long look. "His feeling for you is very strong. How do you feel about him? Or is that too personal a question?"

"No, not from you. Perhaps I should just say I am married to Stephen. We have many binding ties. As for Nicolaus, I no longer feel any anger toward him."

"I'm glad you feel that way. I was hoping you'd be kind. He's been waiting for word from you. Hoping, I'm afraid, that it was all over between you and Stephen."

"I'll be kind."

"Hurry, now, before the children return."

When she knocked on the manor-house door, Nicolaus himself opened it. "I've been waiting for you."

"I came to tell you that—"

"It isn't necessary. The children have already told me." He took her wrap, indicated a chair, and sat facing her. "They say you're going to the Grants or to the Mohawk Valley."

"Yes. Right now we're unsure exactly where."

He tapped the papers in his hand. "How would you like to stay right here in the Hudson Valley?"

"Nicolaus I've told you—"

"Not in Van Badenswyck. Farther north. Up between Livingston Manor and Rensselaerswyck. I have a piece of land up there. Cornelia's brother built a house on it, partially furnished it, then died before his marriage. No one has ever lived in it. He left it to Cornelia. We had planned that if we had a son, he would run the manor here. Our daughter would be given the place upriver. I want to give it to you, Margretta. It's right on the river. You would love it there."

She was stunned, but not too stunned to say proudly, "I cannot accept."

"Why not?"

"Because I would feel forever beholden to you."

He raised one angular eyebrow. "You'd rather have me forever feel that I owed *you* something, forever feel guilt for the sorrow I've caused you? Don't misunderstand me, Margretta. I'm not trying to buy you off. In no way can I make up to you for what happened. But by doing this for you and your children, I can perhaps make your future a little easier."

"You may remarry, Nicolaus. Have children."

"No. I will not marry again. Not unless you . . ."

"It is too much for you to do. You could sell the property."

"I'd rather have a family there that is connected with mine. Our lives and our families are linked, Margretta. If we had a child together, then is it not natural that I should love his brother and sister? Catherine is charming, by the way, and Jonas a fine little lad. While Belle took Catherine through the house, he and I looked at my maps here. We had a good talk. I'd like to in some way ensure their future."

She felt tears start. "Oh, Nicolaus, Nicolaus, I'm crying again. I never cry. In all our years of marriage Stephen has seen me cry only once or twice. Why do I so often cry when I'm near you?"

He came over, and kneeling by her chair, put his arms around her waist. "Don't you know, Margretta, my darling? It's because when you're with me you open up to some of your deepest feelings. We were meant to be together." After holding her a moment, he rose and pulled a chair close to her, sat watching her dab at her eyes.

"Nicolaus, forgive my weakness. I could not help being moved by your generosity and your feeling for my children."

"And for you. A man wants to do something for the woman he loves, for the woman he ought to have married. Give me your hands, Margretta." He took them, turned them over, kissed them. "Look at them, Margretta. Look at how red and chapped they are." She tried to draw them away then, but he held them tighter. "I love them anyway. But I want you to have white hands. You've drudged away long enough. I want you to have some leisure. If you go to some new place, you'll have to build a house, start all over. You may prosper, but it will take years. I want a better life for you right now."

"Even if you can't share it with me?"

"Even if I can't share it with you."

She shook her head. "Stephen would never accept such a gift. He is too proud."

"Would you if I could persuade him?"

"I think I would. But you will not succeed."

She stood up then. It was the wrong move, for it made it all too easy, as he too rose, for them to step into each other's arms. She closed her eyes as his lips touched hers, gave herself up for a moment to a force so powerful that it invaded every cell of her body with tenderness and longing. She drew away, but it was like trying to draw a magnet away from a piece of iron. She was in his arms again.

"It's very hard to say good-bye to you, Nicolaus."

"You must?"

"You know that I must. Already in these past moments I've been more unfaithful to my husband than I was . . . that other time."

Again he kissed her, but this time she held a part of herself back, checking the advancing tide of emotion while trying at the same time to memorize the feel of his lips and the touch of his hands.

"I must go now. Thank you for what you wanted to do for me—for us. I'll always remember it. Let me go quickly now."

She did not cry again until she reached Judith's; after she had finished, Judith put compresses on her eyes. "The children will never know the difference," she said.

By the time the children came, her eyes were clear, though tears came again when she said good-bye to Judith and to the dominie

On the way home she let the children canter ahead. It gave her time alone to sort her feelings and quiet her spirits so she could present Stephen with the calm visage of a wife who has been off on no more than an errand.

Love two men? Was it possible? But she loved both Judith and Sara, though each in a different way: Judith for her intelligence and ironic comments, Sara for her homespun humor and directness. Stephen had long ago made a permanent place for himself in her heart. Then Nicolaus had come storming in—somehow she had allowed it—and found his own place. Whether they were right or wrong, she could not deny her feelings. But she did have the strength to do what was right.

They were hardly in the house before Catherine told Stephen about their visit to the manor house.

"Did you tell Lord Van Baden we were leaving?"

"Yes. Shouldn't I have?"

"It's all right. But in that case I think I ought to go in right away and settle things. I'll go tomorrow."

"That's a good idea," Margretta said, and when he left the next day, she added, "Get a good price for the leasehold, Stephen. Remind him of all the improvements you've made."

He was gone longer than she expected, not returning until late afternoon.

Catherine said, "Did you get a good price?"

"Yes. Far better than I expected."

Beyond that he was uncommunicative, his gaze inward.

Margretta fretted all through supper and afterward. She was prepared for almost any possibility: that Nicolaus had offered the property and Stephen had rejected it; that Nicolaus had inadvertently revealed his feelings for her; that, worst of all, Stephen had seen, as they spoke together, the remarkable resemblance to Paulus.

They worked into the evening, then went to bed, and once again it was in the marriage bed that words of confession were most easily spoken.

"I did something today you may never forgive me for," Stephen said. Then, while darkness concealed her impatience, he told her in detail of the offer Nicolaus had made him.

"And what was your response?"

"I refused immediately."

She suppressed her disappointment. Hadn't she known that was what he, in his pride, would do?

"But then," Stephen went on, "he spoke of how he felt about our child. The guilt he felt, as if he had blood on his hands. He had given his overseer too much authority, he said, hadn't wanted to be bothered by business matters." He moved restlessly. "I know what guilt is, Margretta. If I hadn't stayed to drink with my comrades the night Prendergast was freed, I would have been here when the posse came."

"Don't torture yourself with that. It's in the past."

"The past never leaves us. But what I'm trying to say is that as he spoke of his guilt, hate him though I always had, I began to feel sympathy for him. I knew how he felt because I have felt the same way."

He was quiet a long time. She wanted to shake him and say, *What did you do? What did you do?* But she waited.

At last he said, "I accepted, Margretta. I accepted because I felt maybe he did owe us something for what had been done. But I accepted also for another reason, and that's what makes me ashamed. I feel as though I've broken a promise to you."

"I think I know the other reason, Stephen. You did not want to leave the Hudson Valley. You love it too much."

"I do, but I had promised you we would go elsewhere."

"Stephen, I don't care where we go as long as we're together and as long as we're free and on our own land."

She moved close to him then and gave him the reassurance of her love, as if, with her body—that body that only yesterday had yearned toward infidelity—she was now renewing the vows she had made twenty-three years before.

It was the right thing to do. Her feeling for Nicolaus would gradually subside beneath the layers of daily life in the months and years ahead, eventually no more stirring than her memories of her early years with Stephen. And what was it really but passion?—the beginning of love rather than the deeper feeling that grows out of shared experiences. She would get over it. She was already, as the days passed and she and her family packed and planned for their future, beginning to get over it.

Gradually, one after another, things were settled.

Except for Catherine. She alternately sulked and raged. She did not want to go. She would not go, she said. She wanted to stay with the Vanzuyders.

Margretta coaxed her, spoke of the excitement of travel and of having a new home—all theirs. She spoke of independence. Of change.

"I don't want anything to change. I will not go. I won't. I won't." Over and over.

Finally Stephen said firmly—by then only a week remained before their departure—"But you *are* going. And I do not want to hear you speak of it again."

Catherine, hearing this new authority in Stephen's voice, subsided into quietness. She still sulked, though, and more than once Margretta saw traces of tears on her face and understood the reason for her despair.

"Catherine," she said to her four days before they were to leave, "why don't you ride over to the Vanzuyders'? Stay a couple of days. Take your time saying good-bye."

Catherine went, but she returned the next day with Pieter on a second horse behind her. She came alone into the house where Margretta and Stephen were packing.

"Pieter wants to ask you something."

Margretta looked at the suppressed excitement in the blue of her eyes. No, it was quite impossible. Catherine was still a child despite the growing maturity of her body. And Pieter little older. She would not accede to anything so foolish. Nor must Stephen.

"Go out and bring him in," she said.

When they were alone, she said to Stephen, "I think they want to marry. We must not let them. You must back me up when I say no. Or you must yourself say no with authority."

"Married? You are right. They are far too young."

They came in holding hands, but Pieter came forward alone and stood in front of Stephen. Very straight. Had she seen him from the back, she might have thought he was Paulus.

"Sir, I have a request to make of you."

"Yes?" Stephen's eyebrows lifted.

"I would like to go away with you. Paulus . . . is it all right if I speak of him?"

"It is all right."

"Paulus and I often spoke of leaving here. When we were alone, we spoke of little else. We planned to go even if you did not. I still want to. It would be almost, sir, like making . . . his dream come true."

Stephen bent over the hemp rope he was tying around some implements, tying and retying the knot. When it was exactly right, he looked up, looked at Catherine, then at Pieter. "Is that the only reason?"

Although a deep color suffused Pieter's cheeks, he remained straight and confident. "No, sir. It is also because I am fond of Catherine. When we are older, we may think seriously about each other. And Jonas. I feel closer to him than to anyone in my own family. I've always spent so much time here that it . . . well, it just seems as though I'm more a part of this family than my own."

Stephen put a hand on Pieter's shoulder. "Go outside awhile. I need time to think." When they had gone, he said to Margretta, "What do you think?"

"I would say yes. He could be a great help if we need to clear land. And company for Catherine and Jonas. Have you noticed that they don't argue when he's around?"

"You were wrong about the marriage."

"I don't think so. It's what they want, or think right now they want. But they are either smart enough to be silent about it or sensible enough to know they have to wait. We'd have to keep an eye on them. But otherwise I think it would be a good idea. If it's all right with William and Sara, I can think of no reason to refuse. Can you?"

"Yes." His eyes were shadowed with pain. "We'd be leaving here and I'd no longer have to look at his bed, his tree, his . . . grave. But every time I looked at Pieter, I'd think of him. The same age. So much like him in so many ways."

She placed her hands flat against his chest. "And is that such a bad thing? If a little bit of him remains in or with Pieter, then we have that much more of him than we would otherwise. Certainly you do not want to banish him from your memory."

"No, no, it was not that. Not a banishing."

"Then what?"

He shook his head. "I don't know. Maybe you are right. It's just that remembering is . . ."

"Painful. But we must learn to bear that pain. We are already learning." She kissed him on the cheek. "Go outside now and tell them. Quickly now."

With that too settled, they finished during the next three days selling or giving away the furnishings they had no room to take. On the day before their departure, Margretta brought out the backgammon game Paulus had made, his bow and arrow, his christening dress.

"Shall we take these?" she asked Stephen.

"Surely you would not leave them."

"It depends on what would give you the most ease."

He moved his fingers on the backgammon board. "So smooth. He did such good work."

"Only because you taught him how."

She remembered how Paulus had always been at his heels begging to be taken with him, begging to share whatever work he was doing, begging to be shown how. And the way they had worked together as Paulus had grown older: planting, cultivating, reaping, their arms swinging in the same rhythm, as if, inside their heads, they heard the same music.

"We will take them," she said. "After all, the other children used them also. And someday their children will. Think of it, Stephen—this marriage of ours and the generations that will multiply from it." She moved close to him, excited by a new vision of the future.

"It happens to everybody."

"I suppose so. But to me it seems special."

Their lips were touching when the door swung open and the children came in. "Really," Catherine said. "Aren't you a little old for that kind of thing?"

"Not at all," Margretta said briskly. "But we should be using our time to get the packing done. Shall we dismantle the marriage bed right now?"

"Not until tomorrow morning."

"The marriage bed?" Catherine said. "You call it the *marriage* bed?"

"Your father built it for me before our marriage. It was he who named it that."

"I began it the day I first laid eyes on your mother."

"The marriage bed," Catherine said, touching the tall, graceful bedpost. "How lovely the words sound. To me it was just something that was always there." She paused, her eyes newly aware. "I suppose a bed *is* important to a marriage."

"Indeed it is." A smile twitched at the corner of Stephen's mouth. "Everyone needs a good sleep every night in a comfortable bed."

"Papa. You're teasing me."

He was. But it made all the difference.

They worked until suppertime, then afterward on into the brightness of the June evening. When they finally crawled tiredly into bed, everything was packed except for the food they would eat in the morning, the clothes they would wear, and the bedding. And, of course, the bed.

After breakfast Stephen took it apart and carefully wrapped the pieces in blankets. Pieter arrived, helped hitch the oxen to the loaded wagon, saddled the other two horses.

Early, before breakfast, Margretta had visited Paulus' grave. Now she saw Stephen do so, saw him stand there, his head bowed. On his way back, he bent and scooped up a handful of dirt from the garden plot and let it sift through his fingers.

In the dooryard Jonas crouched under Paulus' tree, digging. He looked up at her. "I'm taking his arbutus. I'll make it grow just like he did."

They were ready now. The cow was tied behind the wagon. Behind it were Catherine, Jonas, and Pieter. Standing by the wagon, Margretta looked back at them. Jonas was adjusting his saddlebags, concerned with the minutiae of travel. Pieter was gazing at Catherine, his gentle brown eyes aglow with worship—and no wonder. She sat straight on her horse, her hair gleaming like a fall of satin, her eyes bright with dreams of the adventure ahead.

Margretta took one last look at the small stone house that had sheltered her and those she loved for so long. The graceful roof extension at the back, the tulips and lilacs massed in the dooryard, Paulus' tree pointing to the heavens—all of these caught her heart in a new way as it came to her she was seeing them for the last time.

"Come, Margretta," Stephen said.

She tucked her notebook into the folds of the feather mattress that, along with the blankets, protected the carefully turned posts of the bed, reflecting at the same time that the bed itself could tell far more of their marriage than the account she had written. It had known it all—all the hope, all the sorrow, all the love.

Then, the sun warm on her back, she climbed up into the wagon. As the oxen ambled down the lane, Stephen took her hand and held it briefly before picking up the reins.